Disney

Tim Burton's THE NIGHTMARE BEFORE CHRISTMAS

MANGA BY JUN ASUKA
COVER ILLUSTRATION BY NATSUKI MINAMI

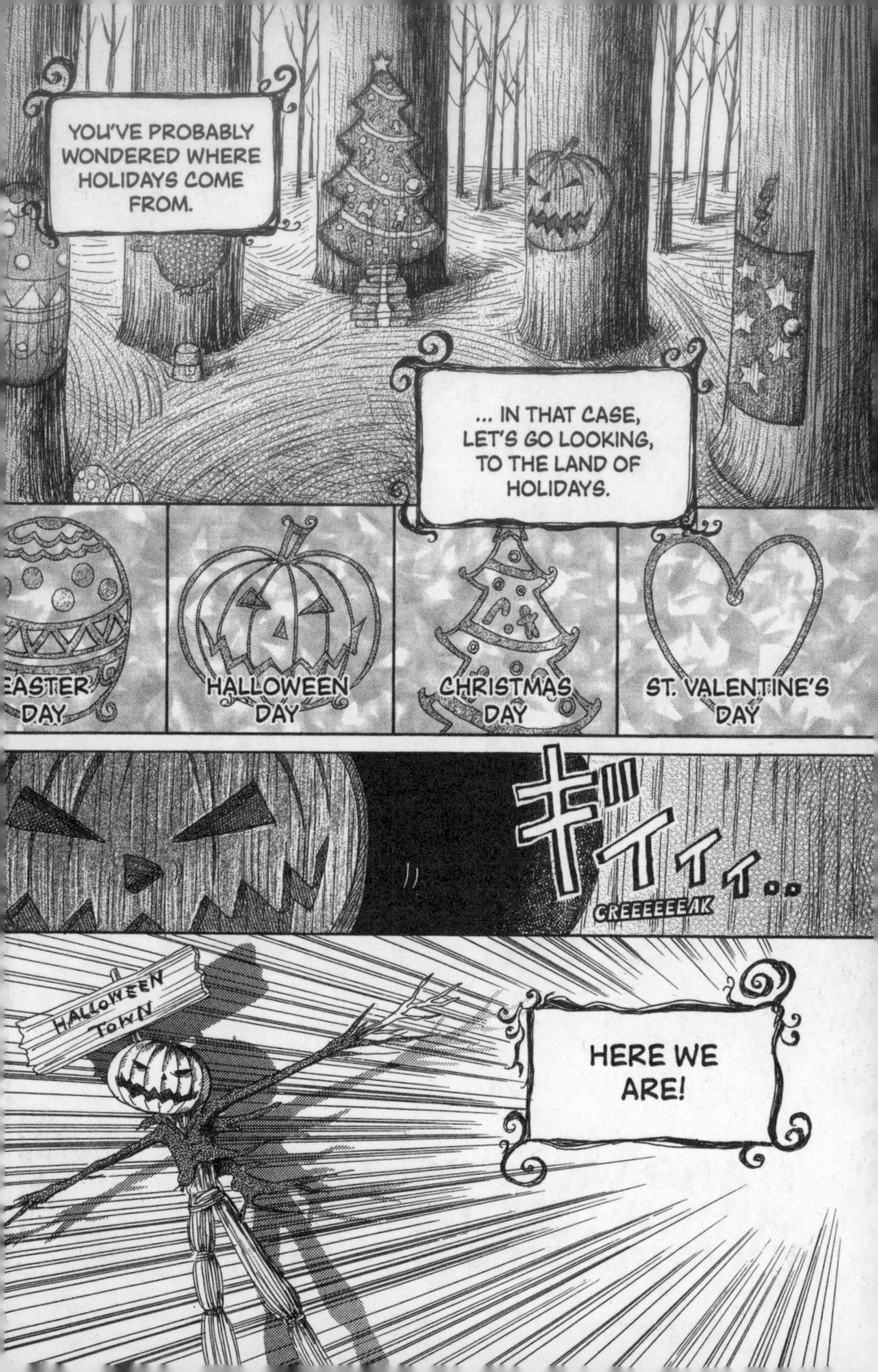
YOU'VE PROBABLY WONDERED WHERE HOLIDAYS COME FROM.
... IN THAT CASE, LET'S GO LOOKING, TO THE LAND OF HOLIDAYS.
ST. VALENTINE'S DAY
CHRISTMAS DAY
HALLOWEEN DAY
EASTER DAY
ギイイイ..
CREEEEEEAK
HALLOWEEN TOWN
HERE WE ARE!

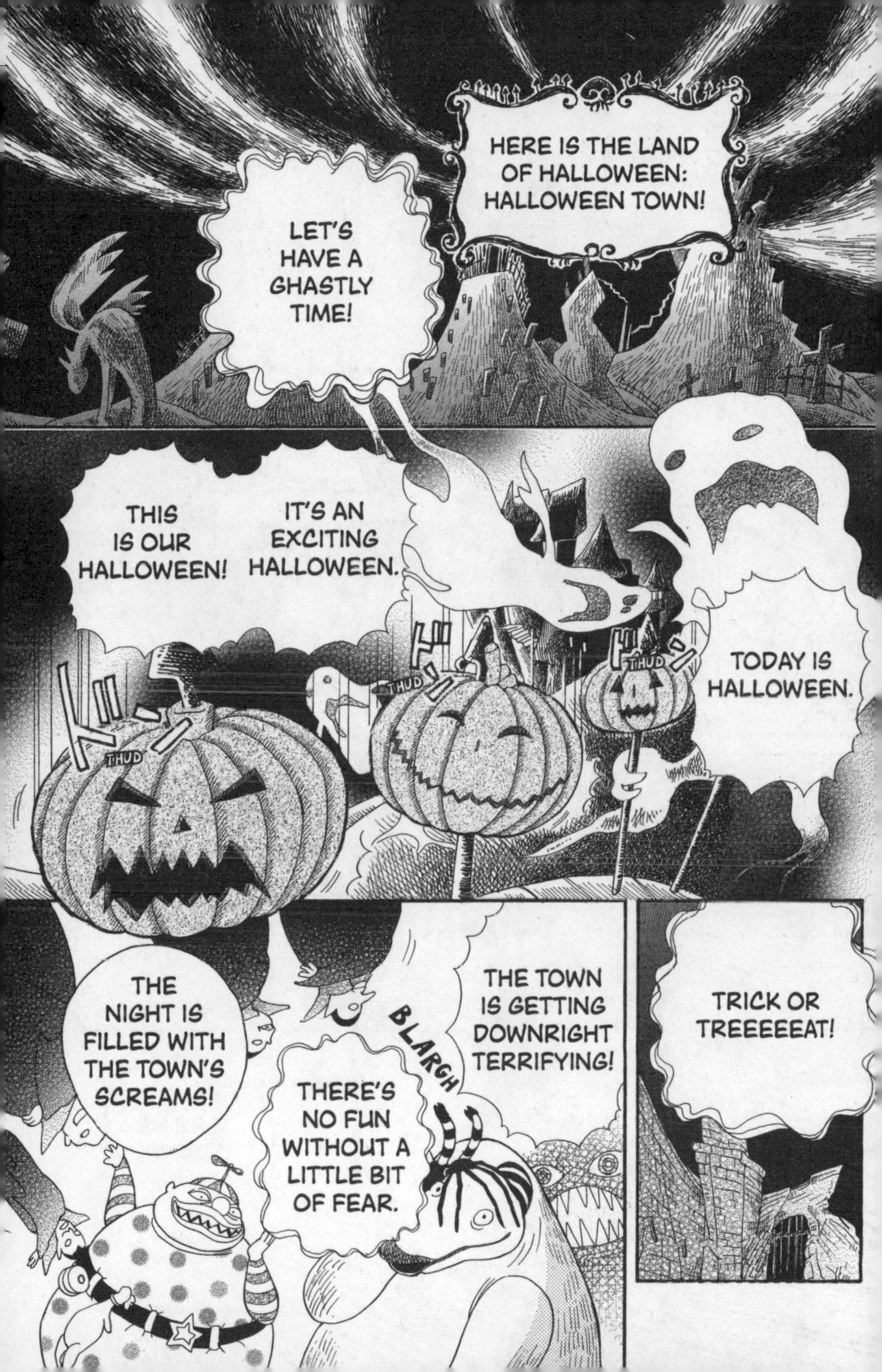
HERE IS THE LAND OF HALLOWEEN: HALLOWEEN TOWN!
LET'S HAVE A GHASTLY TIME!
TODAY IS HALLOWEEN.
THUD
THUD
IT'S AN EXCITING HALLOWEEN.
THIS IS OUR HALLOWEEN!
THUD
TRICK OR TREEEEEAT!
THE TOWN IS GETTING DOWNRIGHT TERRIFYING!
BLARGH
THERE'S NO FUN WITHOUT A LITTLE BIT OF FEAR.
THE NIGHT IS FILLED WITH THE TOWN'S SCREAMS!

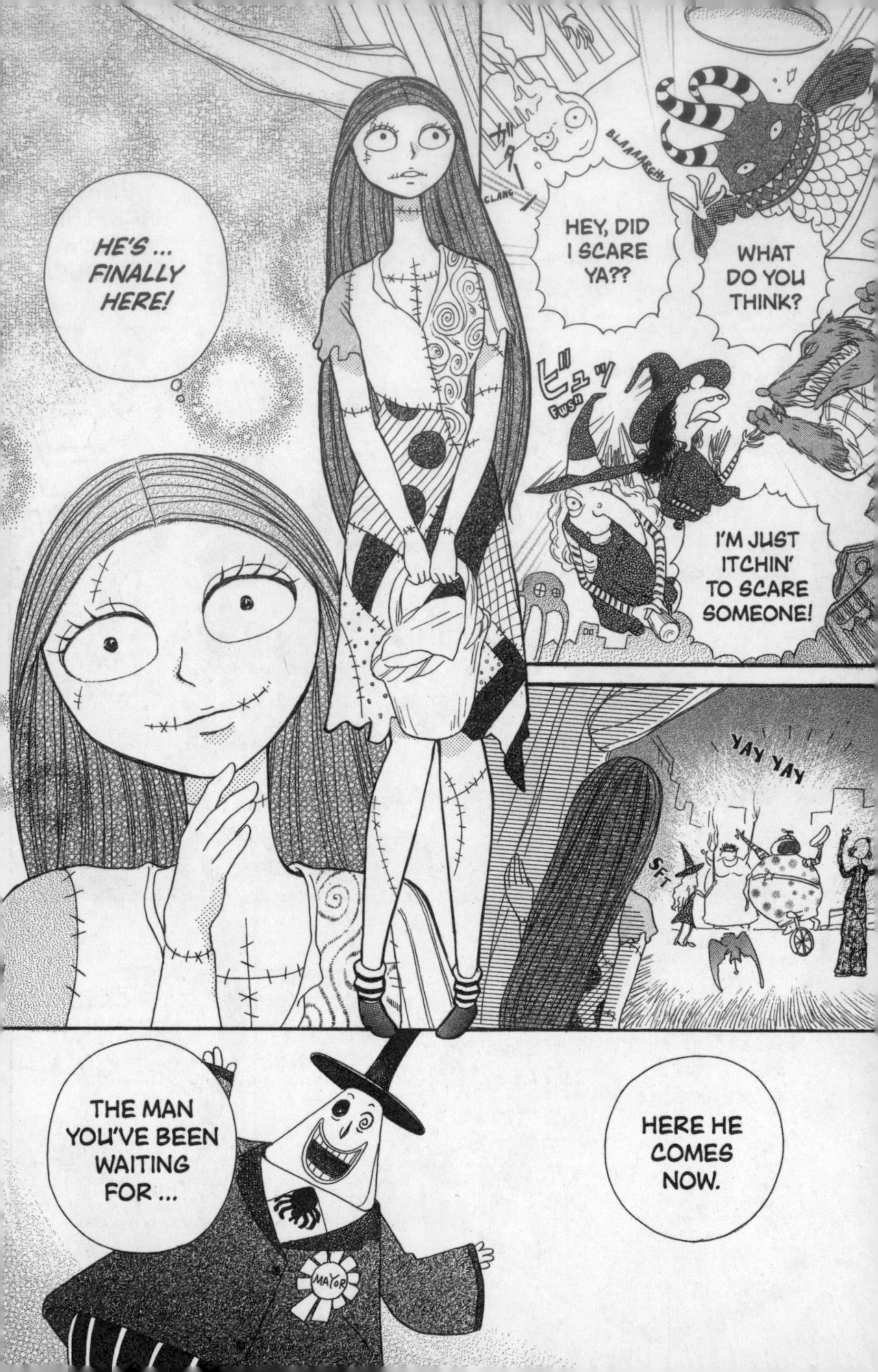
BLAAAARGH
CLANG
WHAT DO YOU THINK?
HEY, DID I SCARE YA??
ビュッ
FWSH
I'M JUST ITCHIN' TO SCARE SOMEONE!
YAY YAY
SFT
HE'S ... FINALLY HERE!
HERE HE COMES NOW.
THE MAN YOU'VE BEEN WAITING FOR ...
MAYOR

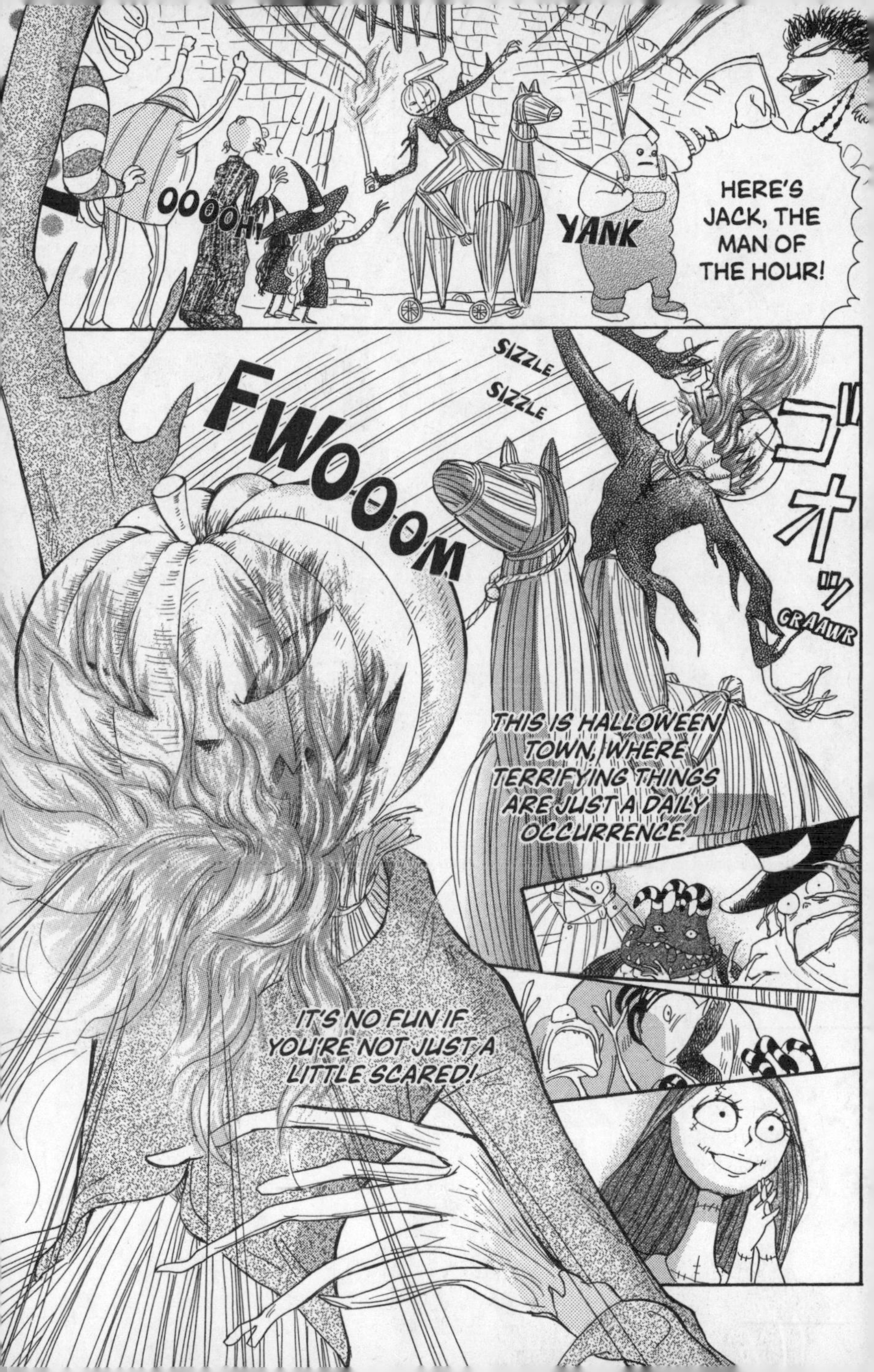
HERE'S JACK, THE MAN OF THE HOUR!
YANK
OOOOOH!
ゴオッ
GRAAWR
SIZZLE
SIZZLE
FWOOOOM
THIS IS HALLOWEEN TOWN, WHERE TERRIFYING THINGS ARE JUST A DAILY OCCURRENCE.
IT'S NO FUN IF YOU'RE NOT JUST A LITTLE SCARED!

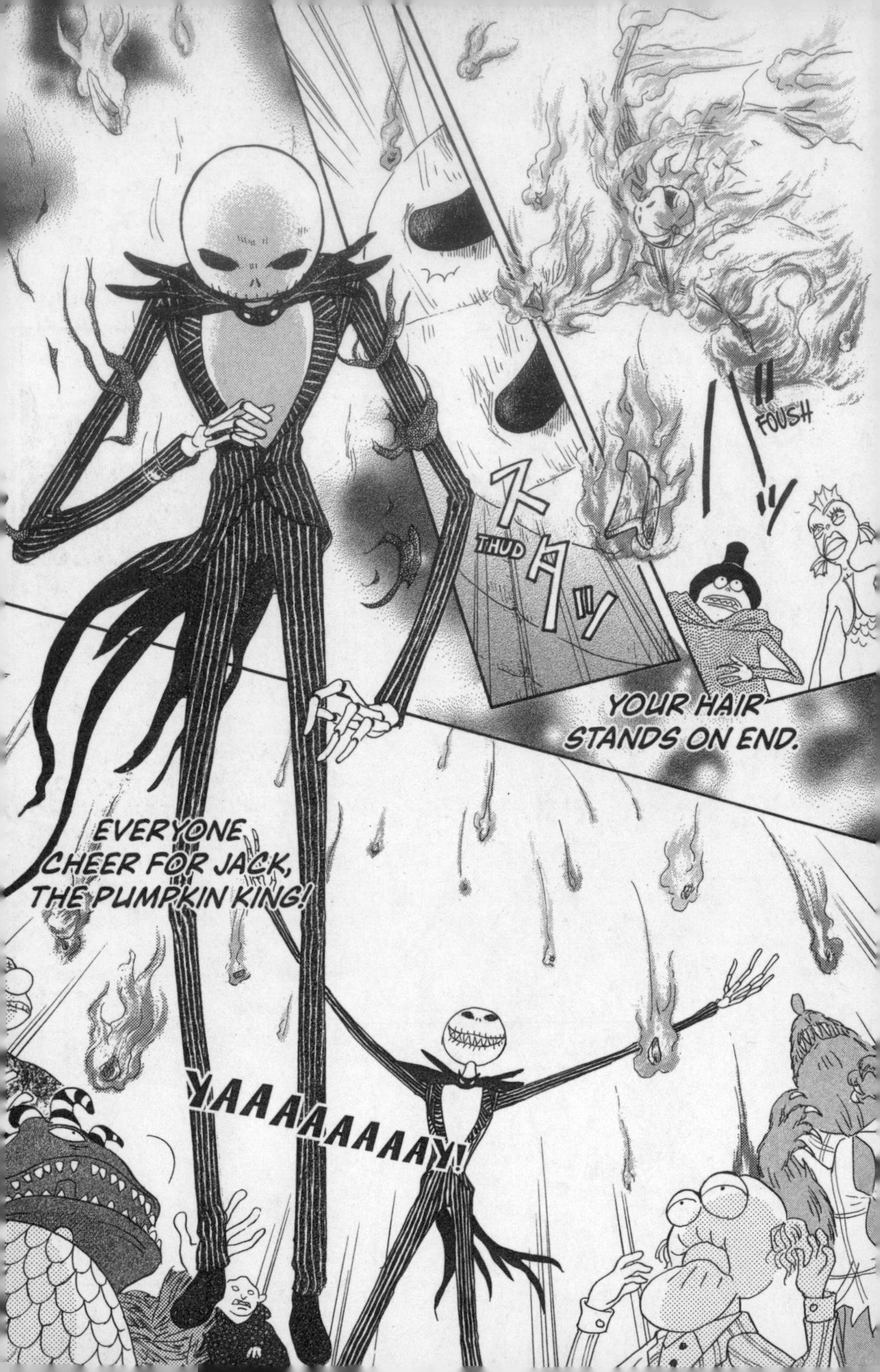
FOUSH
THUD
YOUR HAIR STANDS ON END.
EVERYONE CHEER FOR JACK, THE PUMPKIN KING!
YAAAAAAAAY!

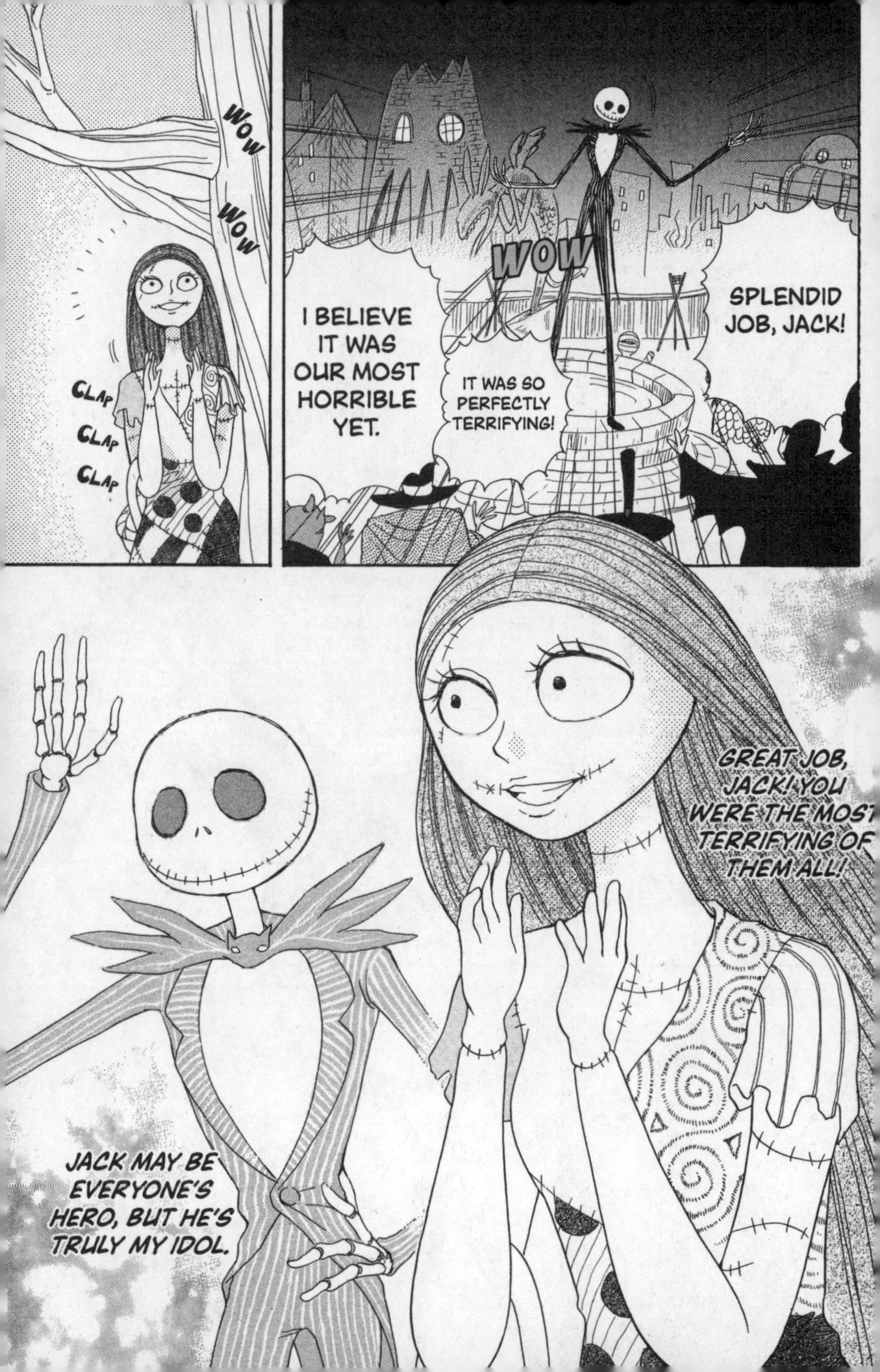
SPLENDID JOB, JACK!
WOW
IT WAS SO PERFECTLY TERRIFYING!
I BELIEVE IT WAS OUR MOST HORRIBLE YET.
WOW
WOW
CLAP
CLAP
CLAP
GREAT JOB, JACK! YOU WERE THE MOST TERRIFYING OF THEM ALL!
JACK MAY BE EVERYONE'S HERO, BUT HE'S TRULY MY IDOL.

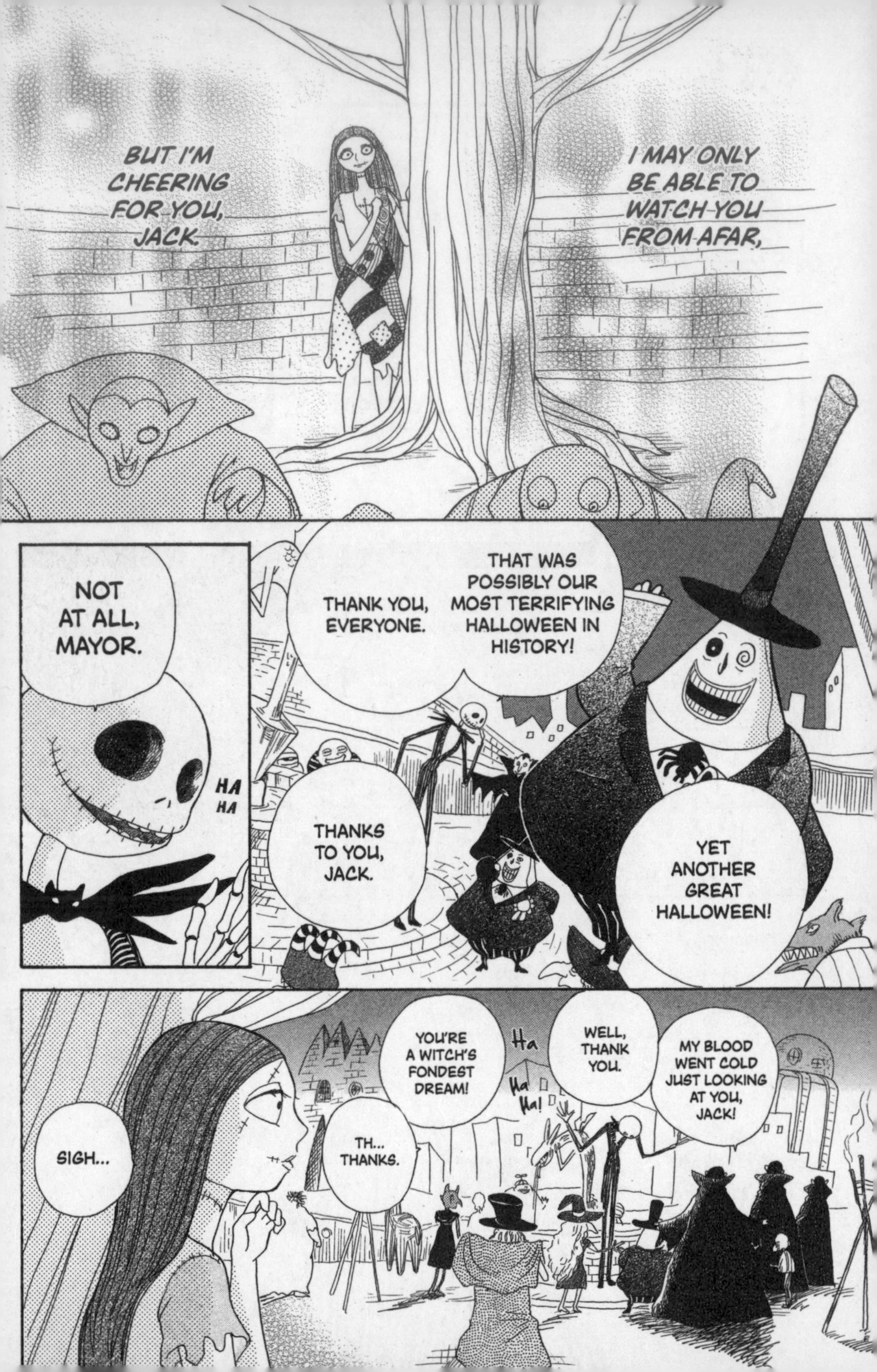
I MAY ONLY BE ABLE TO WATCH YOU FROM AFAR,
BUT I'M CHEERING FOR YOU, JACK.
THAT WAS POSSIBLY OUR MOST TERRIFYING HALLOWEEN IN HISTORY!
THANK YOU, EVERYONE.
YET ANOTHER GREAT HALLOWEEN!
THANKS TO YOU, JACK.
NOT AT ALL, MAYOR.
HA HA
MY BLOOD WENT COLD JUST LOOKING AT YOU, JACK!
WELL, THANK YOU.
Ha Ha Ha!
YOU'RE A WITCH'S FONDEST DREAM!
TH... THANKS.
SIGH...

READ THIS WAY

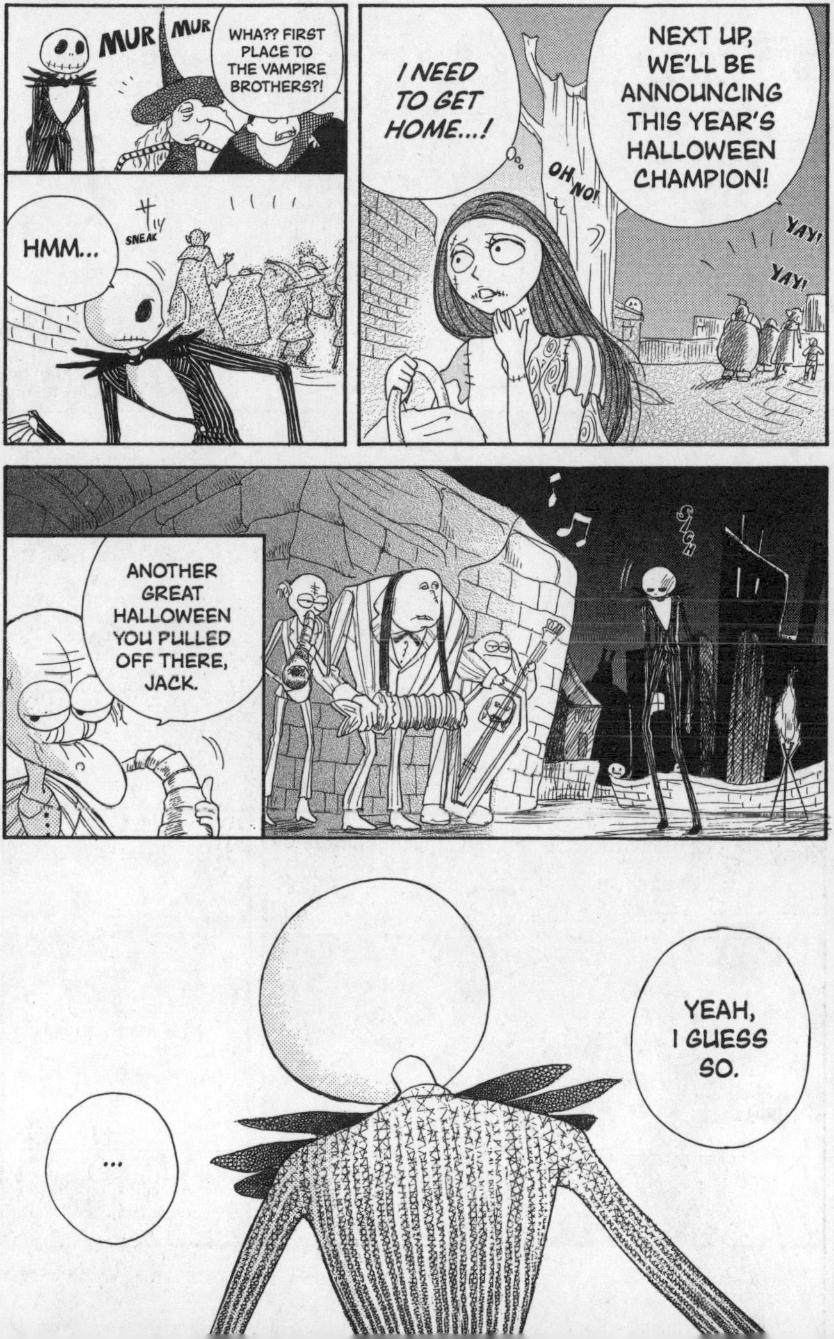

NEXT UP, WE'LL BE ANNOUNCING THIS YEAR'S HALLOWEEN CHAMPION!
I NEED TO GET HOME...!
OH NO!
YAY!
YAY!
MUR MUR
WHA?? FIRST PLACE TO THE VAMPIRE BROTHERS?!
HMM...
SNEAK
SIGH
ANOTHER GREAT HALLOWEEN YOU PULLED OFF THERE, JACK.
YEAH, I GUESS SO.
...

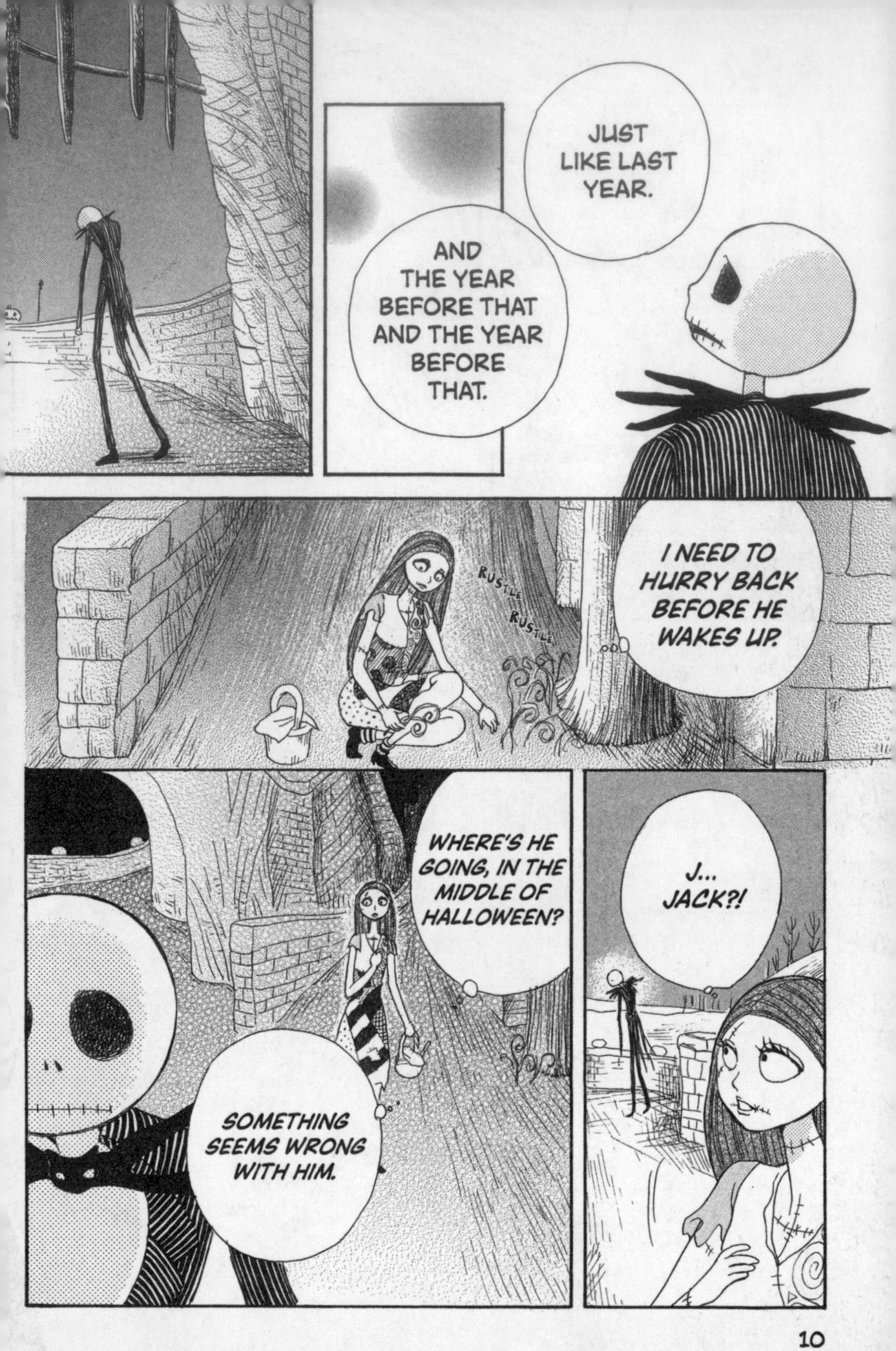
JUST LIKE LAST YEAR.
AND THE YEAR BEFORE THAT AND THE YEAR BEFORE THAT.
I NEED TO HURRY BACK BEFORE HE WAKES UP.
RUSTLE
RUSTLE
J... JACK?!
WHERE'S HE GOING, IN THE MIDDLE OF HALLOWEEN?
SOMETHING SEEMS WRONG WITH HIM.

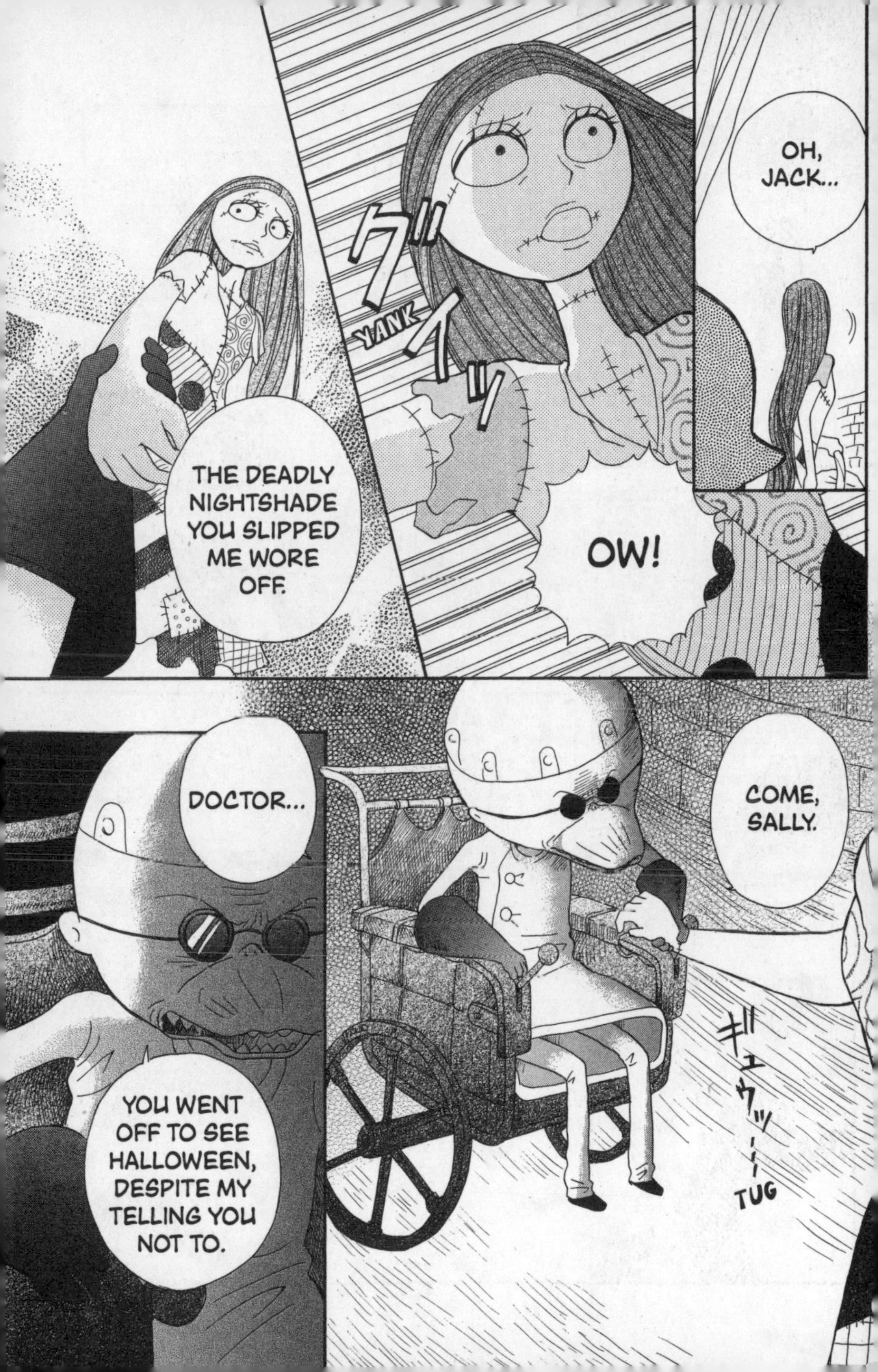
OH, JACK...
グイッ
YANK
OW!
THE DEADLY NIGHTSHADE YOU SLIPPED ME WORE OFF.
COME, SALLY.
ギュウッ
TUG
DOCTOR...
YOU WENT OFF TO SEE HALLOWEEN, DESPITE MY TELLING YOU NOT TO.

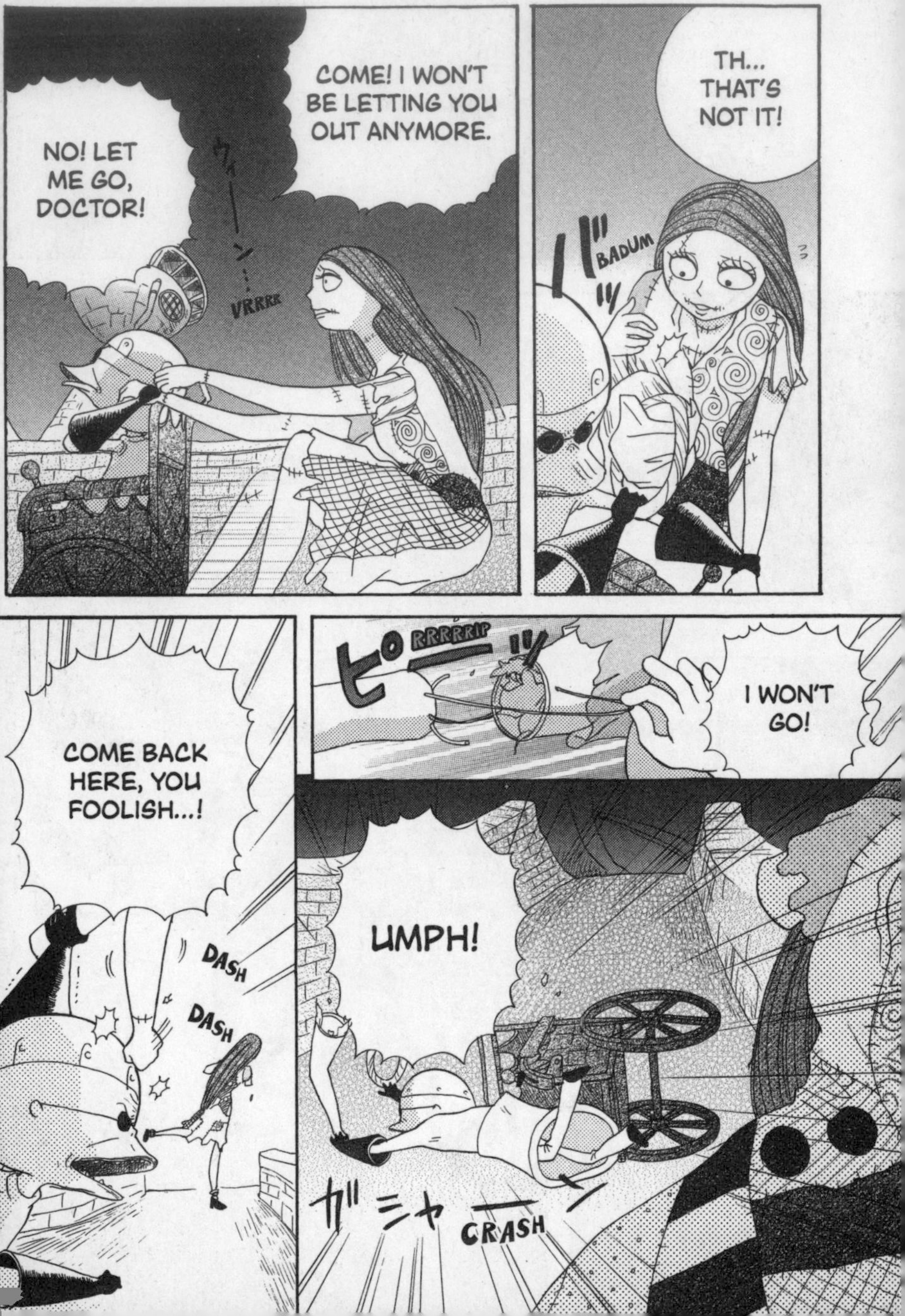
TH... THAT'S NOT IT!
BADUM
COME! I WON'T BE LETTING YOU OUT ANYMORE.
NO! LET ME GO, DOCTOR!
VRRRR
I WON'T GO!
RRRRRIP
UMPH!
CRASH
COME BACK HERE, YOU FOOLISH...!
DASH
DASH

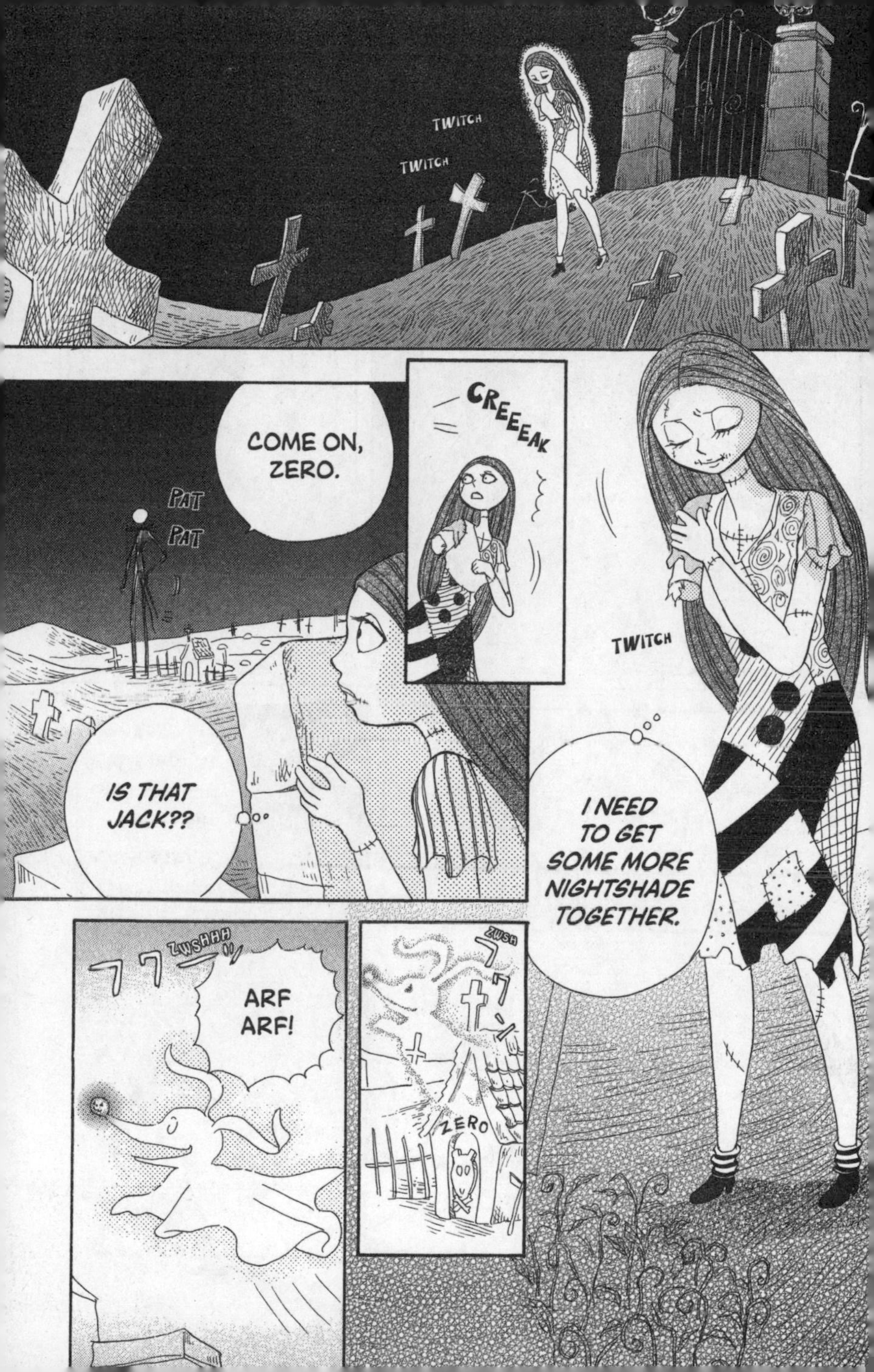
TWITCH
TWITCH
TWITCH
I NEED TO GET SOME MORE NIGHTSHADE TOGETHER.
CREEEAK
COME ON, ZERO.
PAT
PAT
IS THAT JACK??
ZWSH
ZERO
ZWSHHH
ARF ARF!

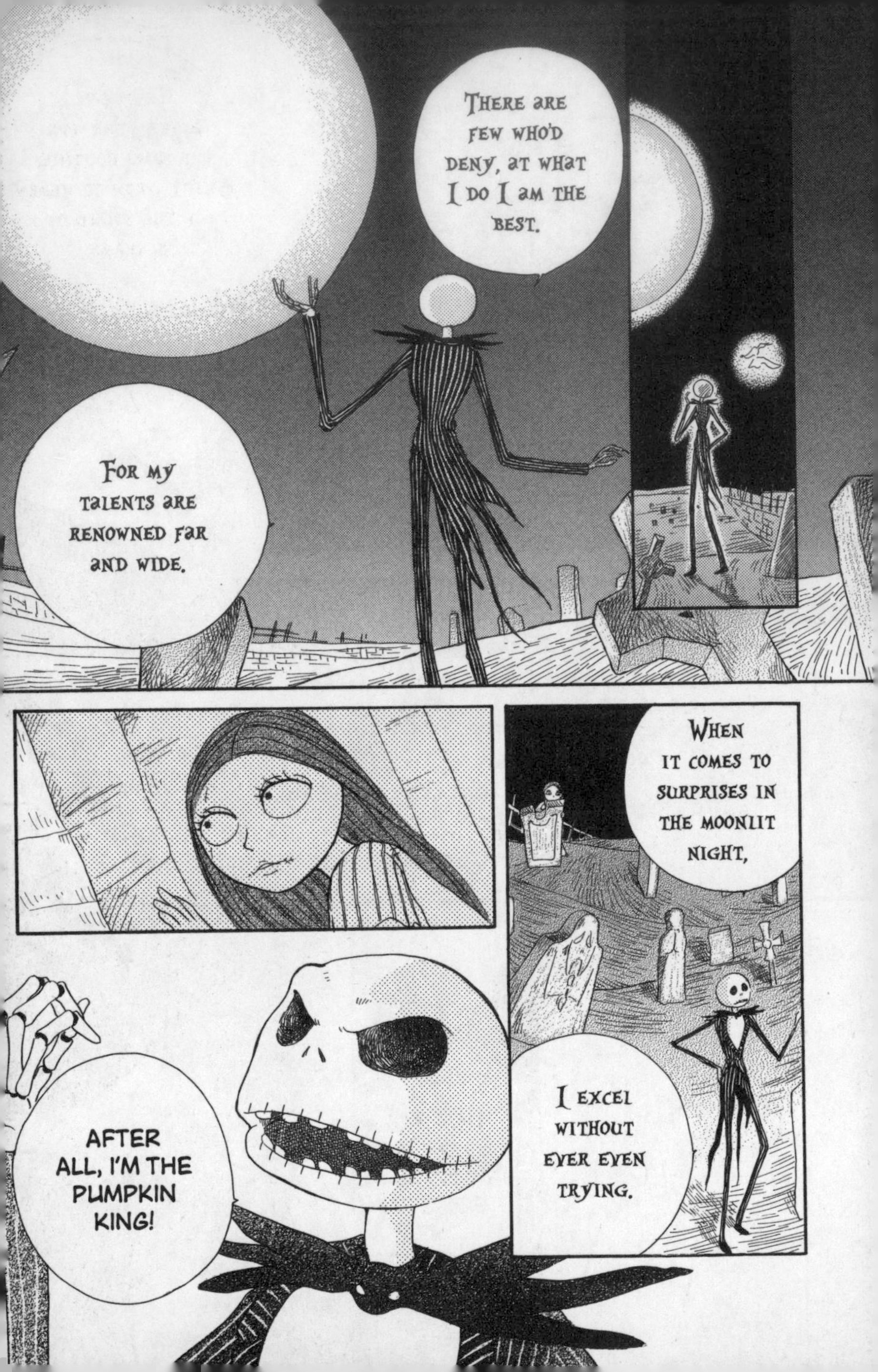
There are few who'd deny, at what I do I am the best.
For my talents are renowned far and wide.
When it comes to surprises in the moonlit night,
I excel without ever even trying.
After all, I'm the Pumpkin King!

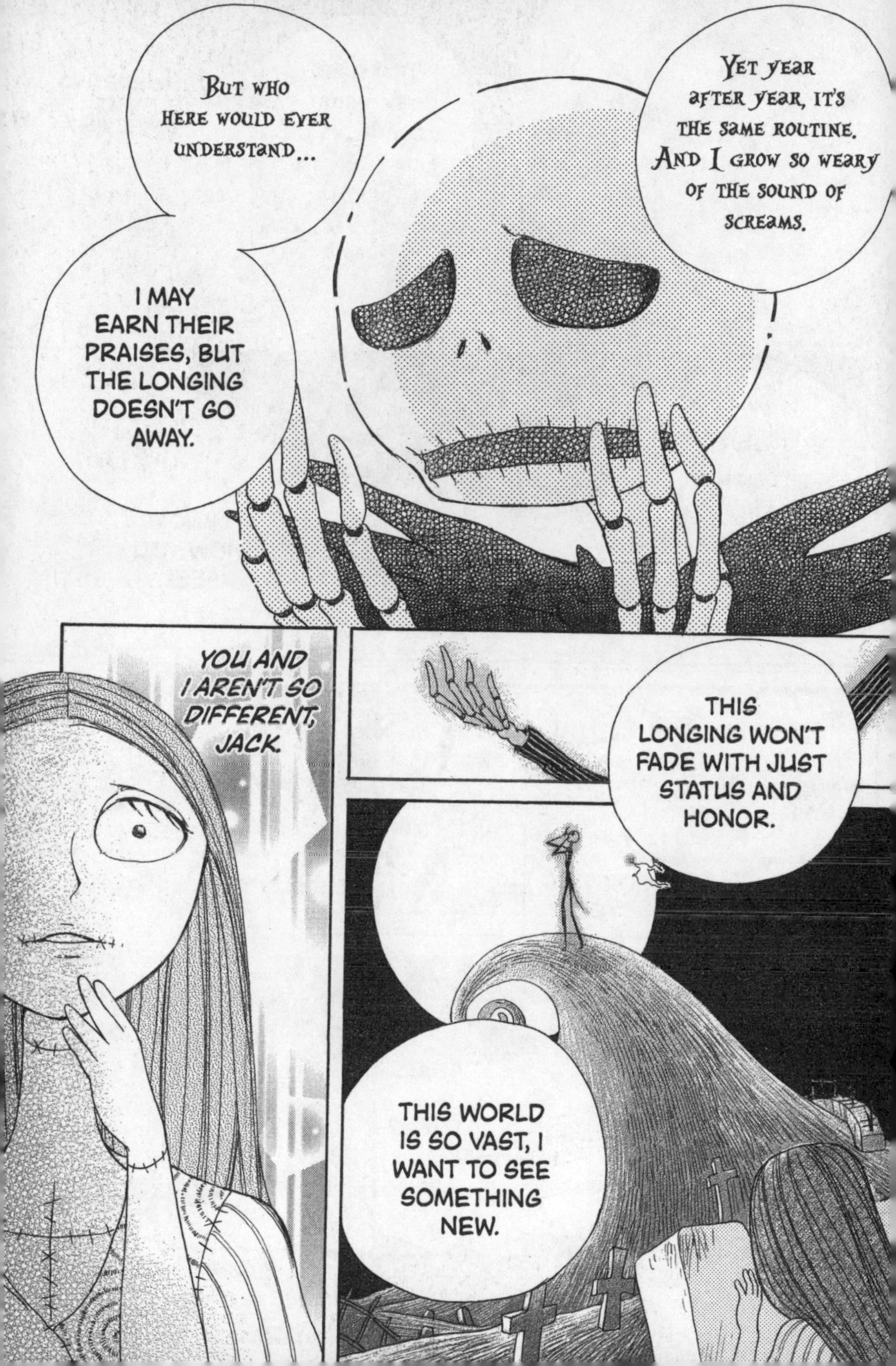
Yet year after year, it's the same routine. And I grow so weary of the sound of screams.
But who here would ever understand...
I may earn their praises, but the longing doesn't go away.
This longing won't fade with just status and honor.
This world is so vast, I want to see something new.
You and I aren't so different, Jack.

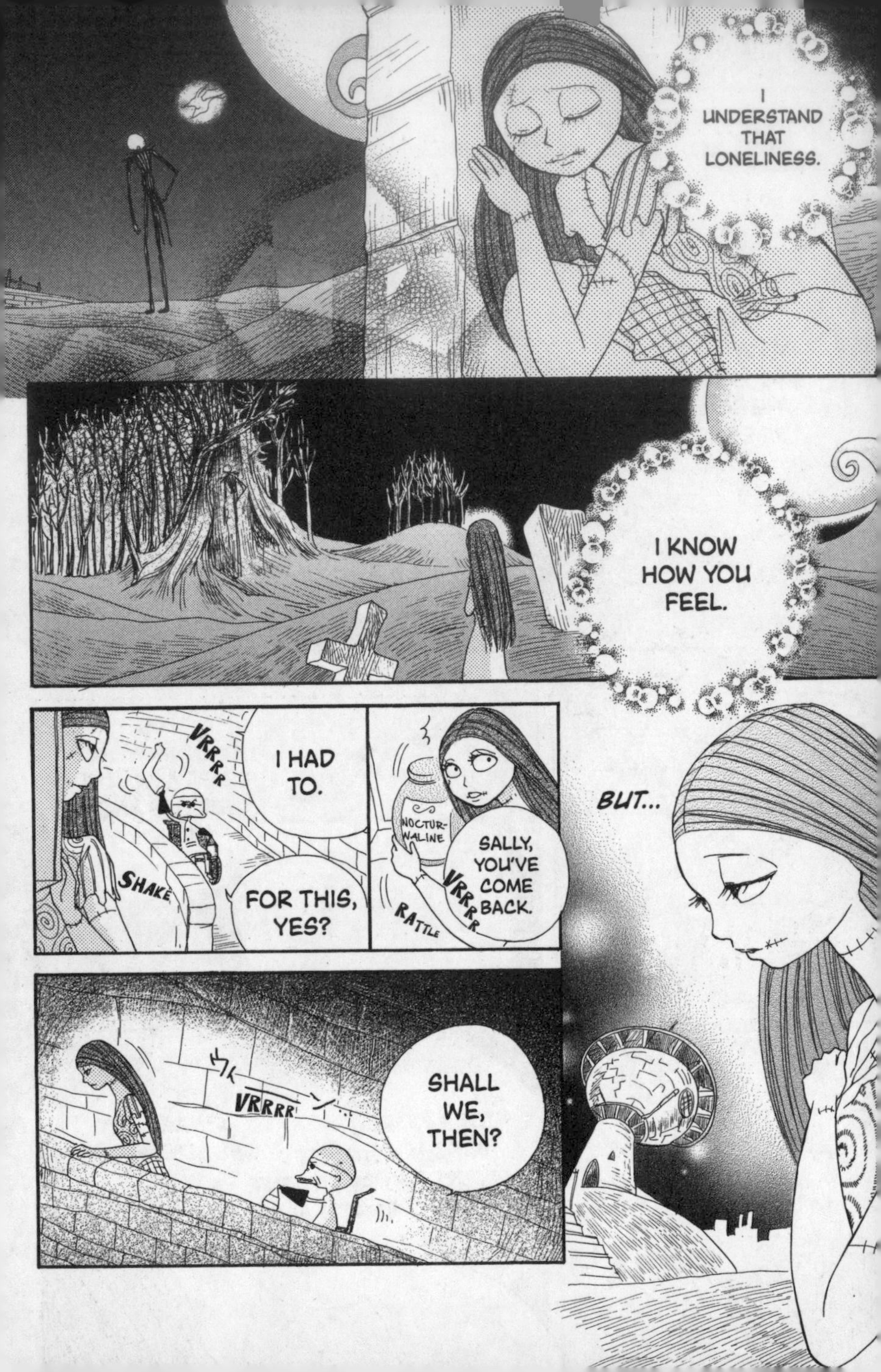
I UNDERSTAND THAT LONELINESS.
I KNOW HOW YOU FEEL.
BUT...
VRRRR
NOCTUR-WALINE
SALLY, YOU'VE COME BACK.
RATTLE
VRRRR
I HAD TO.
FOR THIS, YES?
SHAKE
VRRRR
SHALL WE, THEN?

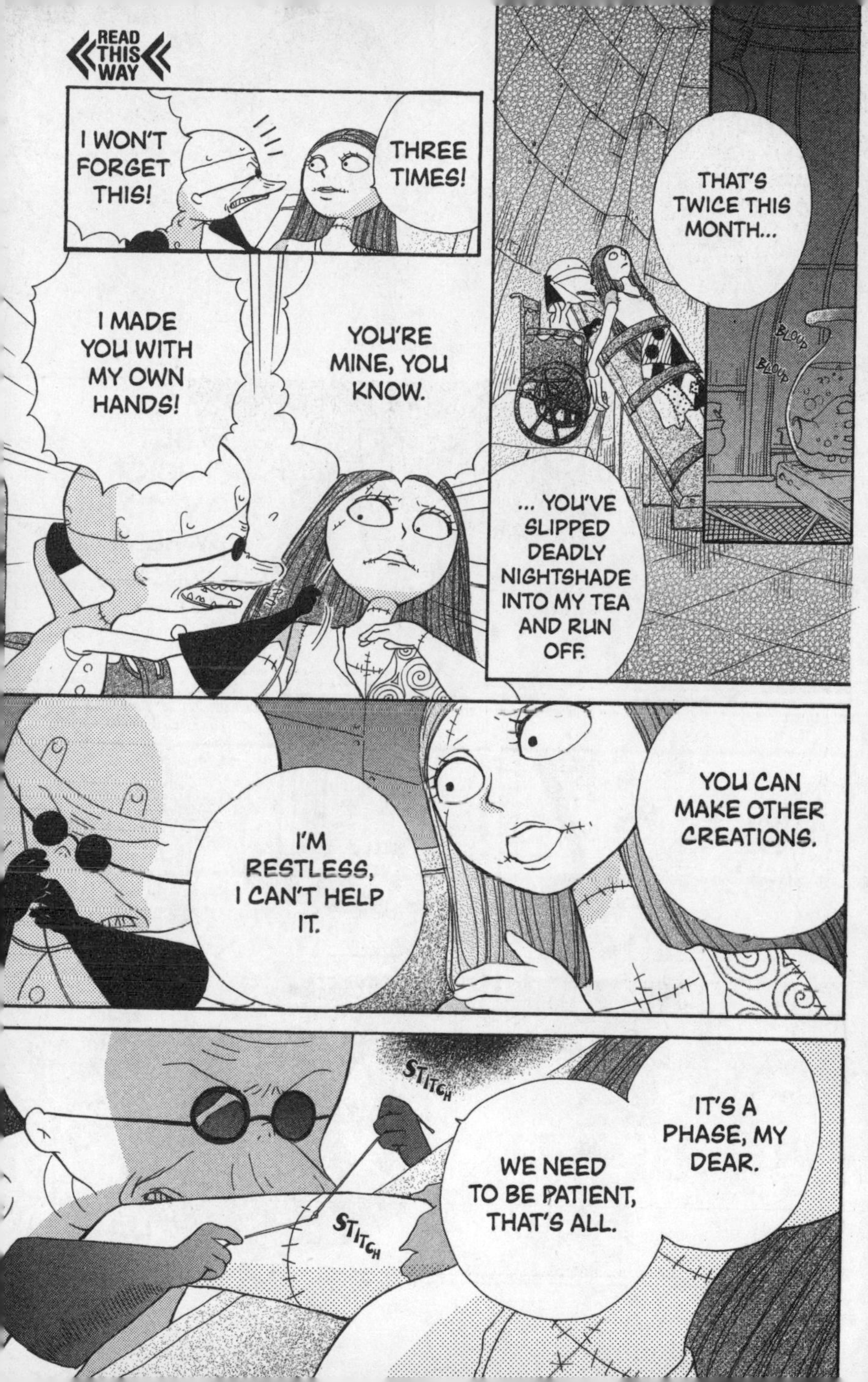
READ THIS WAY
THAT'S TWICE THIS MONTH...
BLOUP
BLOUP
... YOU'VE SLIPPED DEADLY NIGHTSHADE INTO MY TEA AND RUN OFF.
THREE TIMES!
I WON'T FORGET THIS!
YOU'RE MINE, YOU KNOW.
I MADE YOU WITH MY OWN HANDS!
YOU CAN MAKE OTHER CREATIONS.
I'M RESTLESS, I CAN'T HELP IT.
STITCH
IT'S A PHASE, MY DEAR.
WE NEED TO BE PATIENT, THAT'S ALL.
STITCH

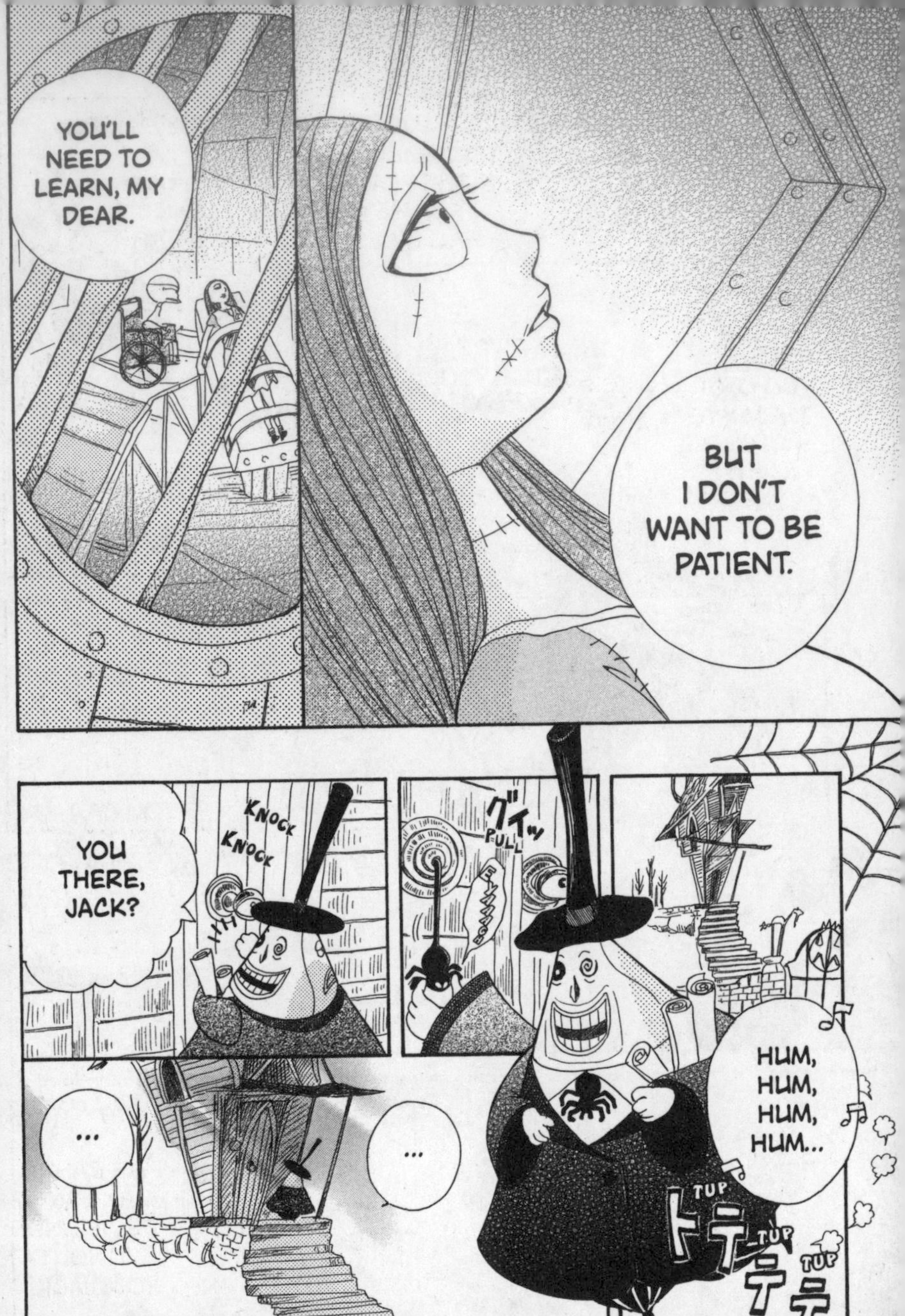
BUT I DON'T WANT TO BE PATIENT.
YOU'LL NEED TO LEARN, MY DEAR.
HUM, HUM, HUM, HUM...
トテ TUP
テ TUP
テ TUP
グイッ PULL
KNOCK KNOCK
YOU THERE, JACK?
...
...

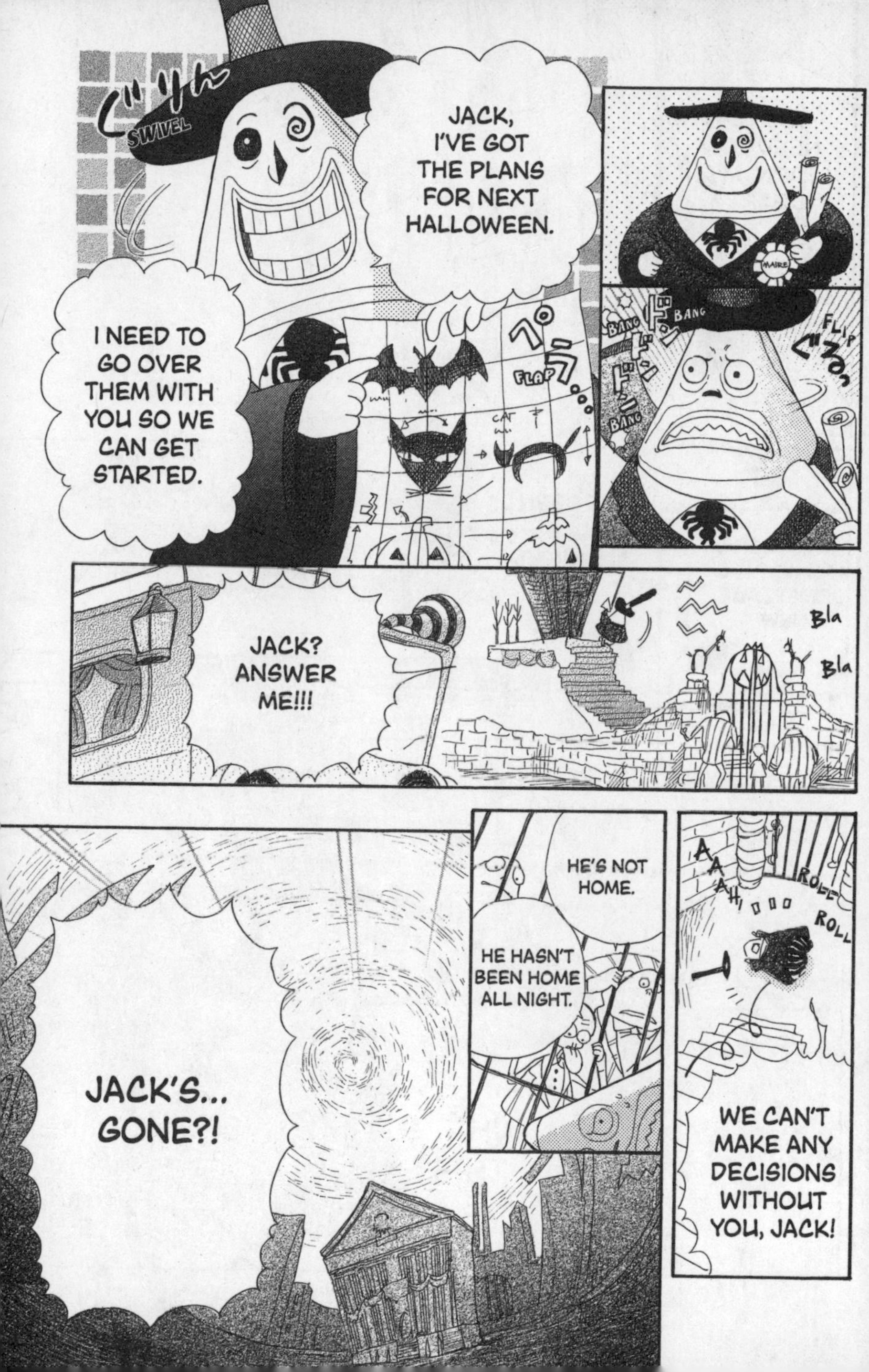
BANG
BANG
BANG
BANG
FLIP
ぐりん
SWIVEL
JACK, I'VE GOT THE PLANS FOR NEXT HALLOWEEN.
I NEED TO GO OVER THEM WITH YOU SO WE CAN GET STARTED.
FLAP
Bla
Bla
JACK? ANSWER ME!!!
AAAH...
ROLL
ROLL
WE CAN'T MAKE ANY DECISIONS WITHOUT YOU, JACK!
HE'S NOT HOME.
HE HASN'T BEEN HOME ALL NIGHT.
JACK'S... GONE?!

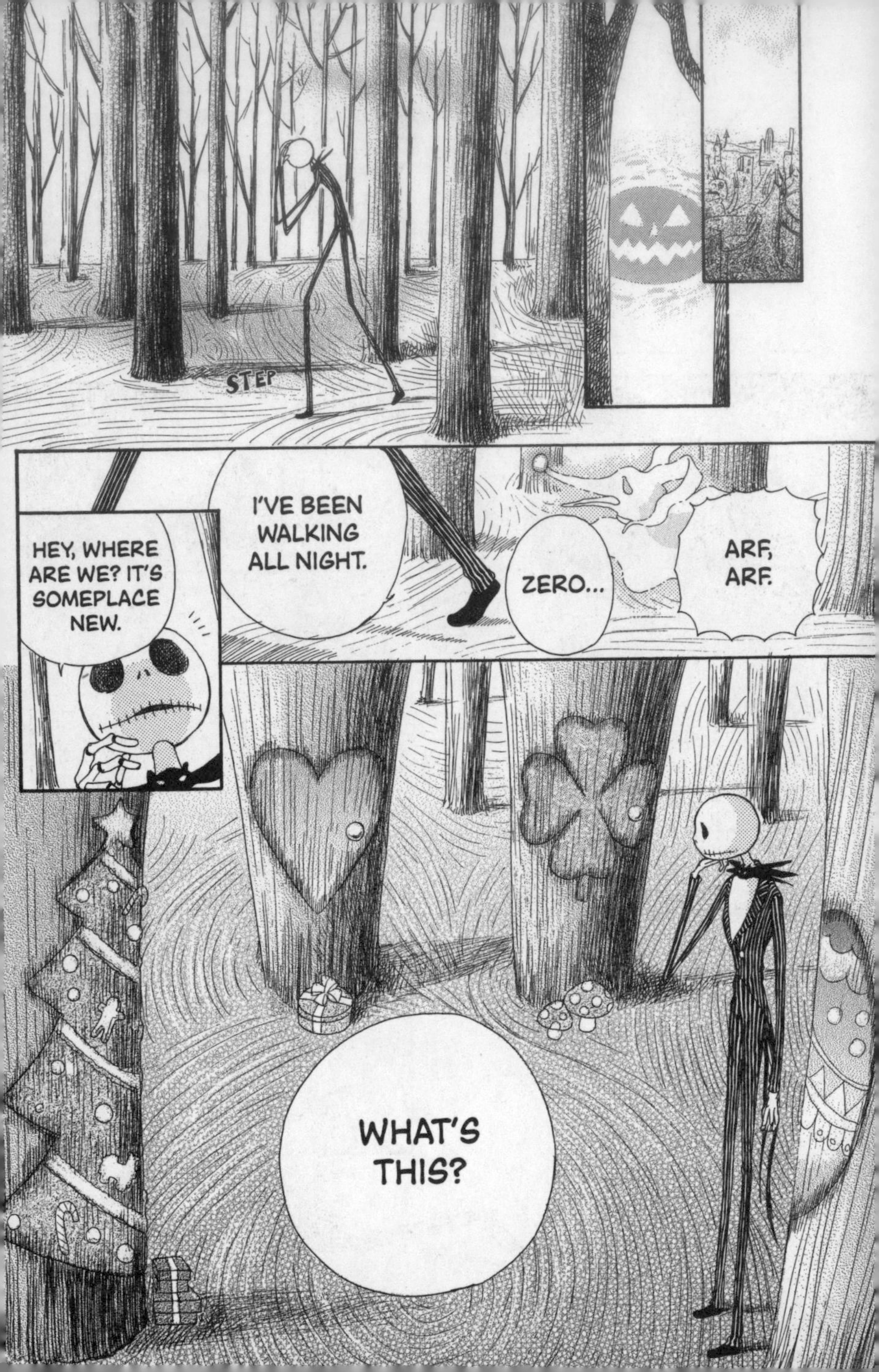
STEP
ARF, ARF.
ZERO...
I'VE BEEN WALKING ALL NIGHT.
HEY, WHERE ARE WE? IT'S SOMEPLACE NEW.
WHAT'S THIS?

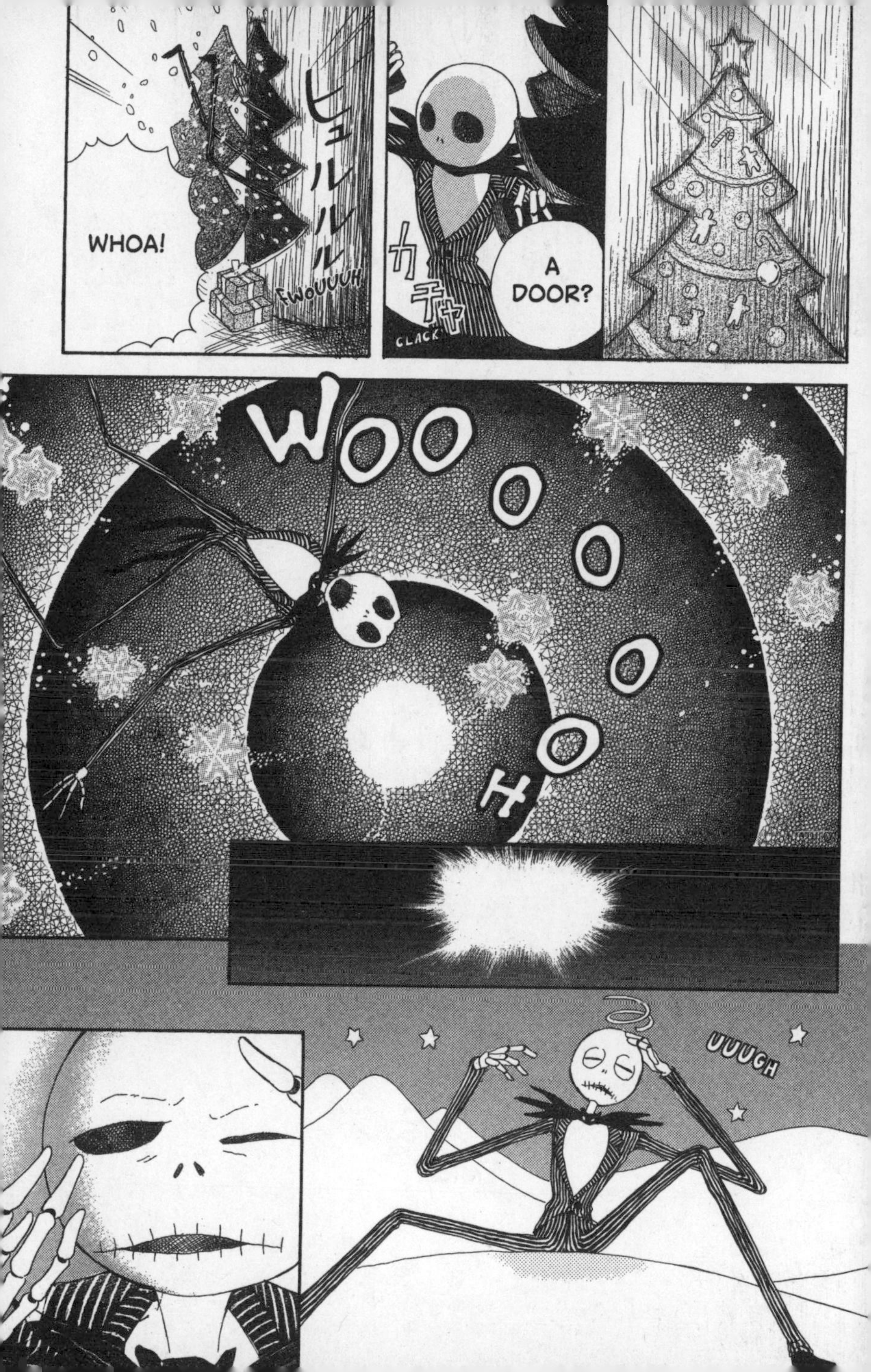
カチャ
CLACK
A DOOR?
WHOA!
ヒュルルル
FWOUUUH
WOOOOOOOH
UUUGH

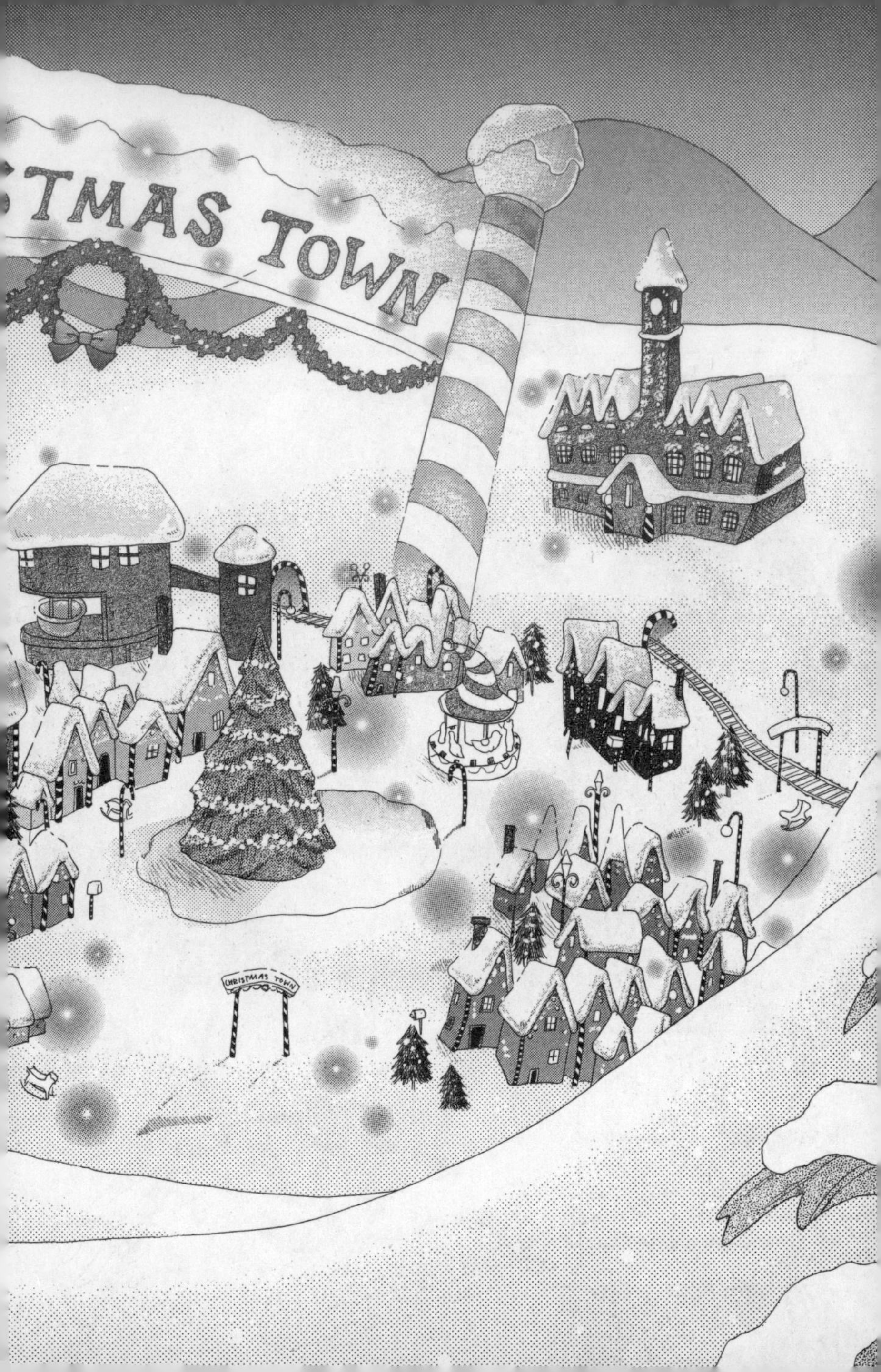
STMAS TOWN
CHRISTMAS TOWN

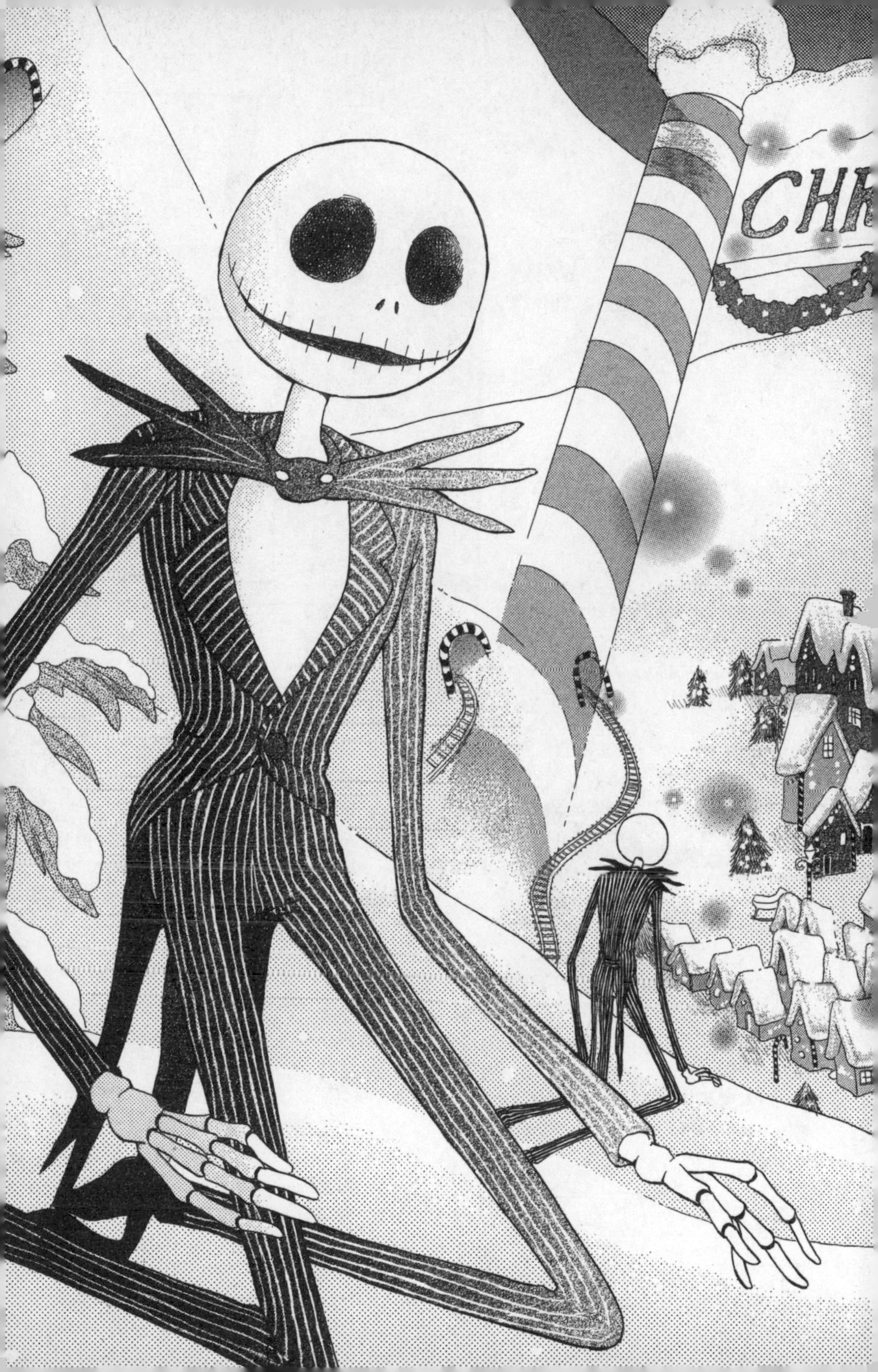
CHR

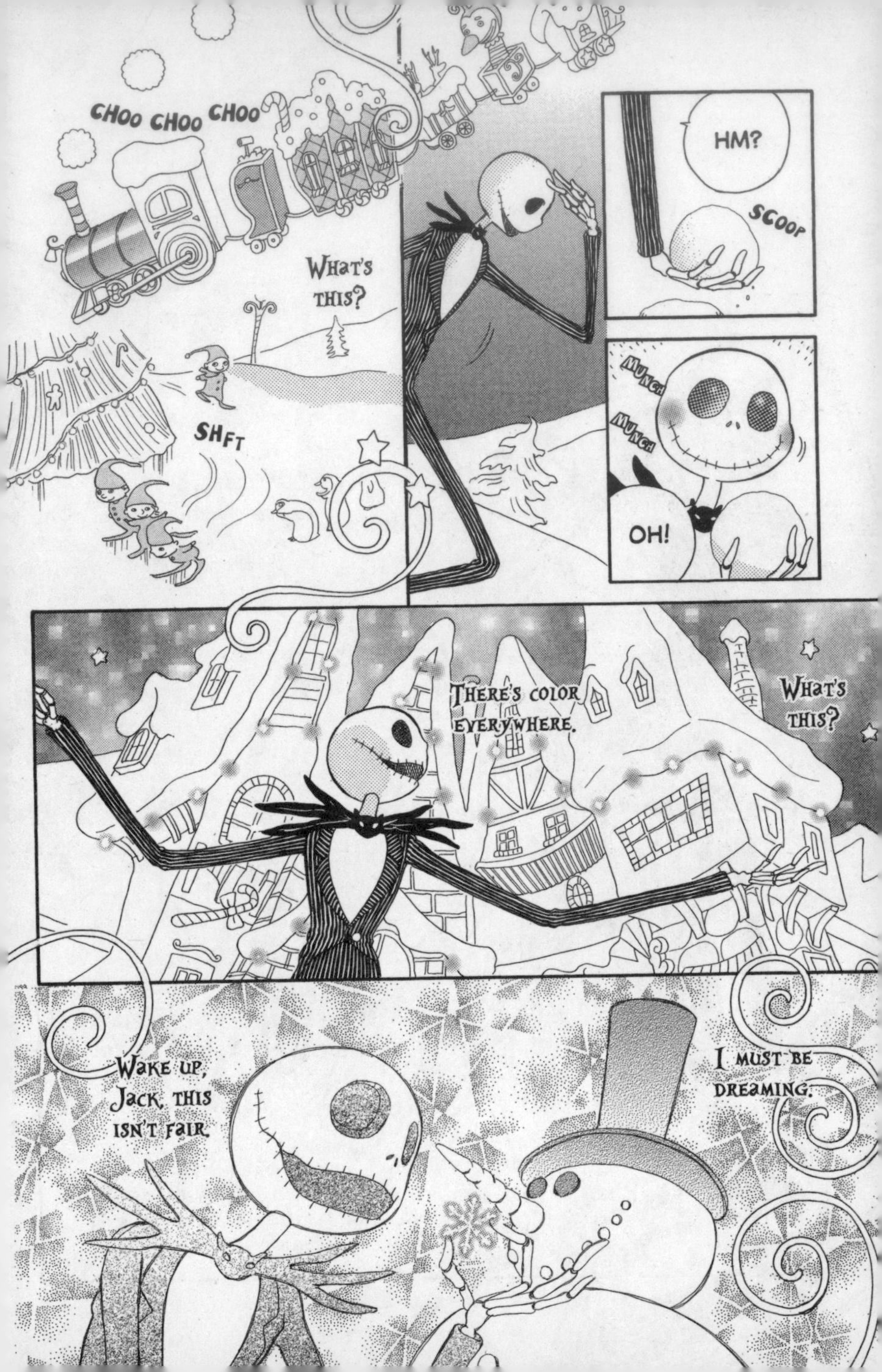
HM?
SCOOP
MUNCH
MUNCH
OH!
CHOO CHOO CHOO
WHAT'S THIS?
SHFT
WHAT'S THIS?
THERE'S COLOR EVERYWHERE.
I MUST BE DREAMING.
WAKE UP, JACK, THIS ISN'T FAIR.

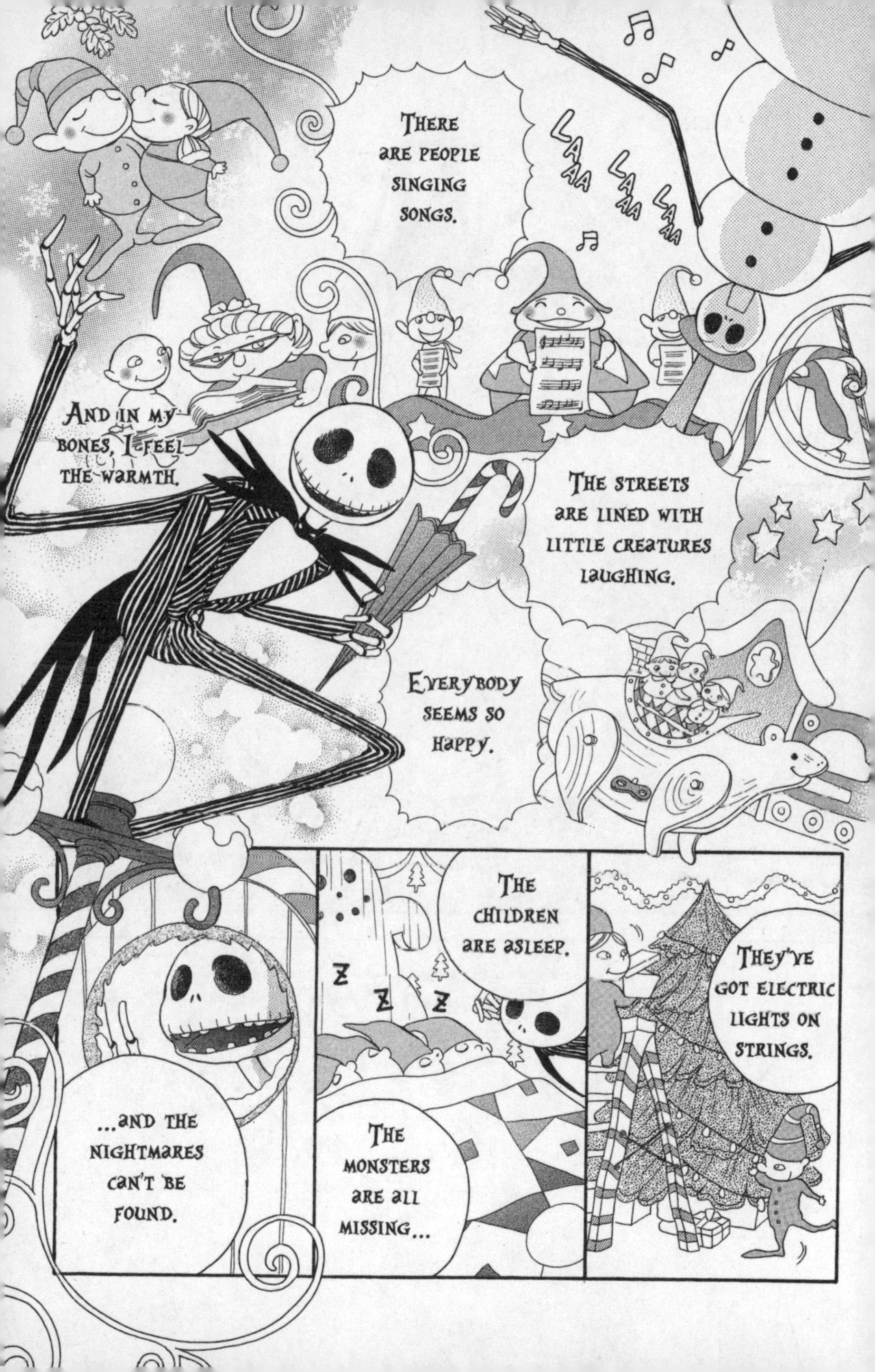
LAAA LAAA LAAA
There are people singing songs.
The streets are lined with little creatures laughing.
Everybody seems so happy.
And in my bones, I feel the warmth.
They've got electric lights on strings.
The children are asleep.
Z Z Z
The monsters are all missing...
...and the nightmares can't be found.

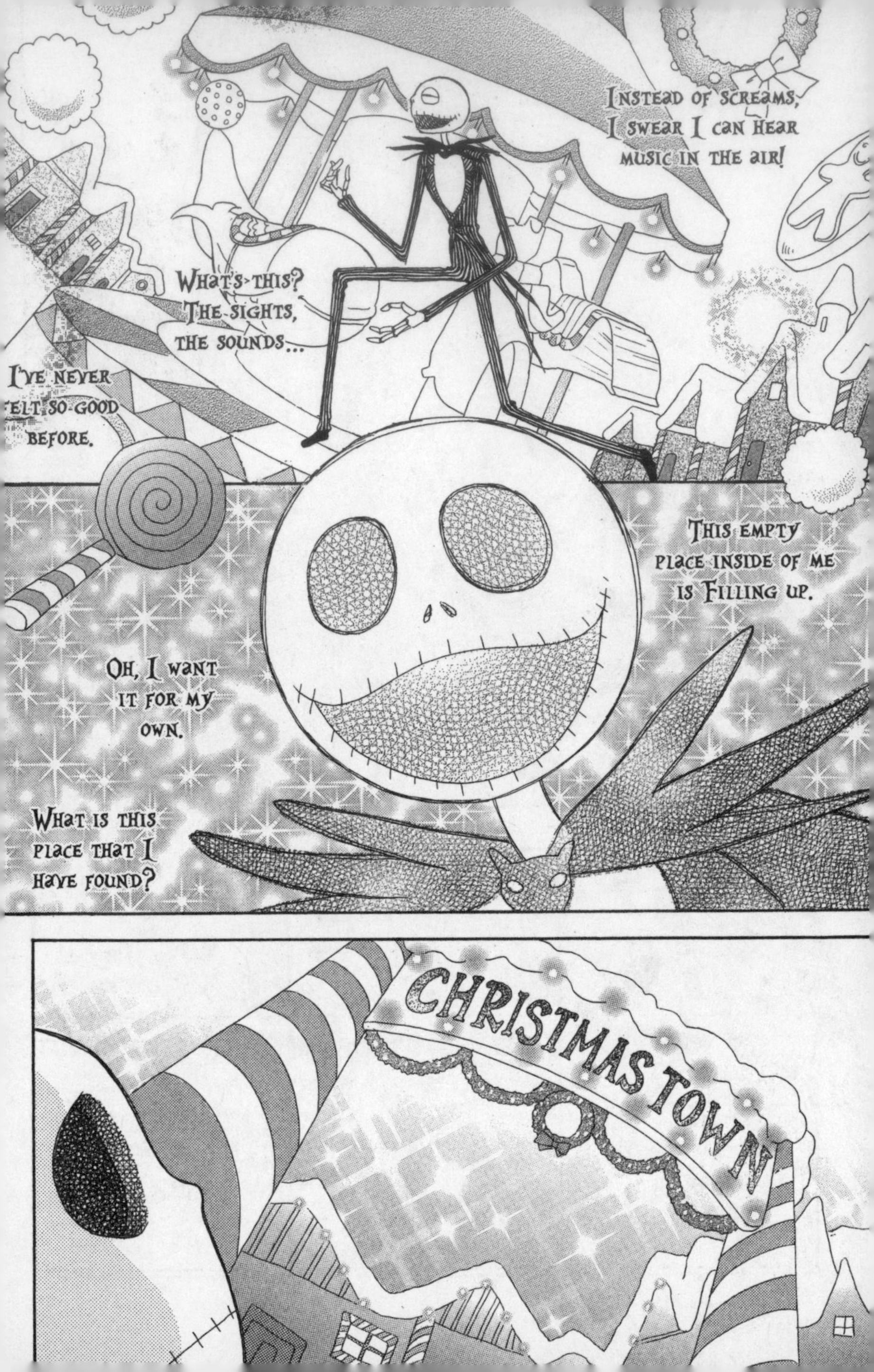
INSTEAD OF SCREAMS, I SWEAR I CAN HEAR MUSIC IN THE AIR!
WHAT'S THIS? THE SIGHTS, THE SOUNDS...
I'VE NEVER FELT SO GOOD BEFORE.
THIS EMPTY PLACE INSIDE OF ME IS FILLING UP.
OH, I WANT IT FOR MY OWN.
WHAT IS THIS PLACE THAT I HAVE FOUND?
CHRISTMAS TOWN

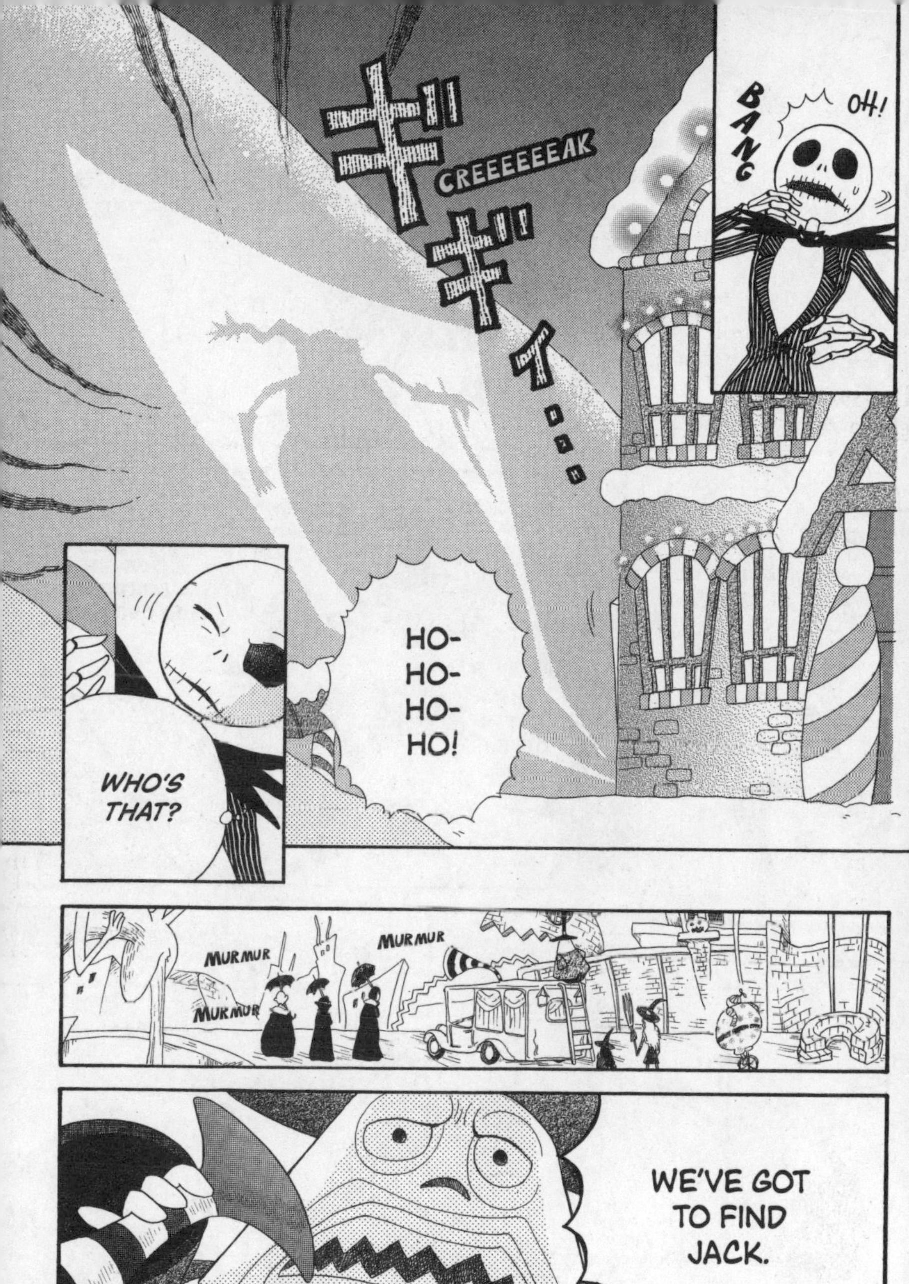
BANG
OH!
ギギギイ…
CREEEEEEAK
HO-HO-HO-HO!
WHO'S THAT?
MURMUR
MURMUR
MURMUR
WE'VE GOT TO FIND JACK.

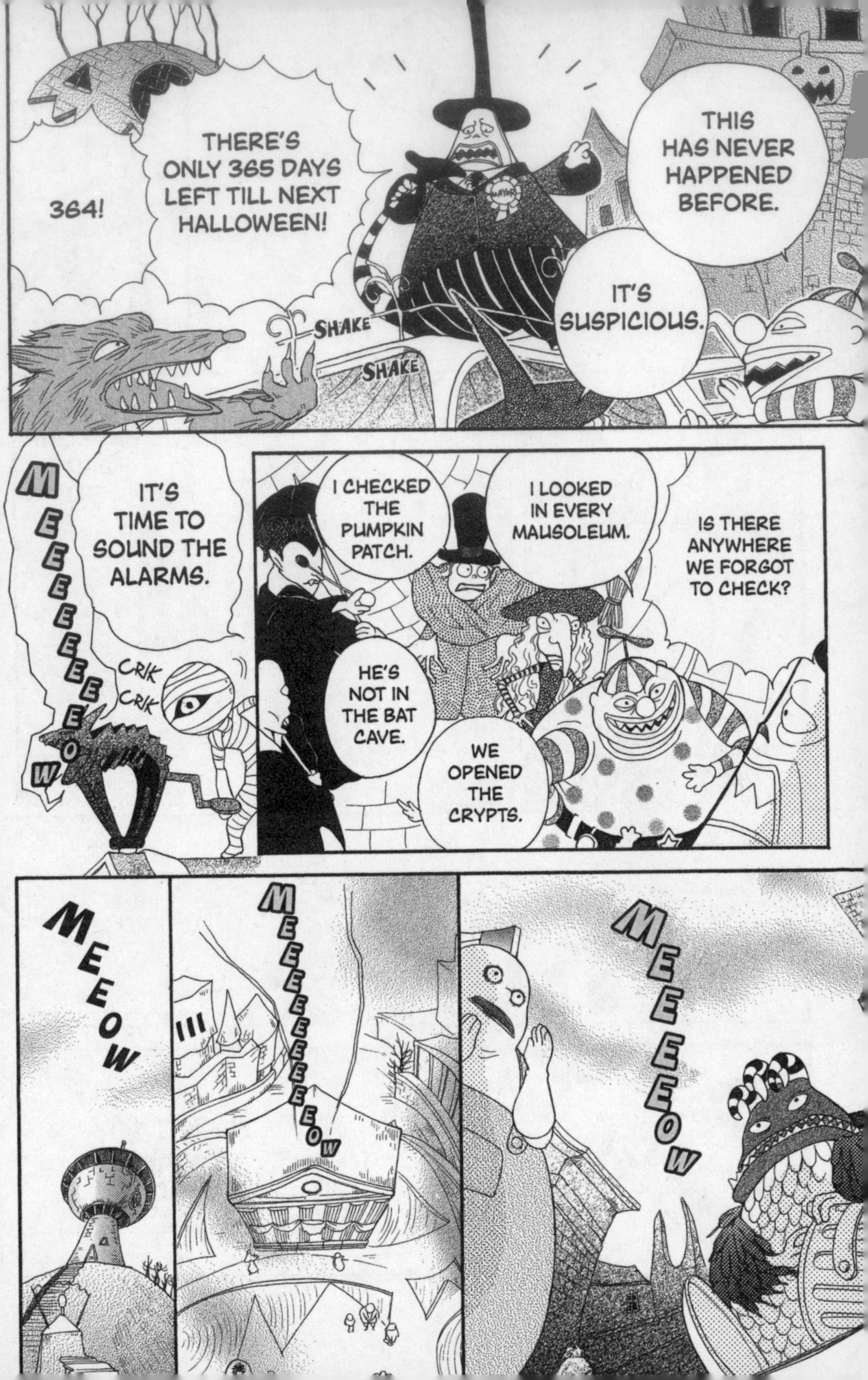
THIS HAS NEVER HAPPENED BEFORE.
IT'S SUSPICIOUS.
THERE'S ONLY 365 DAYS LEFT TILL NEXT HALLOWEEN!
364!
SHAKE
SHAKE
IS THERE ANYWHERE WE FORGOT TO CHECK?
I LOOKED IN EVERY MAUSOLEUM.
I CHECKED THE PUMPKIN PATCH.
HE'S NOT IN THE BAT CAVE.
WE OPENED THE CRYPTS.
IT'S TIME TO SOUND THE ALARMS.
MEEEEEEEEOW
CRIK
CRIK
MEEEEOW
MEEEEEEEEEOW
MEEOW

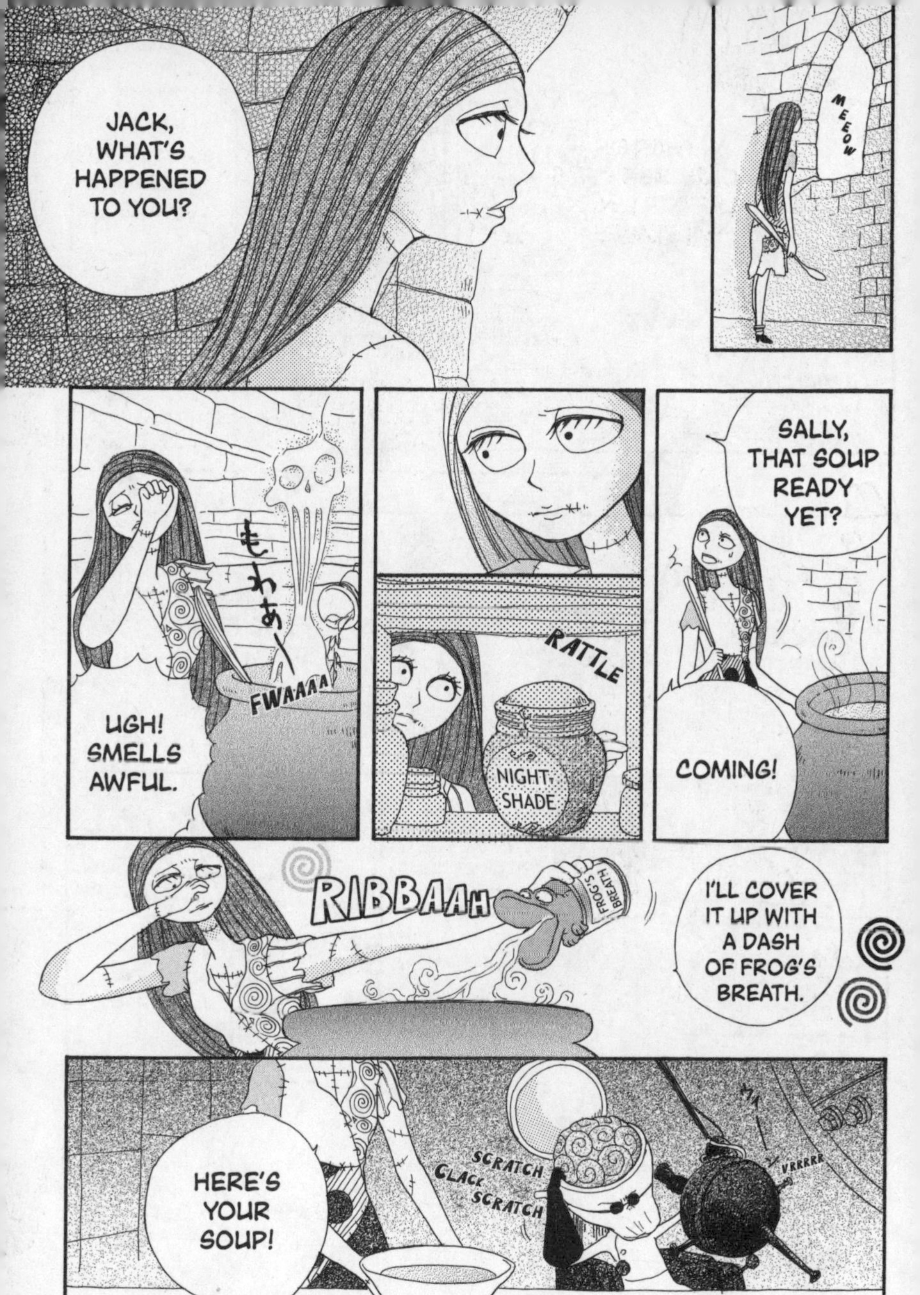
MEEOW
JACK, WHAT'S HAPPENED TO YOU?
SALLY, THAT SOUP READY YET?
COMING!
RATTLE
NIGHT-SHADE
もわあ～
FWAAAA
UGH! SMELLS AWFUL.
I'LL COVER IT UP WITH A DASH OF FROG'S BREATH.
FROG'S BREATH
RIBBAAH
VRRRRR
SCRATCH
CLACK
SCRATCH
HERE'S YOUR SOUP!

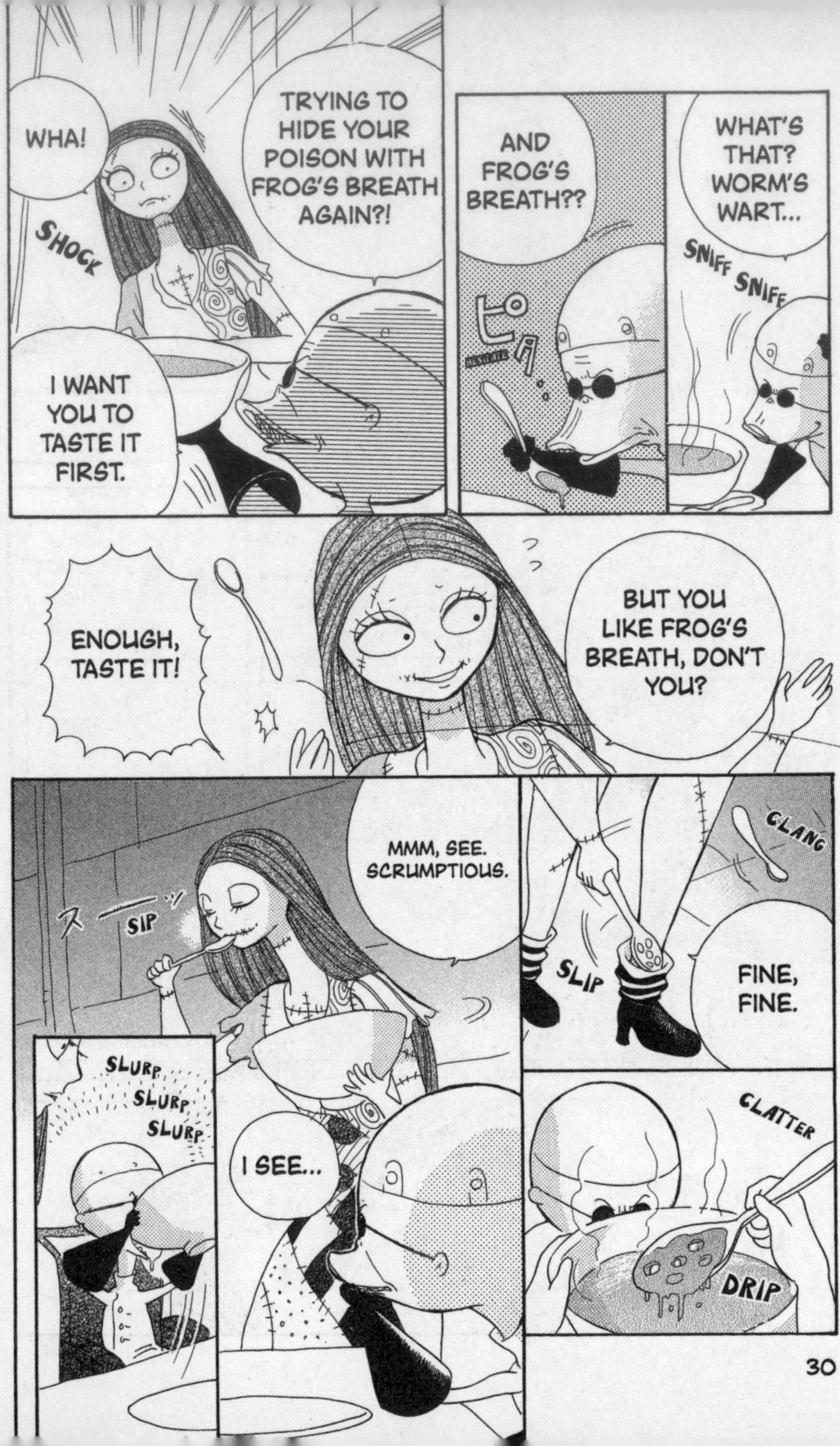
WHAT'S THAT? WORM'S WART...
SNIFF SNIFF
AND FROG'S BREATH??
ピタ
HESITATE
TRYING TO HIDE YOUR POISON WITH FROG'S BREATH AGAIN?!
WHA!
SHOCK
I WANT YOU TO TASTE IT FIRST.
BUT YOU LIKE FROG'S BREATH, DON'T YOU?
ENOUGH, TASTE IT!
CLANG
FINE, FINE.
SLIP
MMM, SEE. SCRUMPTIOUS.
スーッ
SIP
CLATTER
DRIP
I SEE...
SLURP
SLURP
SLURP

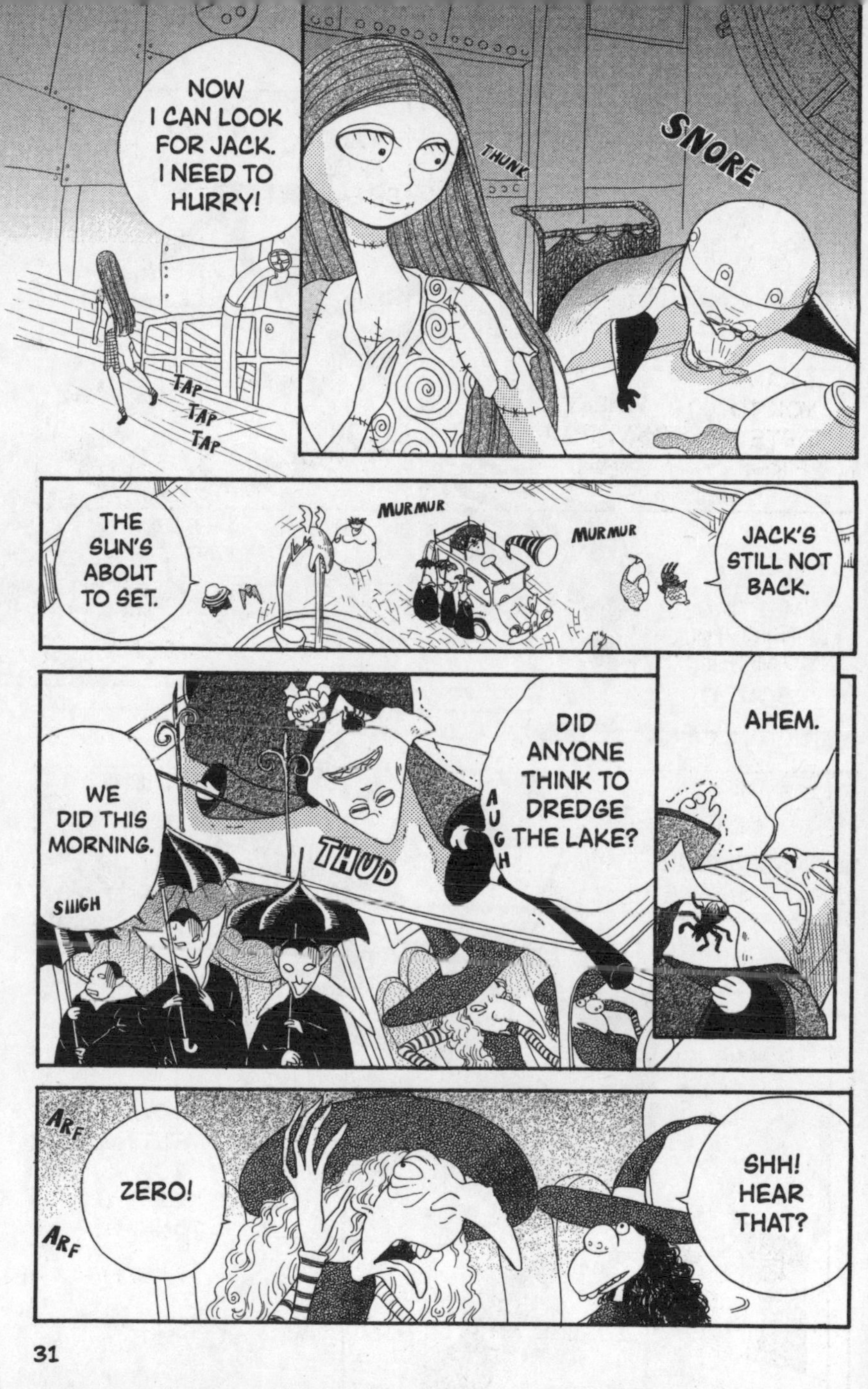
SNORE
THUNK
NOW I CAN LOOK FOR JACK. I NEED TO HURRY!
TAP TAP TAP
JACK'S STILL NOT BACK.
MURMUR
MURMUR
THE SUN'S ABOUT TO SET.
AHEM.
DID ANYONE THINK TO DREDGE THE LAKE?
AUGH
THUD
WE DID THIS MORNING.
SIIIGH
SHH! HEAR THAT?
ZERO!
ARF
ARF

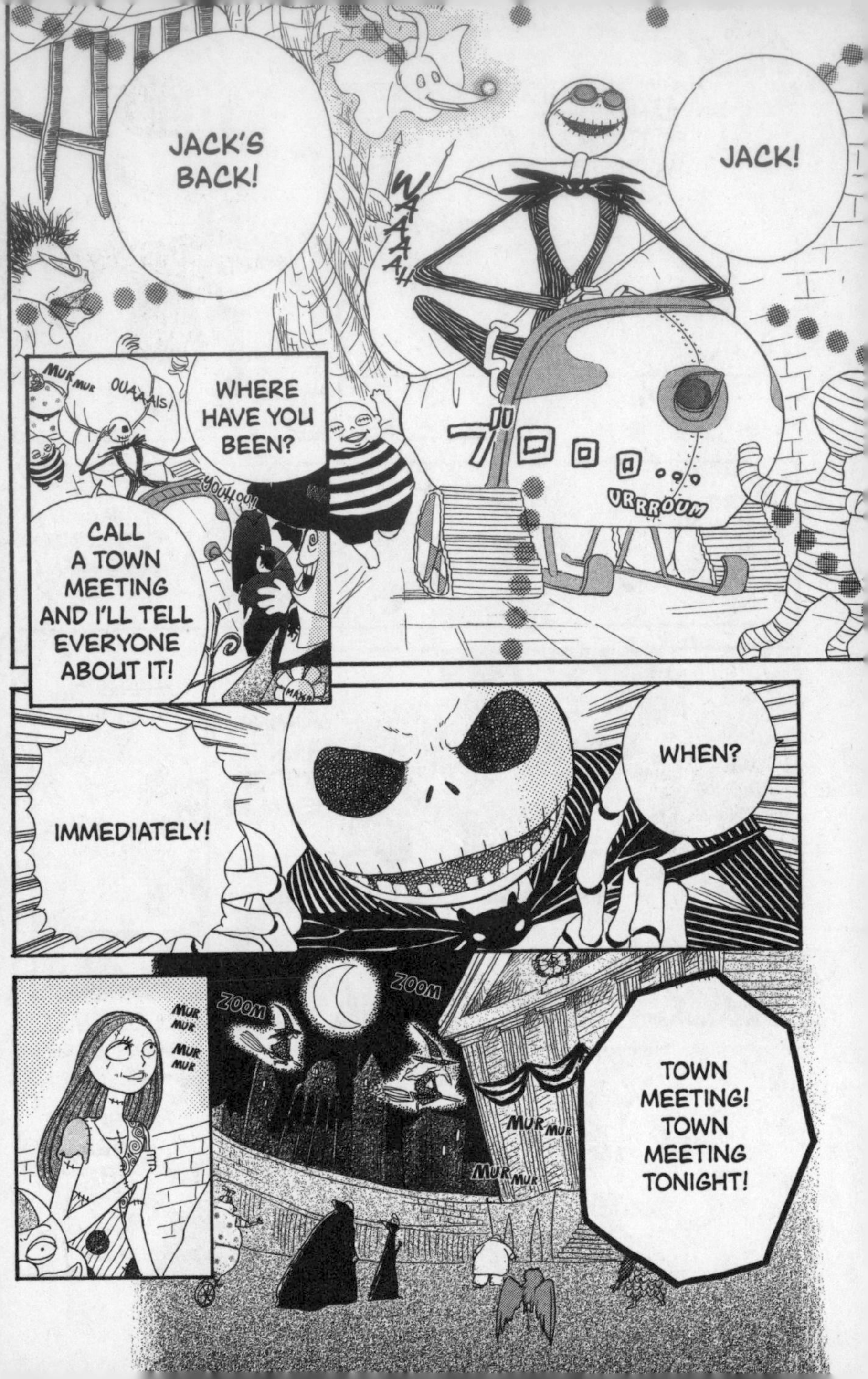
JACK!
JACK'S BACK!
WAAAAH
ブロロロ
VRRROUM
MUR MUR
OUAAAIS!
WHERE HAVE YOU BEEN?
YOUHOU!
CALL A TOWN MEETING AND I'LL TELL EVERYONE ABOUT IT!
WHEN?
IMMEDIATELY!
TOWN MEETING! TOWN MEETING TONIGHT!
ZOOM
ZOOM
MUR MUR
MUR MUR
MUR MUR
MUR MUR

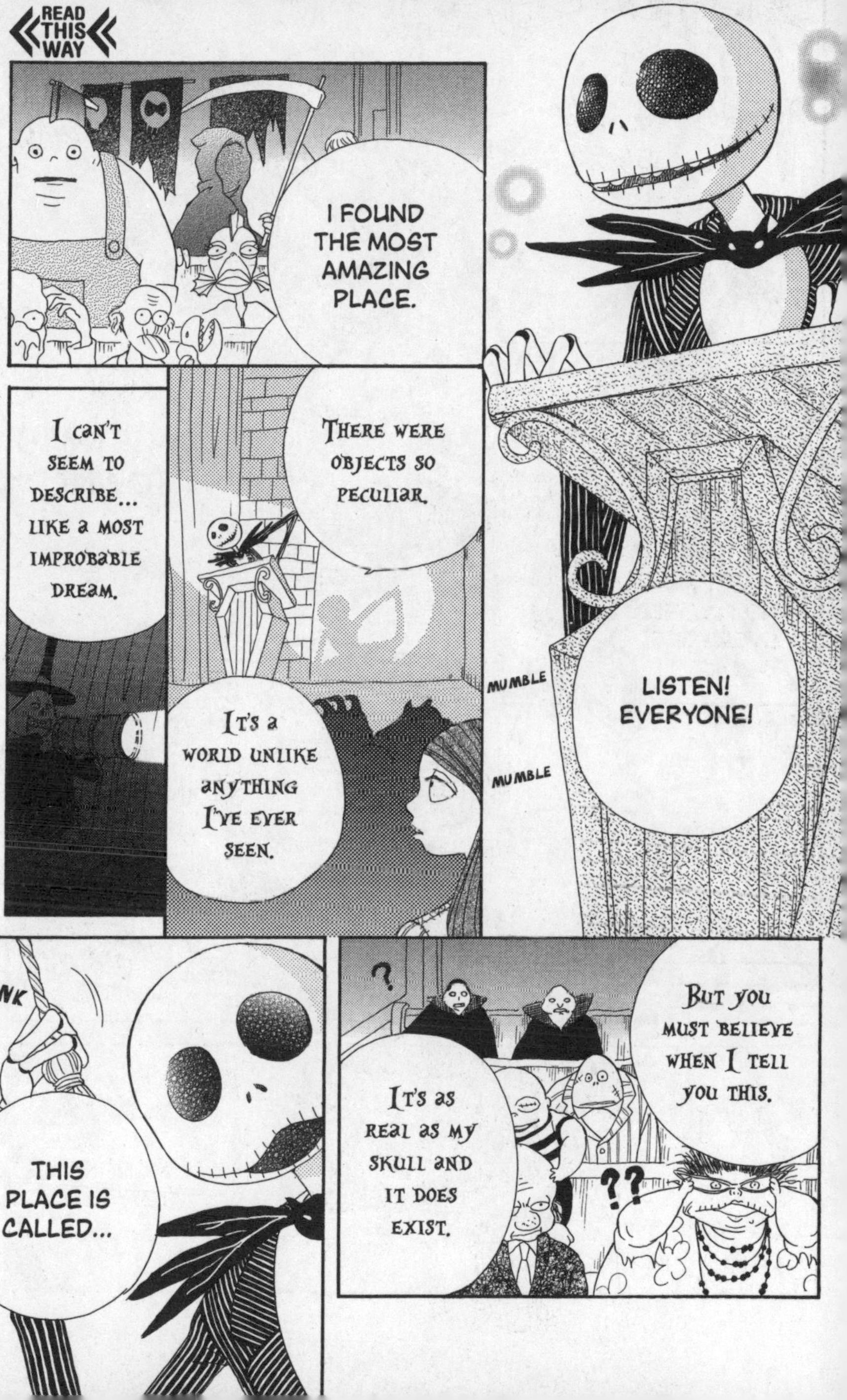
READ THIS WAY
MUMBLE
MUMBLE
LISTEN! EVERYONE!
I FOUND THE MOST AMAZING PLACE.
THERE WERE OBJECTS SO PECULIAR.
IT'S A WORLD UNLIKE ANYTHING I'VE EVER SEEN.
I CAN'T SEEM TO DESCRIBE... LIKE A MOST IMPROBABLE DREAM.
BUT YOU MUST BELIEVE WHEN I TELL YOU THIS.
?
??
IT'S AS REAL AS MY SKULL AND IT DOES EXIST.
YANK
THIS PLACE IS CALLED...

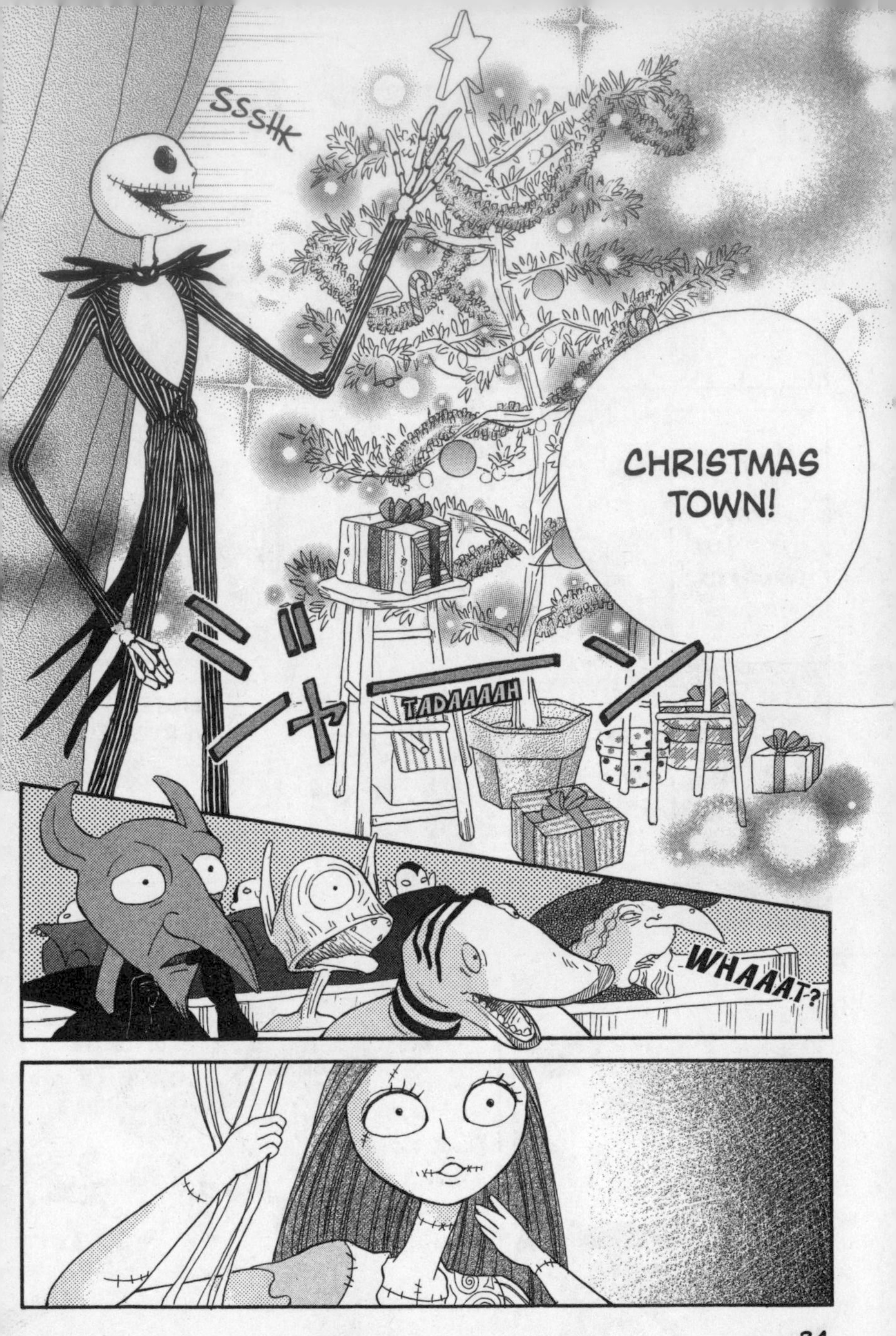
CHRISTMAS TOWN!
SSSHK
TADAAAAH
WHAAAT?

READ THIS WAY

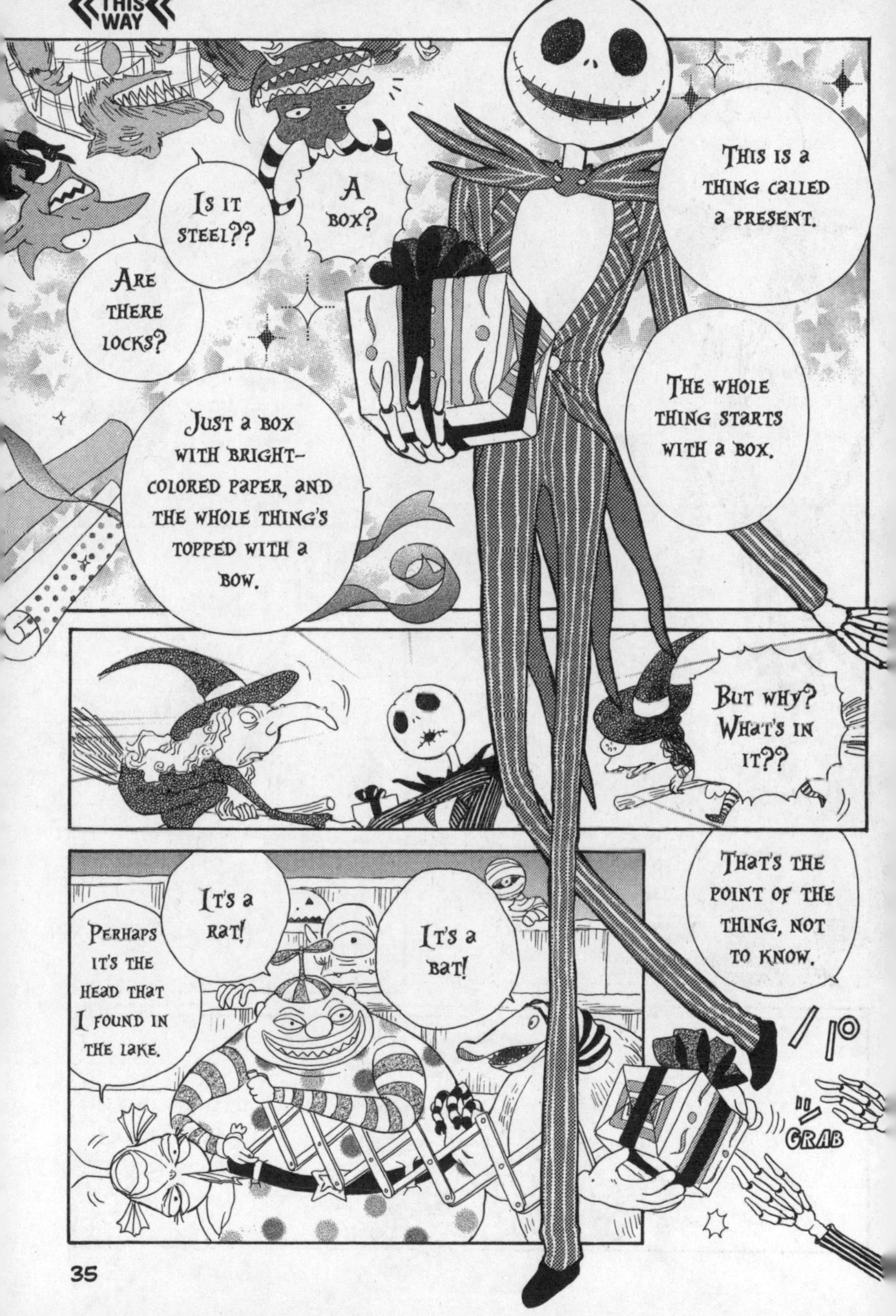

This is a thing called a present.
A box?
Is it steel??
Are there locks?
The whole thing starts with a box.
Just a box with bright-colored paper, and the whole thing's topped with a bow.
But why? What's in it??
That's the point of the thing, not to know.
GRAB
It's a bat!
It's a rat!
Perhaps it's the head that I found in the lake.

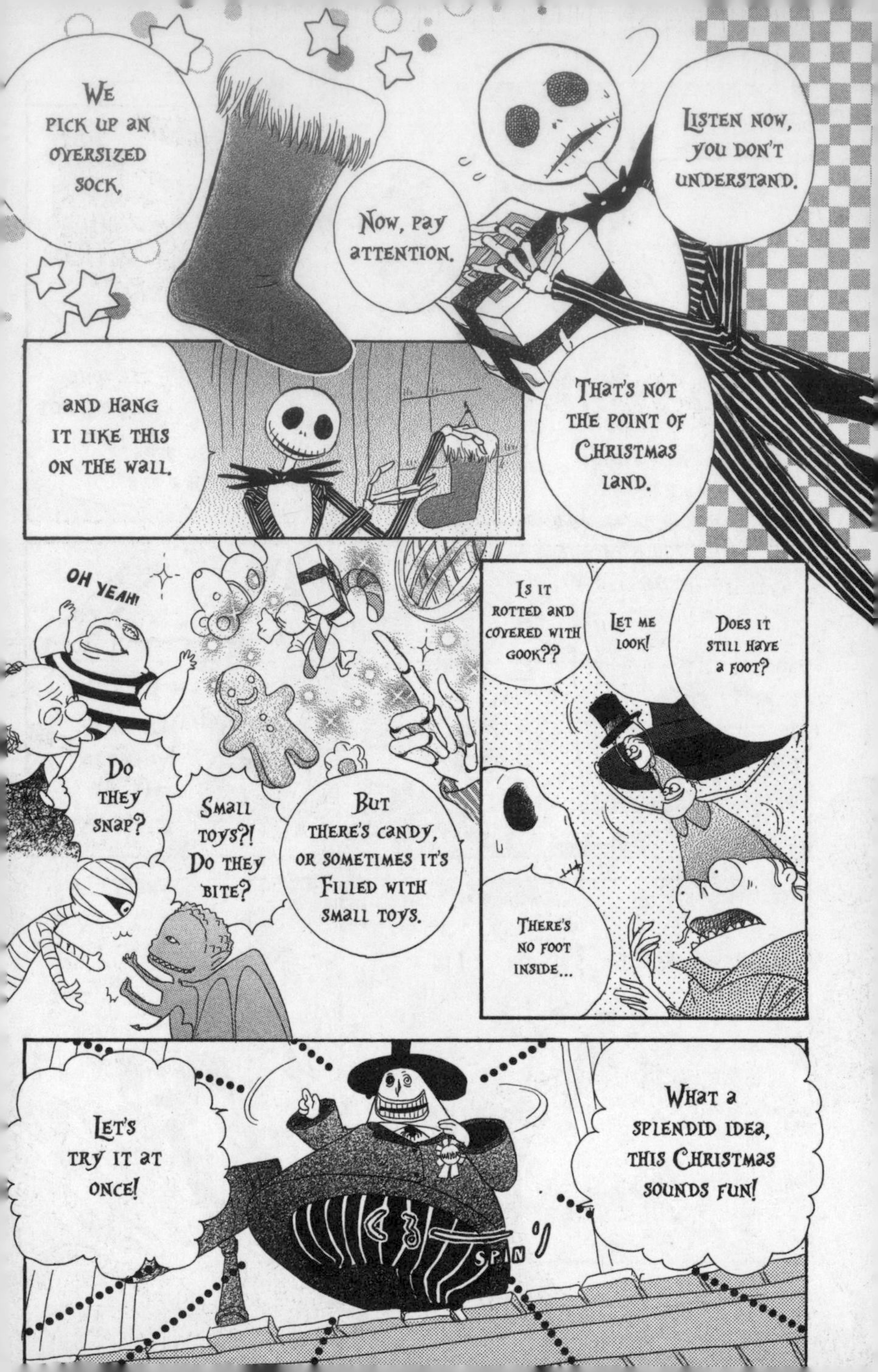
Listen now, you don't understand.
That's not the point of Christmas land.
Now, pay attention.
We pick up an oversized sock,
and hang it like this on the wall.
Does it still have a foot?
Let me look!
Is it rotted and covered with gook??
There's no foot inside...
But there's candy, or sometimes it's filled with small toys.
Small toys?! Do they bite?
Do they snap?
OH YEAH!
What a splendid idea, this Christmas sounds fun!
Let's try it at once!
SPIN

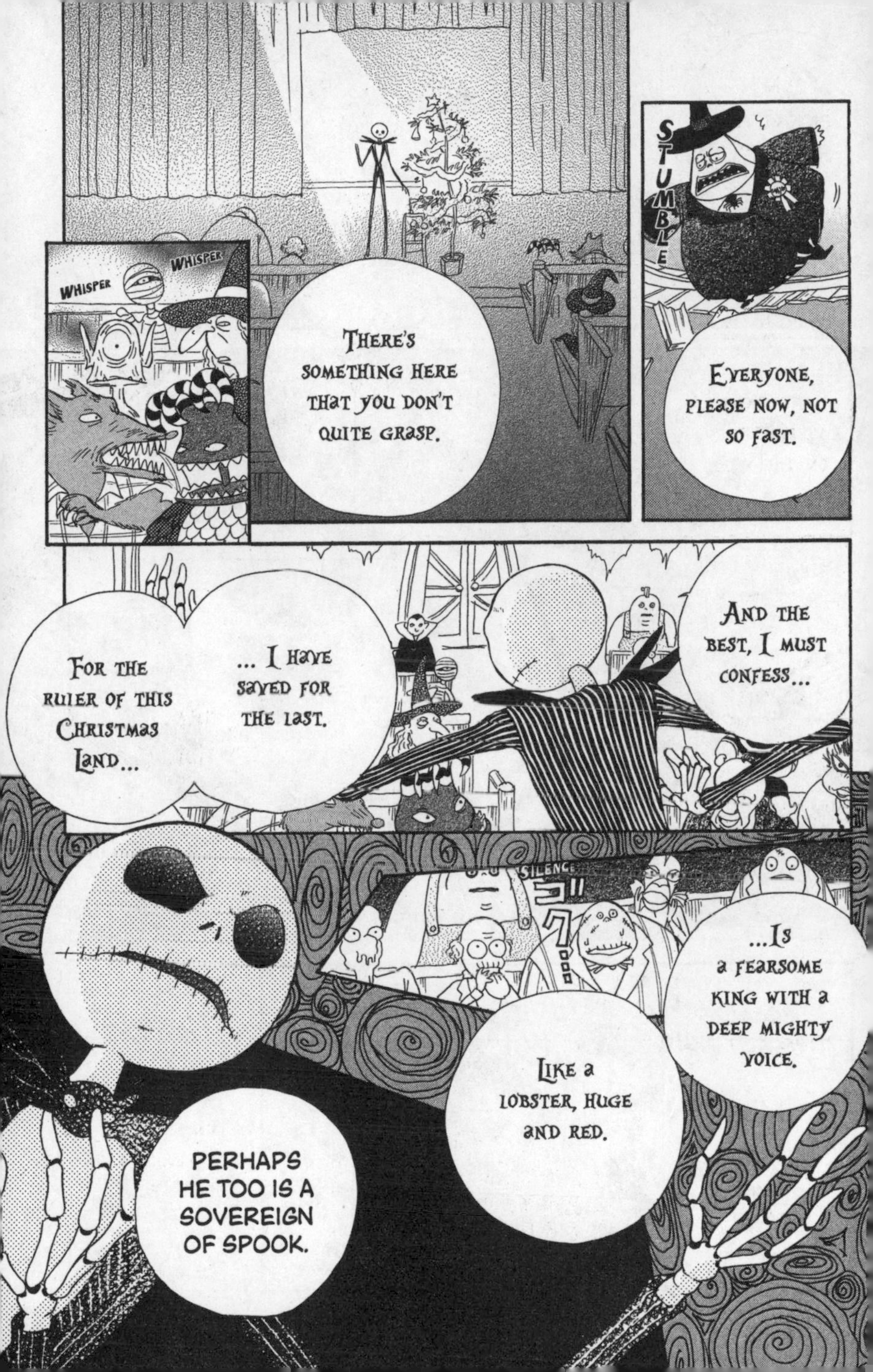
STUMBLE
EVERYONE, PLEASE NOW, NOT SO FAST.
THERE'S SOMETHING HERE THAT YOU DON'T QUITE GRASP.
WHISPER
WHISPER
AND THE BEST, I MUST CONFESS...
... I HAVE SAVED FOR THE LAST.
FOR THE RULER OF THIS CHRISTMAS LAND...
...IS A FEARSOME KING WITH A DEEP MIGHTY VOICE.
SILENC
LIKE A LOBSTER, HUGE AND RED.
PERHAPS HE TOO IS A SOVEREIGN OF SPOOK.

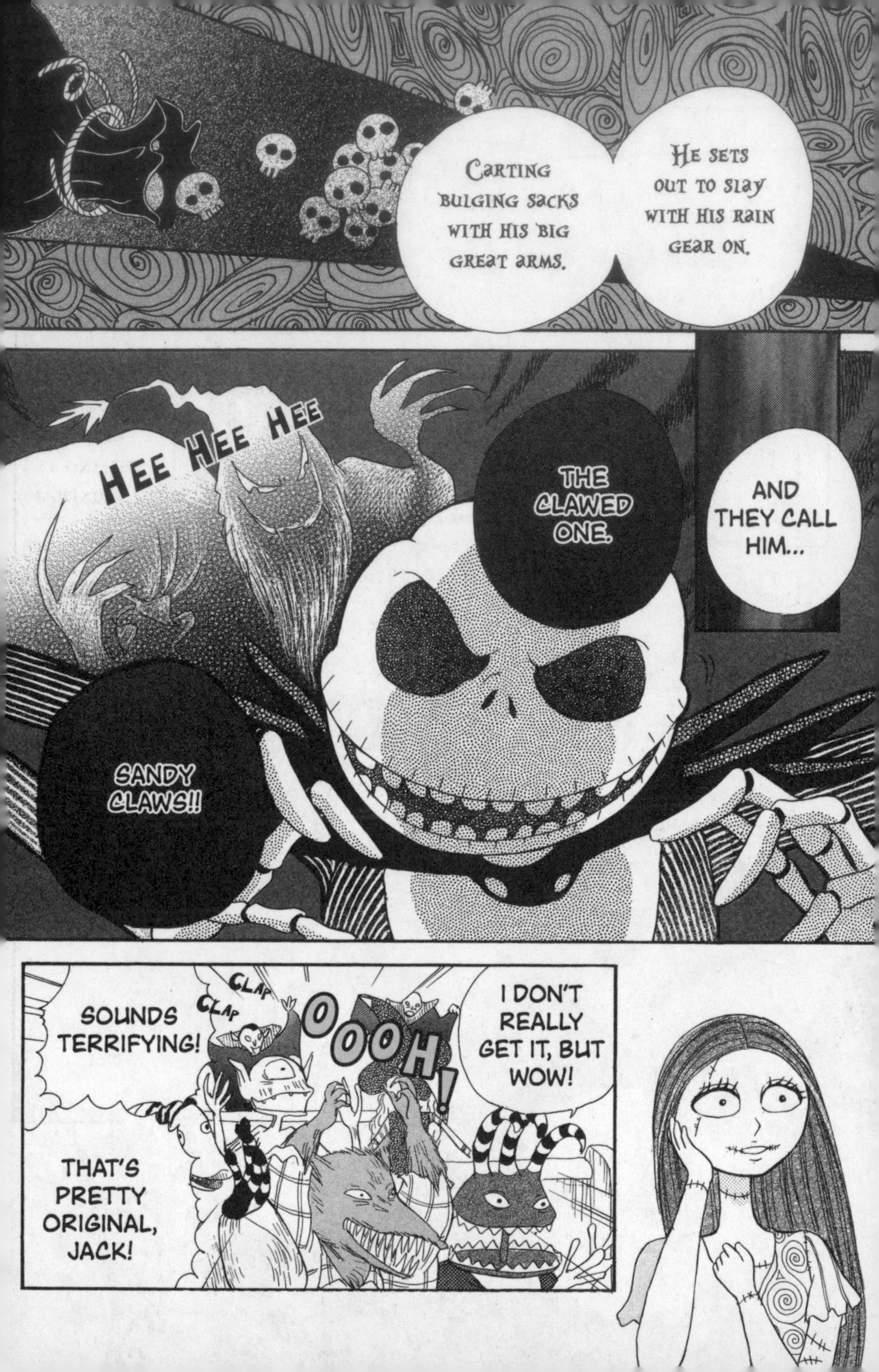
He sets out to slay with his rain gear on.
Carting bulging sacks with his big great arms.
AND THEY CALL HIM...
THE CLAWED ONE.
HEE HEE HEE
SANDY CLAWS!!
I DON'T REALLY GET IT, BUT WOW!
OOOH!
CLAP
CLAP
SOUNDS TERRIFYING!
THAT'S PRETTY ORIGINAL, JACK!

READ THIS WAY

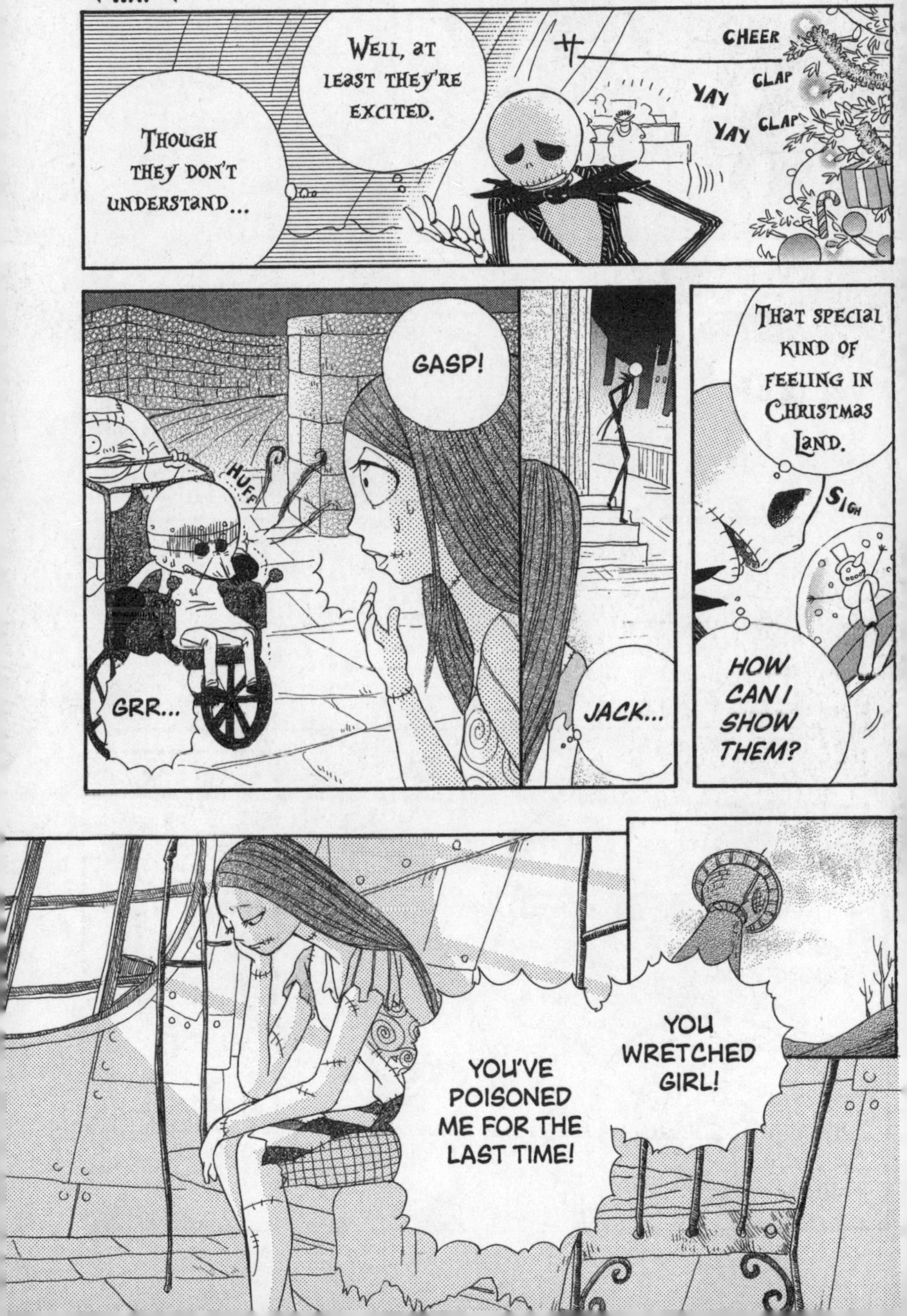
CHEER
CLAP
YAY
CLAP
YAY
WELL, AT LEAST THEY'RE EXCITED.
THOUGH THEY DON'T UNDERSTAND...
THAT SPECIAL KIND OF FEELING IN CHRISTMAS LAND.
SIGH
HOW CAN I SHOW THEM?
JACK...
GASP!
HUFF
GRR...
YOU WRETCHED GIRL!
YOU'VE POISONED ME FOR THE LAST TIME!

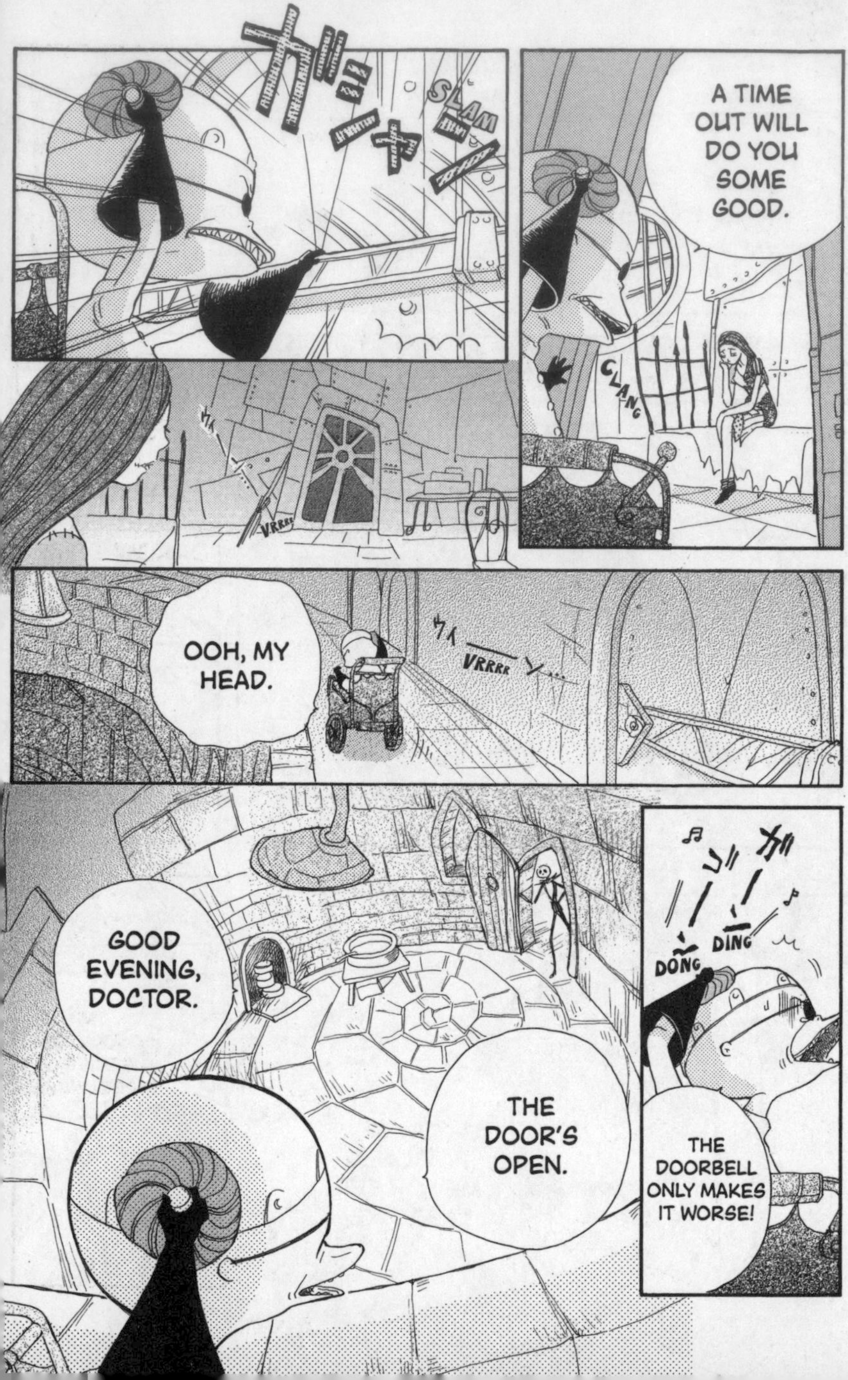
A TIME OUT WILL DO YOU SOME GOOD.
CLANG
SLAM
VRRRR
OOH, MY HEAD.
VRRRR
DING
DONG
THE DOORBELL ONLY MAKES IT WORSE!
GOOD EVENING, DOCTOR.
THE DOOR'S OPEN.

READ THIS WAY

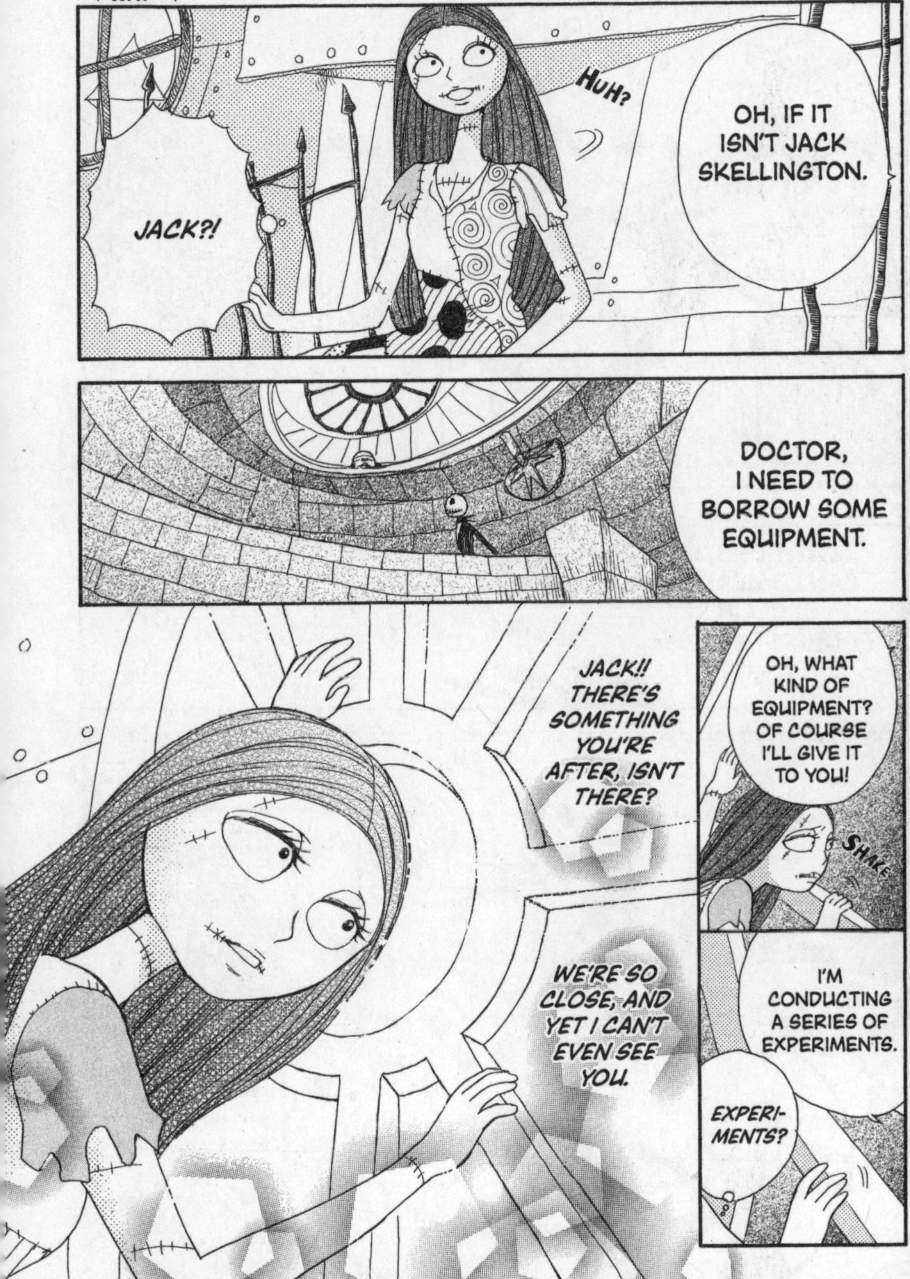
OH, IF IT ISN'T JACK SKELLINGTON.
HUH?
JACK?!
DOCTOR, I NEED TO BORROW SOME EQUIPMENT.
OH, WHAT KIND OF EQUIPMENT? OF COURSE I'LL GIVE IT TO YOU!
SHAKE
I'M CONDUCTING A SERIES OF EXPERIMENTS.
EXPERI-MENTS?
JACK!! THERE'S SOMETHING YOU'RE AFTER, ISN'T THERE?
WE'RE SO CLOSE, AND YET I CAN'T EVEN SEE YOU.

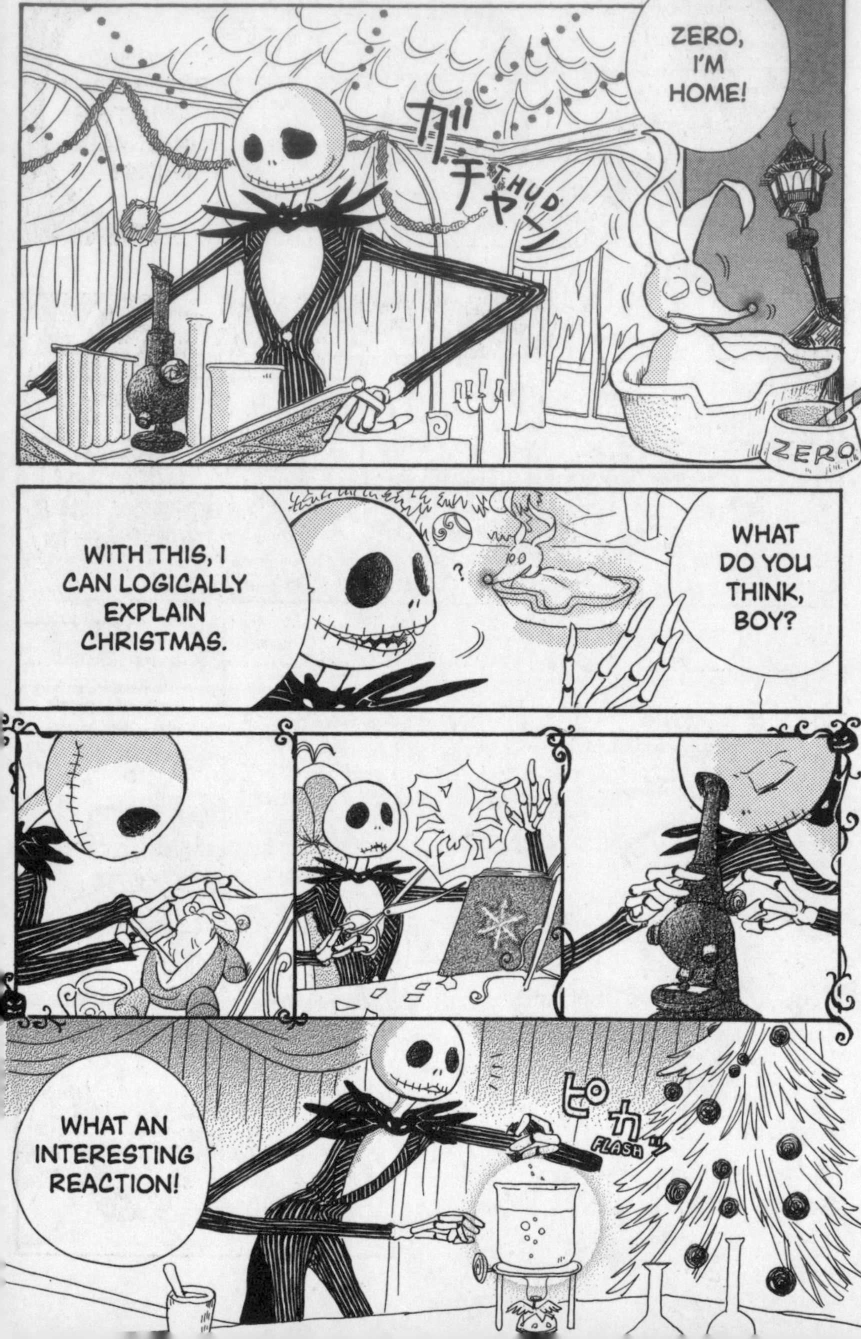
ZERO, I'M HOME!
ガチャン
THUD
WHAT DO YOU THINK, BOY?
WITH THIS, I CAN LOGICALLY EXPLAIN CHRISTMAS.
ZERO
ピカッ
FLASH
WHAT AN INTERESTING REACTION!

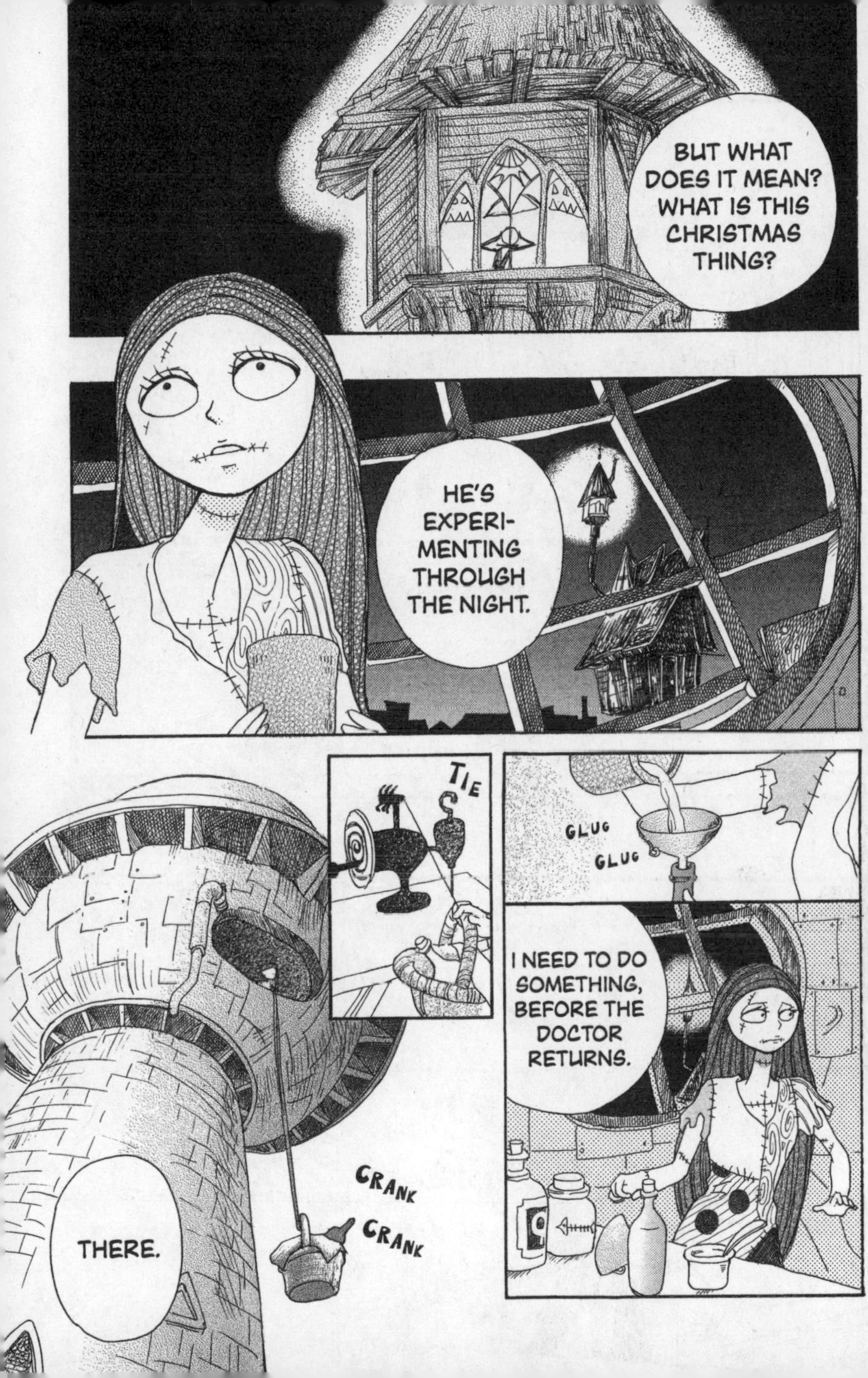
BUT WHAT DOES IT MEAN? WHAT IS THIS CHRISTMAS THING?
HE'S EXPERI-MENTING THROUGH THE NIGHT.
GLUG
GLUG
I NEED TO DO SOMETHING, BEFORE THE DOCTOR RETURNS.
TIE
CRANK
CRANK
THERE.

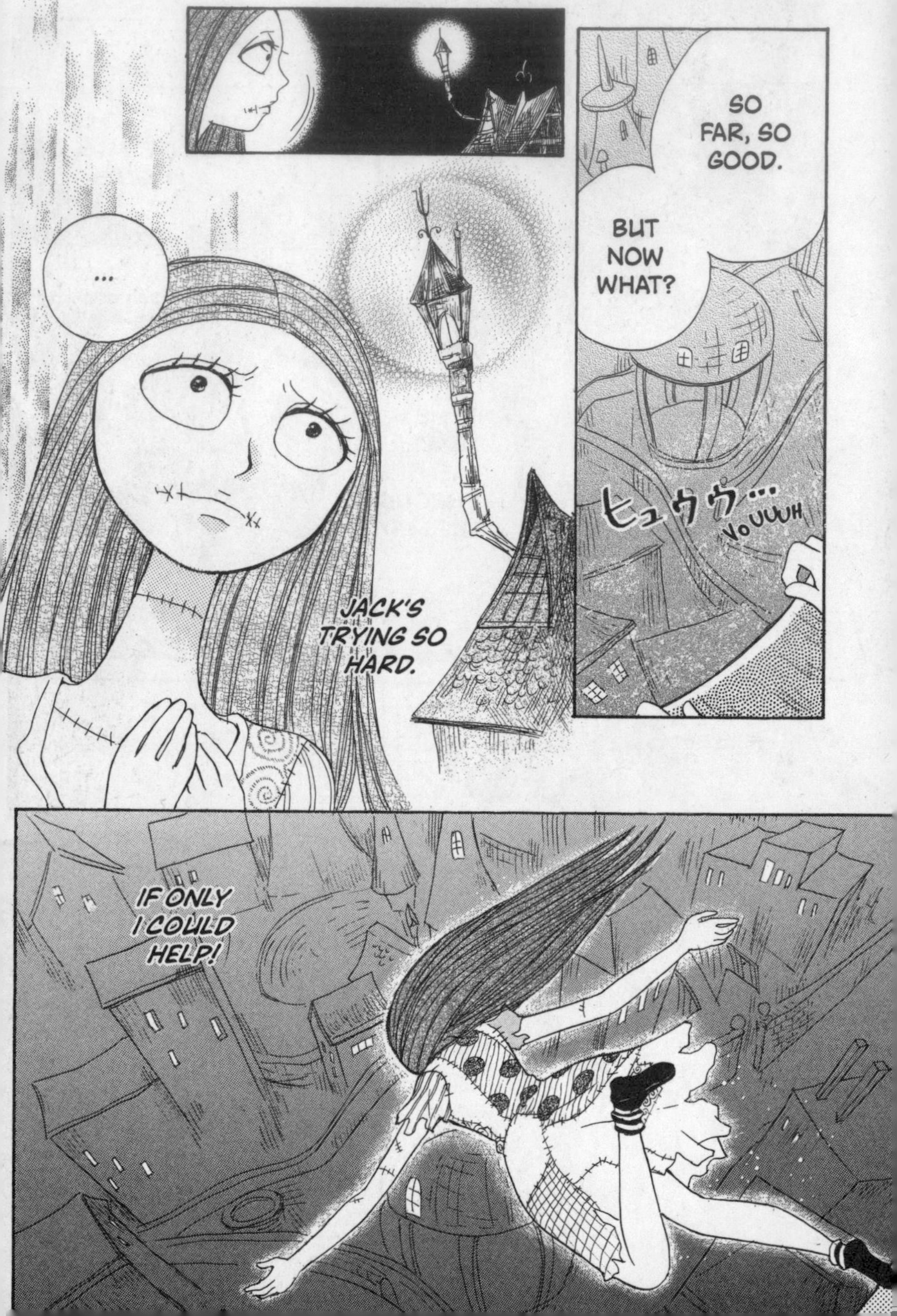
SO FAR, SO GOOD.
BUT NOW WHAT?
ヒュウウ… VOUUUH
...
JACK'S TRYING SO HARD.
IF ONLY I COULD HELP!

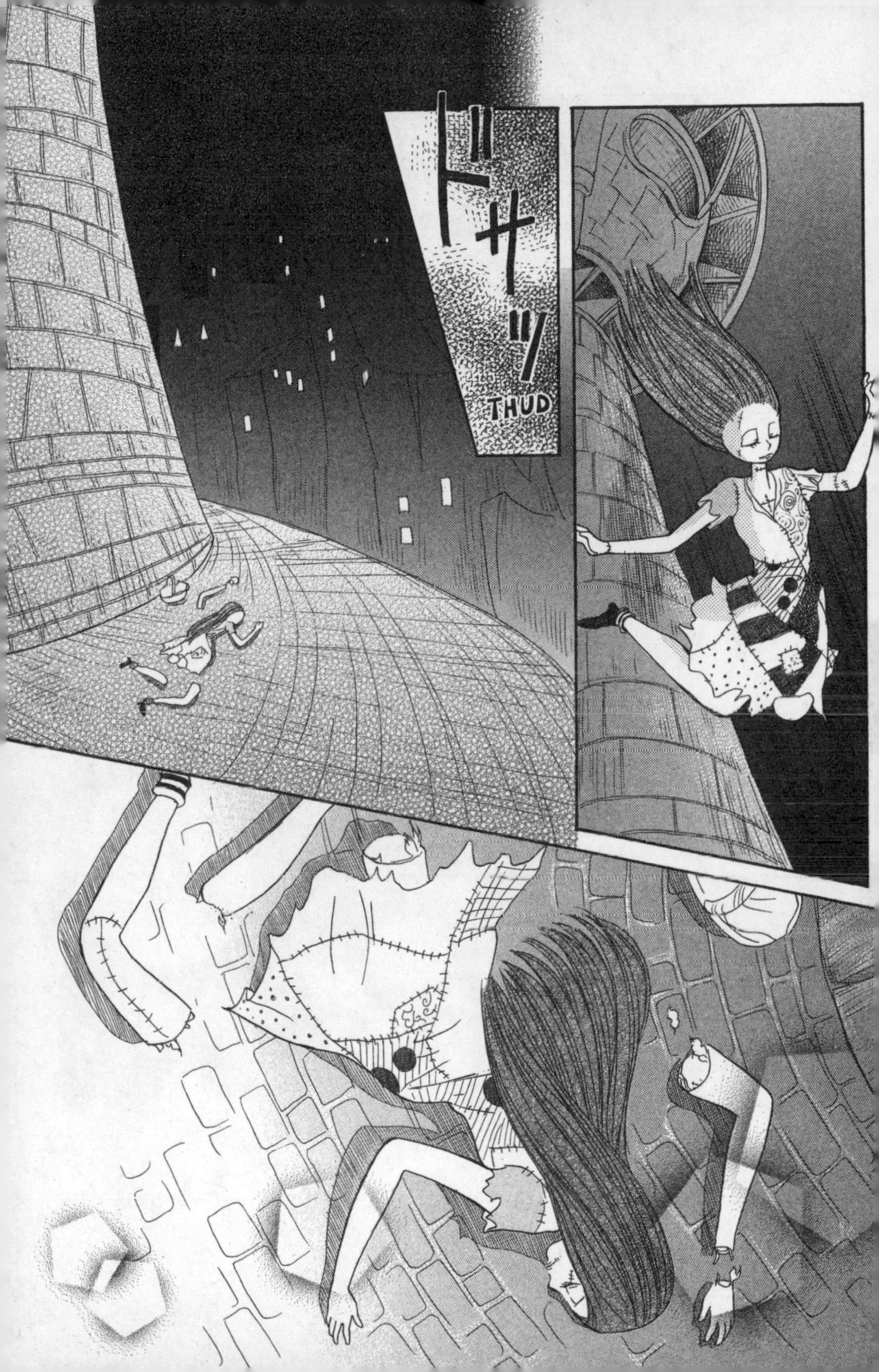
ドサッ
THUD

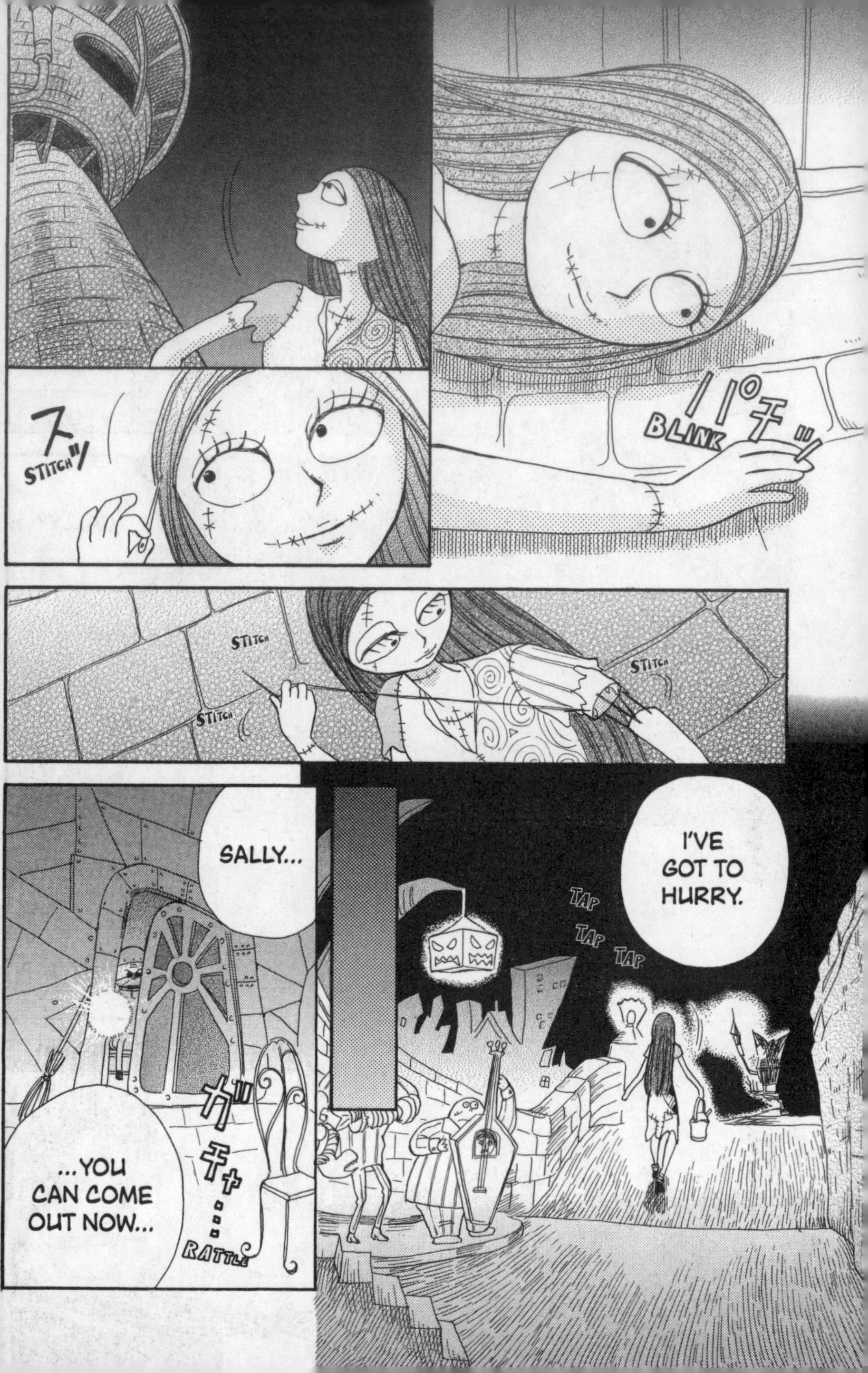

パチッ
BLINK
スッ
STITCH
STITCH
STITCH
STITCH
I'VE GOT TO HURRY.
TAP
TAP
TAP
SALLY...
...YOU CAN COME OUT NOW...
ガチャ...
RATTLE

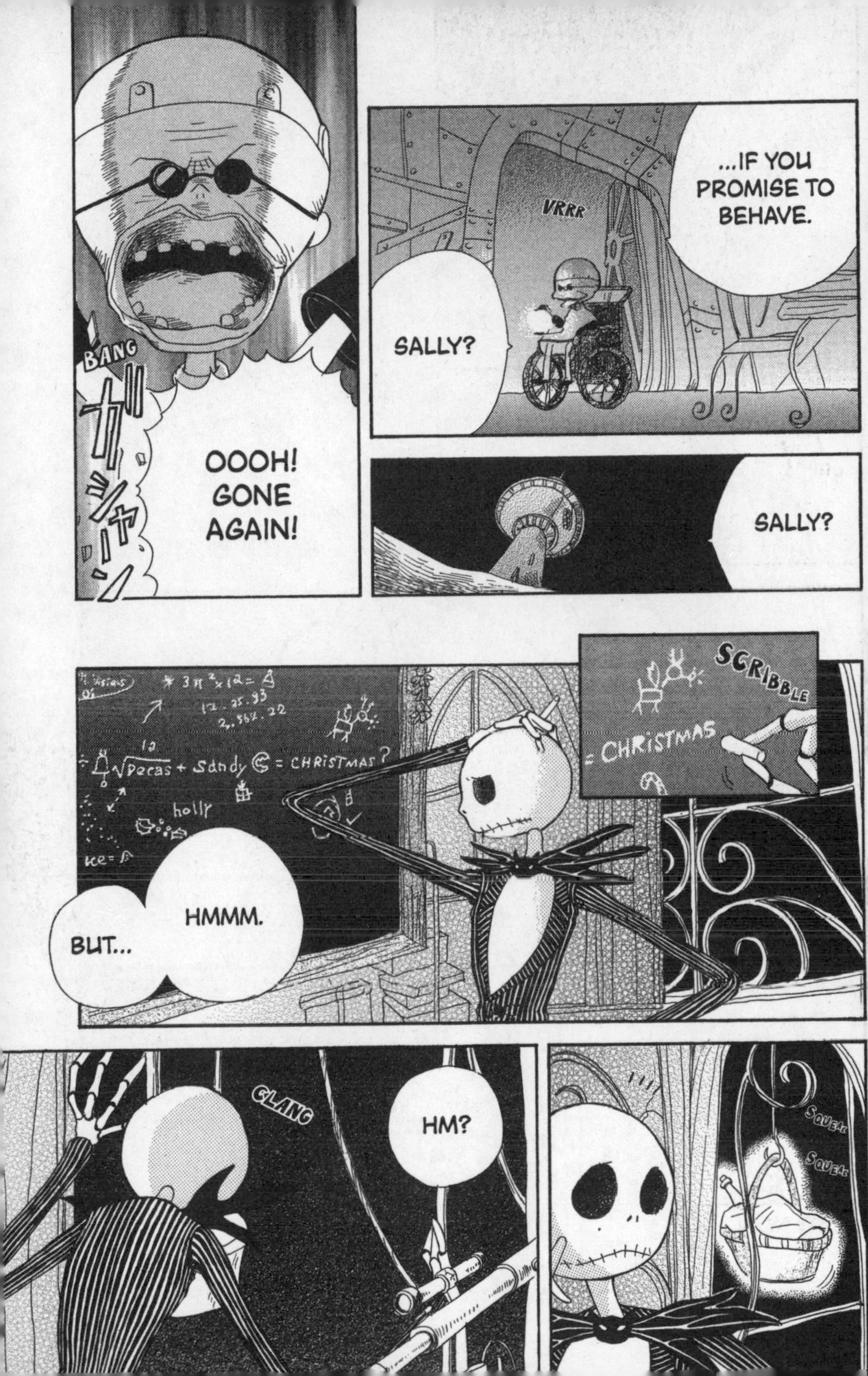
...IF YOU PROMISE TO BEHAVE.
VRRR
SALLY?
SALLY?
BANG
OOOH! GONE AGAIN!
SCRIBBLE
= CHRISTMAS
= CHRISTMAS?
holly
HMMM.
BUT...
SQUEAK
SQUEAK
CLANG
HM?

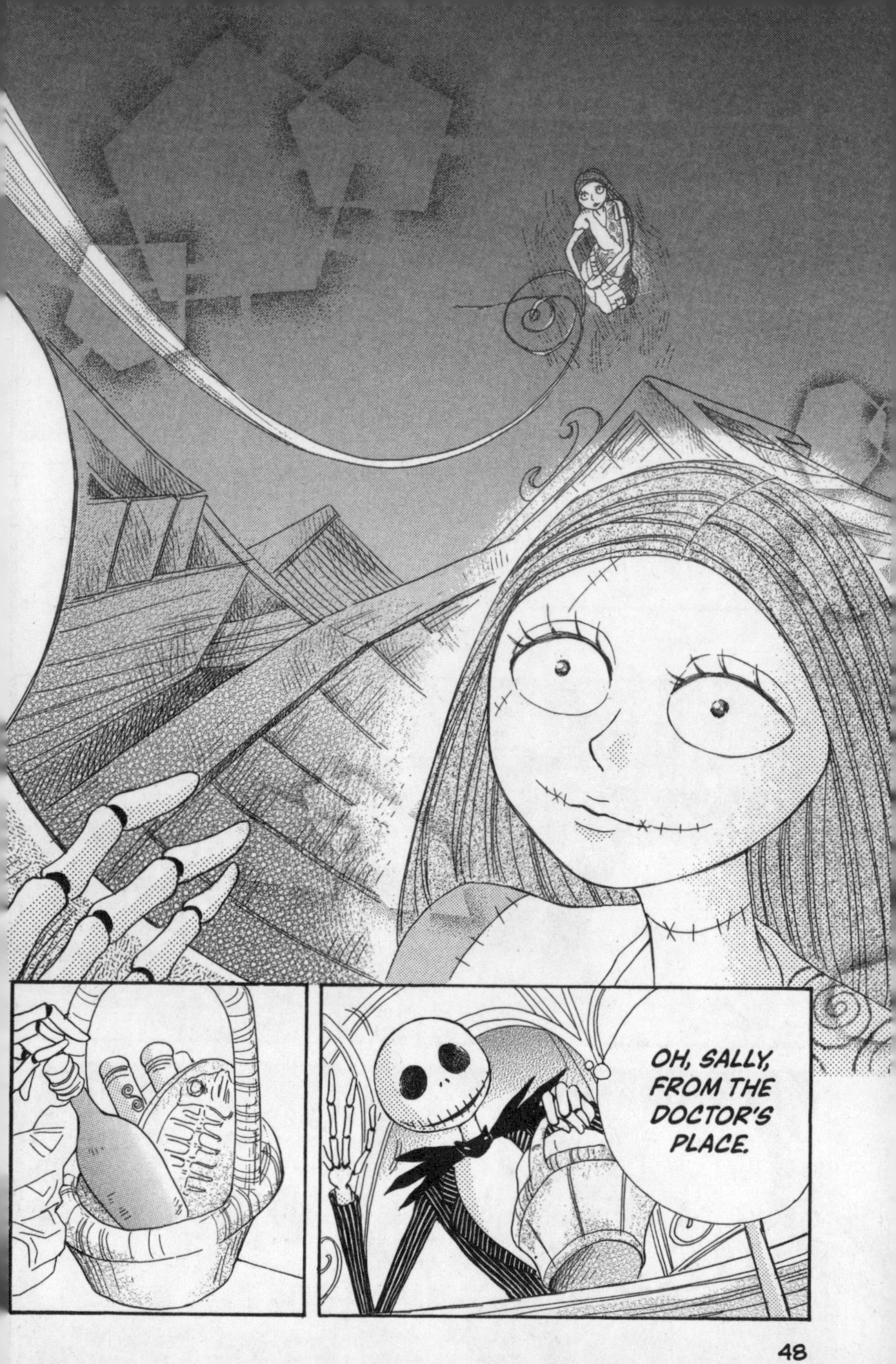
OH, SALLY, FROM THE DOCTOR'S PLACE.

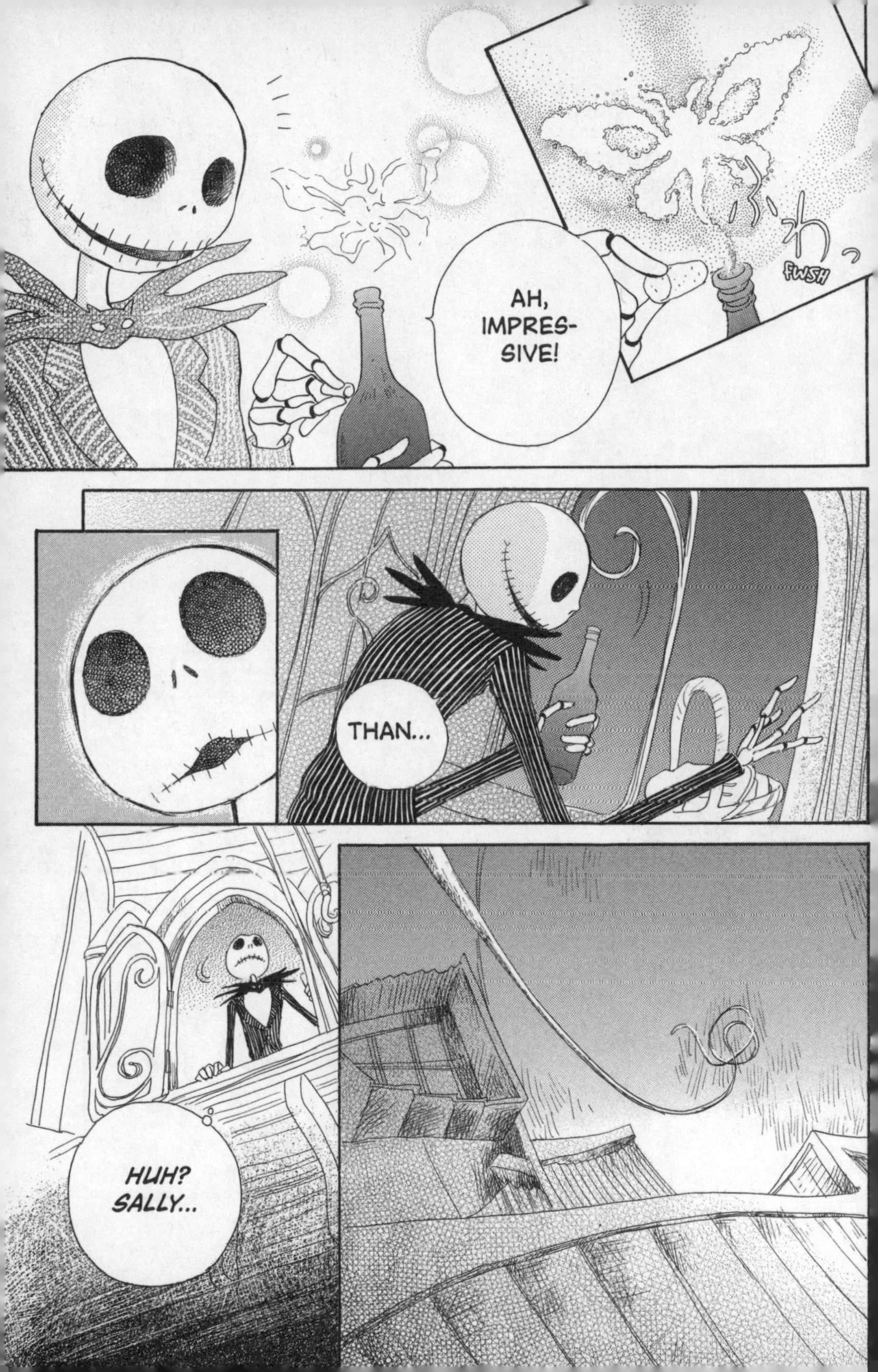
ふわっ
FWSH
AH, IMPRES-SIVE!
THAN...
HUH? SALLY...

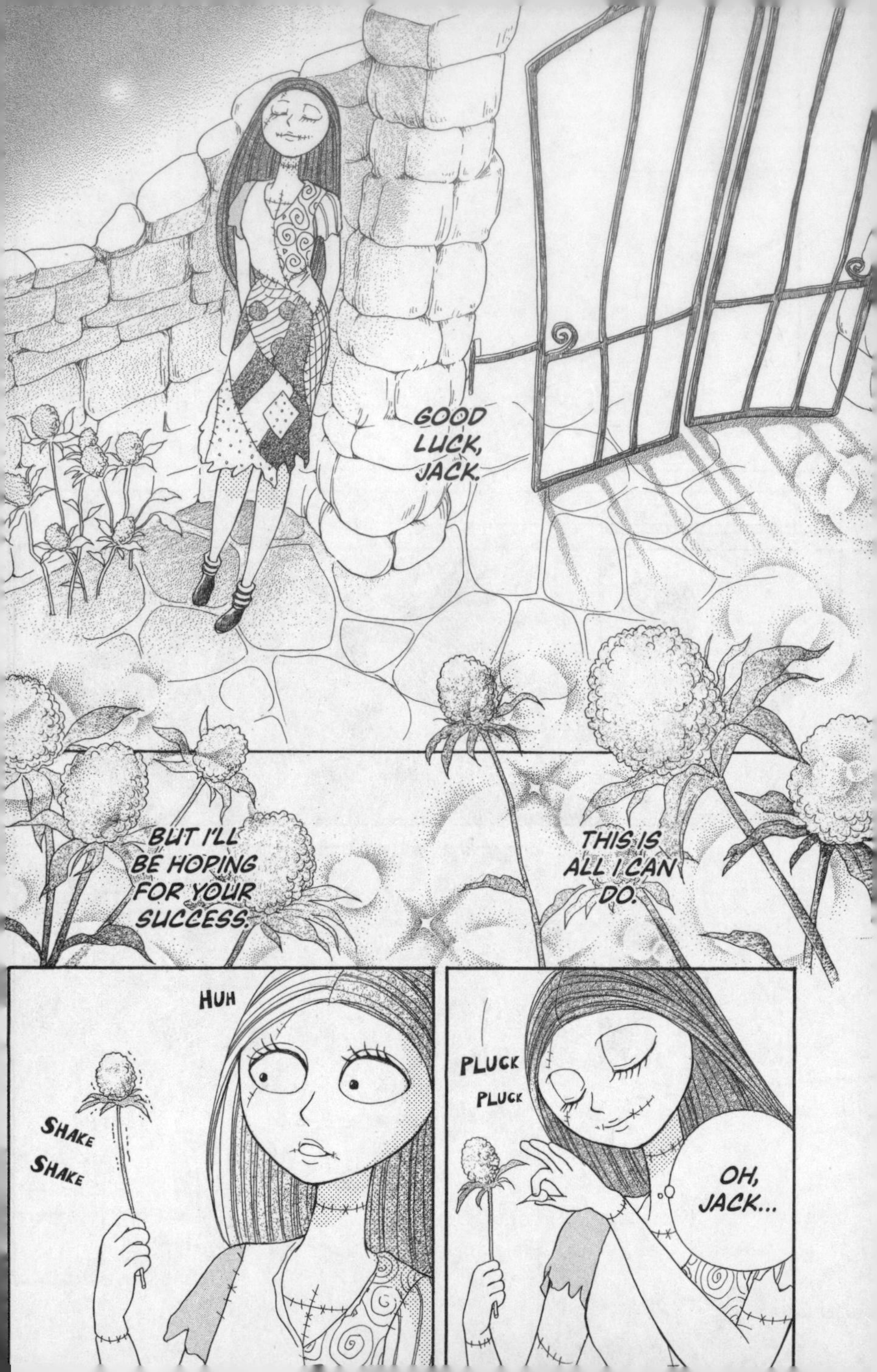
GOOD LUCK, JACK.
THIS IS ALL I CAN DO.
BUT I'LL BE HOPING FOR YOUR SUCCESS.
PLUCK
PLUCK
OH, JACK...
HUH
SHAKE
SHAKE

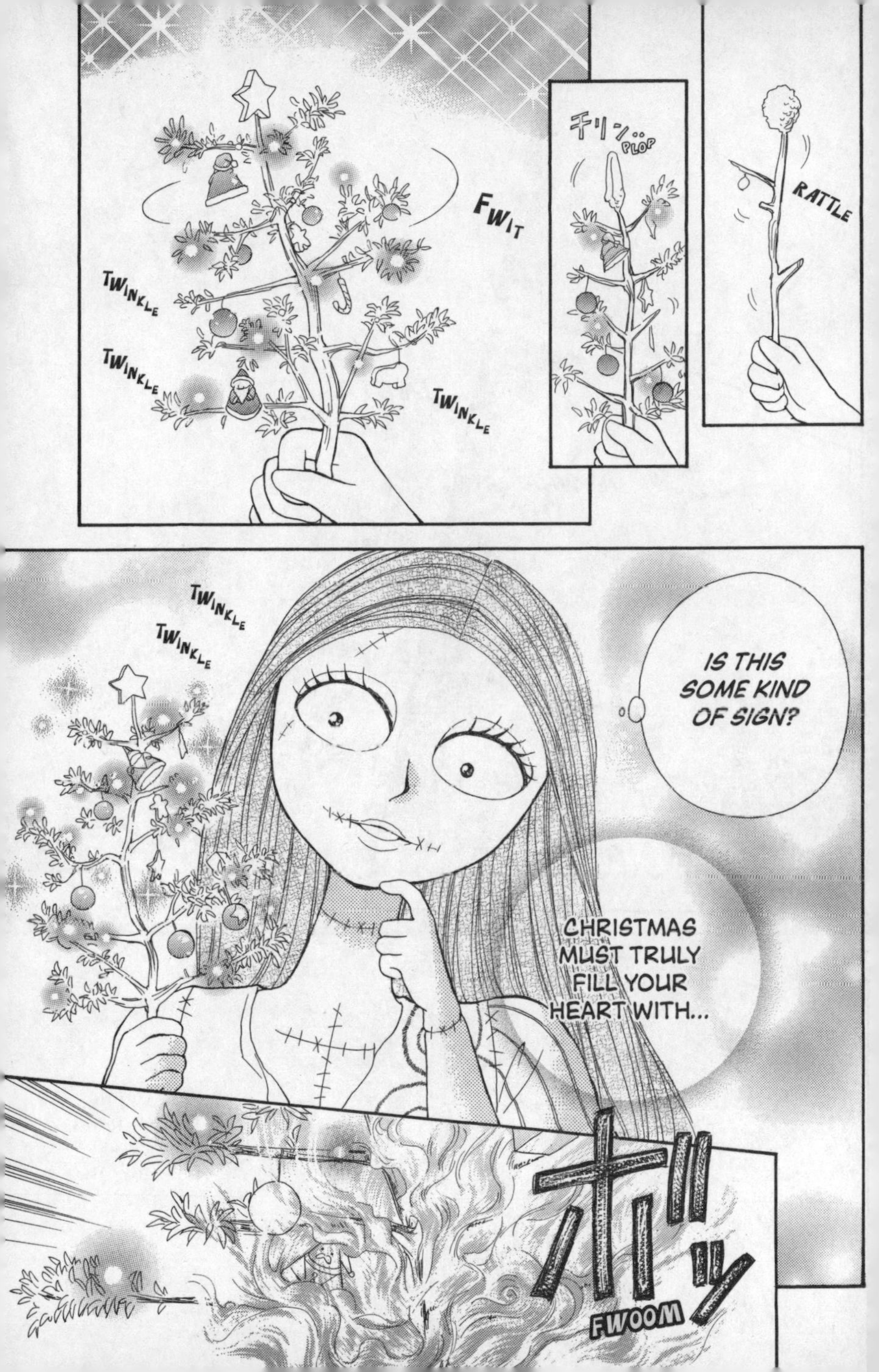
RATTLE
チリン..
PLOP
FWIT
TWINKLE
TWINKLE
TWINKLE
IS THIS SOME KIND OF SIGN?
TWINKLE
TWINKLE
CHRISTMAS MUST TRULY FILL YOUR HEART WITH...
ボッ
FWOOM

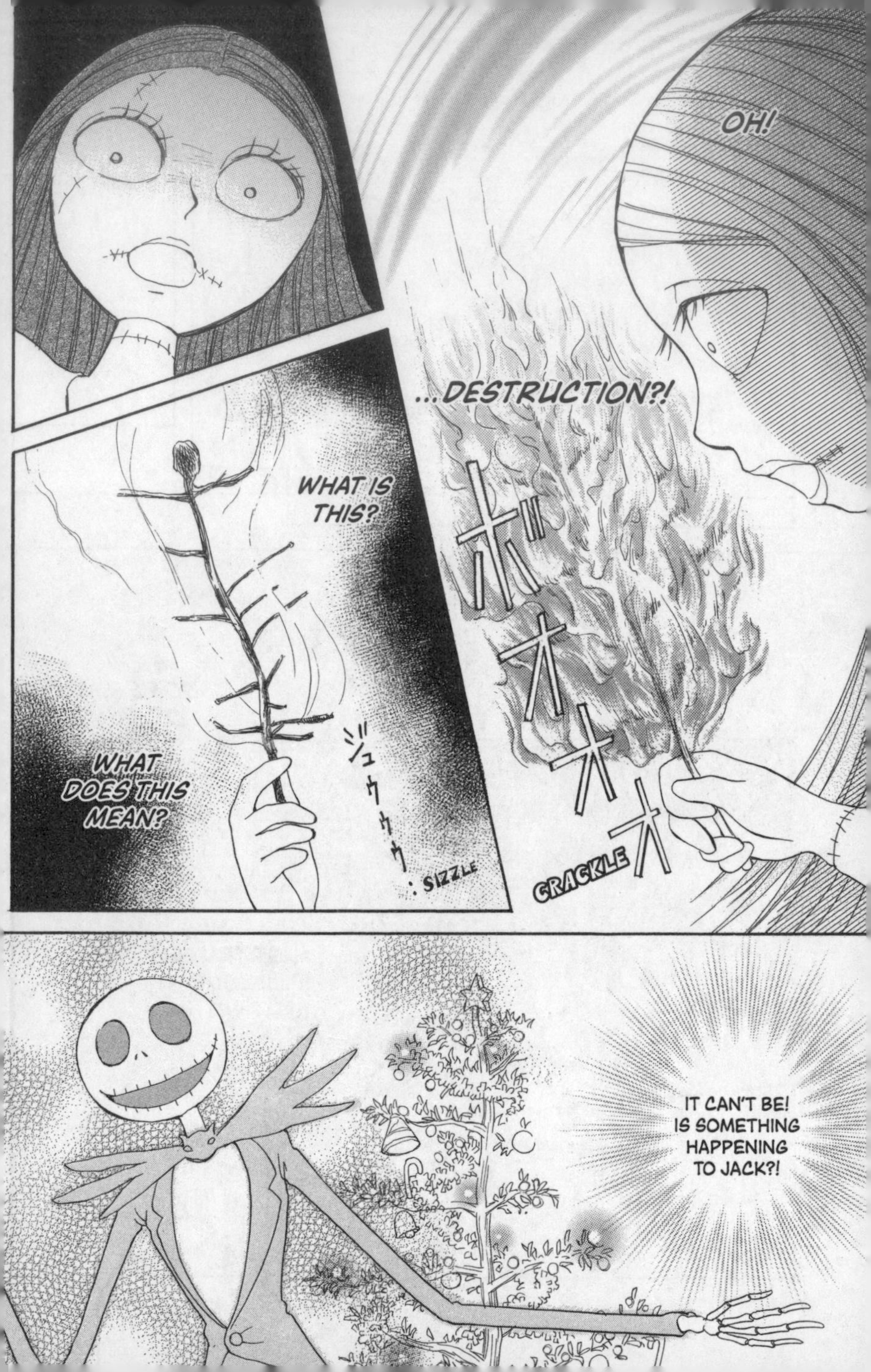

OH!
...DESTRUCTION?!
ボオオオオ
CRACKLE
WHAT IS THIS?
WHAT DOES THIS MEAN?
ジュウウウ
SIZZLE
IT CAN'T BE! IS SOMETHING HAPPENING TO JACK?!

READ THIS WAY

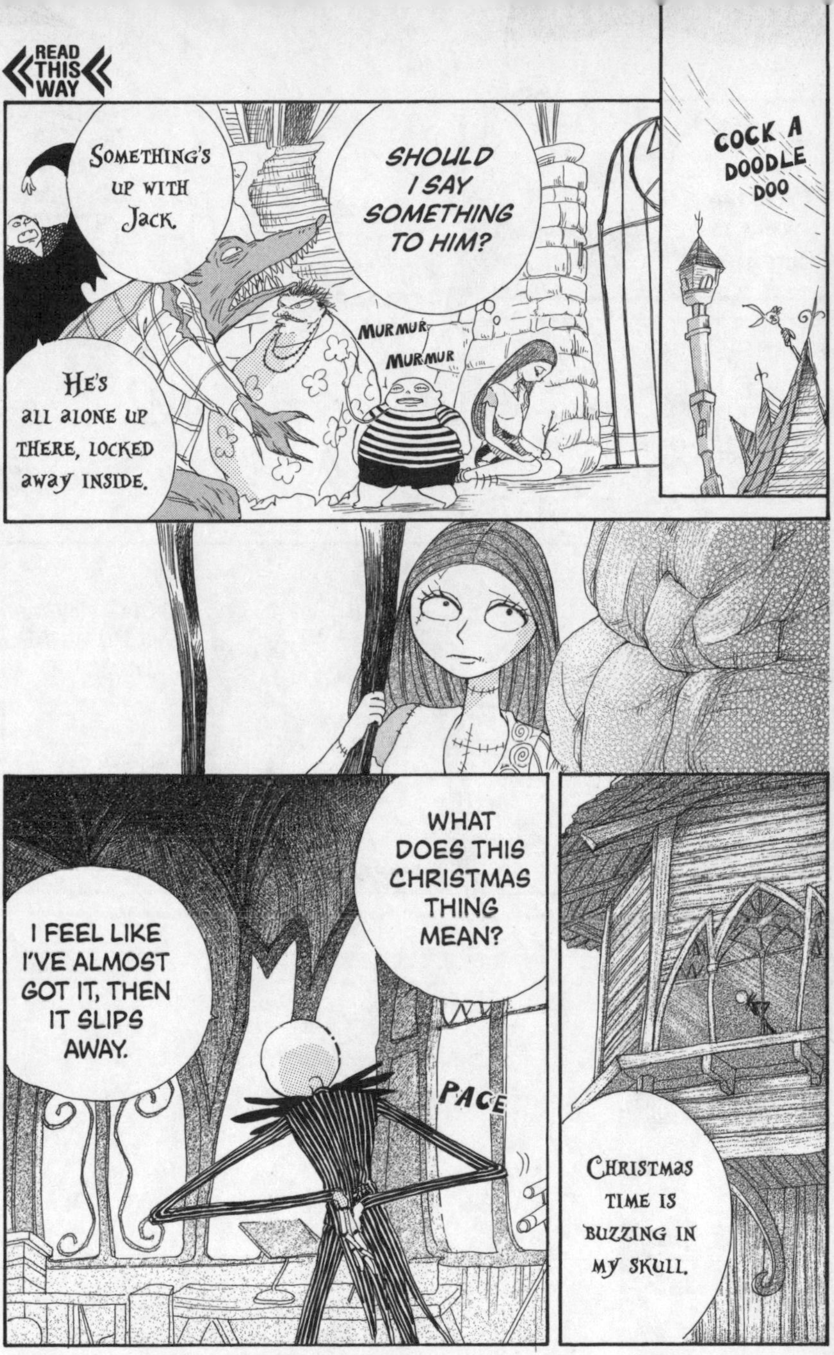
COCK A DOODLE DOO
SHOULD I SAY SOMETHING TO HIM?
Something's up with Jack.
MURMUR
MURMUR
He's all alone up there, locked away inside.
Christmas time is buzzing in my skull.
WHAT DOES THIS CHRISTMAS THING MEAN?
PACE
I FEEL LIKE I'VE ALMOST GOT IT, THEN IT SLIPS AWAY.

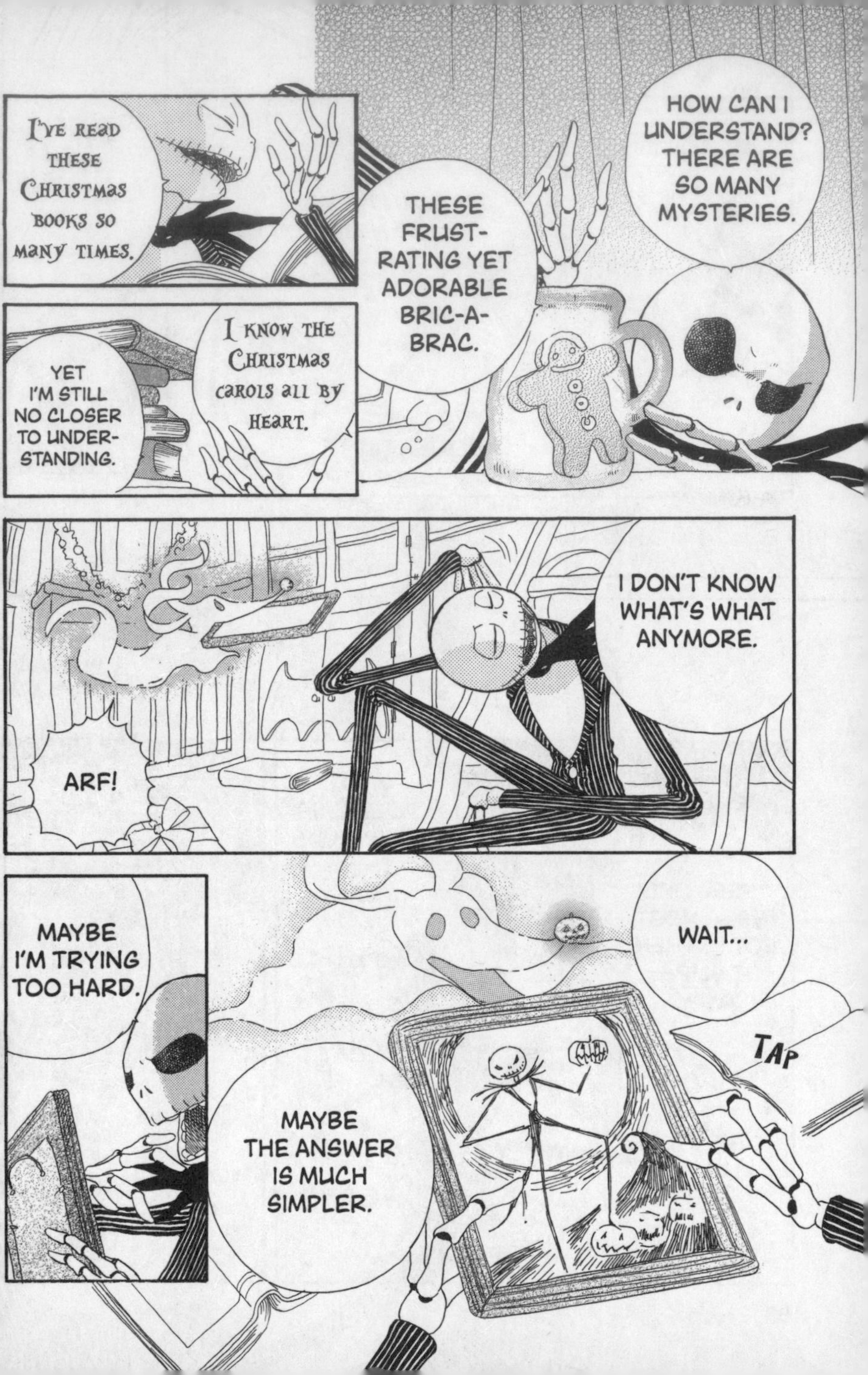
HOW CAN I UNDERSTAND? THERE ARE SO MANY MYSTERIES.
THESE FRUST-RATING YET ADORABLE BRIC-A-BRAC.
I'YE READ THESE CHRISTMAS BOOKS SO MANY TIMES.
I KNOW THE CHRISTMAS CAROLS ALL BY HEART.
YET I'M STILL NO CLOSER TO UNDER-STANDING.
I DON'T KNOW WHAT'S WHAT ANYMORE.
ARF!
WAIT...
TAP
MAYBE THE ANSWER IS MUCH SIMPLER.
MAYBE I'M TRYING TOO HARD.

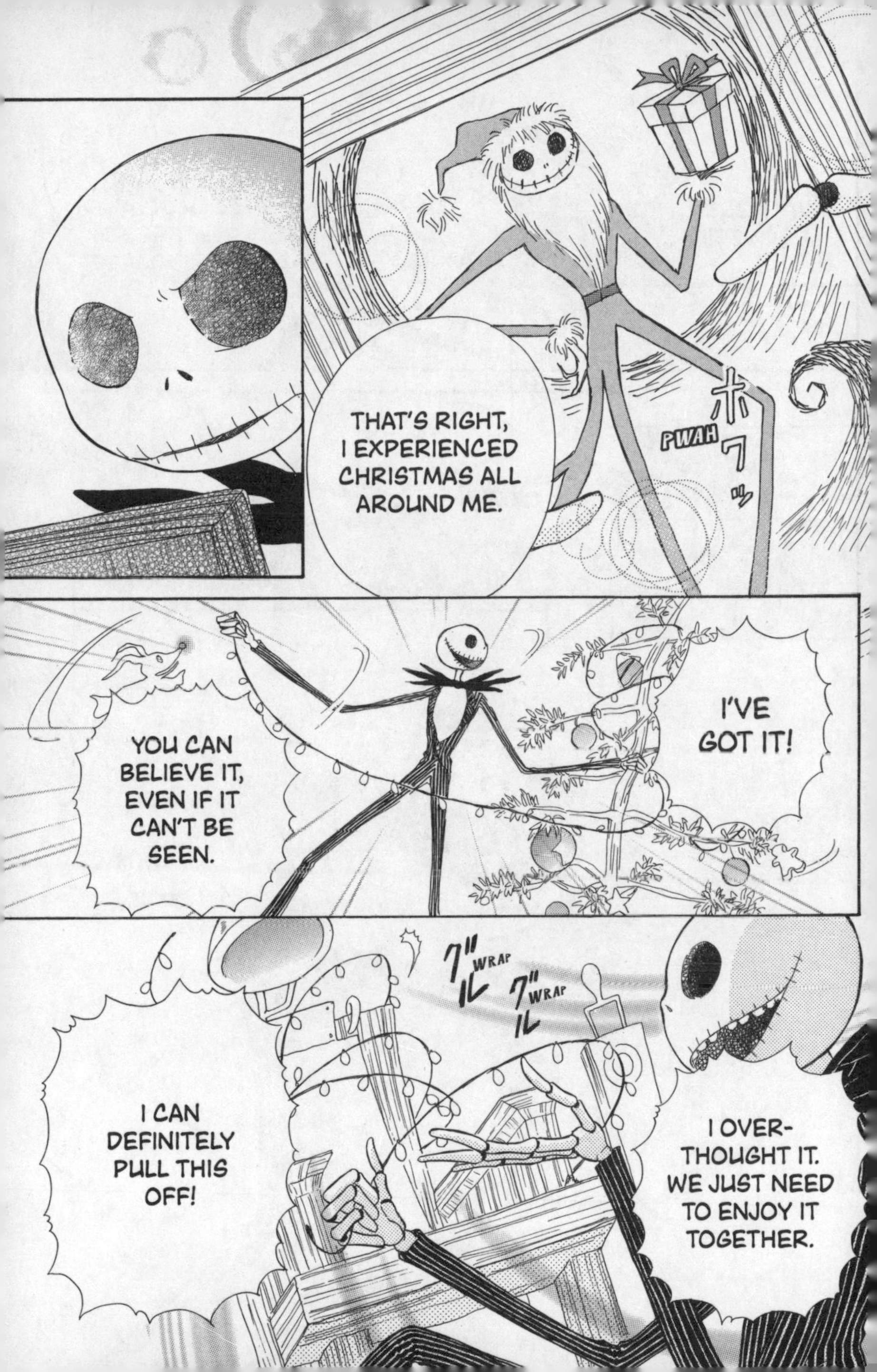

THAT'S RIGHT, I EXPERIENCED CHRISTMAS ALL AROUND ME.
ホワッ PWAH
I'VE GOT IT!
YOU CAN BELIEVE IT, EVEN IF IT CAN'T BE SEEN.
I OVER-THOUGHT IT. WE JUST NEED TO ENJOY IT TOGETHER.
グル WRAP
グル WRAP
I CAN DEFINITELY PULL THIS OFF!

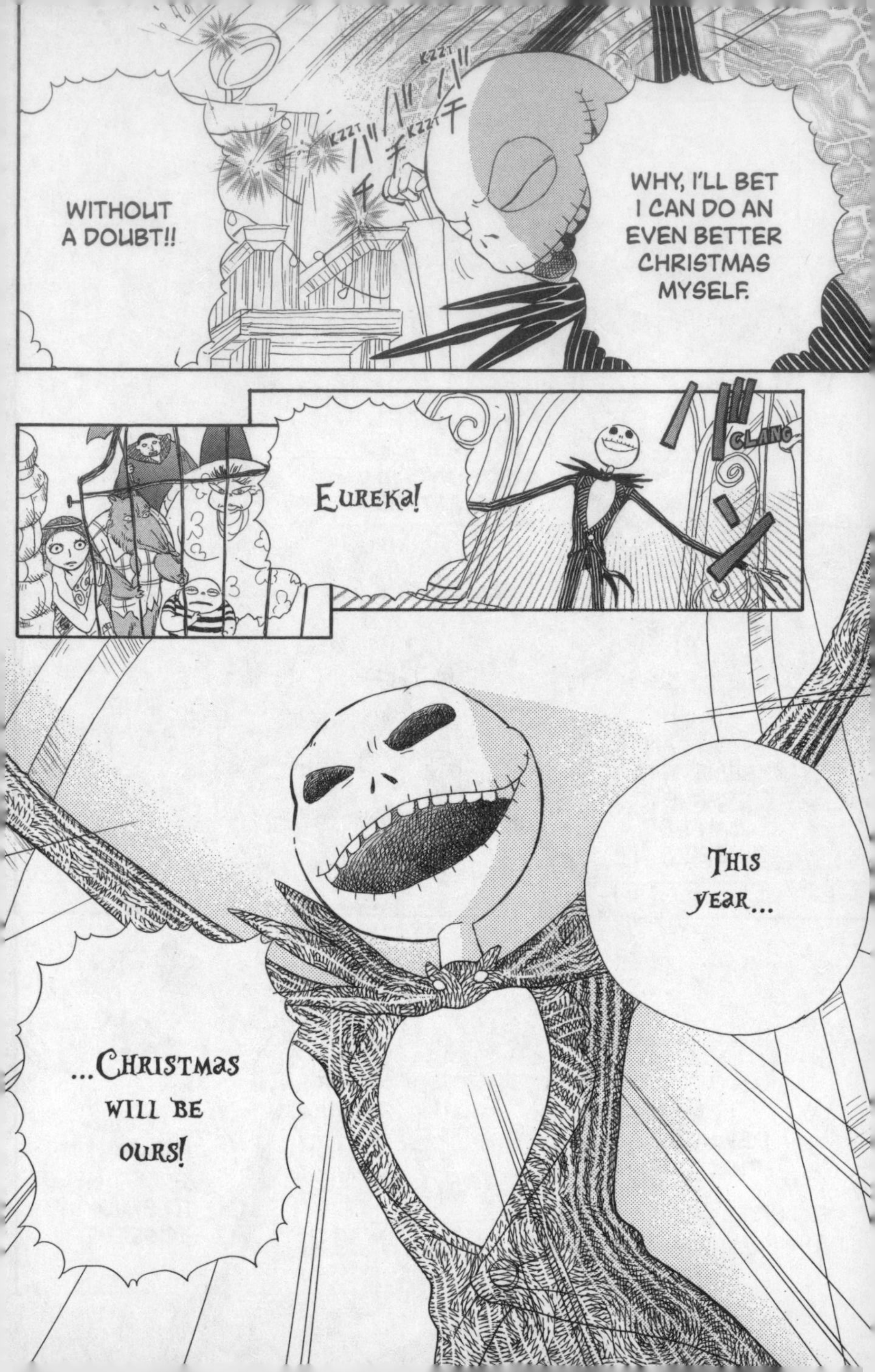
KZZT
KZZT
KZZT
WHY, I'LL BET I CAN DO AN EVEN BETTER CHRISTMAS MYSELF.
WITHOUT A DOUBT!!
CLANG
Eureka!
This year...
...Christmas will be ours!

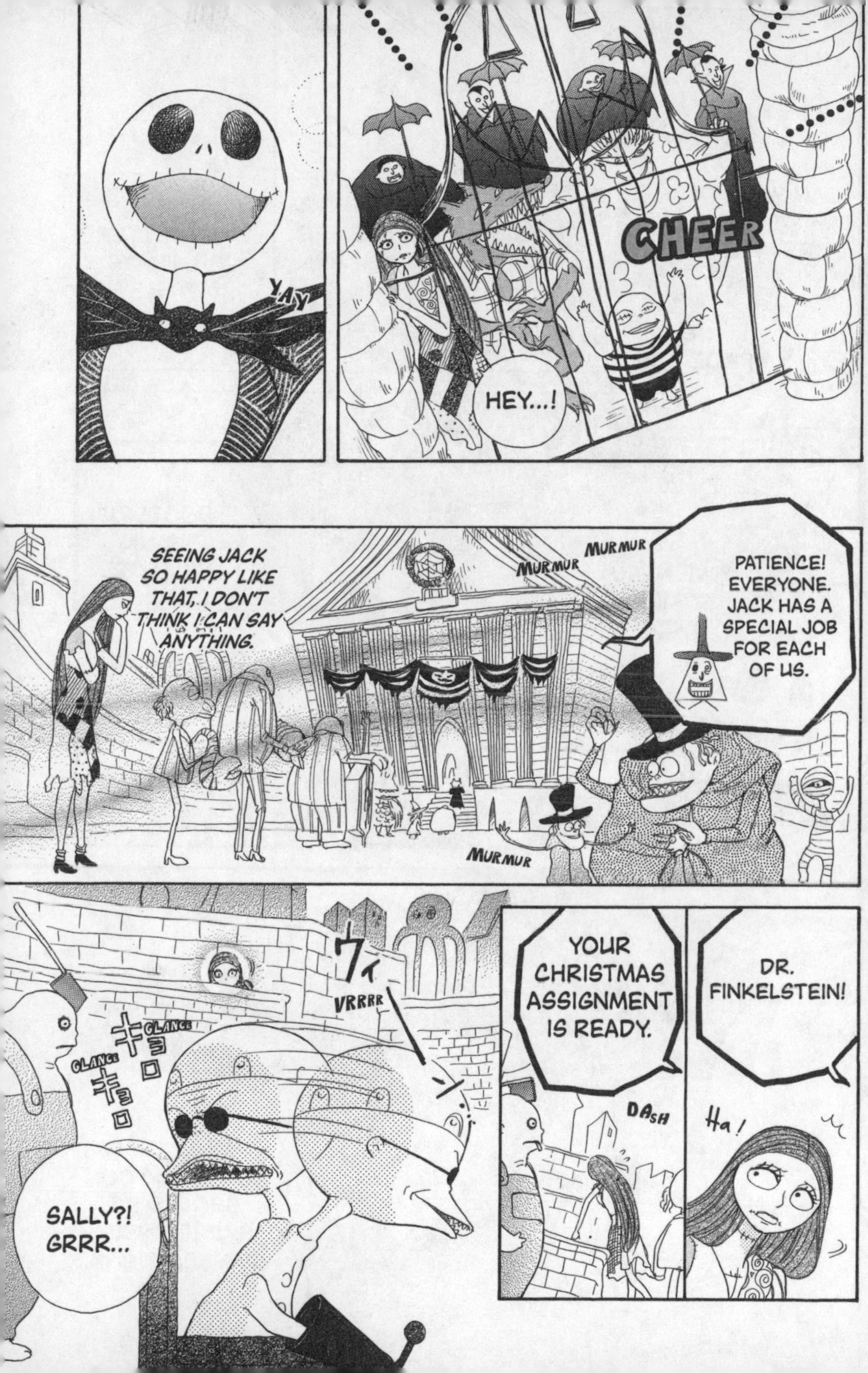
CHEER
HEY...!
YAY
PATIENCE! EVERYONE. JACK HAS A SPECIAL JOB FOR EACH OF US.
MURMUR MURMUR
SEEING JACK SO HAPPY LIKE THAT, I DON'T THINK I CAN SAY ANYTHING.
MURMUR
DR. FINKELSTEIN!
Ha!
YOUR CHRISTMAS ASSIGNMENT IS READY.
DASH
ヴィ
VRRRR
キョロ
GLANCE
キョロ
GLANCE
SALLY?! GRRR...

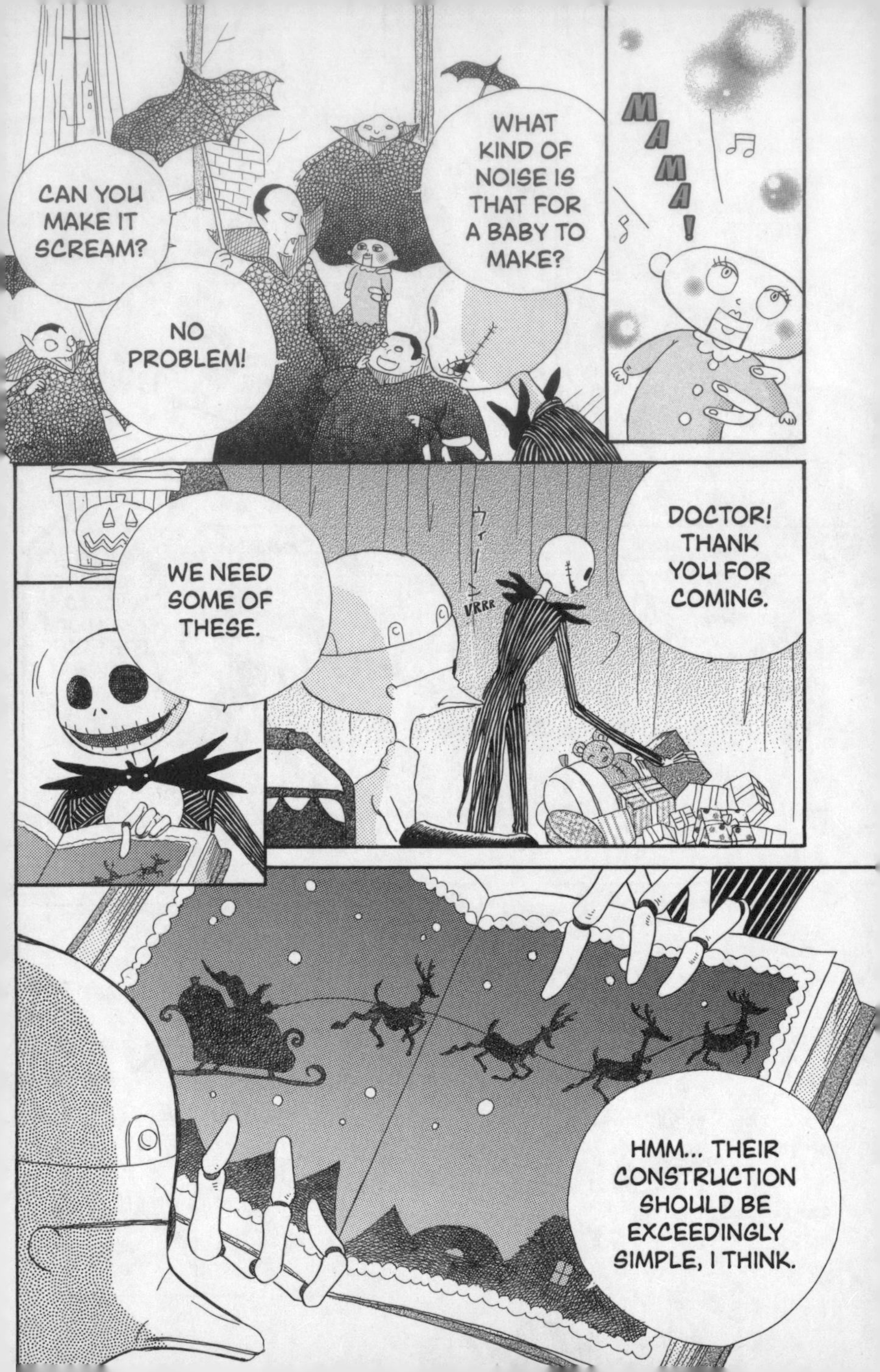
MAMA!
WHAT KIND OF NOISE IS THAT FOR A BABY TO MAKE?
CAN YOU MAKE IT SCREAM?
NO PROBLEM!
DOCTOR! THANK YOU FOR COMING.
VRRR
WE NEED SOME OF THESE.
HMM... THEIR CONSTRUCTION SHOULD BE EXCEEDINGLY SIMPLE, I THINK.

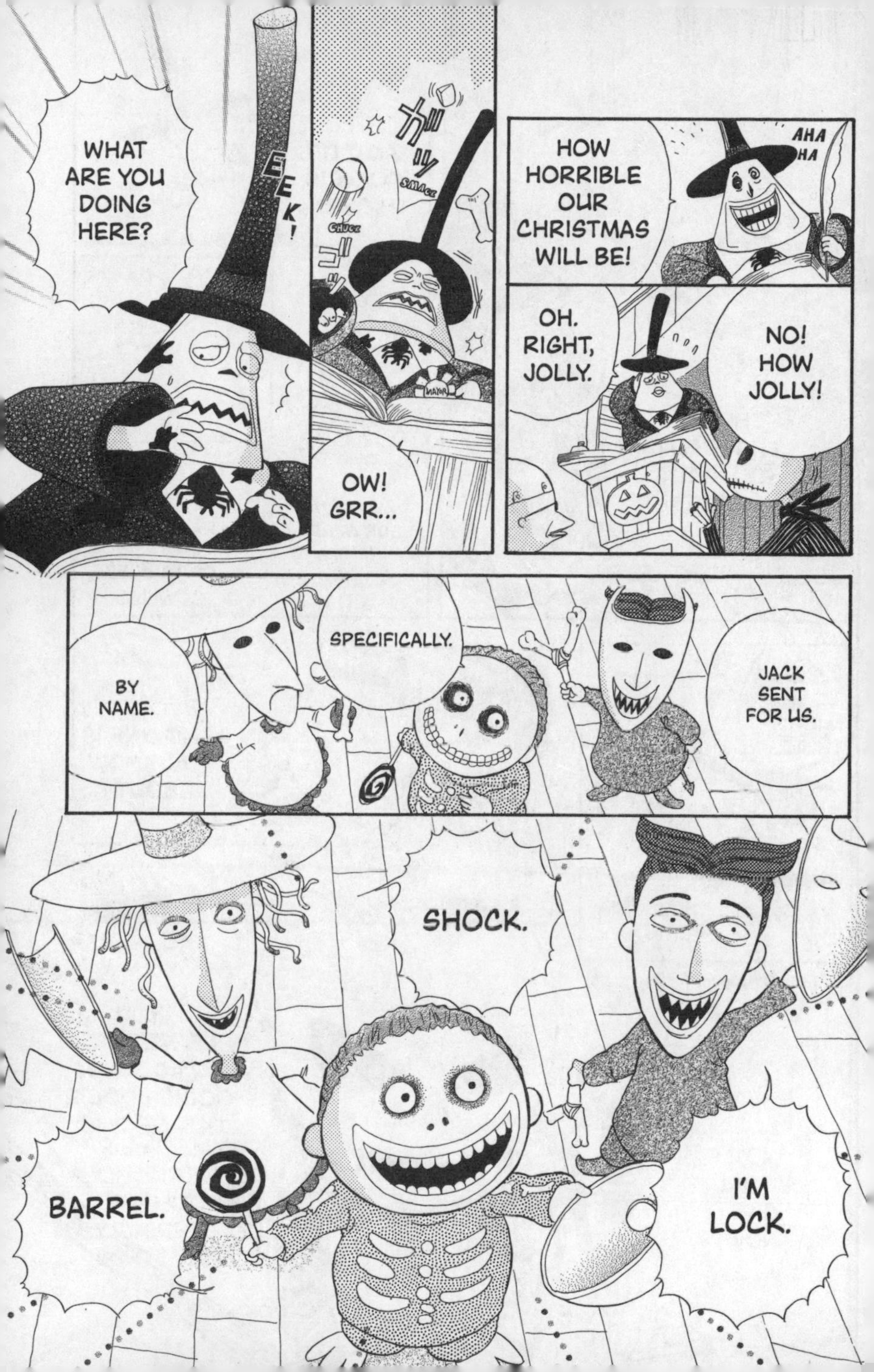
AHA HA
HOW HORRIBLE OUR CHRISTMAS WILL BE!
NO! HOW JOLLY!
OH. RIGHT, JOLLY.
SMACK
CHUCK
OW! GRR...
EEK!
WHAT ARE YOU DOING HERE?
JACK SENT FOR US.
SPECIFICALLY.
BY NAME.
I'M LOCK.
SHOCK.
BARREL.

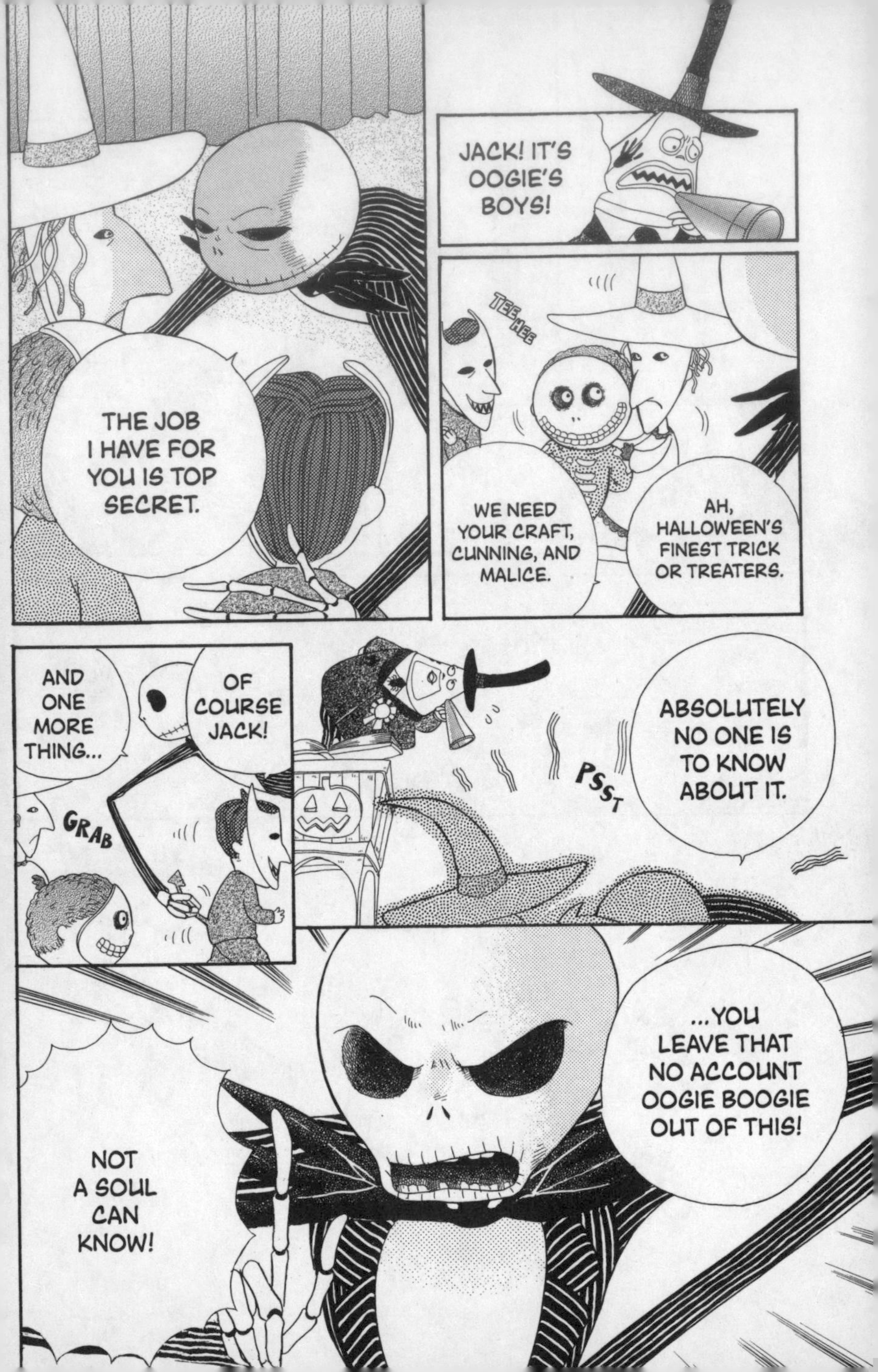
JACK! IT'S OOGIE'S BOYS!
TEE HEE
AH, HALLOWEEN'S FINEST TRICK OR TREATERS.
WE NEED YOUR CRAFT, CUNNING, AND MALICE.
THE JOB I HAVE FOR YOU IS TOP SECRET.
ABSOLUTELY NO ONE IS TO KNOW ABOUT IT.
PSST
OF COURSE JACK!
AND ONE MORE THING...
GRAB
...YOU LEAVE THAT NO ACCOUNT OOGIE BOOGIE OUT OF THIS!
NOT A SOUL CAN KNOW!

READ THIS WAY

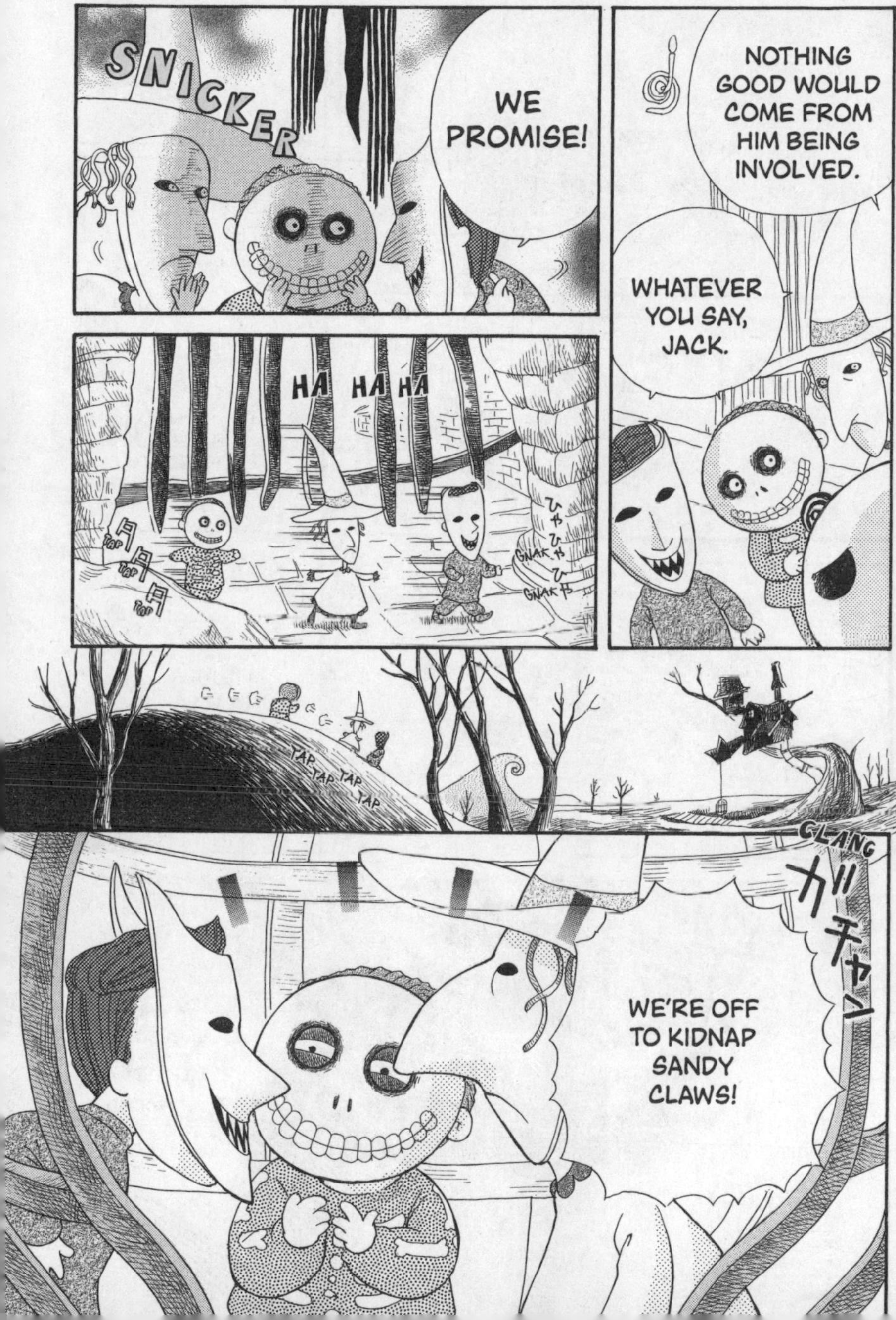
NOTHING GOOD WOULD COME FROM HIM BEING INVOLVED.
WHATEVER YOU SAY, JACK.
SNICKER
WE PROMISE!
HA HA HA
TAP TAP TAP
GNAK GNAK
TAP TAP TAP TAP
CLANG
ガチャン
WE'RE OFF TO KIDNAP SANDY CLAWS!

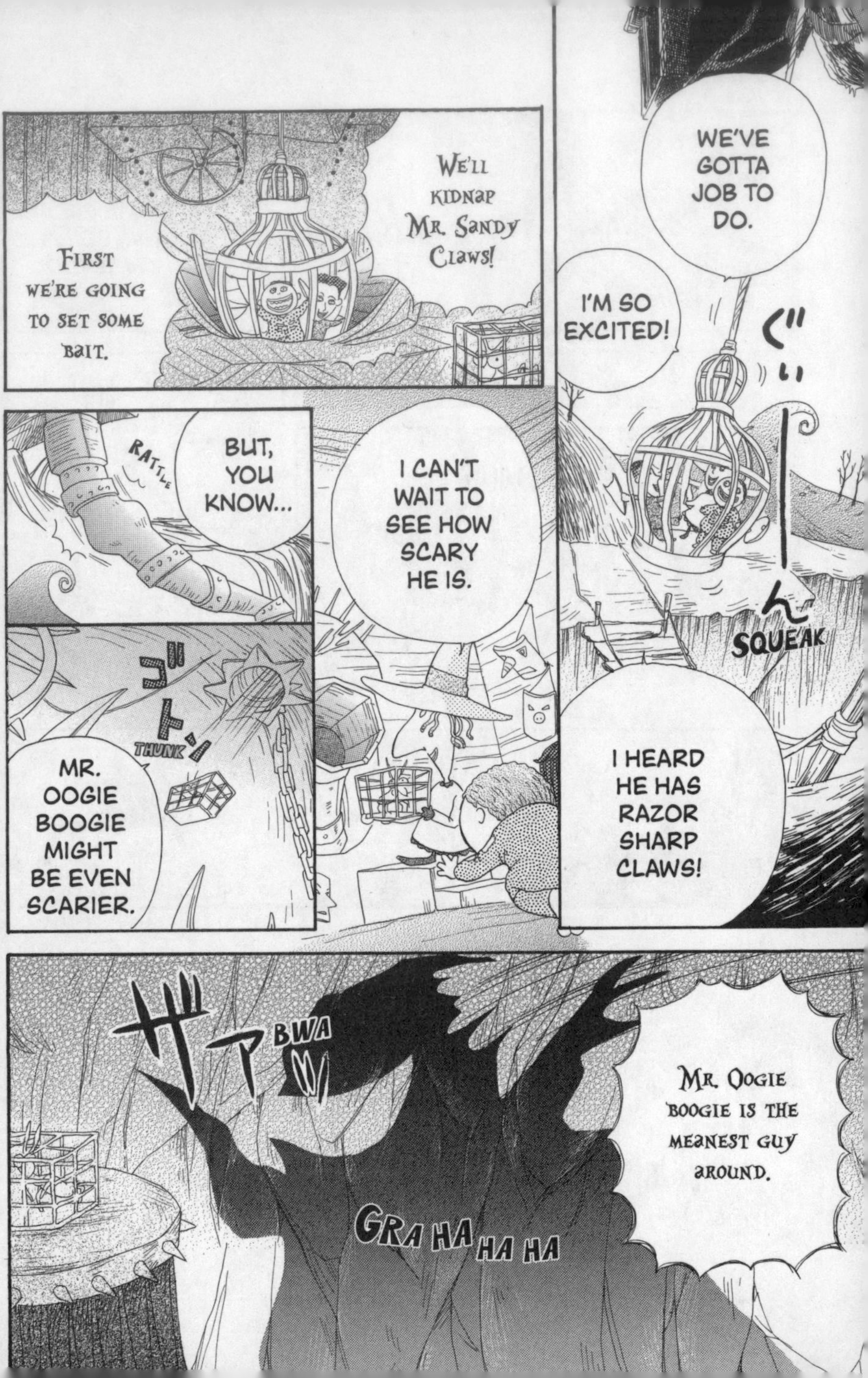
WE'VE GOTTA JOB TO DO.
I'M SO EXCITED!
ぐいーん
SQUEAK
I HEARD HE HAS RAZOR SHARP CLAWS!
We'll kidnap Mr. Sandy Claws!
First we're going to set some bait.
I CAN'T WAIT TO SEE HOW SCARY HE IS.
BUT, YOU KNOW...
RATTLE
ゴトッ
THUNK
MR. OOGIE BOOGIE MIGHT BE EVEN SCARIER.
Mr. Oogie Boogie is the meanest guy around.
ザァ
BWA
GRA HA HA HA HA

READ THIS WAY

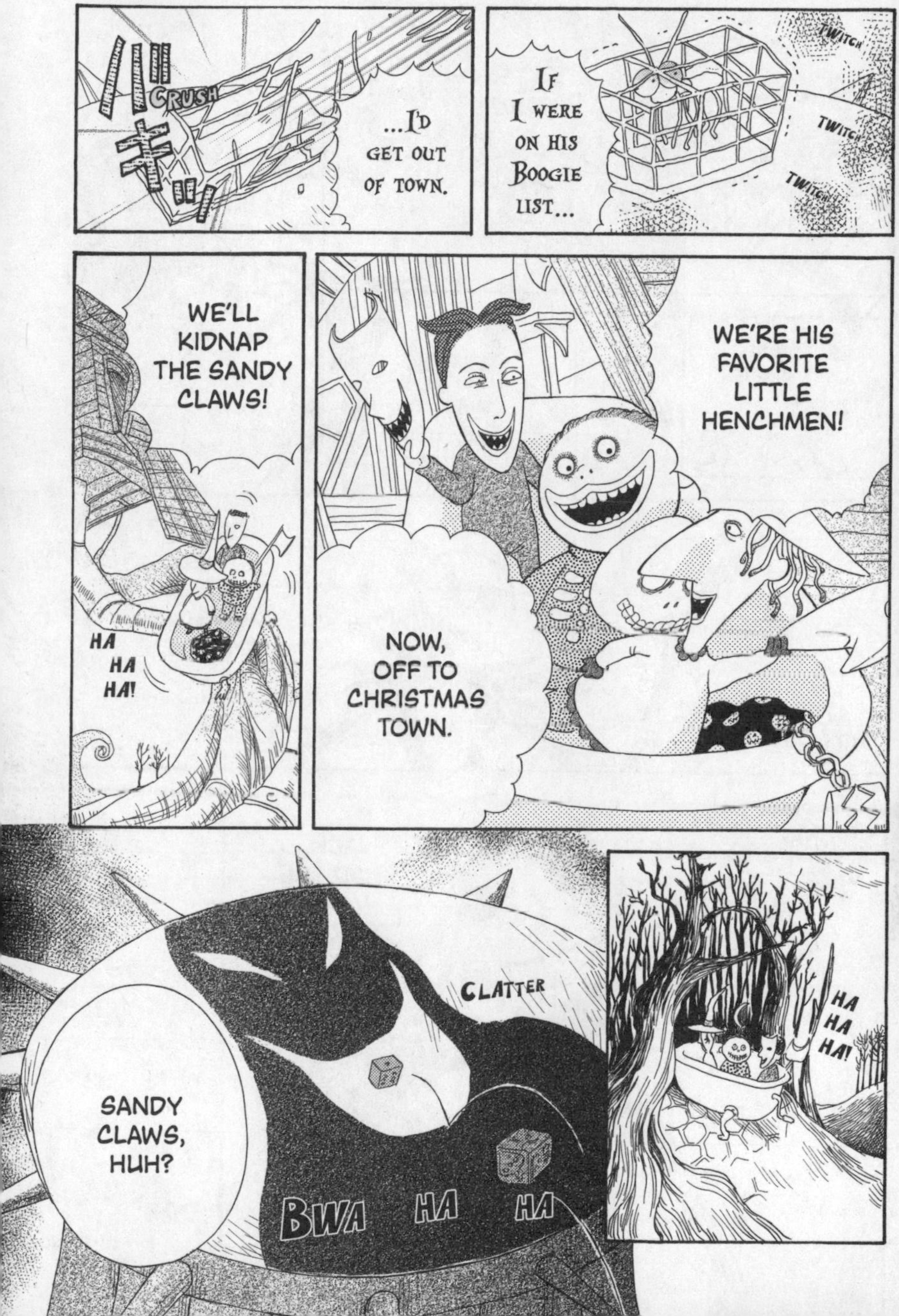
TWITCH
TWITCH
TWITCH
If I were on his Boogie list...
...I'd get out of town.
CRUSH
We're his favorite little henchmen!
Now, off to Christmas Town.
We'll kidnap the Sandy Claws!
HA HA HA!
HA HA HA!
CLATTER
Sandy Claws, huh?
BWA HA HA

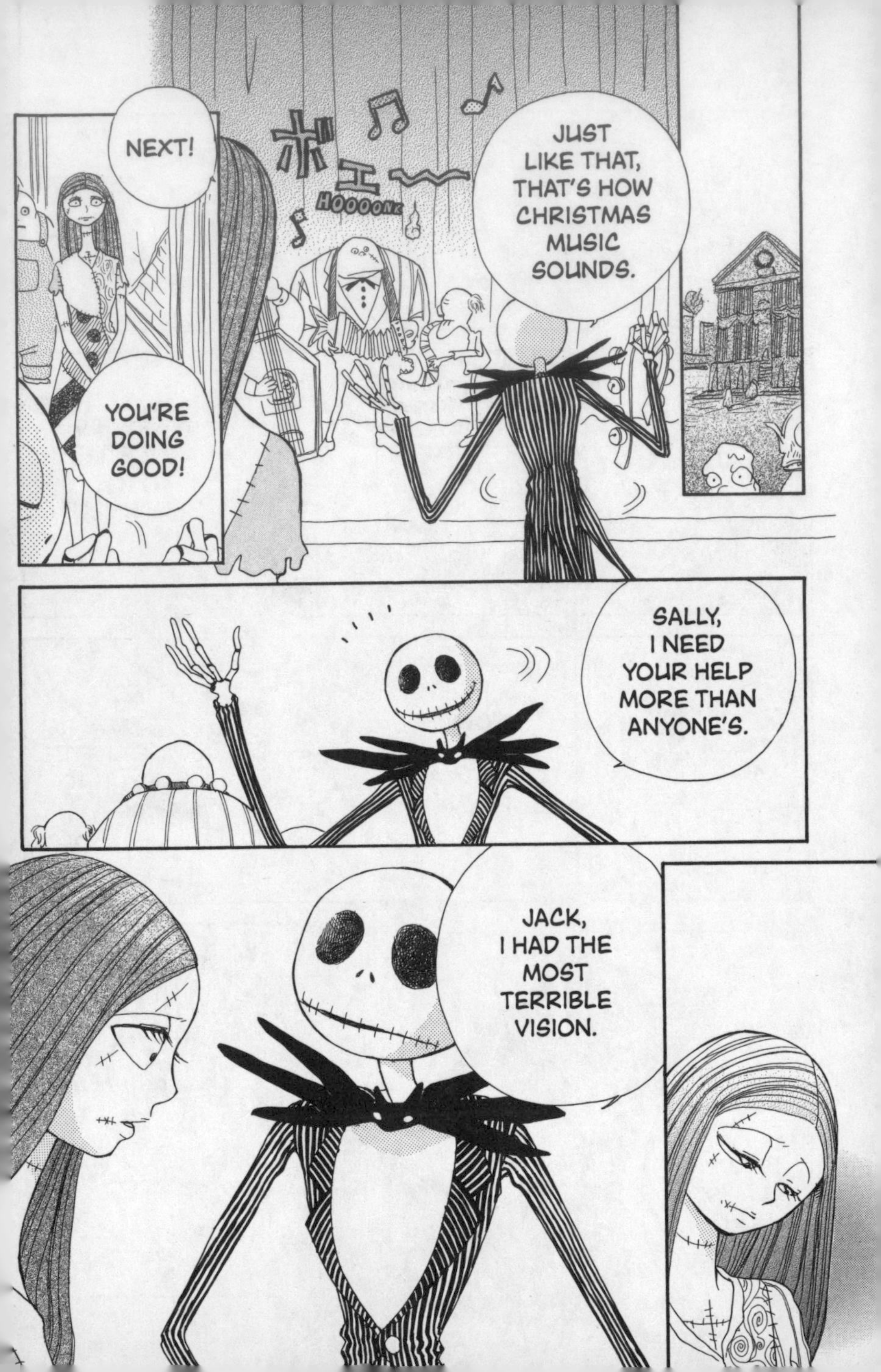
JUST LIKE THAT, THAT'S HOW CHRISTMAS MUSIC SOUNDS.
ボエ〜
HOOOONK
NEXT!
YOU'RE DOING GOOD!
SALLY, I NEED YOUR HELP MORE THAN ANYONE'S.
JACK, I HAD THE MOST TERRIBLE VISION.

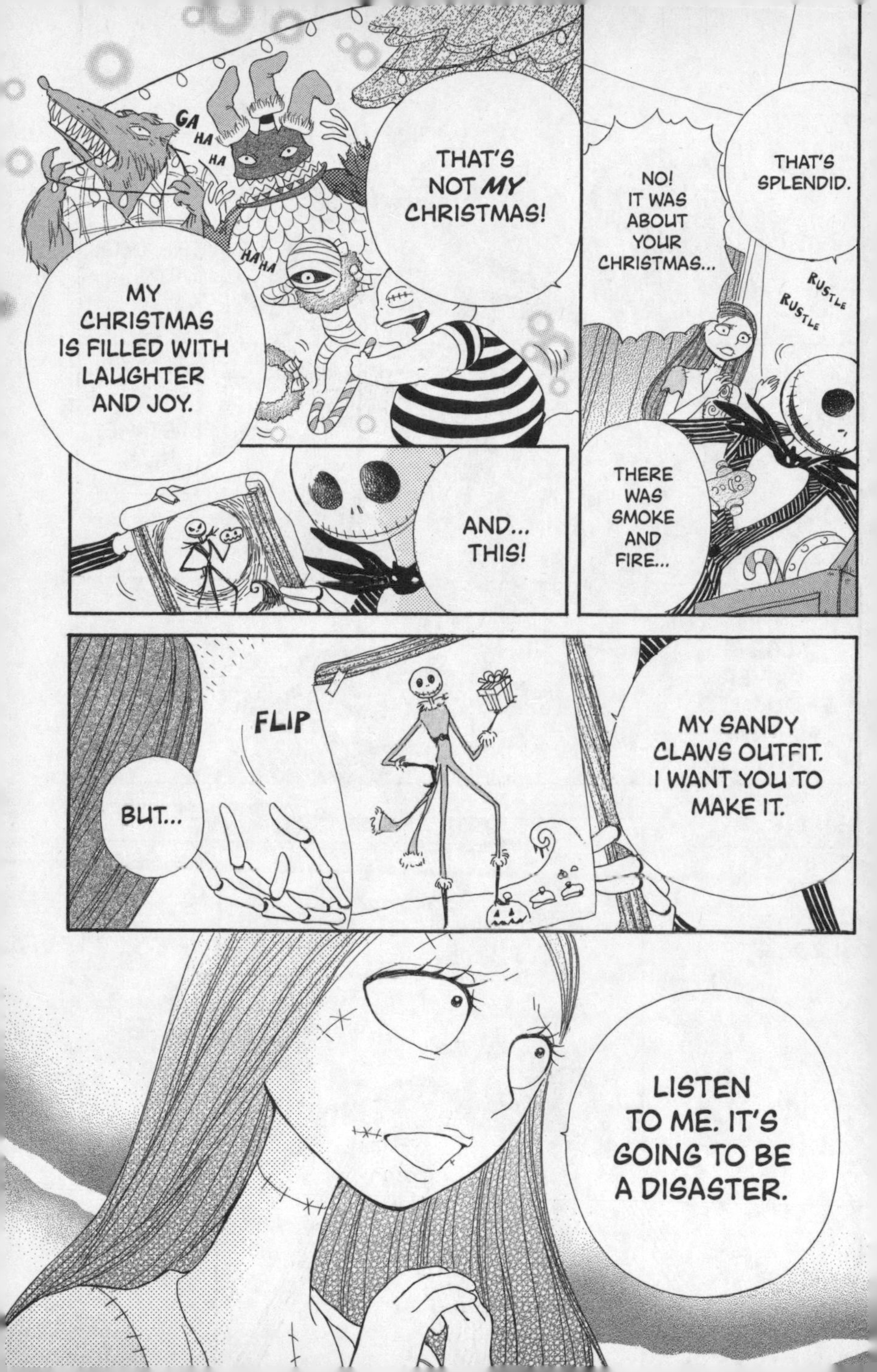
THAT'S SPLENDID.
NO! IT WAS ABOUT YOUR CHRISTMAS...
RUSTLE RUSTLE
THERE WAS SMOKE AND FIRE...
THAT'S NOT MY CHRISTMAS!
GA HA HA
HA HA
MY CHRISTMAS IS FILLED WITH LAUGHTER AND JOY.
AND... THIS!
MY SANDY CLAWS OUTFIT. I WANT YOU TO MAKE IT.
FLIP
BUT...
LISTEN TO ME. IT'S GOING TO BE A DISASTER.

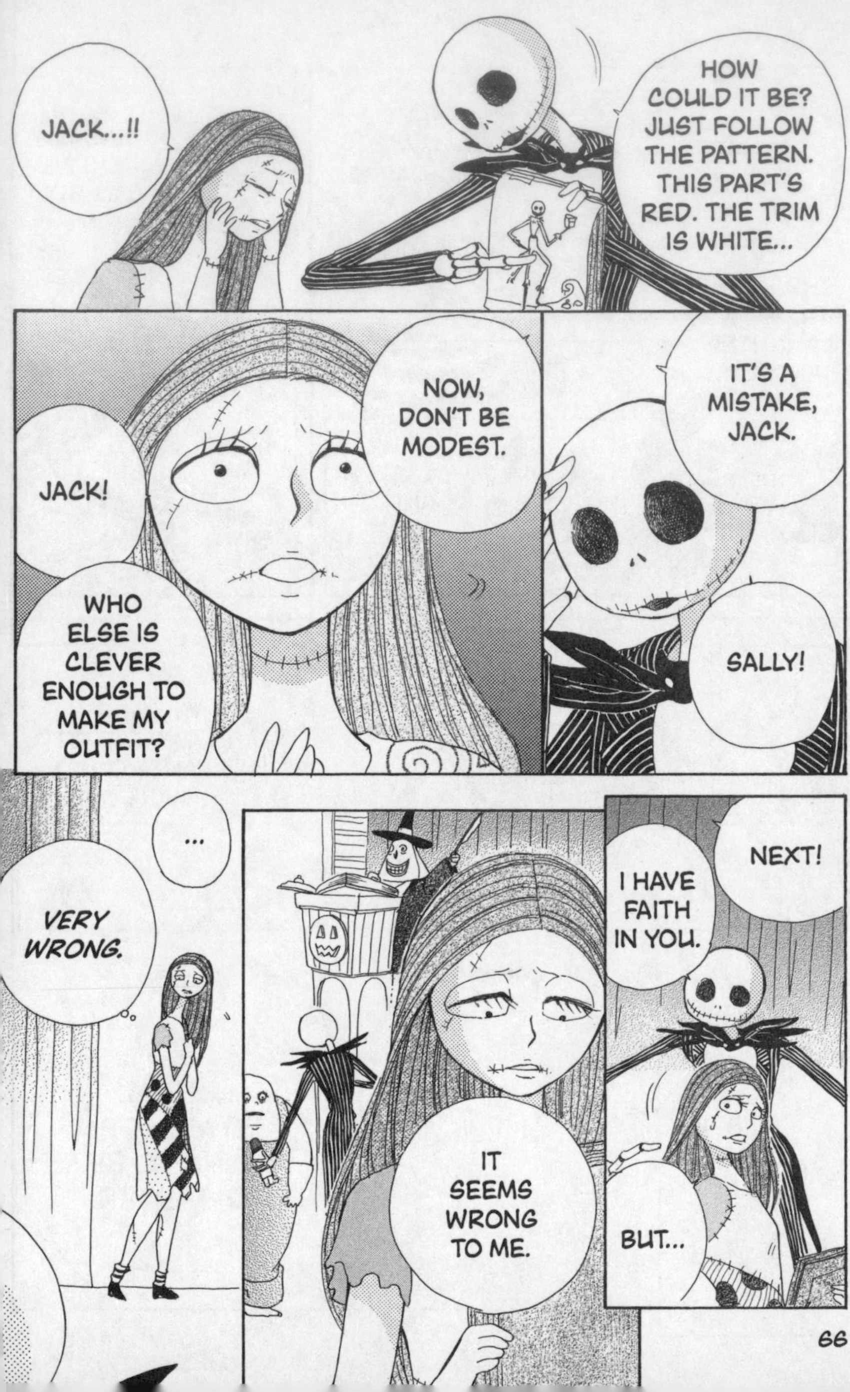
HOW COULD IT BE? JUST FOLLOW THE PATTERN. THIS PART'S RED. THE TRIM IS WHITE...
JACK...!!
IT'S A MISTAKE, JACK.
SALLY!
NOW, DON'T BE MODEST.
JACK!
WHO ELSE IS CLEVER ENOUGH TO MAKE MY OUTFIT?
NEXT!
I HAVE FAITH IN YOU.
BUT...
IT SEEMS WRONG TO ME.
...
VERY WRONG.

READ THIS WAY

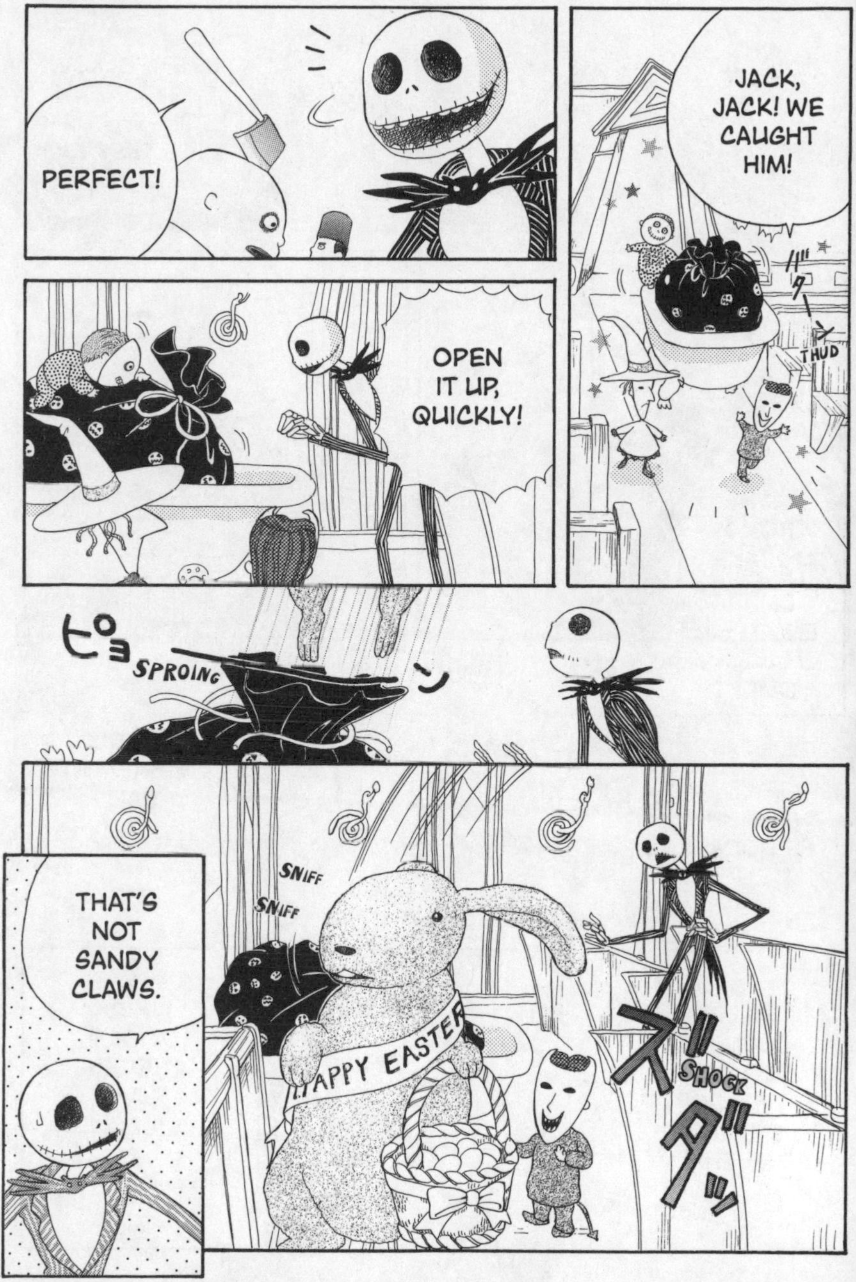
JACK, JACK! WE CAUGHT HIM!
THUD
PERFECT!
OPEN IT UP, QUICKLY!
SPROING
SNIFF
SNIFF
HAPPY EASTER
SHOCK
THAT'S NOT SANDY CLAWS.

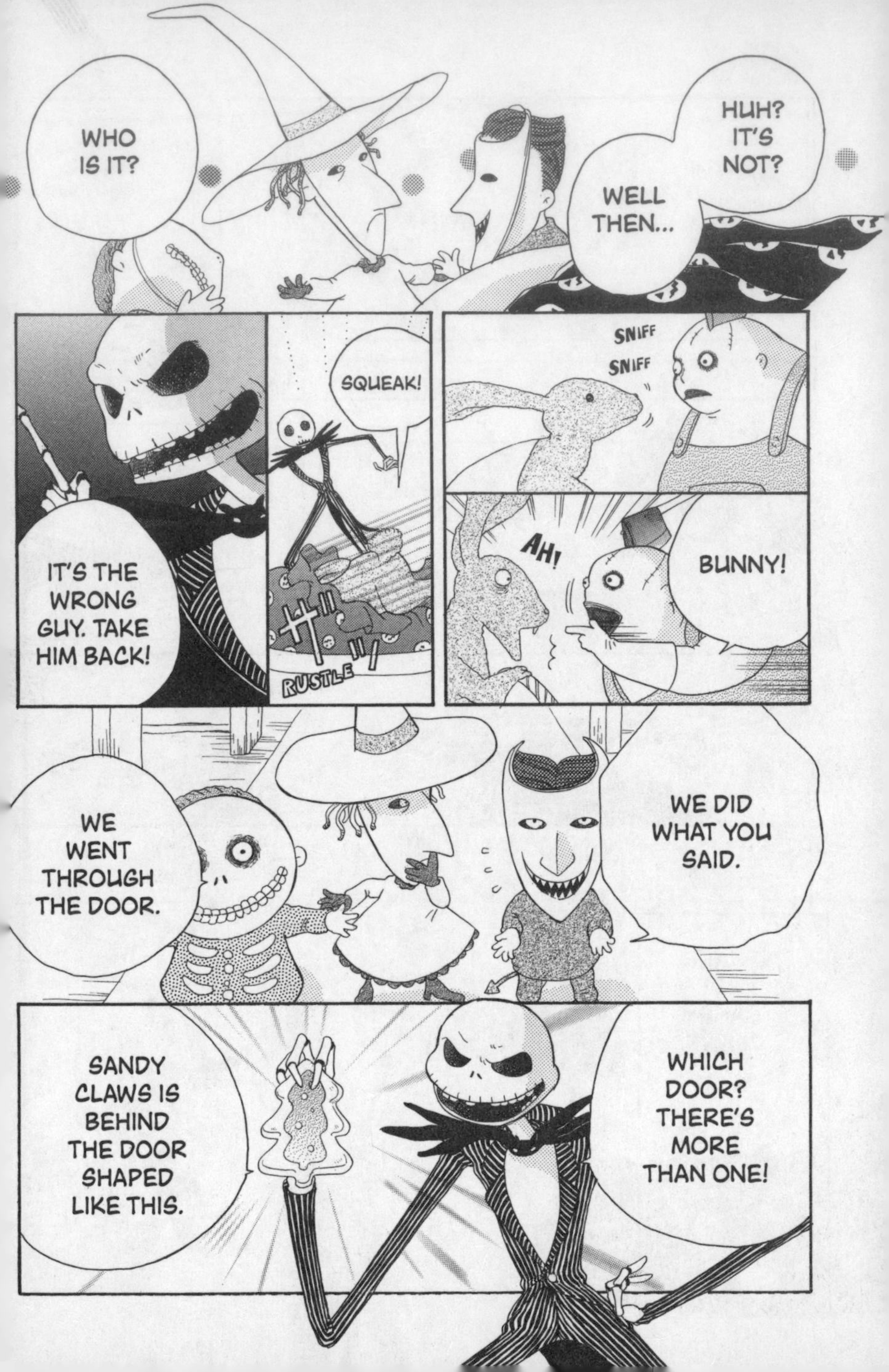
HUH? IT'S NOT?
WELL THEN...
WHO IS IT?
SNIFF SNIFF
BUNNY!
AH!
SQUEAK!
RUSTLE
IT'S THE WRONG GUY. TAKE HIM BACK!
WE DID WHAT YOU SAID.
WE WENT THROUGH THE DOOR.
WHICH DOOR? THERE'S MORE THAN ONE!
SANDY CLAWS IS BEHIND THE DOOR SHAPED LIKE THIS.

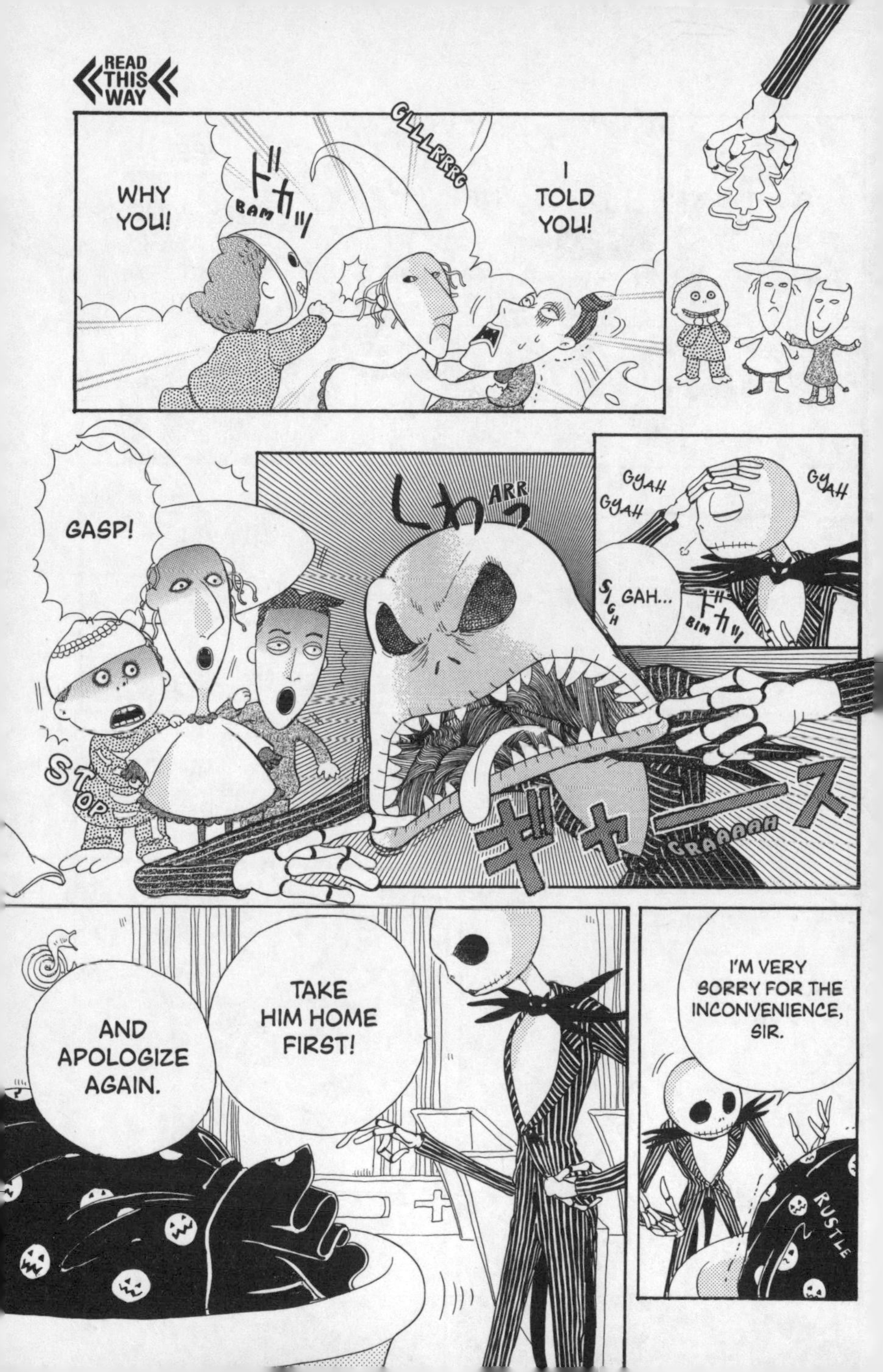
READ THIS WAY
GLLLRRRG
I TOLD YOU!
ドカッ BAM
WHY YOU!
GYAH
GYAH
GYAH
SIGH
GAH...
ドカッ BIM
しわっ ARR
ギャース GRAAAAH
GASP!
STOP
I'M VERY SORRY FOR THE INCONVENIENCE, SIR.
RUSTLE
TAKE HIM HOME FIRST!
AND APOLOGIZE AGAIN.

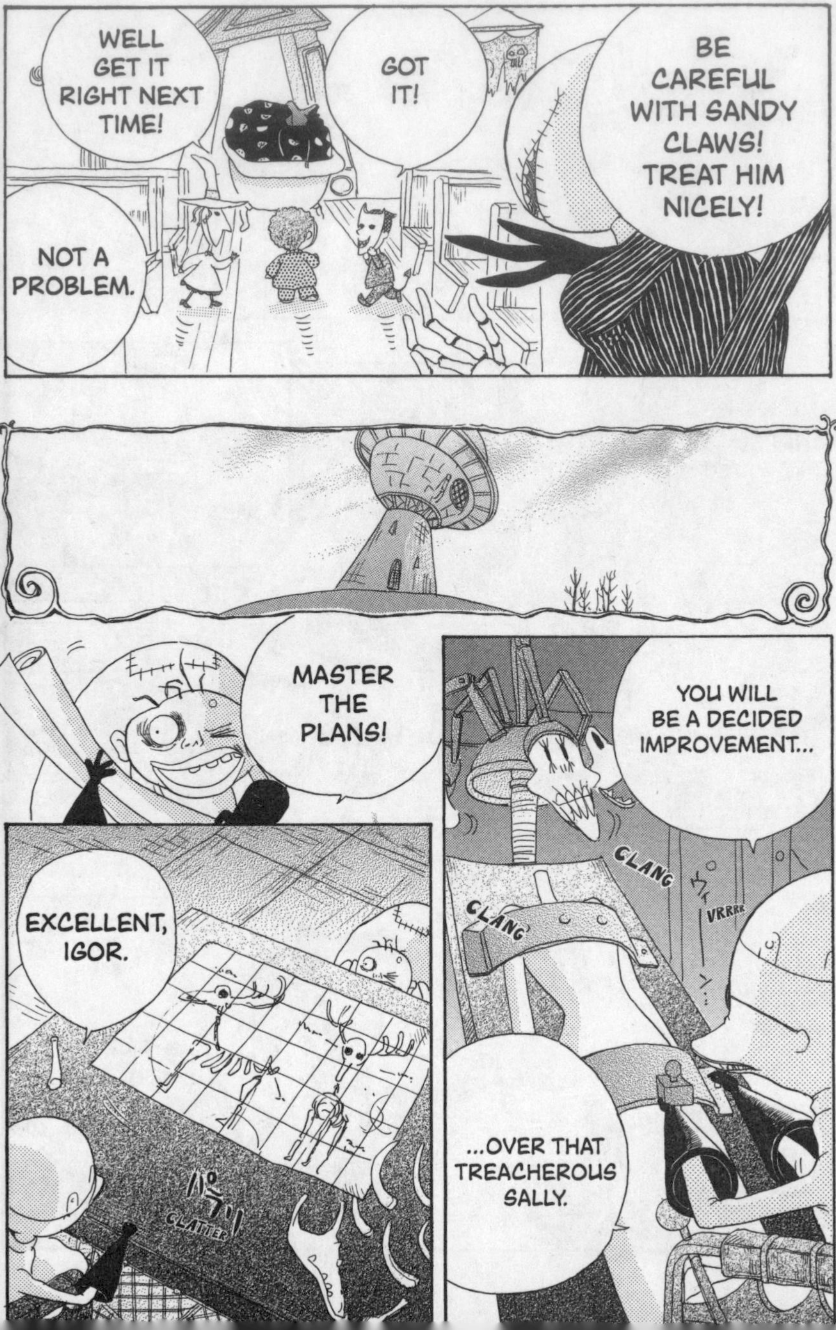
BE CAREFUL WITH SANDY CLAWS! TREAT HIM NICELY!
GOT IT!
WELL GET IT RIGHT NEXT TIME!
NOT A PROBLEM.
YOU WILL BE A DECIDED IMPROVEMENT...
CLANG
VRRRR
CLANG
...OVER THAT TREACHEROUS SALLY.
MASTER THE PLANS!
EXCELLENT, IGOR.
パラリ
CLATTER

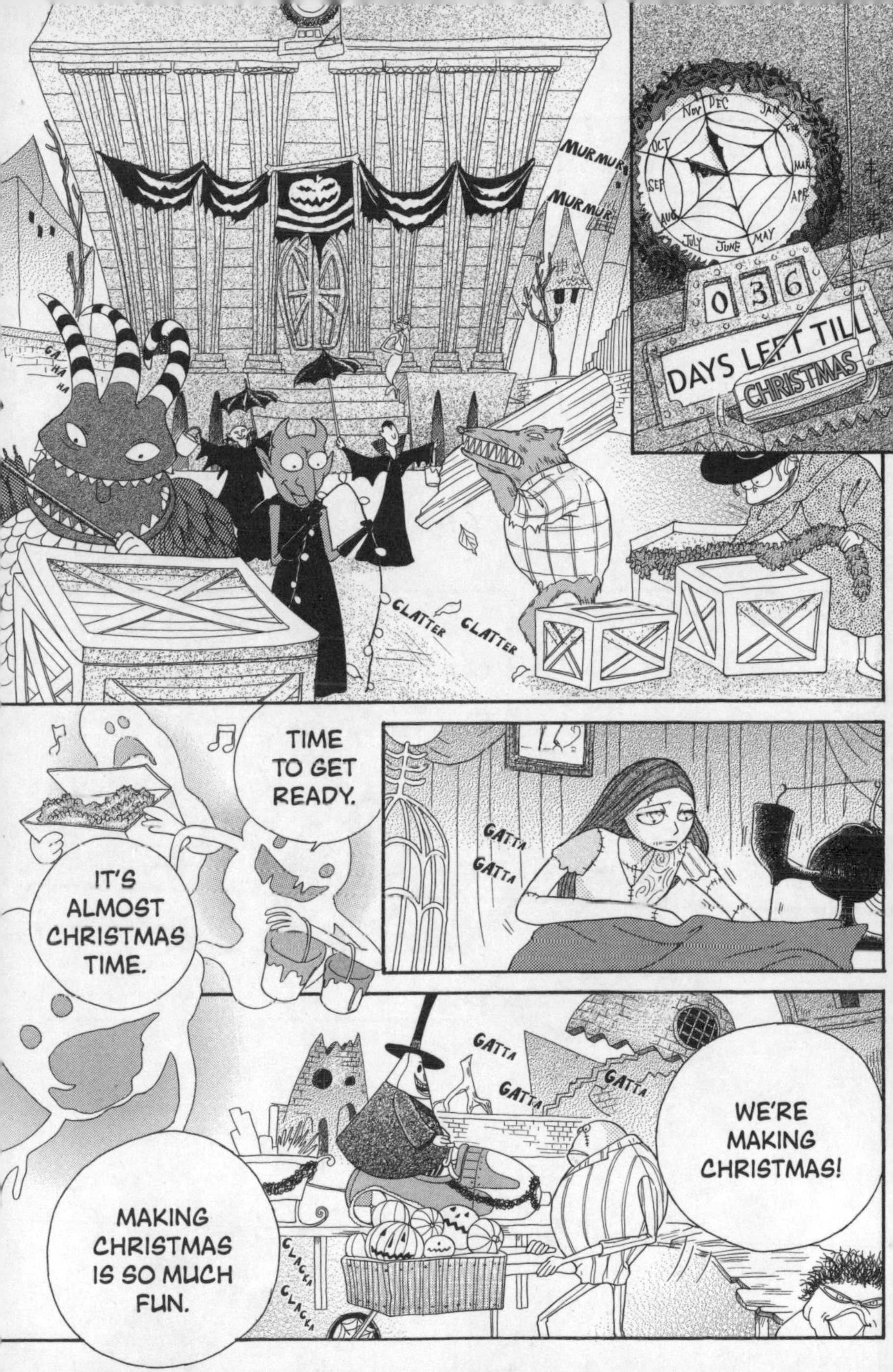
NOV DEC JAN FEB MAR APR MAY JUNE JULY AUG SEP OCT
036
DAYS LEFT TILL
CHRISTMAS
MURMUR
MURMUR
GA HA HA
CLATTER
CLATTER
GATTA
GATTA
TIME TO GET READY.
IT'S ALMOST CHRISTMAS TIME.
WE'RE MAKING CHRISTMAS!
GATTA
GATTA
GATTA
MAKING CHRISTMAS IS SO MUCH FUN.
CLACKA
CLACKA

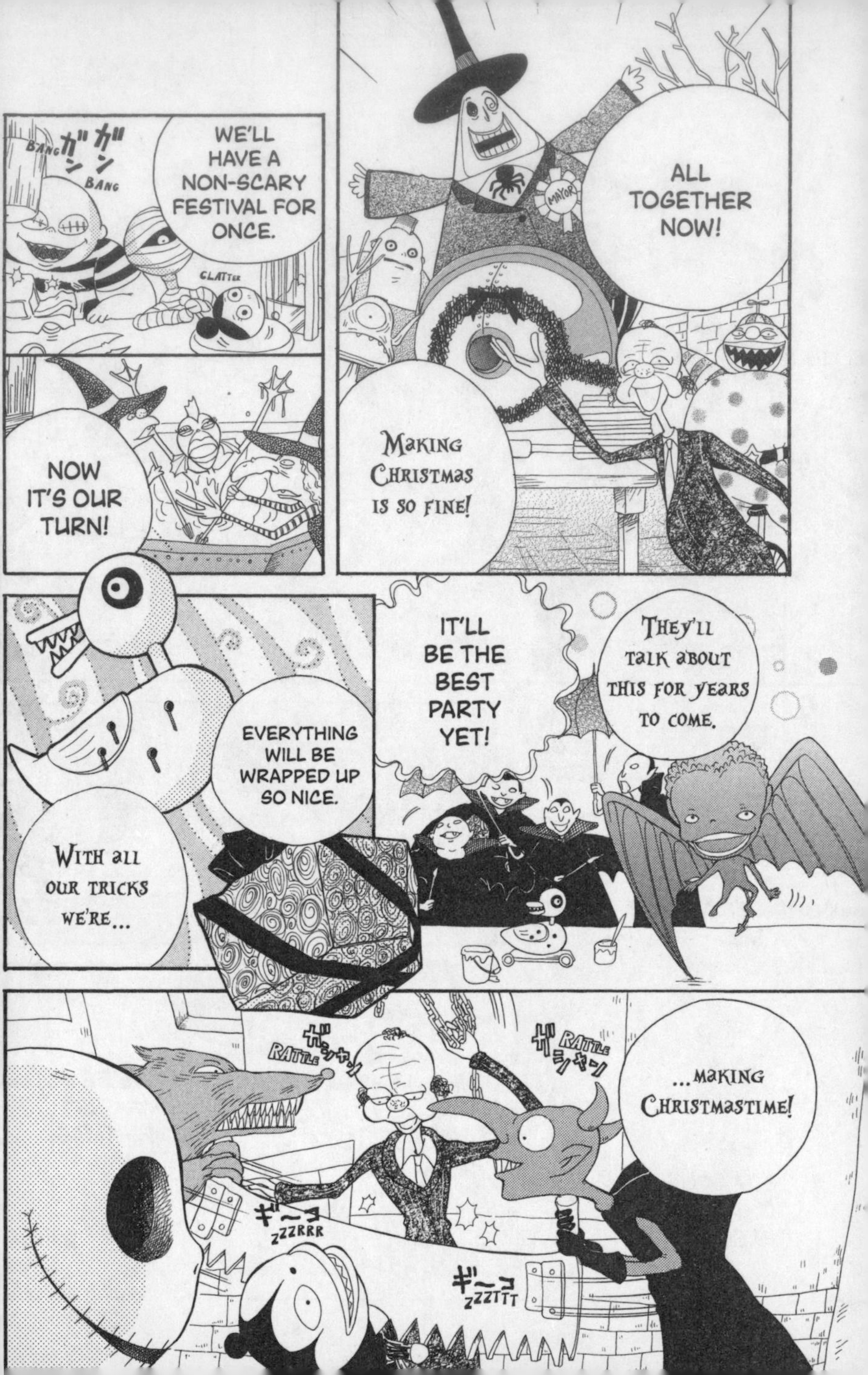
ALL TOGETHER NOW!
MAKING CHRISTMAS IS SO FINE!
BANG BANG
WE'LL HAVE A NON-SCARY FESTIVAL FOR ONCE.
CLATTER
NOW IT'S OUR TURN!
THEY'LL TALK ABOUT THIS FOR YEARS TO COME.
IT'LL BE THE BEST PARTY YET!
EVERYTHING WILL BE WRAPPED UP SO NICE.
WITH ALL OUR TRICKS WE'RE...
...MAKING CHRISTMASTIME!
RATTLE
RATTLE
ZZZRRR
ZZZTTT

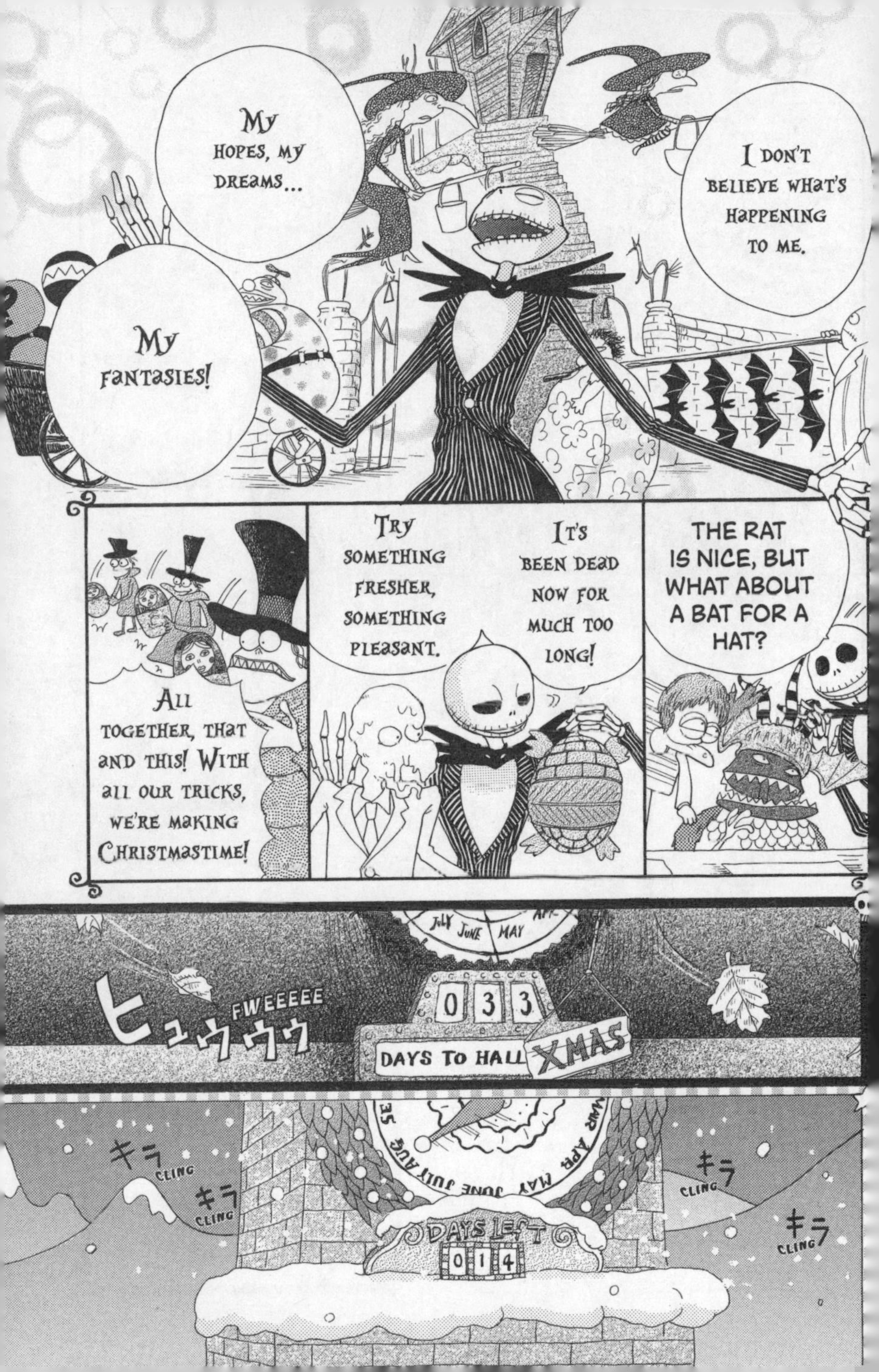
I DON'T BELIEVE WHAT'S HAPPENING TO ME.
MY HOPES, MY DREAMS...
MY FANTASIES!
THE RAT IS NICE, BUT WHAT ABOUT A BAT FOR A HAT?
IT'S BEEN DEAD NOW FOR MUCH TOO LONG!
TRY SOMETHING FRESHER, SOMETHING PLEASANT.
ALL TOGETHER, THAT AND THIS! WITH ALL OUR TRICKS, WE'RE MAKING CHRISTMASTIME!
JULY JUNE MAY
033
DAYS TO HALL XMAS
ヒュウウウ
FWEEEEE
キラ
CLING
キラ
CLING
MAR APR MAY JUNE JULY AUG SE
DAYS LEFT
014
キラ
CLING
キラ
CLING

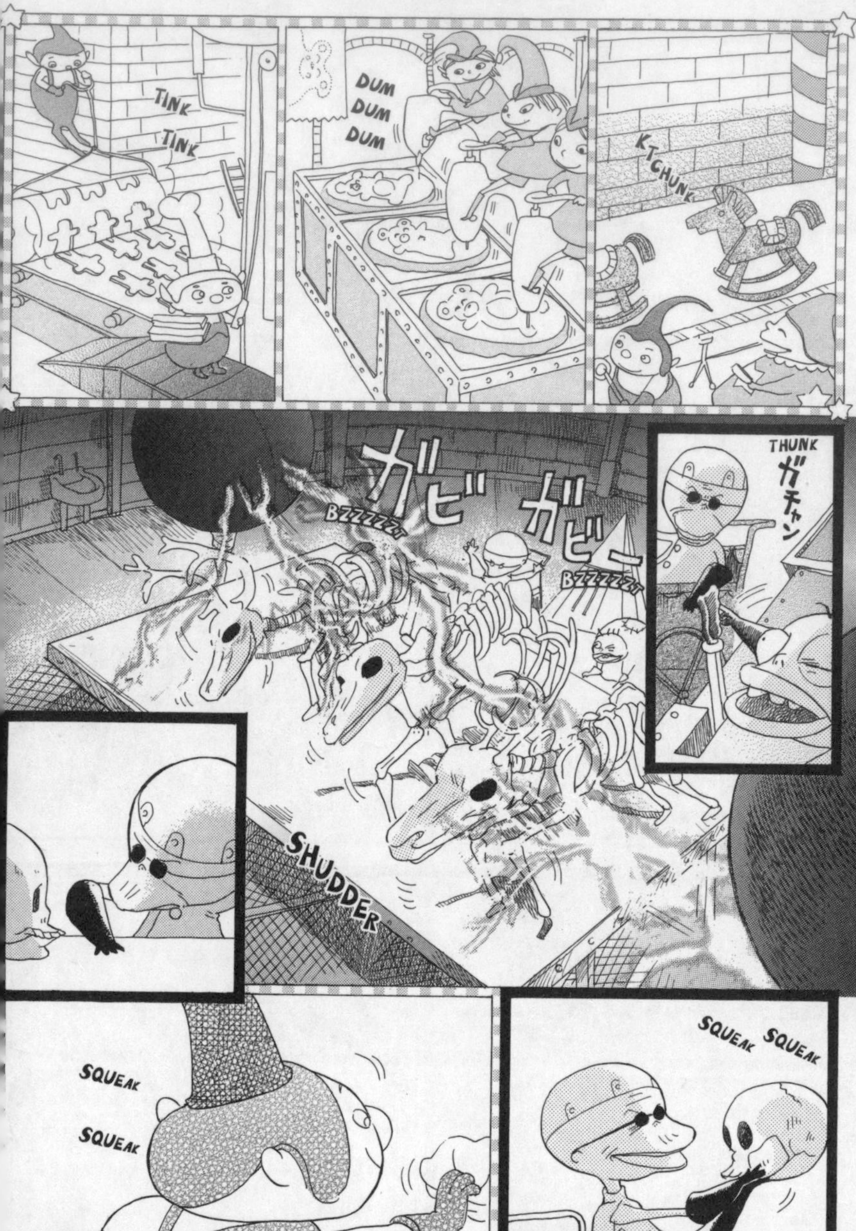
KTCHUNK
DUM
DUM
DUM
TINK
TINK
THUNK
ガチャン
ガビ
BZZZZZT
ガビー
BZZZZZT
SHUDDER
SQUEAK
SQUEAK
SQUEAK
SQUEAK

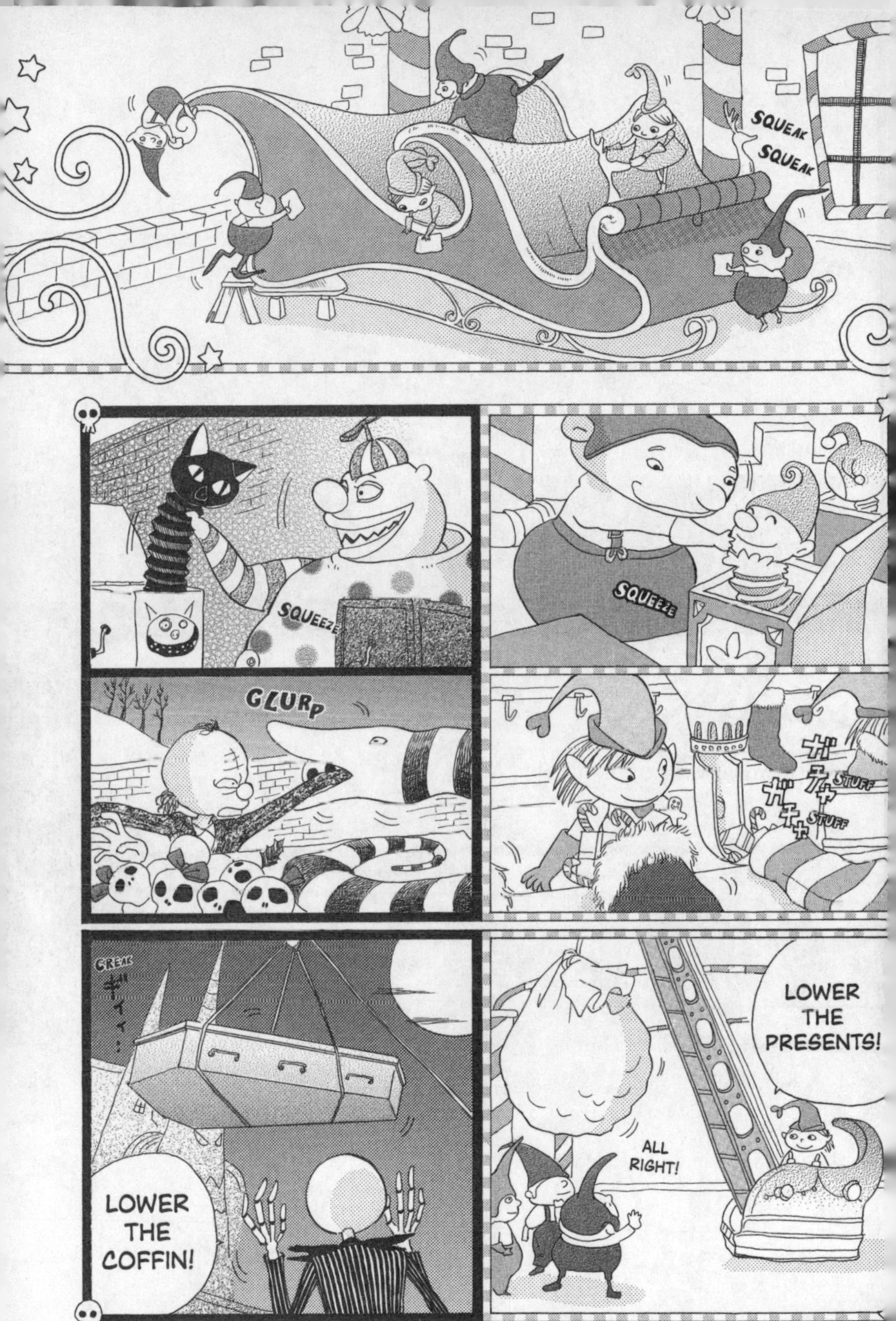
SQUEAK
SQUEAK
SQUEEZE
SQUEEZE
ガチャ
STUFF
ガチャ
STUFF
GLURP
LOWER THE PRESENTS!
ALL RIGHT!
CREAK
ギイイ…
LOWER THE COFFIN!

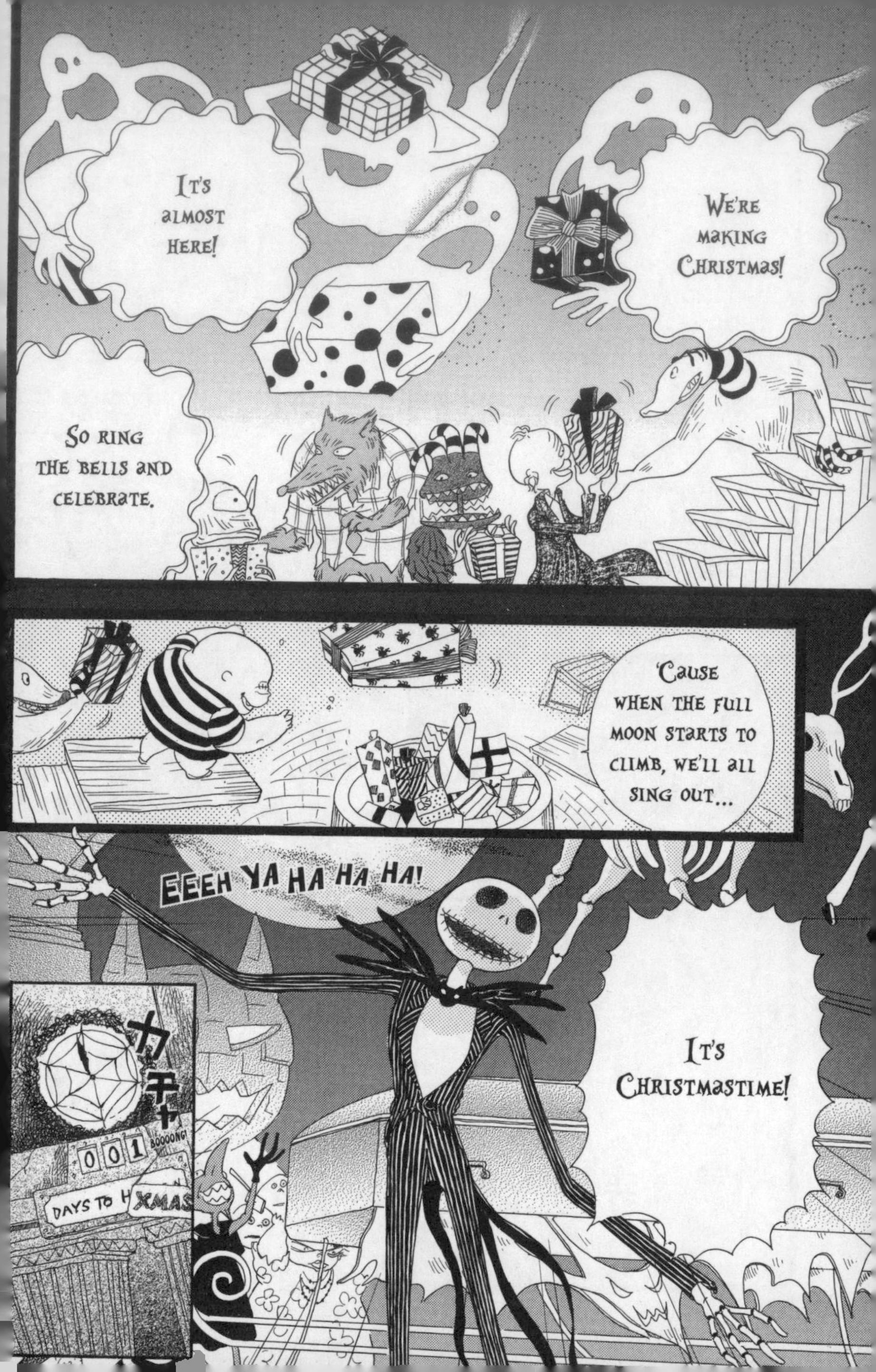
We're making Christmas!
It's almost here!
So ring the bells and celebrate.
'Cause when the full moon starts to climb, we'll all sing out...
It's Christmastime!
EEEH YA HA HA HA!
カチャ
BOOOONG!
001
DAYS TO H
XMAS

READ THIS WAY

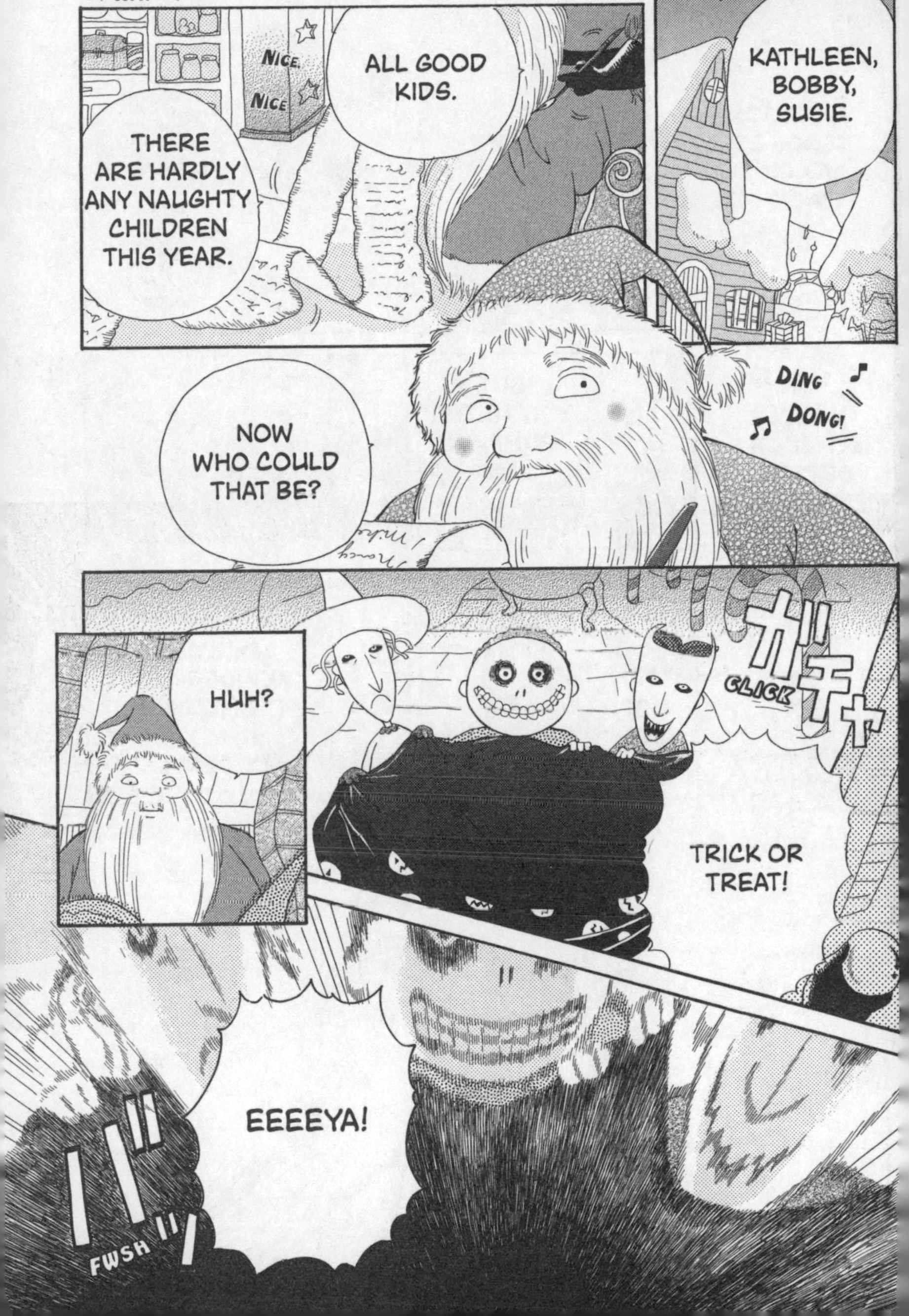
KATHLEEN, BOBBY, SUSIE.
ALL GOOD KIDS.
THERE ARE HARDLY ANY NAUGHTY CHILDREN THIS YEAR.
NICE.
NICE
DING DONG!
NOW WHO COULD THAT BE?
ガチャ
CLICK
TRICK OR TREAT!
HUH?
EEEEYA!
FWSH

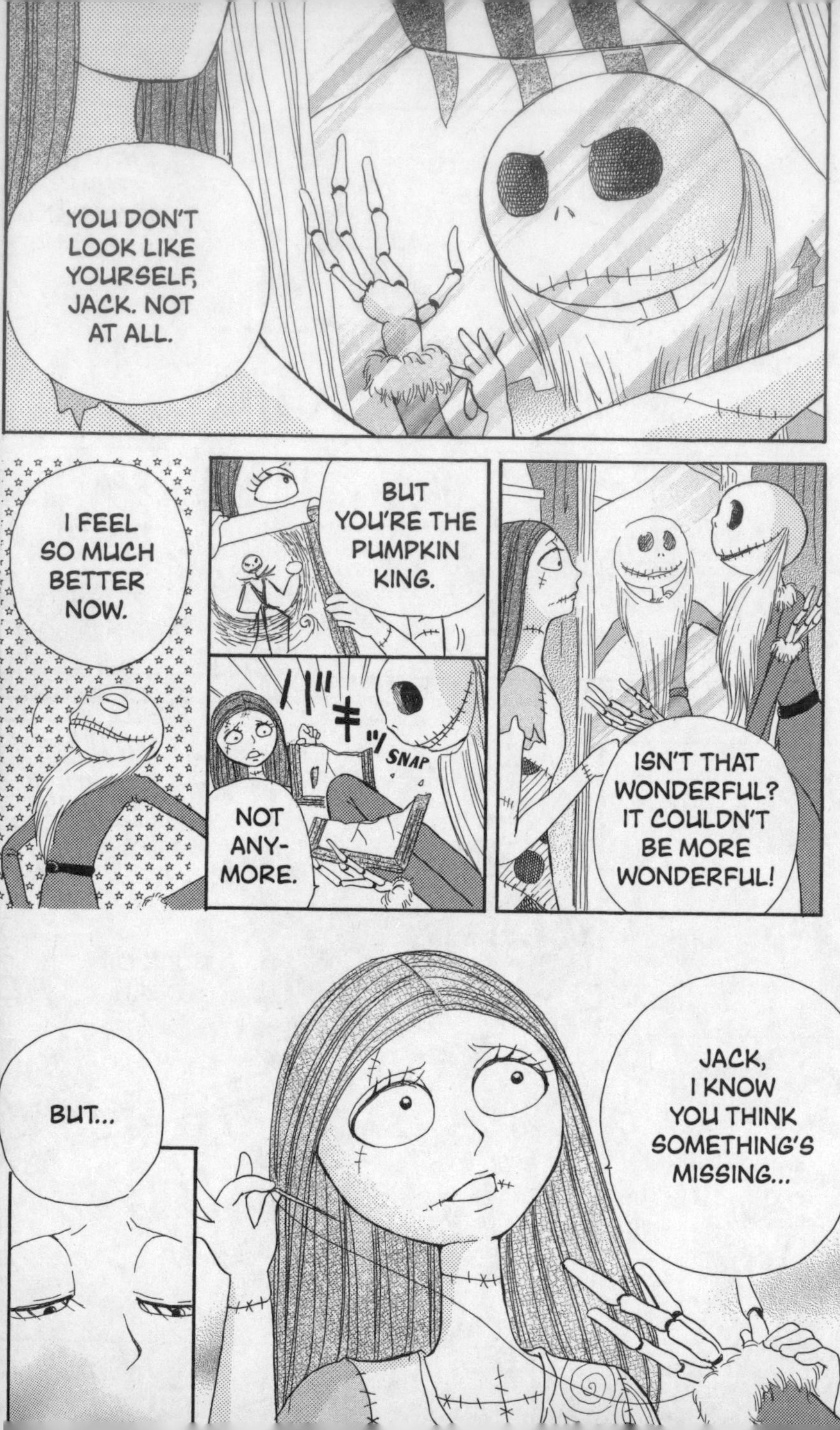
YOU DON'T LOOK LIKE YOURSELF, JACK. NOT AT ALL.
ISN'T THAT WONDERFUL? IT COULDN'T BE MORE WONDERFUL!
BUT YOU'RE THE PUMPKIN KING.
バキッ
SNAP
NOT ANY-MORE.
I FEEL SO MUCH BETTER NOW.
JACK, I KNOW YOU THINK SOMETHING'S MISSING...
BUT...

READ THIS WAY

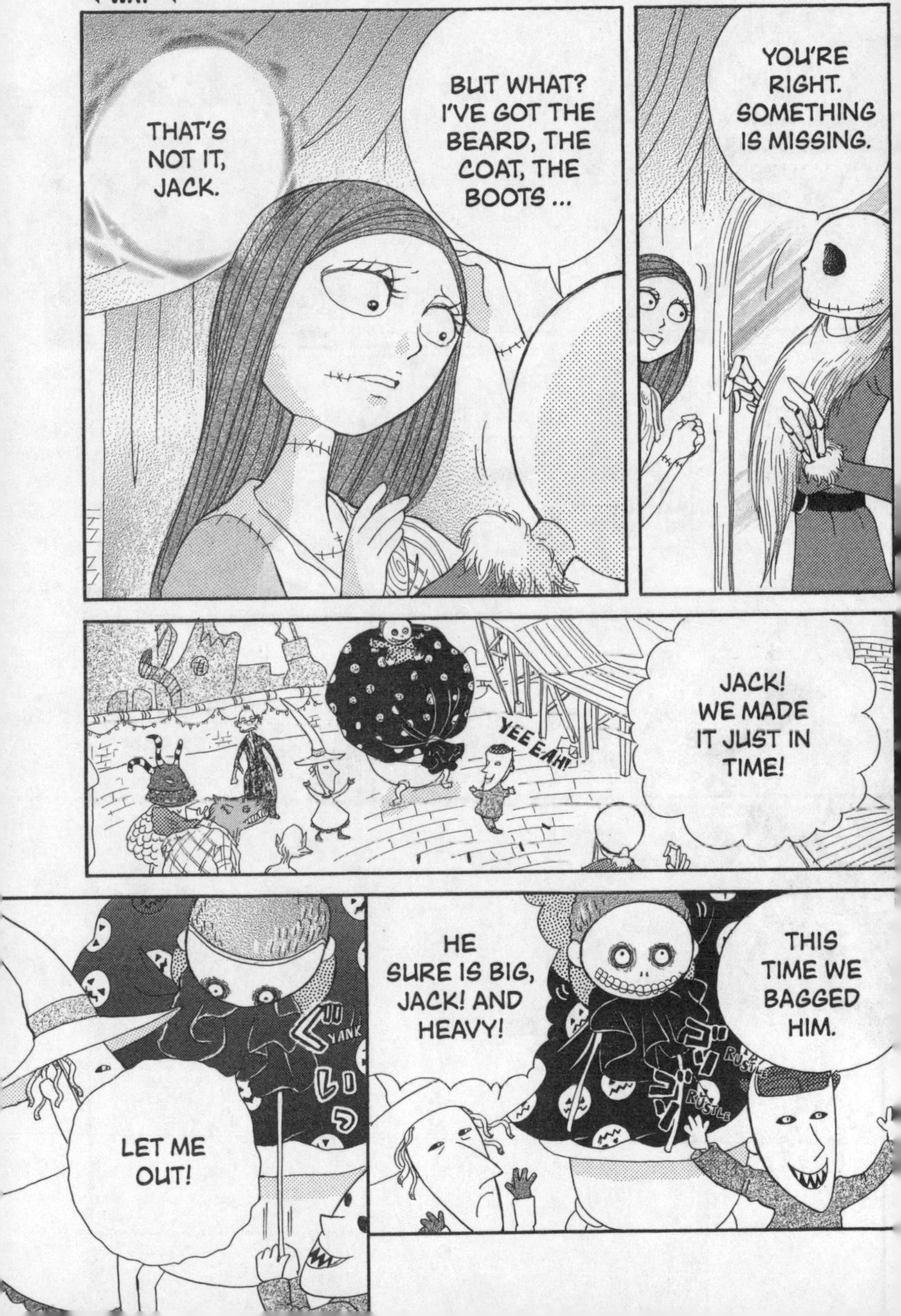
YOU'RE RIGHT. SOMETHING IS MISSING.
BUT WHAT? I'VE GOT THE BEARD, THE COAT, THE BOOTS ...
THAT'S NOT IT, JACK.
JACK! WE MADE IT JUST IN TIME!
YEE EAH!
THIS TIME WE BAGGED HIM.
RUSTLE
RUSTLE
HE SURE IS BIG, JACK! AND HEAVY!
YANK
LET ME OUT!

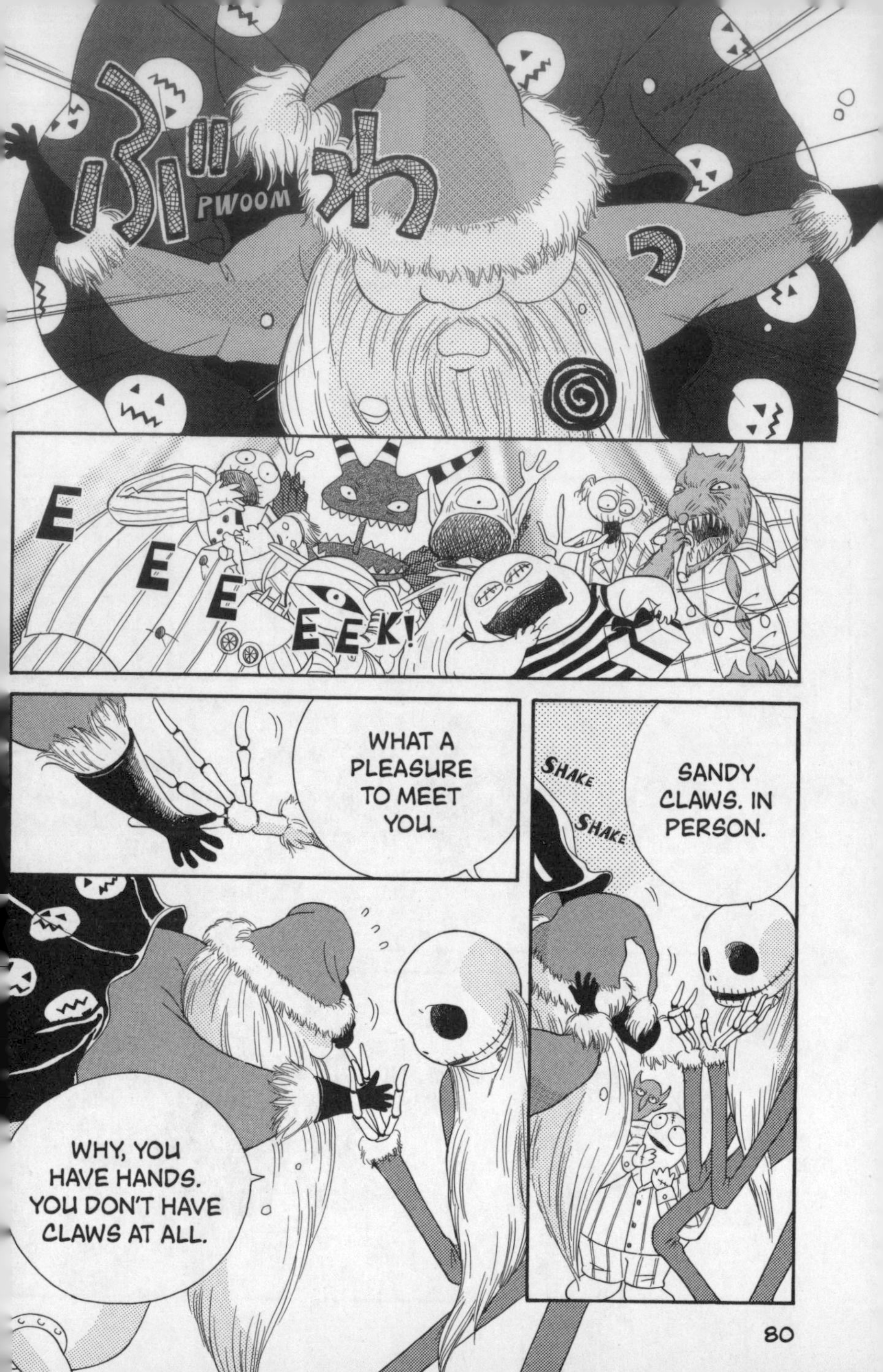
ぶわっ
PWOOM
EEEEEK!
SHAKE SHAKE
SANDY CLAWS. IN PERSON.
WHAT A PLEASURE TO MEET YOU.
WHY, YOU HAVE HANDS. YOU DON'T HAVE CLAWS AT ALL.

READ THIS WAY

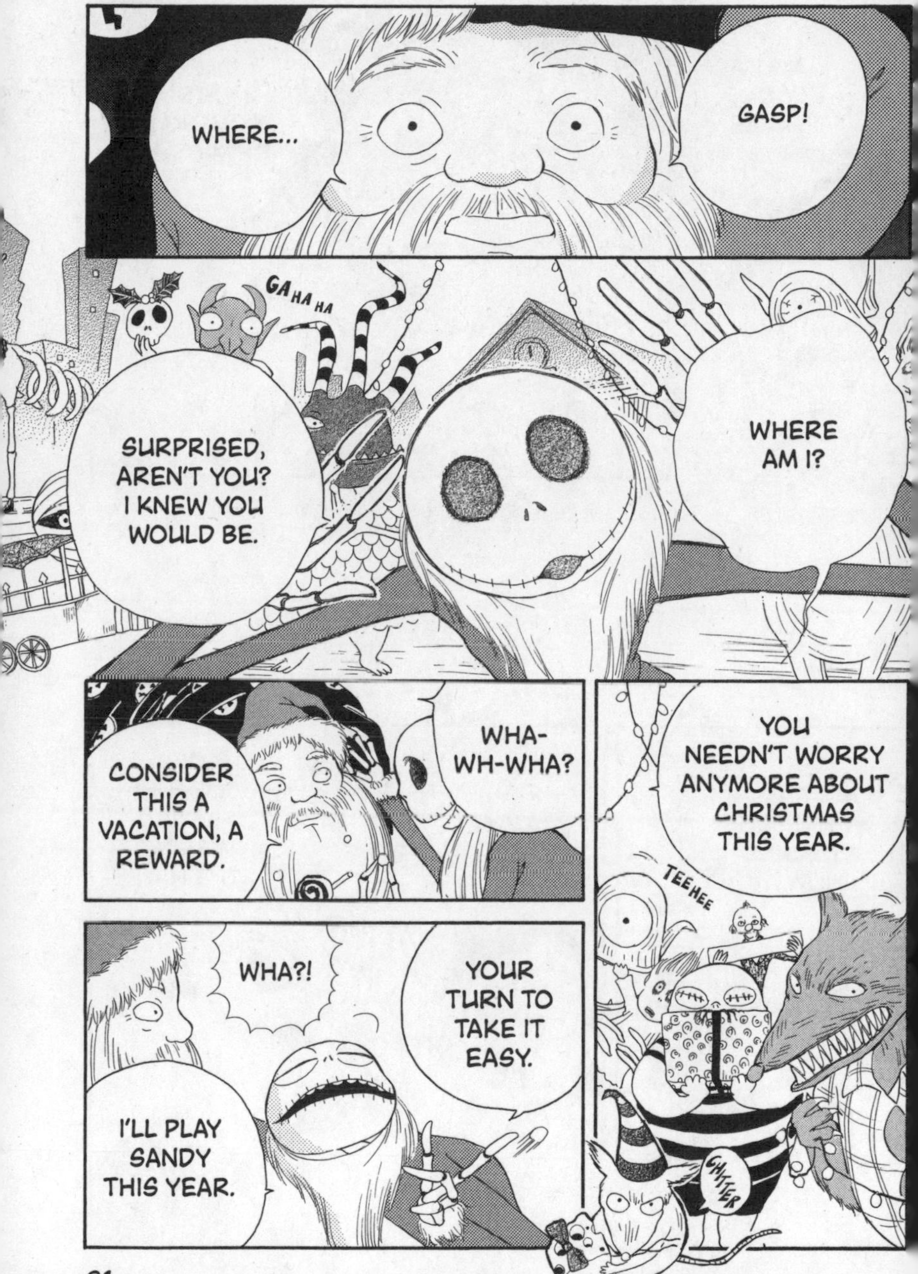
GASP!
WHERE...
WHERE AM I?
SURPRISED, AREN'T YOU? I KNEW YOU WOULD BE.
GA HA HA
YOU NEEDN'T WORRY ANYMORE ABOUT CHRISTMAS THIS YEAR.
TEEHEE
CHITTER
WHA-WH-WHA?
CONSIDER THIS A VACATION, A REWARD.
YOUR TURN TO TAKE IT EASY.
WHA?!
I'LL PLAY SANDY THIS YEAR.

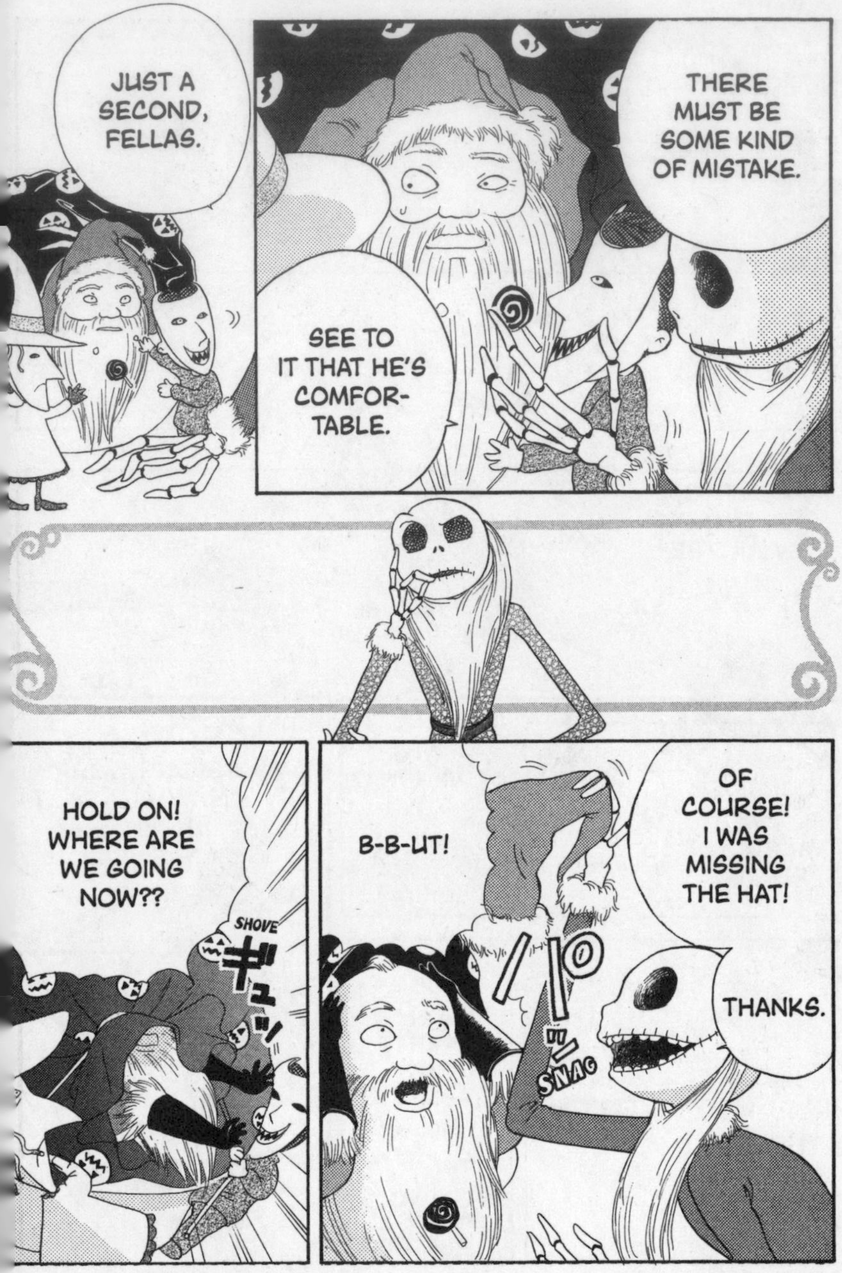
THERE MUST BE SOME KIND OF MISTAKE.
SEE TO IT THAT HE'S COMFORTABLE.
JUST A SECOND, FELLAS.
OF COURSE! I WAS MISSING THE HAT!
B-B-UT!
SNAG
THANKS.
HOLD ON! WHERE ARE WE GOING NOW??
SHOVE

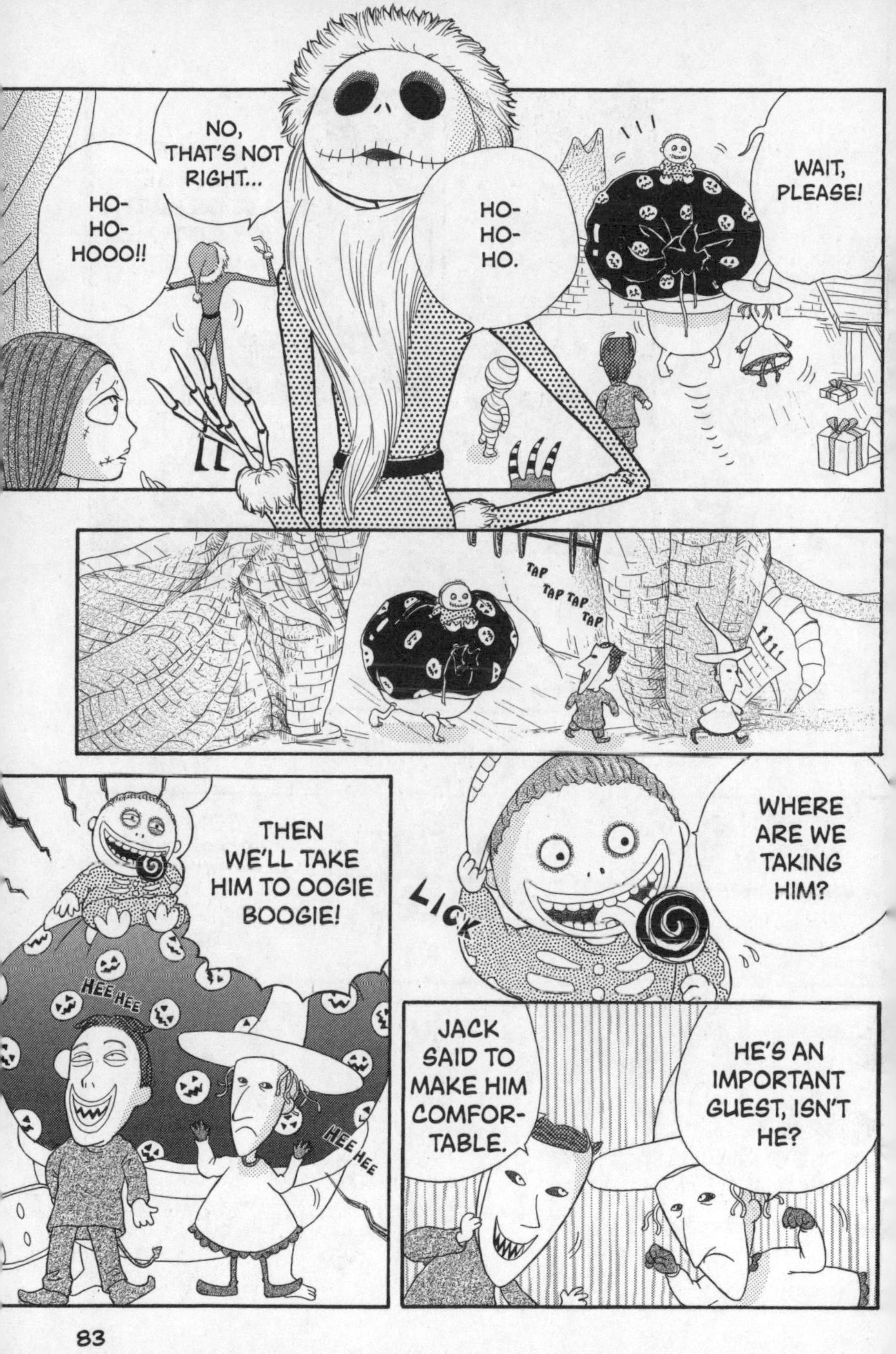
WAIT, PLEASE!
HO-HO-HO.
NO, THAT'S NOT RIGHT...
HO-HO-HOOO!!
TAP TAP TAP TAP
WHERE ARE WE TAKING HIM?
LICK
HE'S AN IMPORTANT GUEST, ISN'T HE?
JACK SAID TO MAKE HIM COMFORTABLE.
THEN WE'LL TAKE HIM TO OOGIE BOOGIE!
HEE HEE
HEE HEE

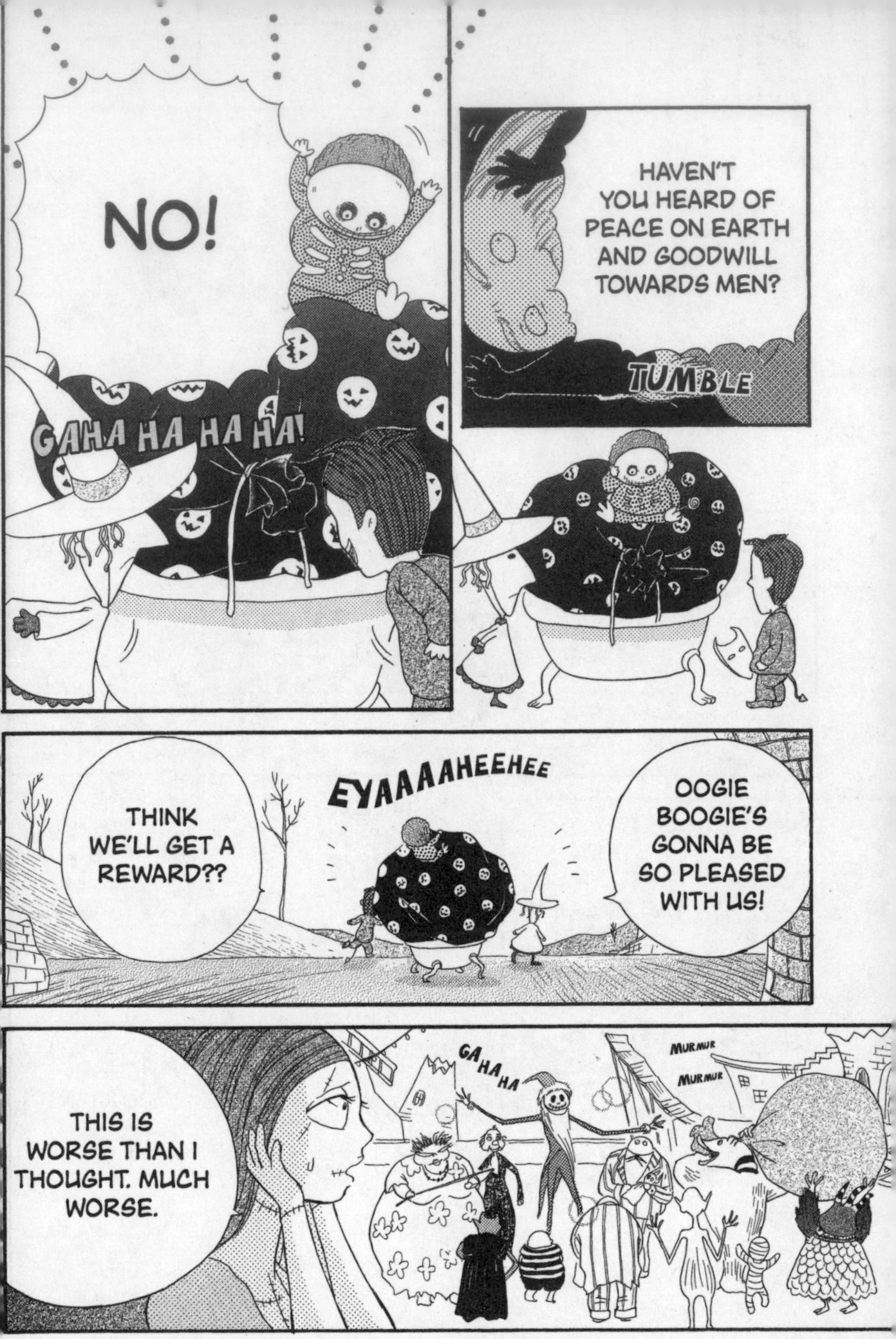
HAVEN'T YOU HEARD OF PEACE ON EARTH AND GOODWILL TOWARDS MEN?
TUMBLE
NO!
GAHA HA HA HA!
OOGIE BOOGIE'S GONNA BE SO PLEASED WITH US!
EYAAAAHEEHEE
THINK WE'LL GET A REWARD??
MURMUR
MURMUR
GAHAHA
THIS IS WORSE THAN I THOUGHT. MUCH WORSE.

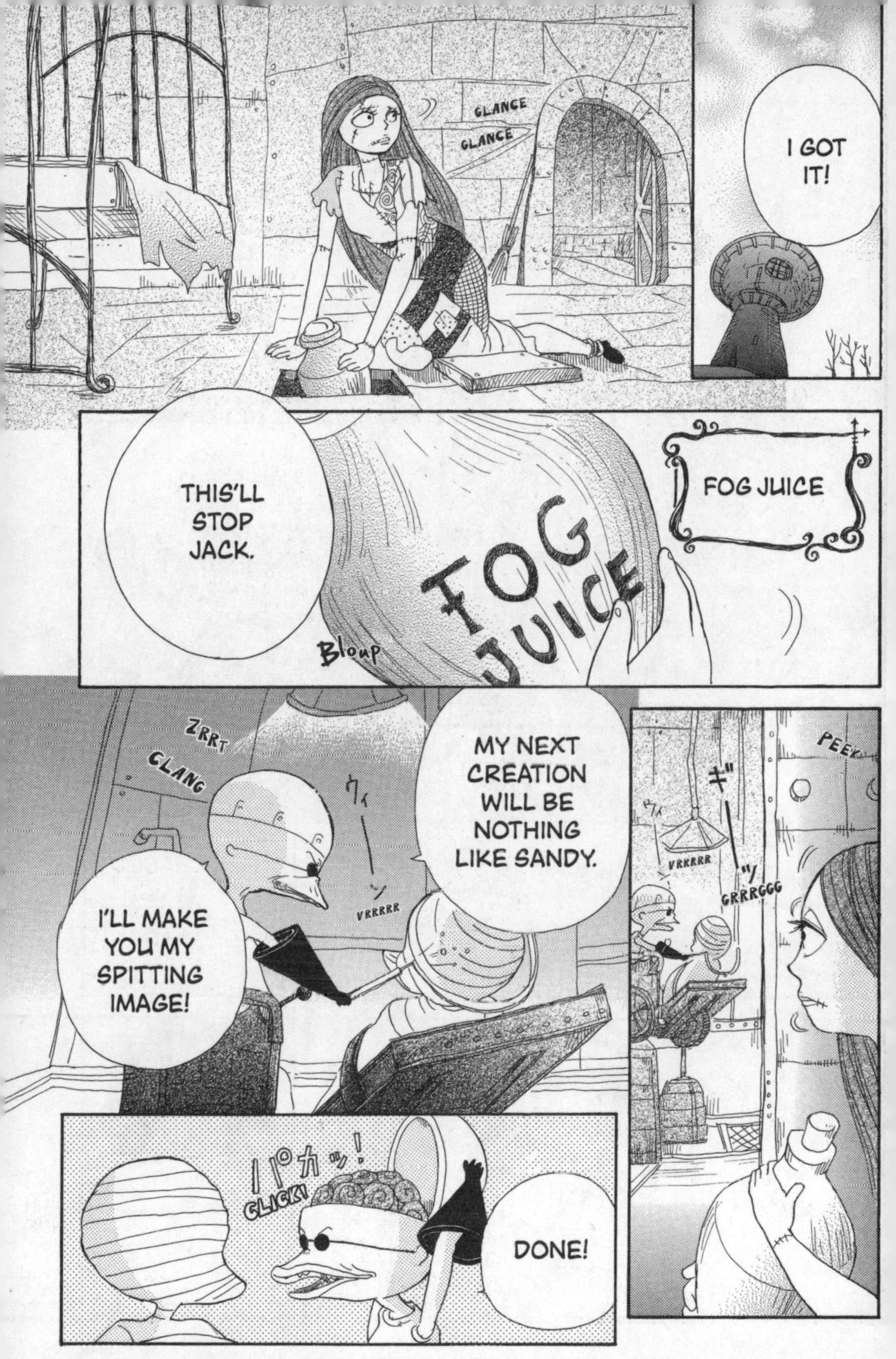

I GOT IT!
GLANCE
GLANCE
FOG JUICE
THIS'LL STOP JACK.
FOG JUICE
Bloup
PEEK
VRRRRR
GRRRGGG
MY NEXT CREATION WILL BE NOTHING LIKE SANDY.
ZRRT
CLANG
VRRRRR
I'LL MAKE YOU MY SPITTING IMAGE!
DONE!
CLICK!

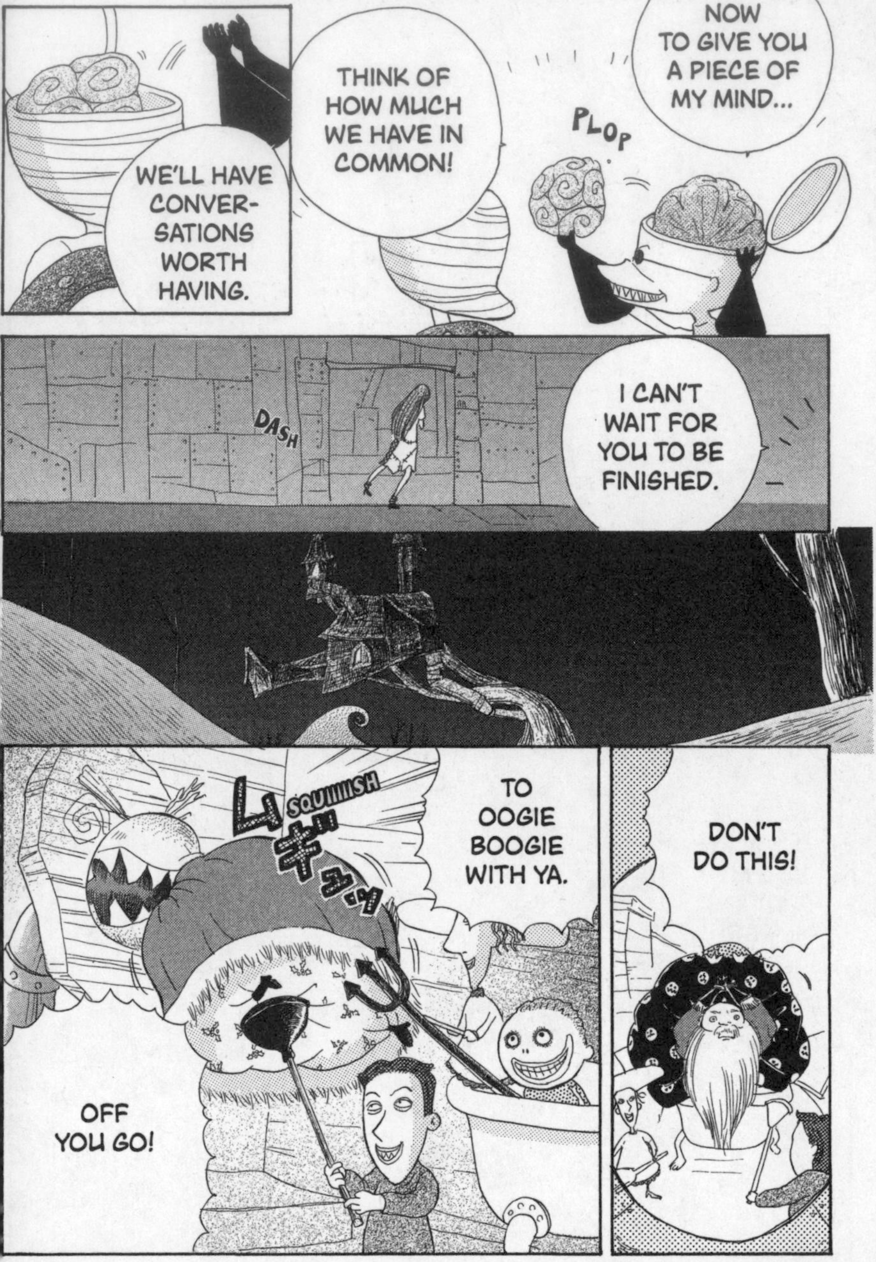
NOW TO GIVE YOU A PIECE OF MY MIND...
PLOP
THINK OF HOW MUCH WE HAVE IN COMMON!
WE'LL HAVE CONVER-SATIONS WORTH HAVING.
I CAN'T WAIT FOR YOU TO BE FINISHED.
DASH
DON'T DO THIS!
TO OOGIE BOOGIE WITH YA.
SQUIIIISH
ムギュッ
OFF YOU GO!

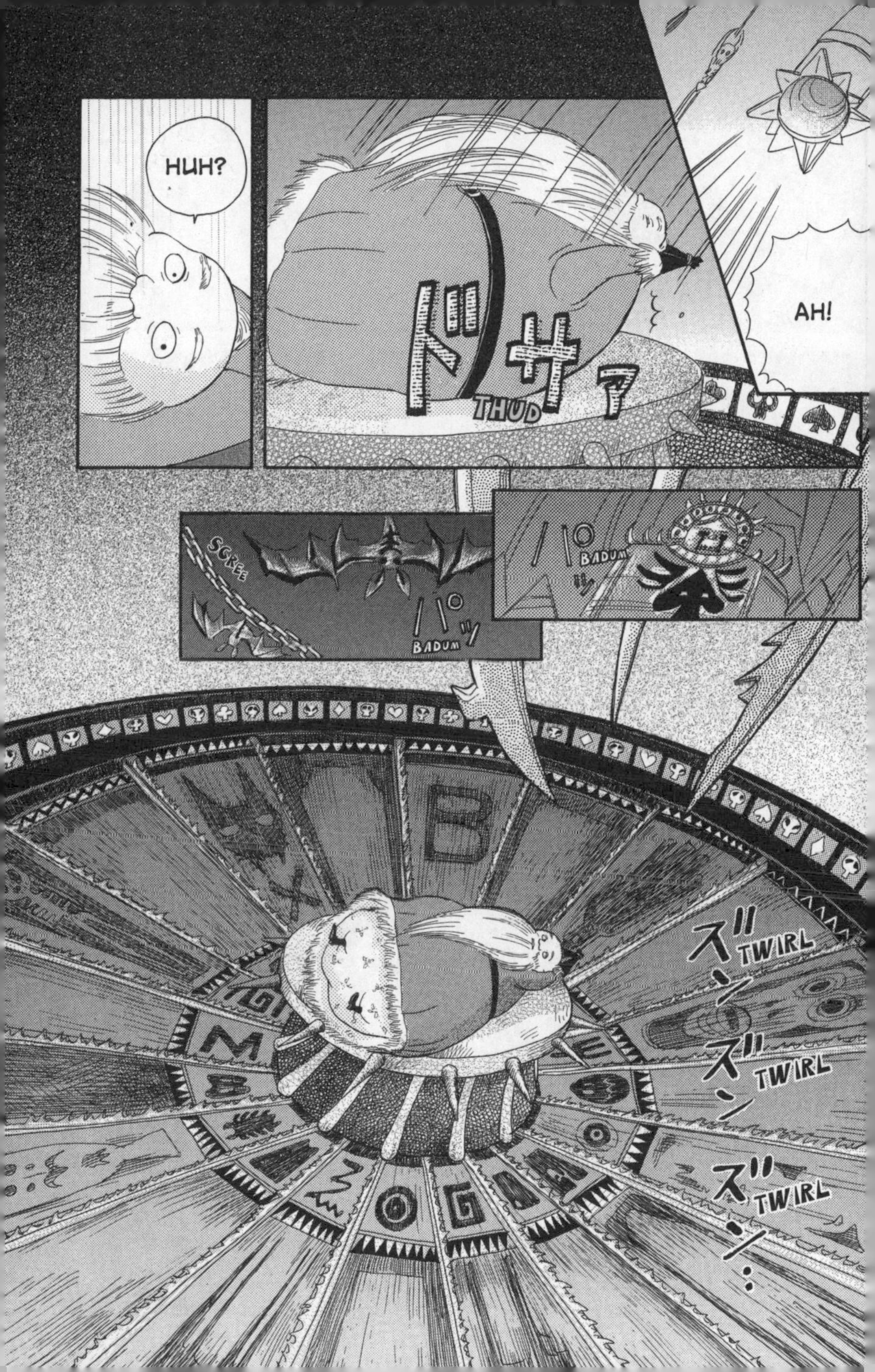
AH!
ドサァ
THUD
HUH?
パ
BADUM
パッ
SCREE
BADUM
ズン
TWIRL
ズン
TWIRL
ズン…
TWIRL

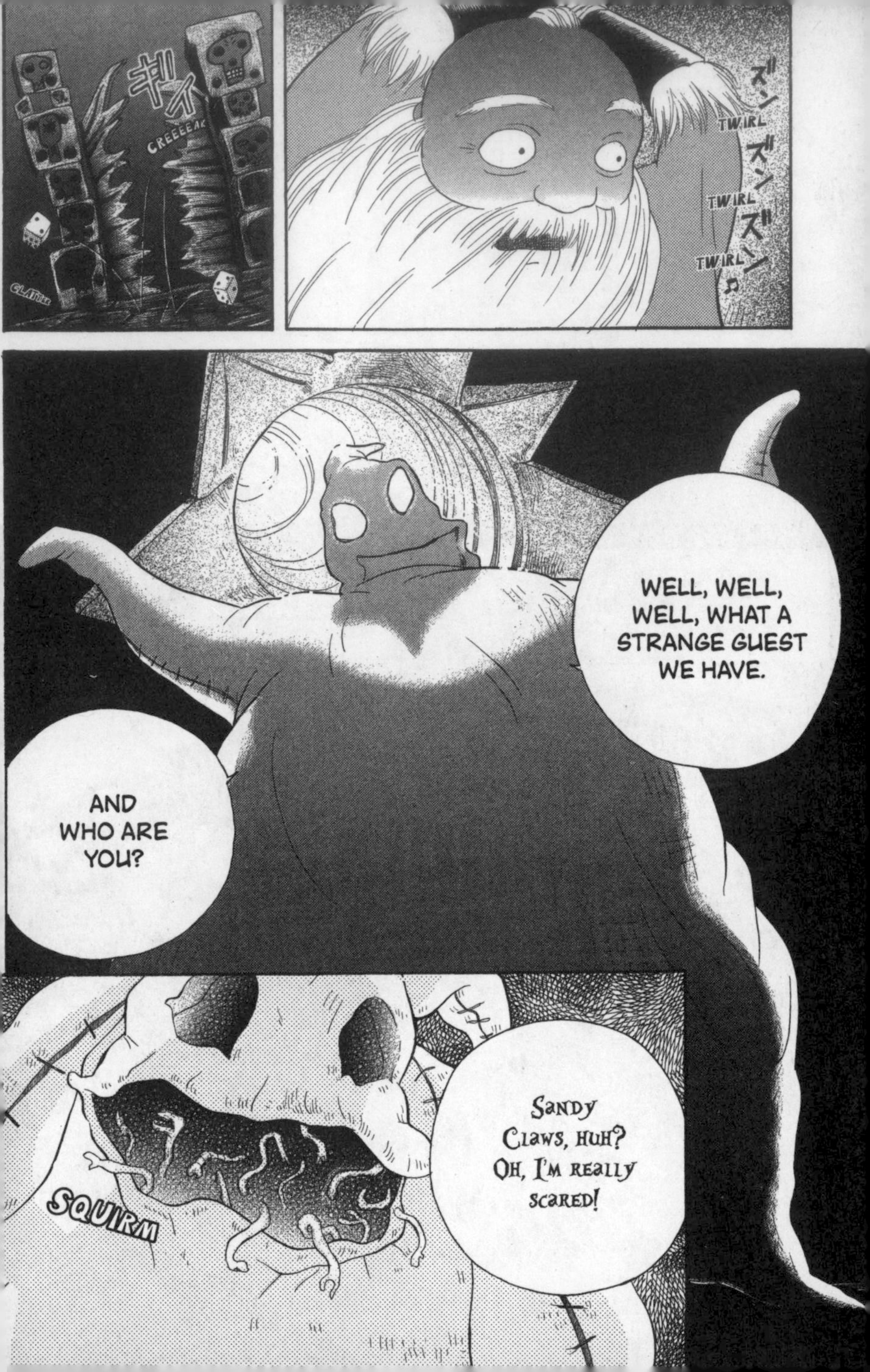

ズンズンズン♪
TWIRL
TWIRL
TWIRL
ギィ
CREEEEAK
CLATTER
WELL, WELL, WELL, WHAT A STRANGE GUEST WE HAVE.
AND WHO ARE YOU?
SANDY CLAWS, HUH? OH, I'M REALLY SCARED!
SQUIRM

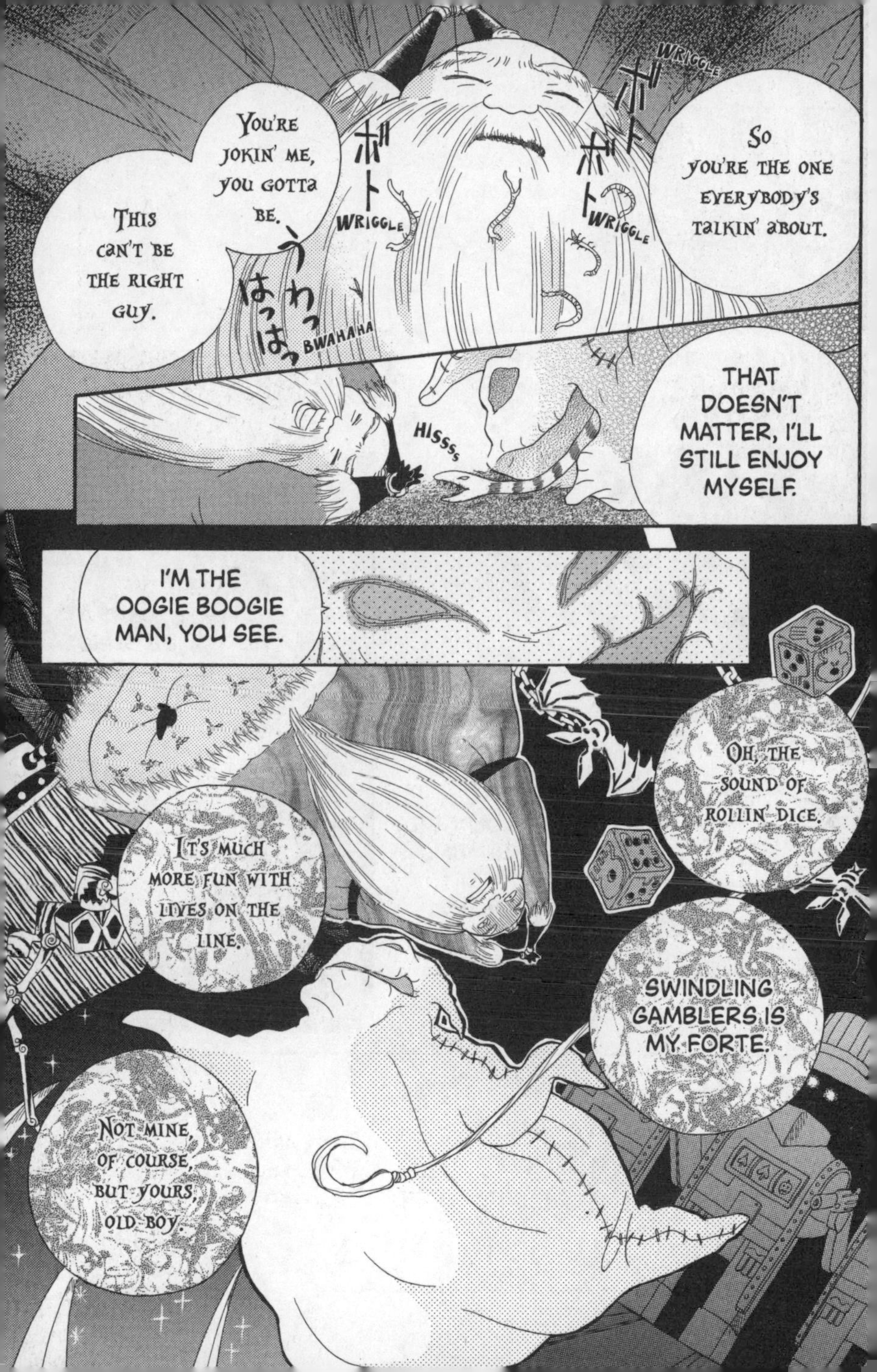
WRIGGLE
ボト
ボト
WRIGGLE
So you're the one everybody's talkin' about.
ボト
WRIGGLE
You're jokin' me, you gotta be.
This can't be the right guy.
うわっはっはっ
BWAHAHA
That doesn't matter, I'll still enjoy myself.
HISSSS
I'm the Oogie Boogie Man, you see.
Oh, the sound of rollin' dice.
It's much more fun with lives on the line.
Swindling gamblers is my forte.
Not mine, of course, but yours, old boy.

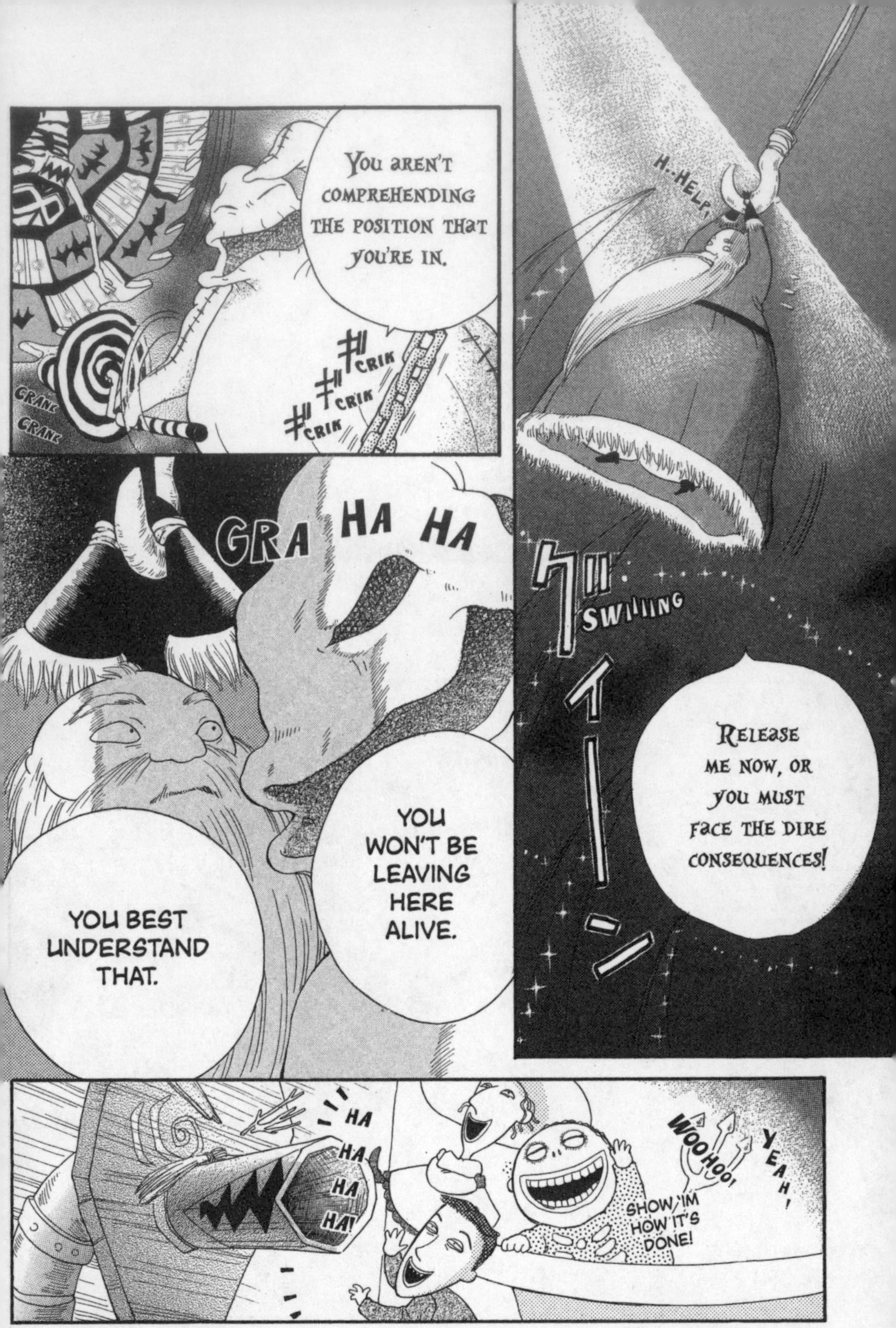
H..HELP,
クイーン
SWIIIING
Release me now, or you must face the dire consequences!
You aren't comprehending the position that you're in.
CRIK CRIK CRIK
CRANK CRANK
GRA HA HA
You won't be leaving here alive.
You best understand that.
YEAH!
WOOHOO!
SHOW 'IM HOW IT'S DONE!
HA HA HA HA!

READ THIS WAY

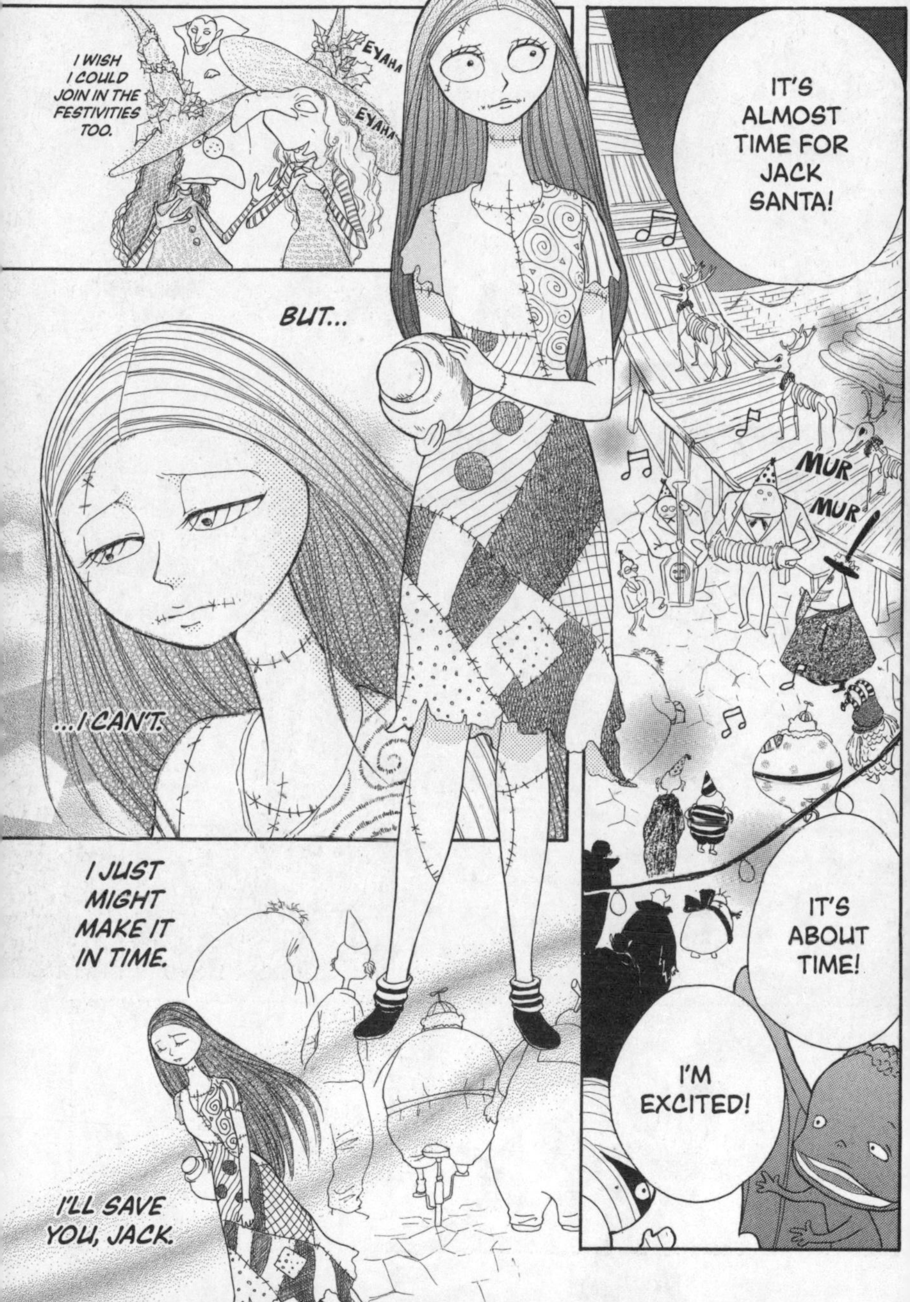
IT'S ALMOST TIME FOR JACK SANTA!
MUR
MUR
EYAHA
EYAHA
I WISH I COULD JOIN IN THE FESTIVITIES TOO.
BUT...
...I CAN'T.
IT'S ABOUT TIME!
I'M EXCITED!
I JUST MIGHT MAKE IT IN TIME.
I'LL SAVE YOU, JACK.

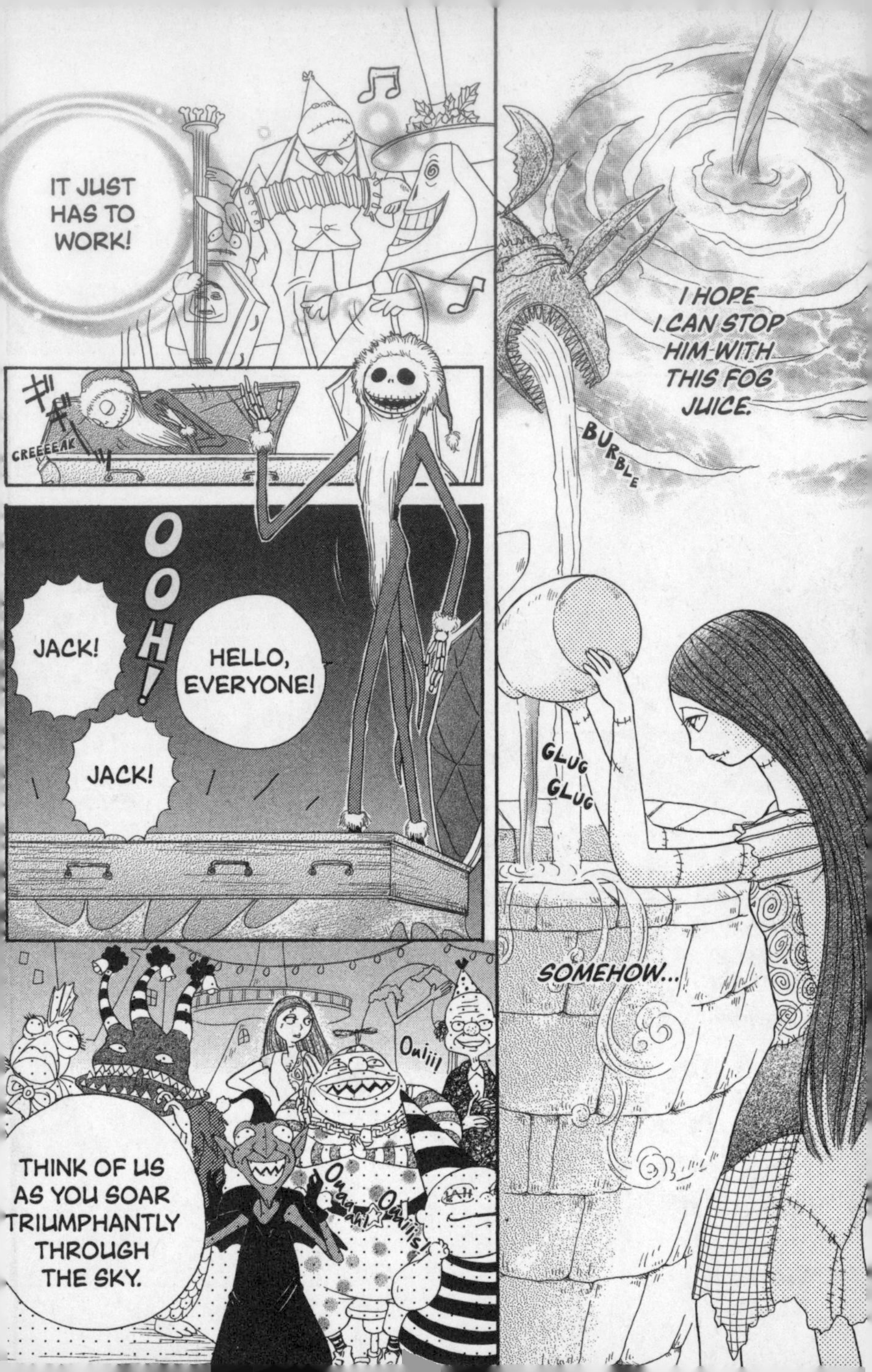
I HOPE I CAN STOP HIM WITH THIS FOG JUICE.
BURBLE
GLUG GLUG
SOMEHOW...
IT JUST HAS TO WORK!
CREEEEAK
HELLO, EVERYONE!
OOH!
JACK!
JACK!
THINK OF US AS YOU SOAR TRIUMPHANTLY THROUGH THE SKY.

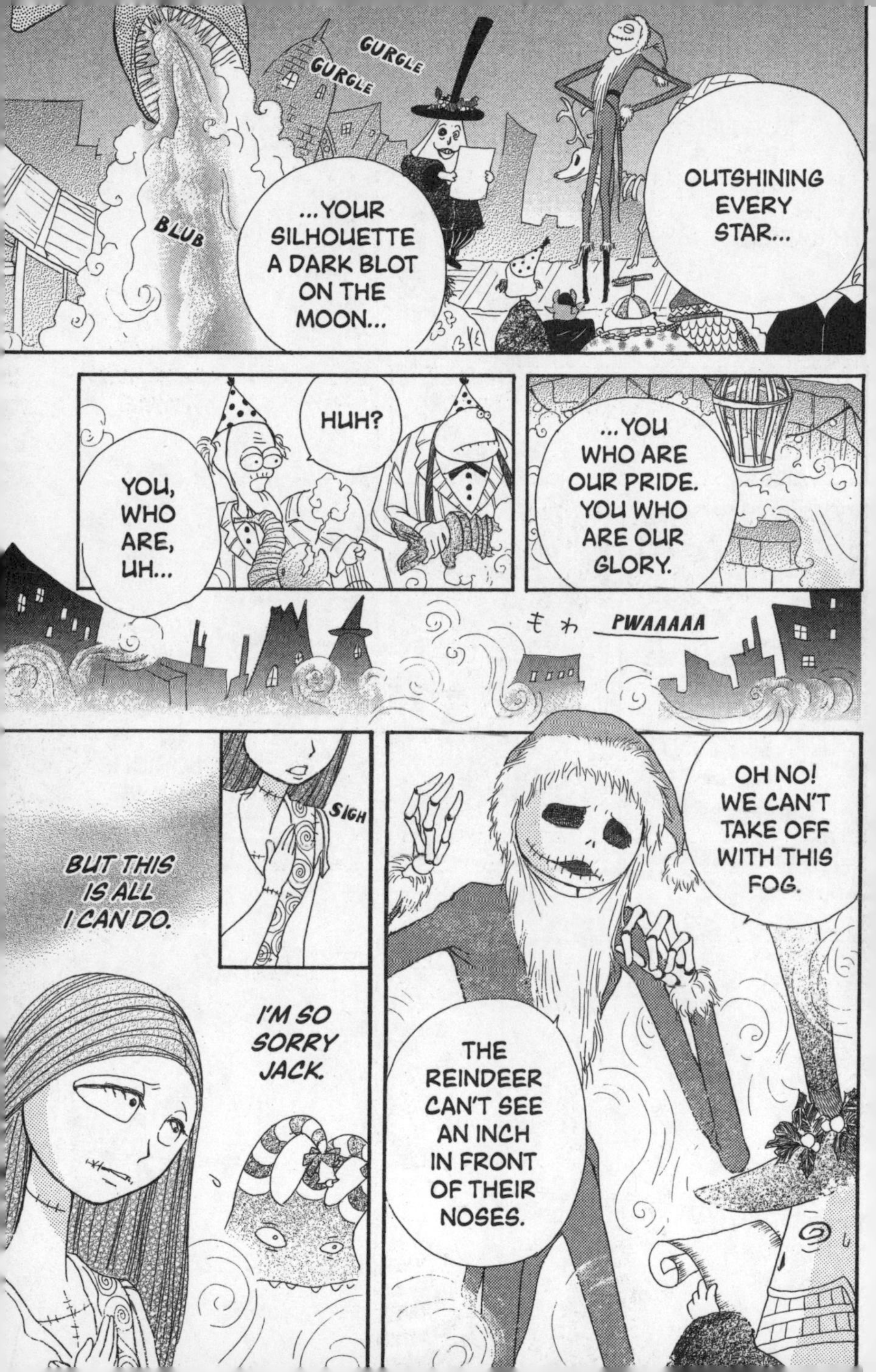
GURGLE
GURGLE
BLUB
...YOUR SILHOUETTE A DARK BLOT ON THE MOON...
OUTSHINING EVERY STAR...
YOU, WHO ARE, UH...
HUH?
...YOU WHO ARE OUR PRIDE. YOU WHO ARE OUR GLORY.
もわ
PWAAAAA
BUT THIS IS ALL I CAN DO.
SIGH
I'M SO SORRY JACK.
OH NO! WE CAN'T TAKE OFF WITH THIS FOG.
THE REINDEER CAN'T SEE AN INCH IN FRONT OF THEIR NOSES.

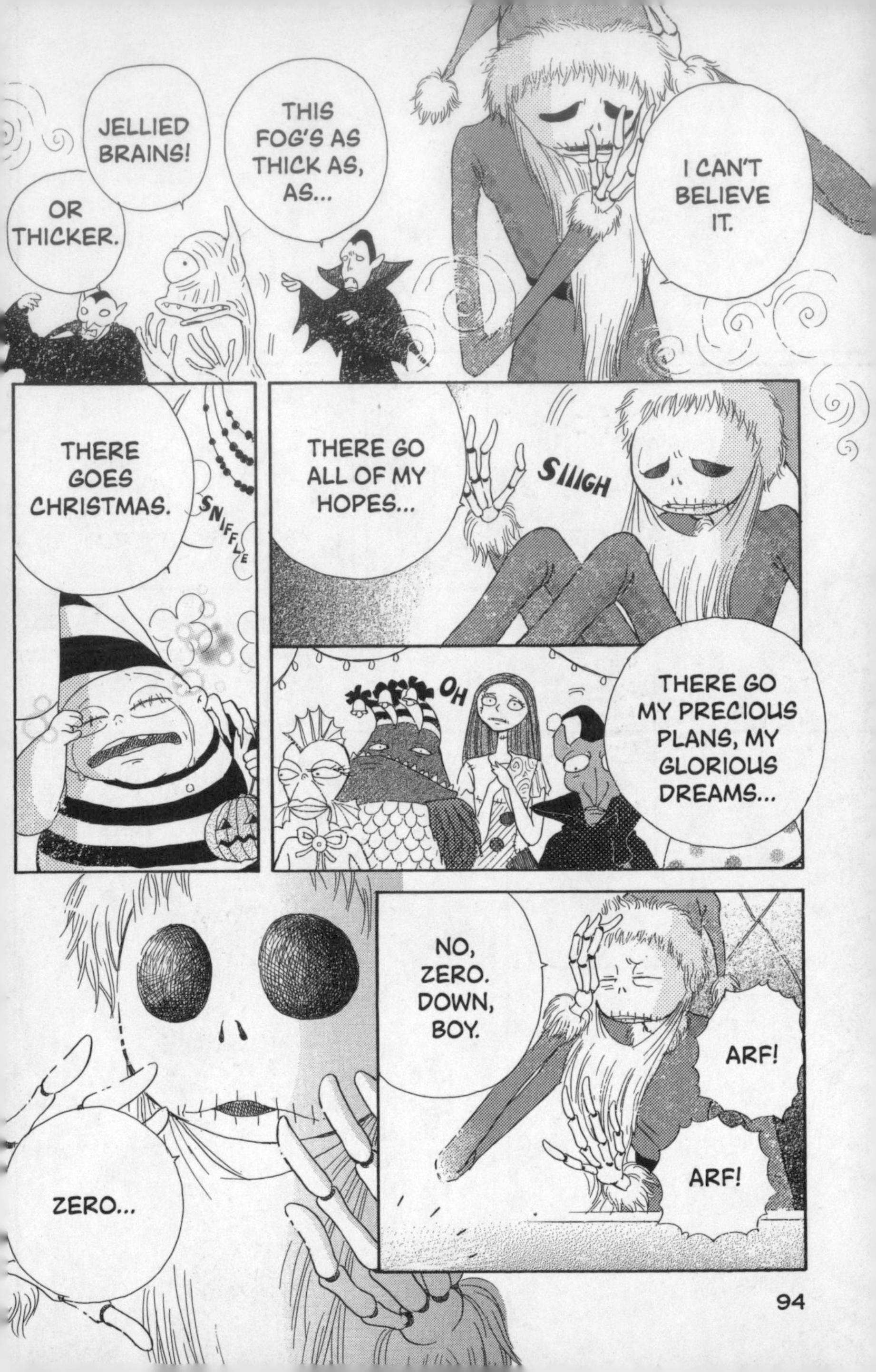

I CAN'T BELIEVE IT.
THIS FOG'S AS THICK AS, AS...
JELLIED BRAINS!
OR THICKER.
THERE GO ALL OF MY HOPES...
SIIIGH
THERE GO MY PRECIOUS PLANS, MY GLORIOUS DREAMS...
OH
THERE GOES CHRISTMAS.
SNIFFLE
ARF!
NO, ZERO. DOWN, BOY.
ARF!
ZERO...

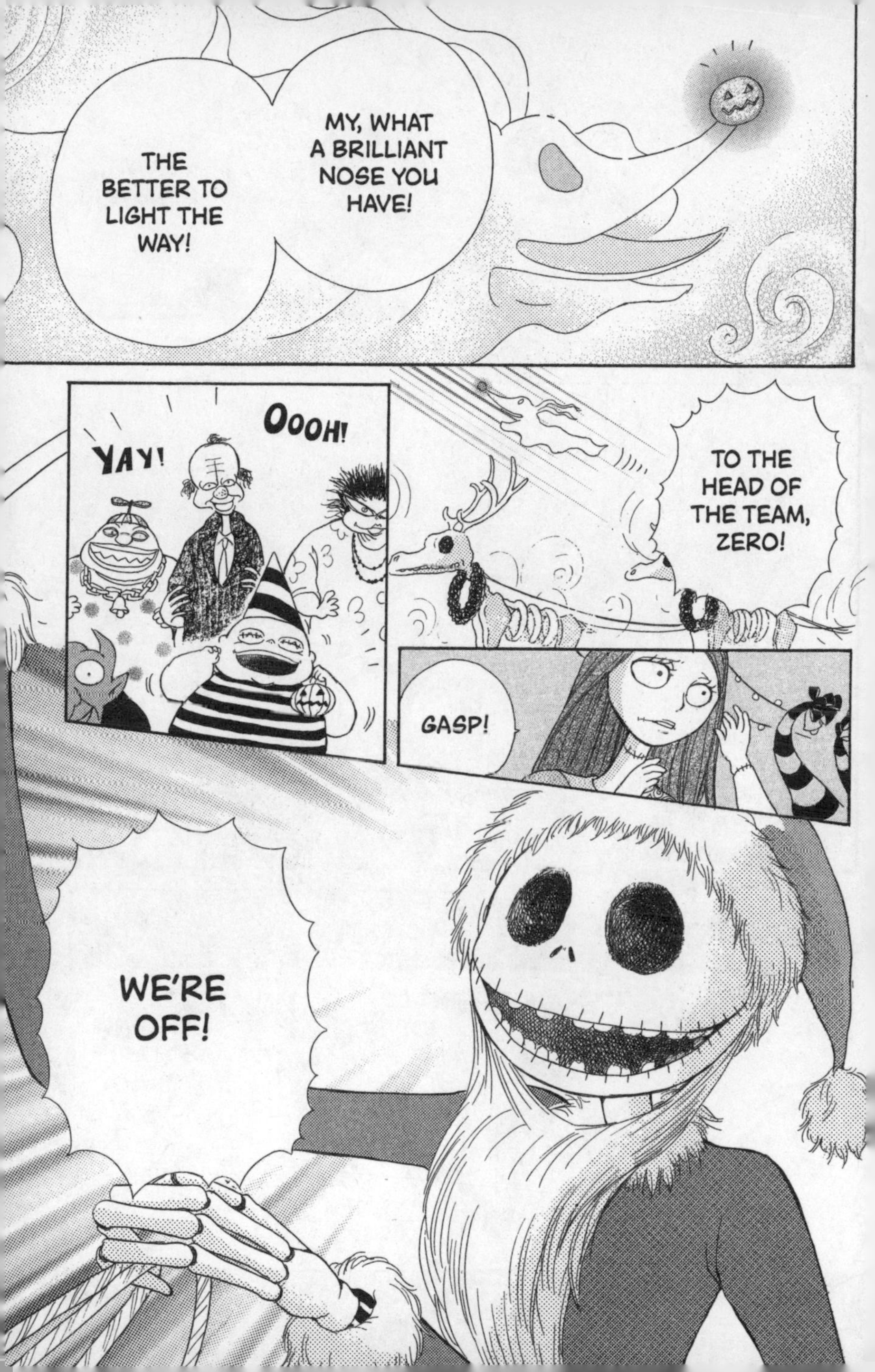
MY, WHAT A BRILLIANT NOSE YOU HAVE!
THE BETTER TO LIGHT THE WAY!
TO THE HEAD OF THE TEAM, ZERO!
GASP!
OOOH!
YAY!
WE'RE OFF!

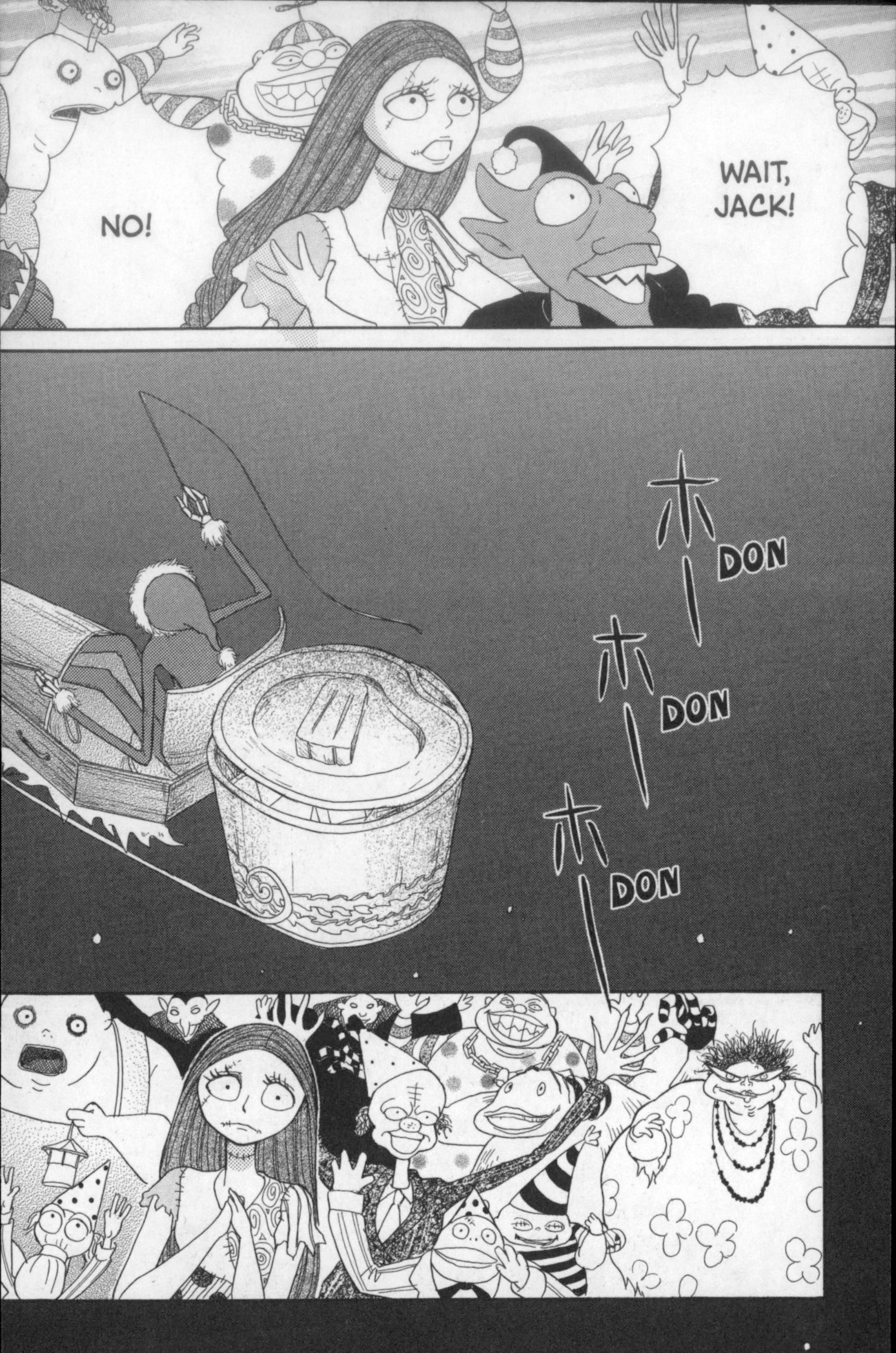
WAIT, JACK!
NO!
ホー
DON
ホー
DON
ホー
DON

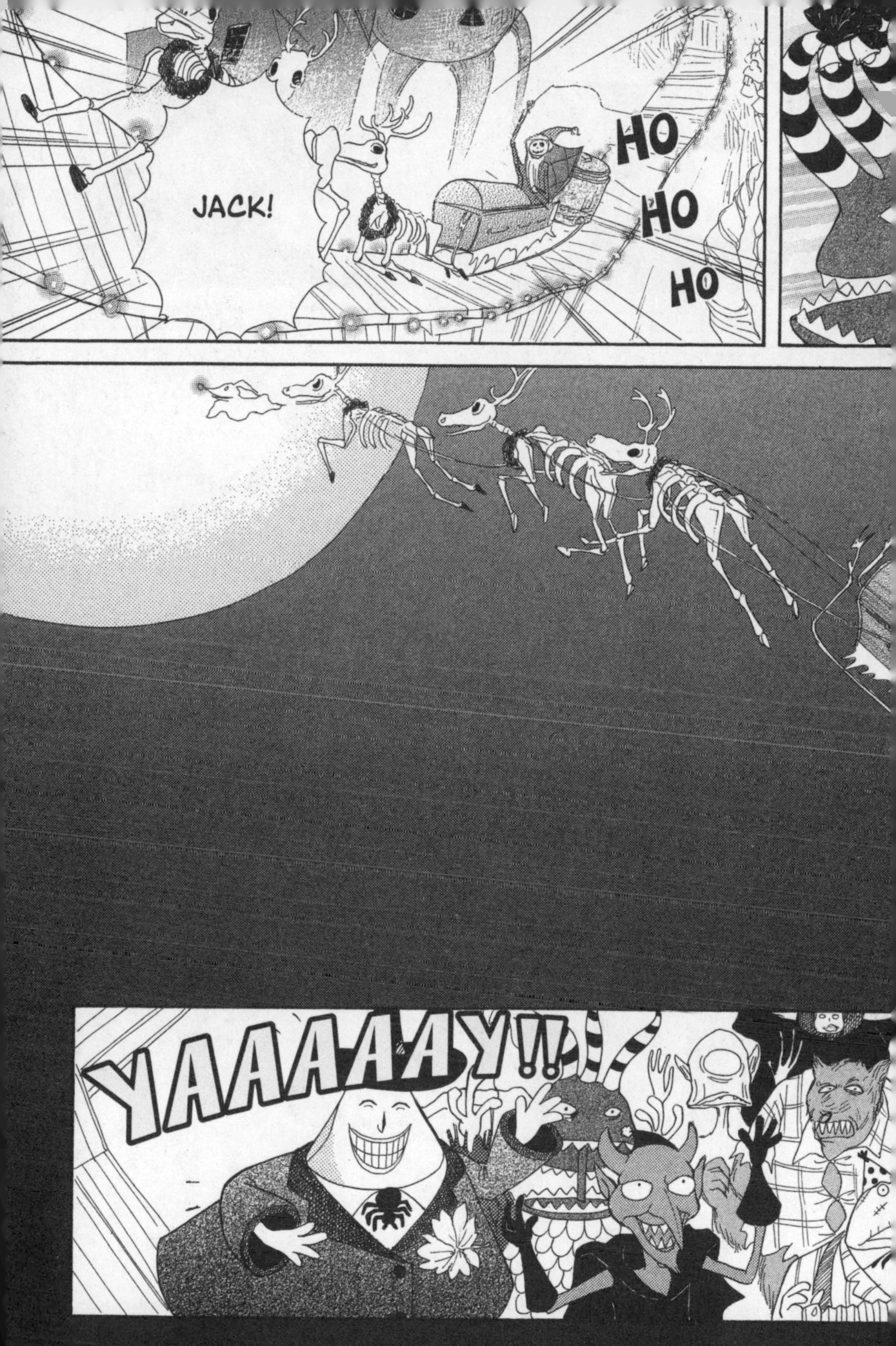
HO
HO
HO
JACK!
YAAAAAY!!

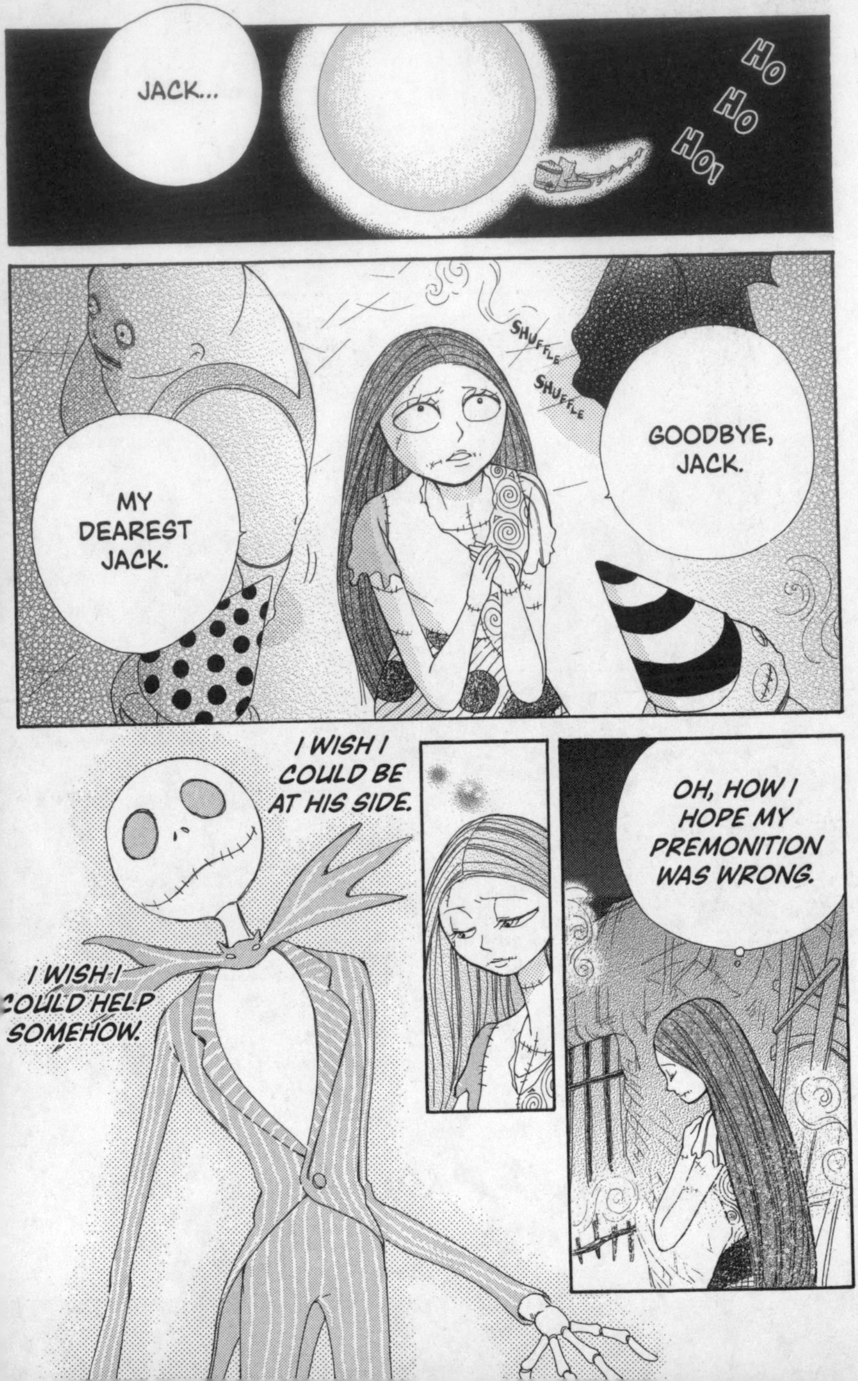
HO HO HO!
JACK...
GOODBYE, JACK.
SHUFFLE SHUFFLE
MY DEAREST JACK.
OH, HOW I HOPE MY PREMONITION WAS WRONG.
I WISH I COULD BE AT HIS SIDE.
I WISH I COULD HELP SOMEHOW.

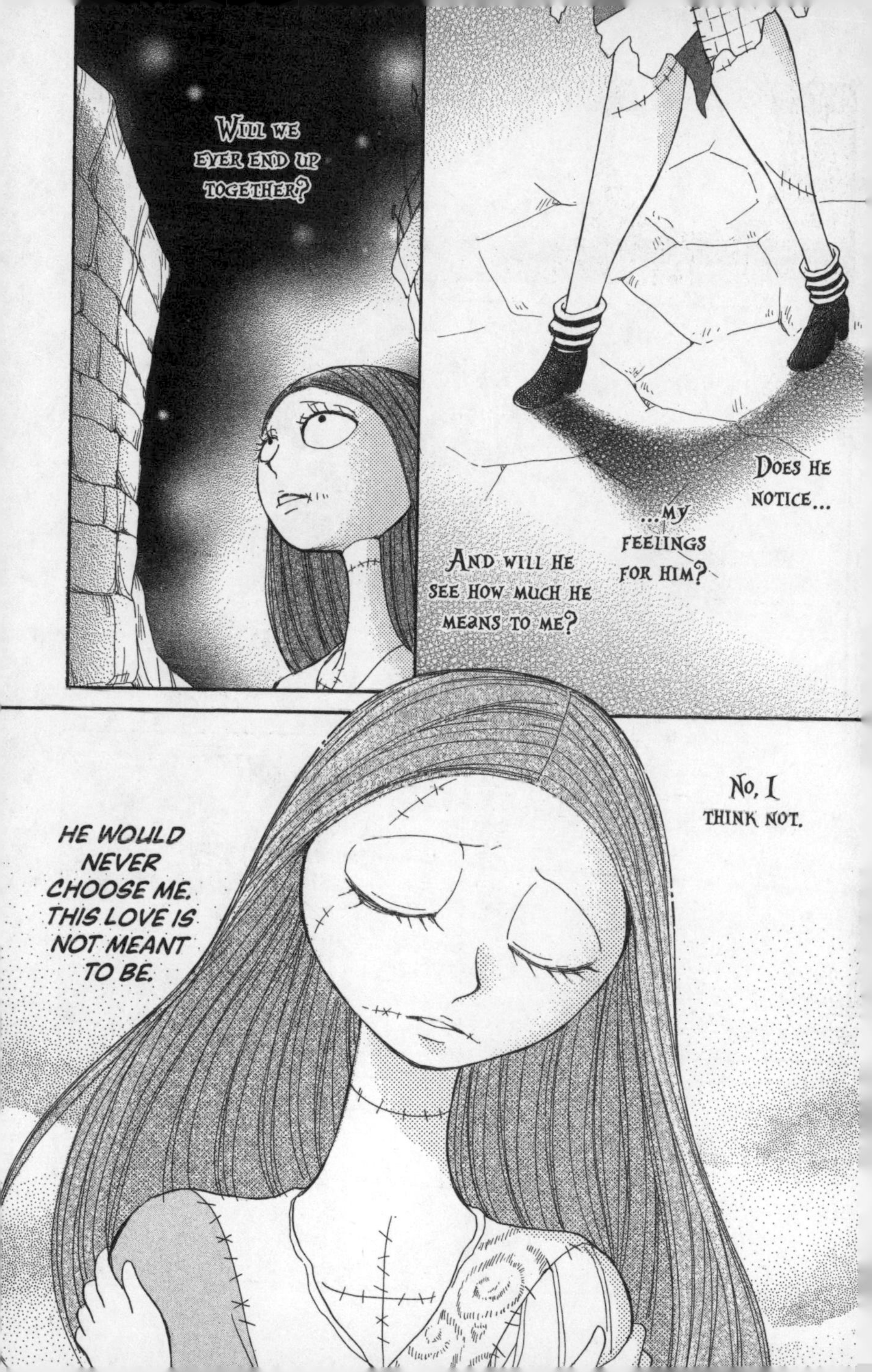
Does he notice...
...my feelings for him?
And will he see how much he means to me?
Will we ever end up together?
No, I think not.
He would never choose me. This love is not meant to be.

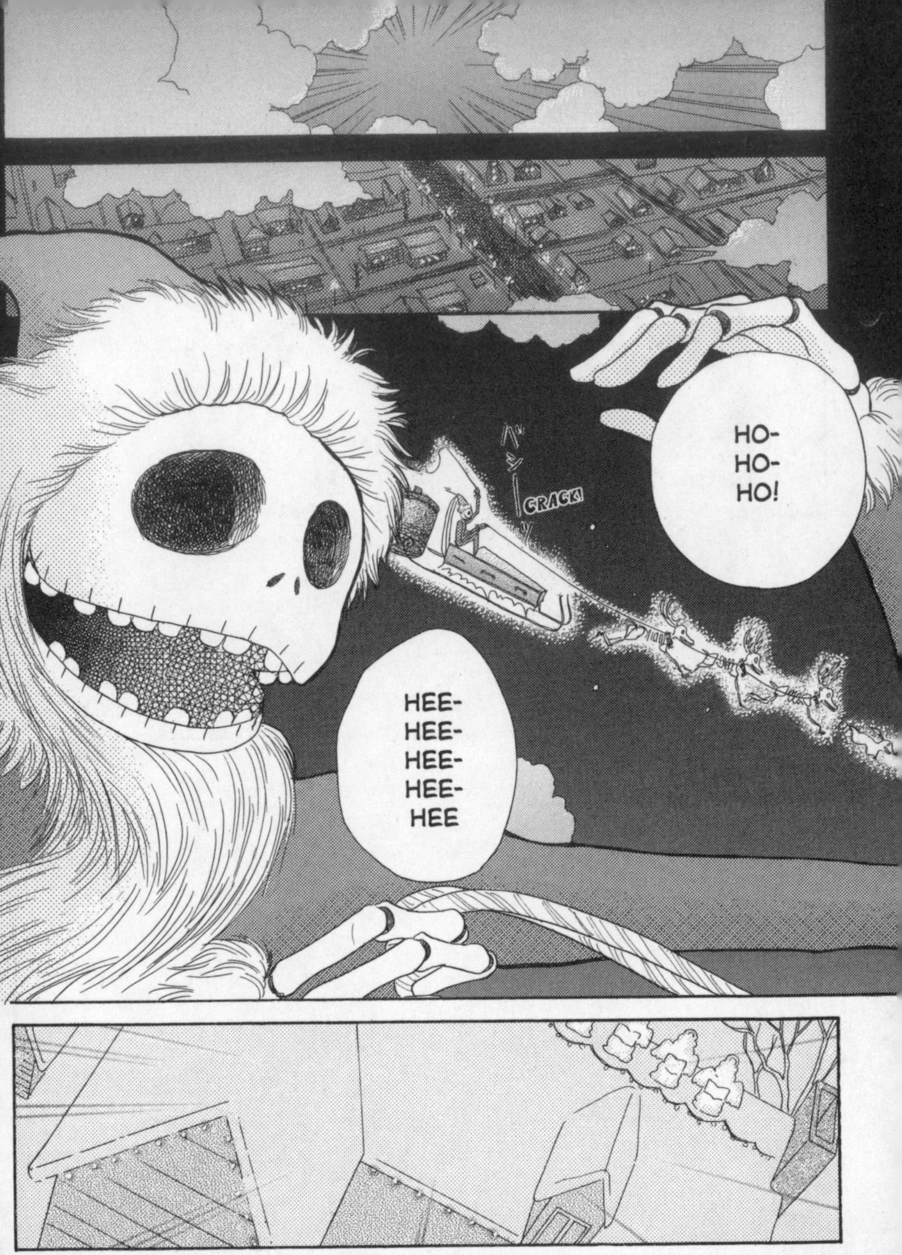
HO-HO-HO!
CRACK!
HEE-HEE-HEE-HEE-HEE

READ THIS WAY

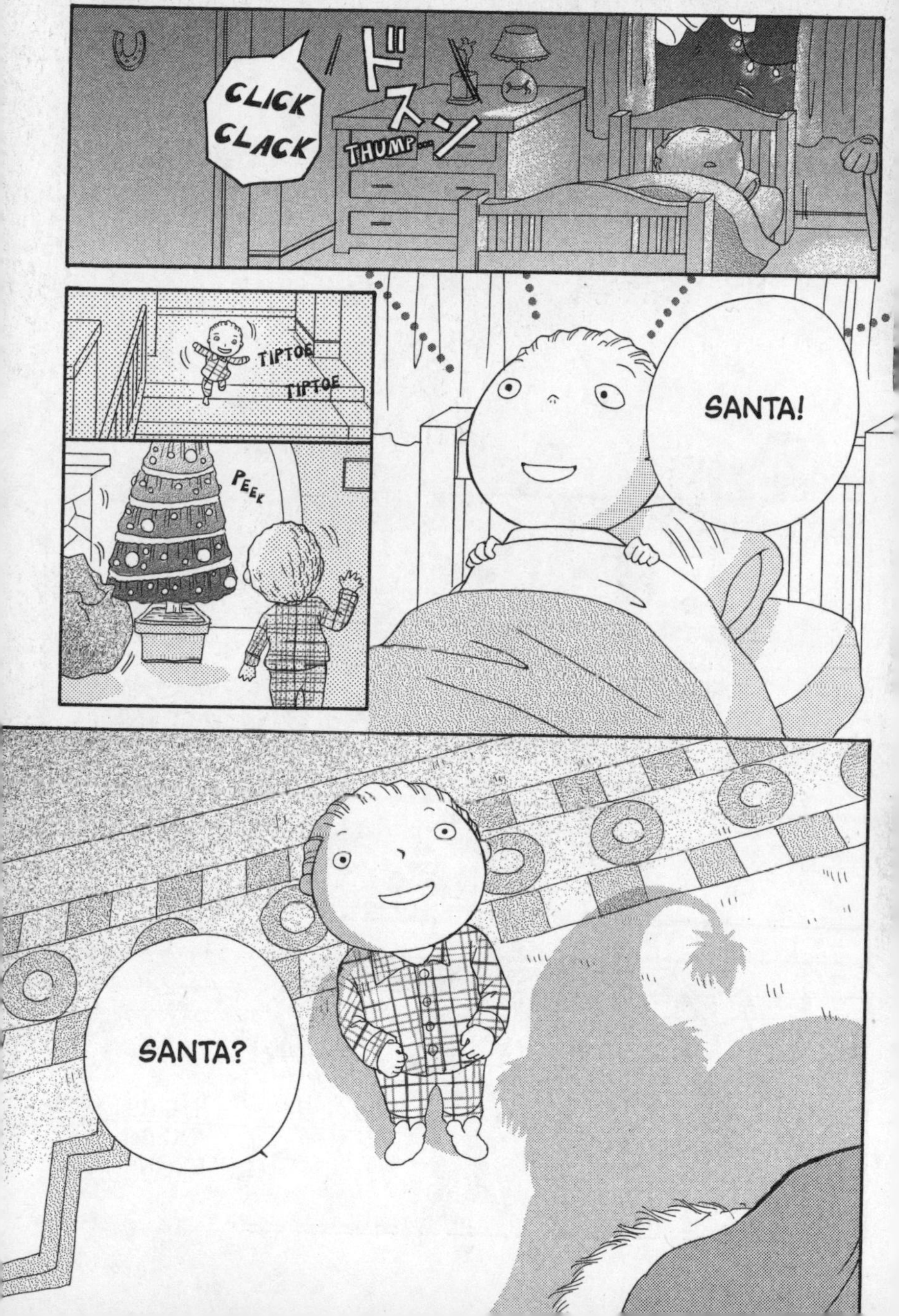

ドスン
THUMP...
CLICK CLACK
SANTA!
TIPTOE
TIPTOE
PEEK
SANTA?

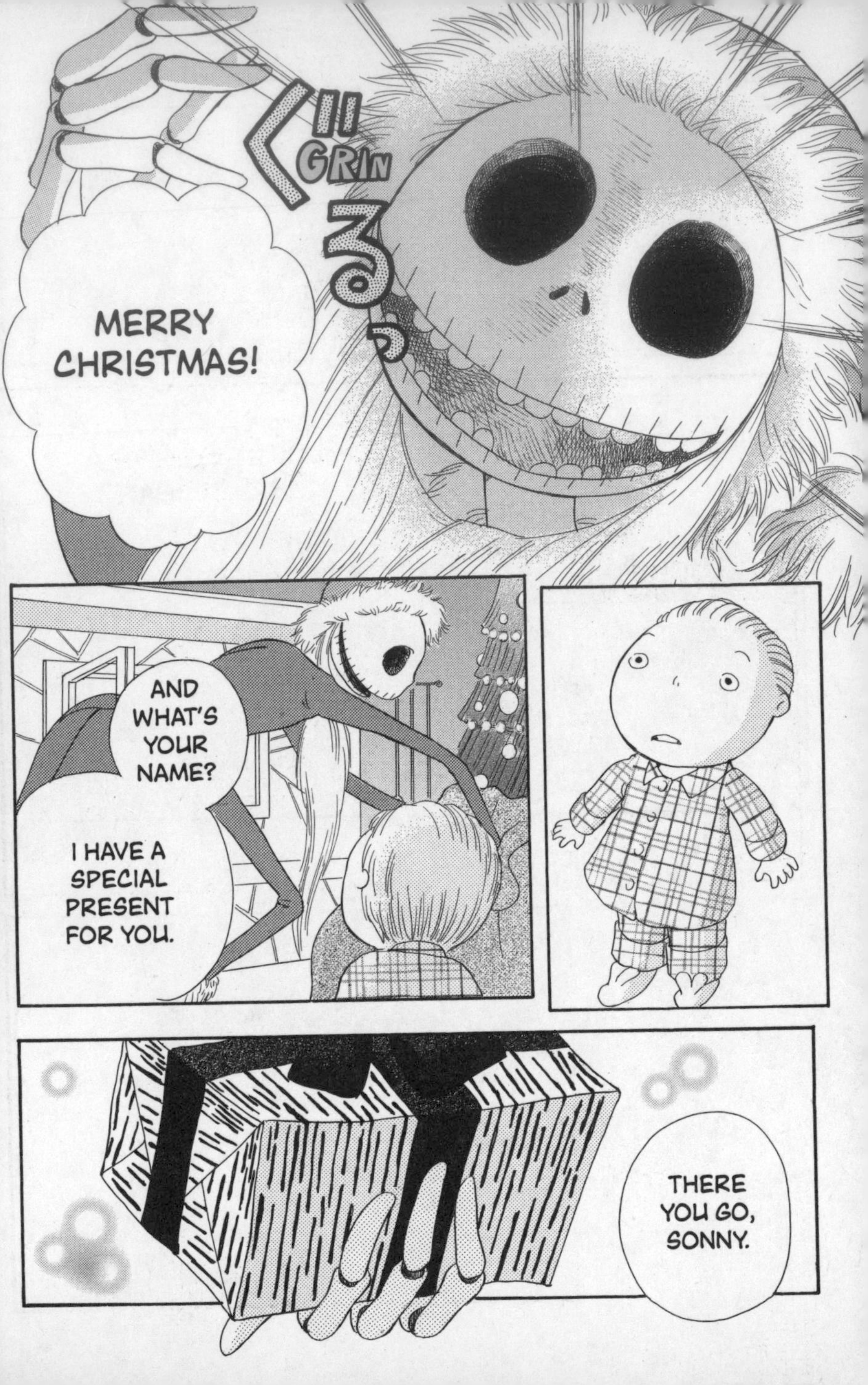
くるっ
GRIN
MERRY CHRISTMAS!
AND WHAT'S YOUR NAME?
I HAVE A SPECIAL PRESENT FOR YOU.
THERE YOU GO, SONNY.

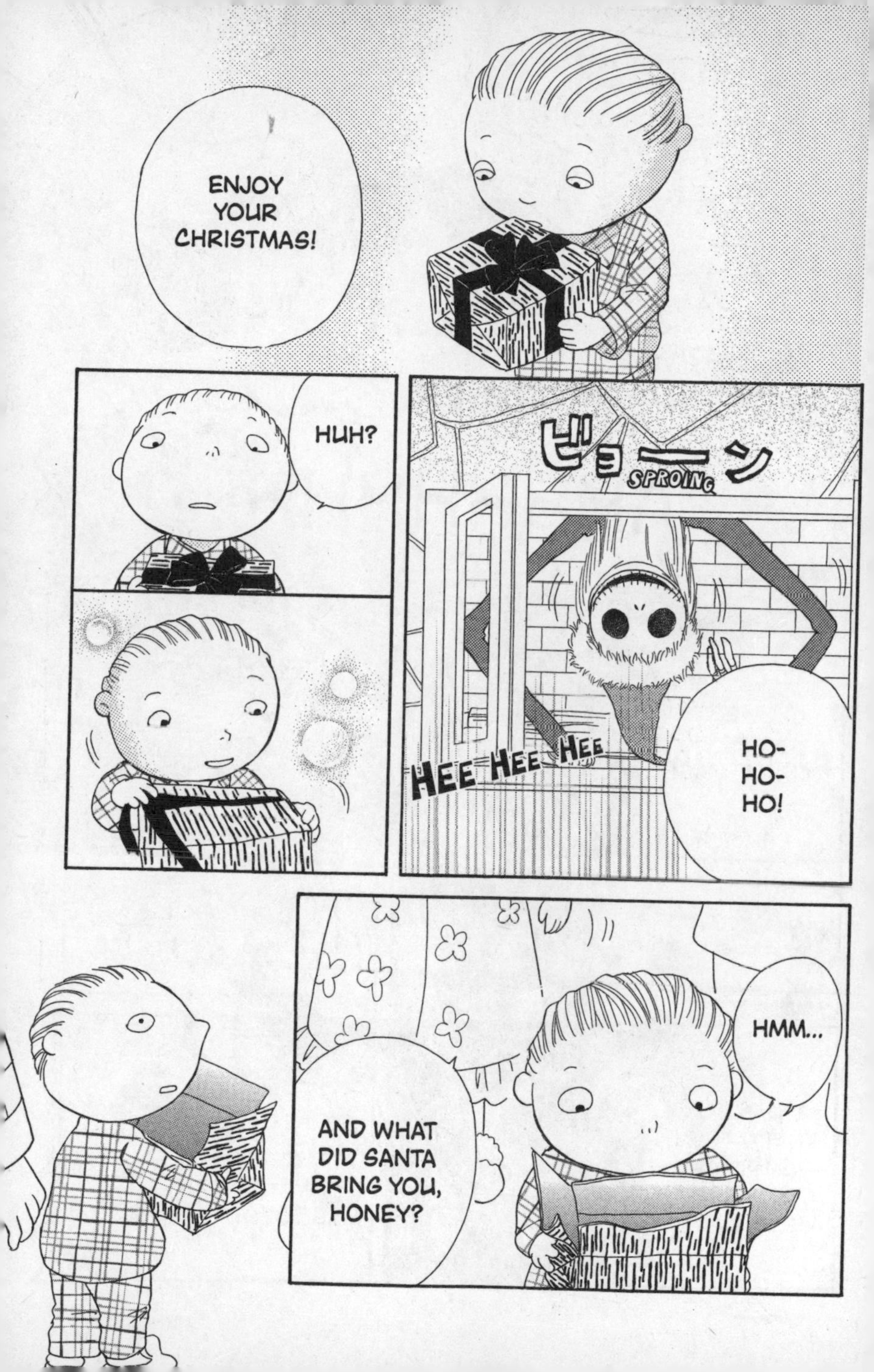
ENJOY YOUR CHRISTMAS!
ビョーン
SPROING
HO-HO-HO!
HEE HEE HEE
HUH?
HMM...
AND WHAT DID SANTA BRING YOU, HONEY?

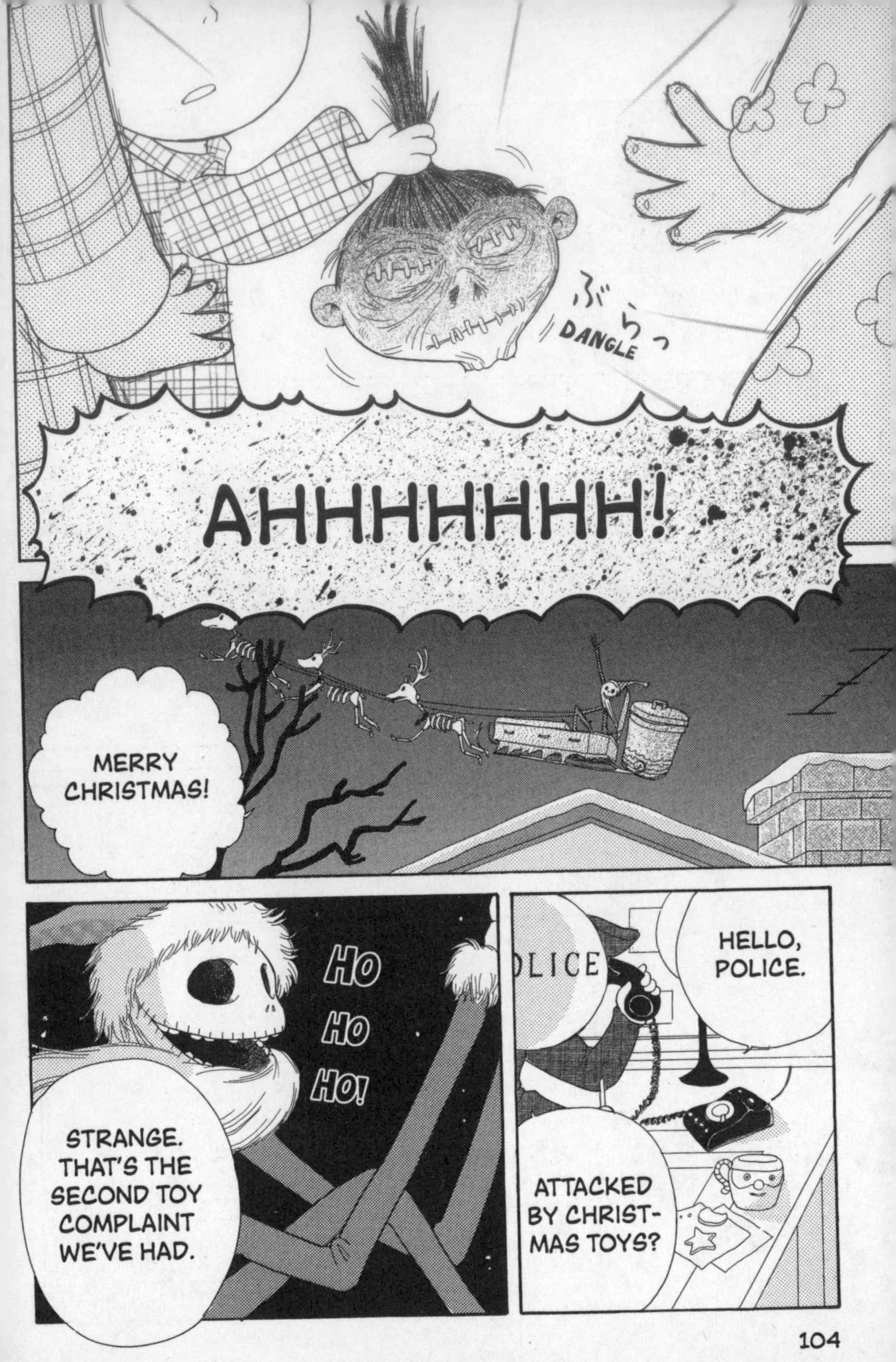
ぶらっ
DANGLE
AHHHHHHH!
MERRY CHRISTMAS!
HELLO, POLICE.
ATTACKED BY CHRIST-MAS TOYS?
HO HO HO!
STRANGE. THAT'S THE SECOND TOY COMPLAINT WE'VE HAD.

READ THIS WAY

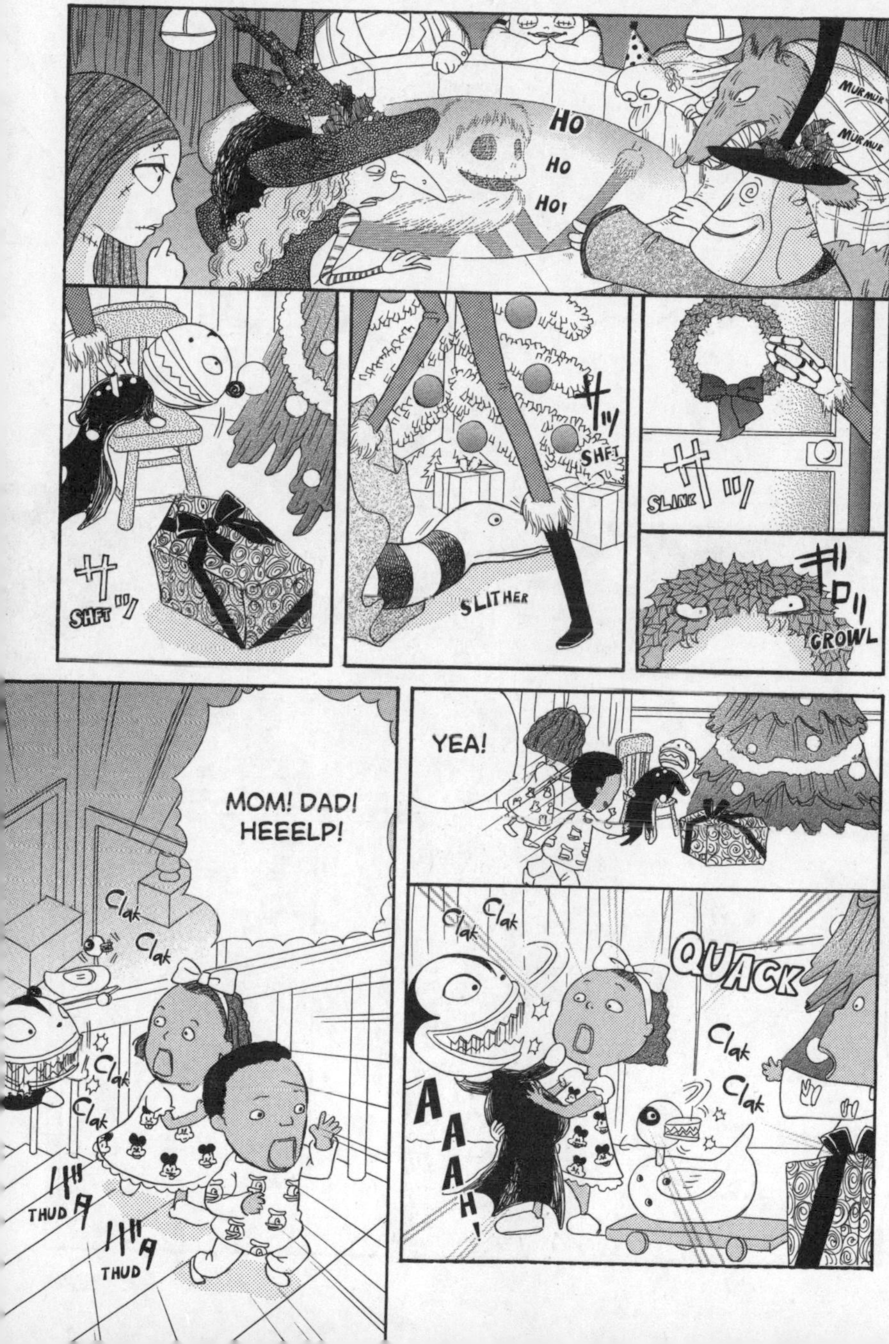

MURMUR
MURMUR
HO
HO
HO!
SLINK
GROWL
SHFT
SLITHER
SHFT
YEA!
Clak
Clak
QUACK
Clak
Clak
AAAH!
MOM! DAD! HEEELP!
Clak
Clak
Clak
Clak
THUD
THUD

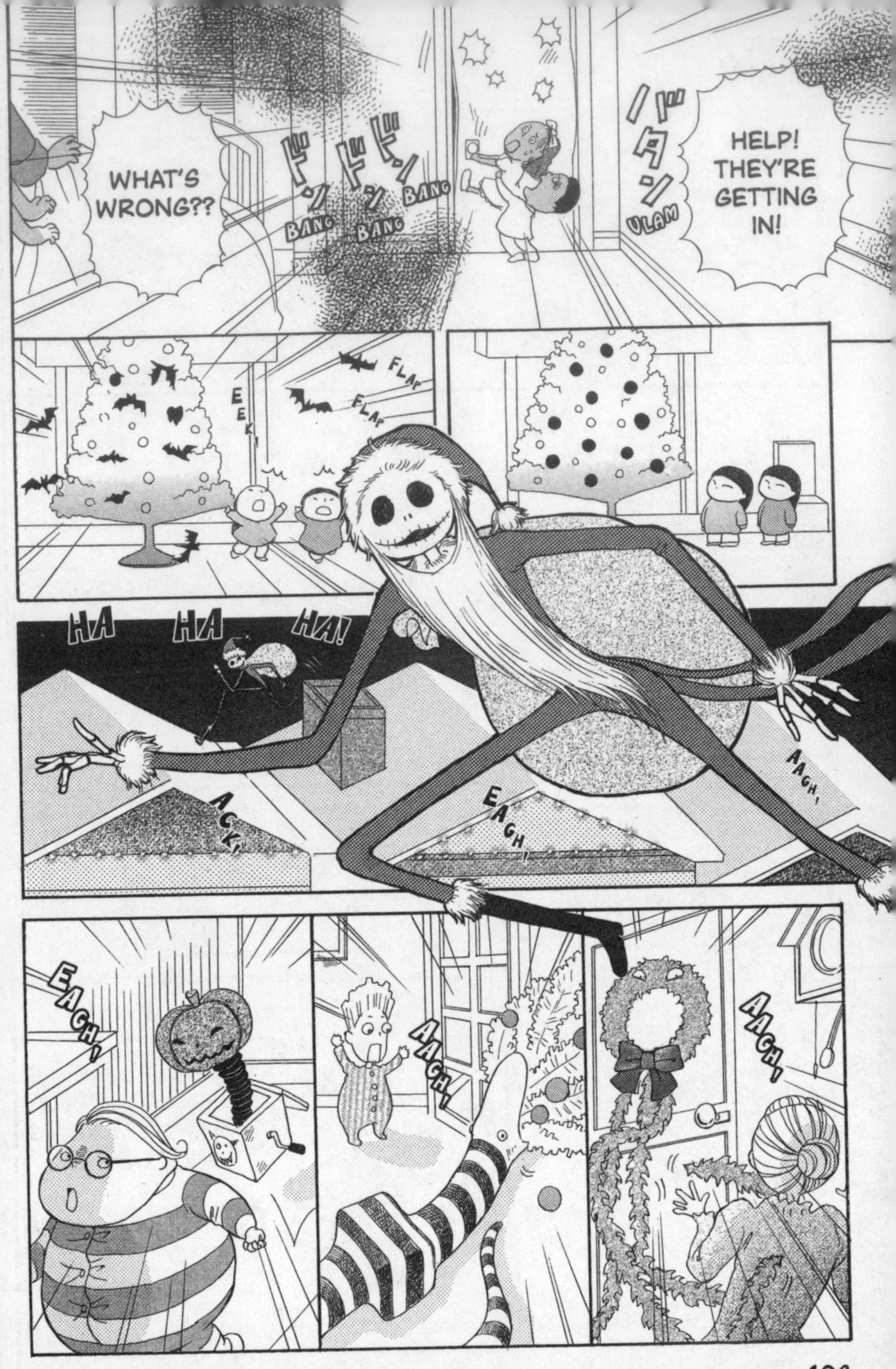
HELP! THEY'RE GETTING IN!
バタン
BANG BANG BANG
WHAT'S WRONG??
FLAP FLAP
EEK!
HA HA HA!
AAGH!
EAGH!
ACK!
AAGH!
AAGH!
EAGH!

READ THIS WAY

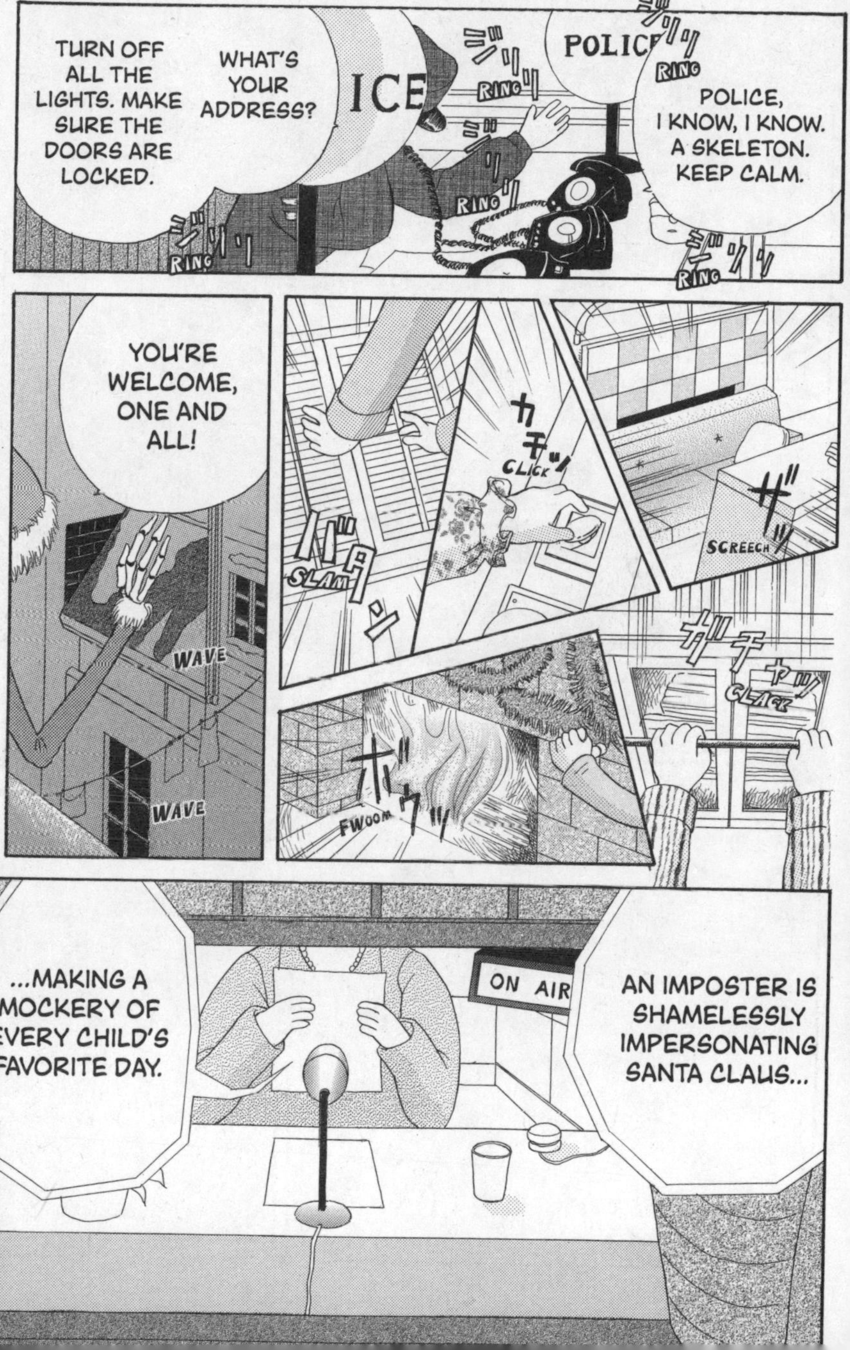

POLICE
RING
POLICE, I KNOW, I KNOW. A SKELETON. KEEP CALM.
RING
ICE
WHAT'S YOUR ADDRESS?
RING
RING
TURN OFF ALL THE LIGHTS. MAKE SURE THE DOORS ARE LOCKED.
RING
SCREECH
CLICK
SLAM
CLACK
FWOOM
YOU'RE WELCOME, ONE AND ALL!
WAVE
WAVE
AN IMPOSTER IS SHAMELESSLY IMPERSONATING SANTA CLAUS...
ON AIR
...MAKING A MOCKERY OF EVERY CHILD'S FAVORITE DAY.

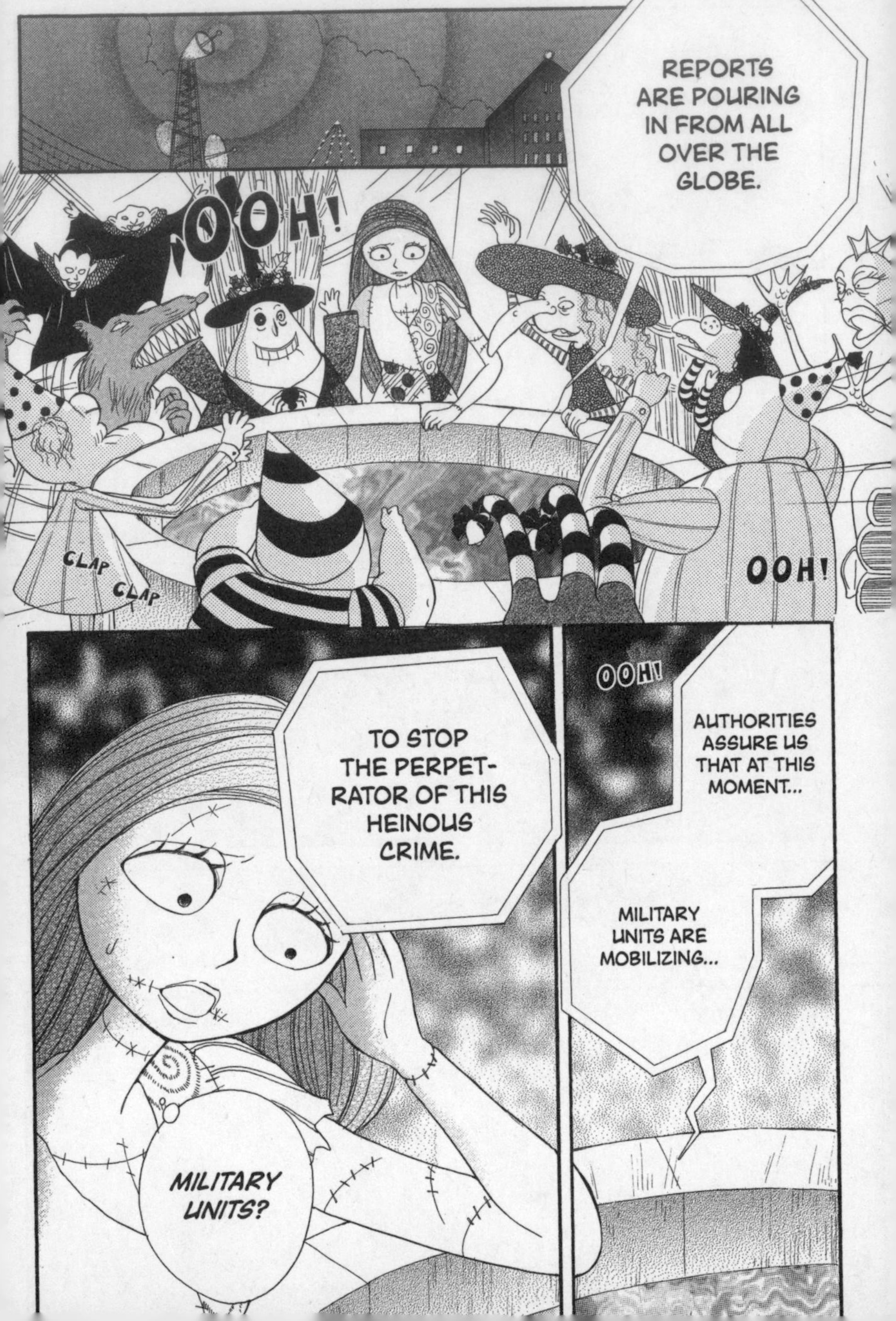

REPORTS ARE POURING IN FROM ALL OVER THE GLOBE.
OOH!
OOH!
CLAP
CLAP
OOH!
AUTHORITIES ASSURE US THAT AT THIS MOMENT...
MILITARY UNITS ARE MOBILIZING...
TO STOP THE PERPET-RATOR OF THIS HEINOUS CRIME.
MILITARY UNITS?

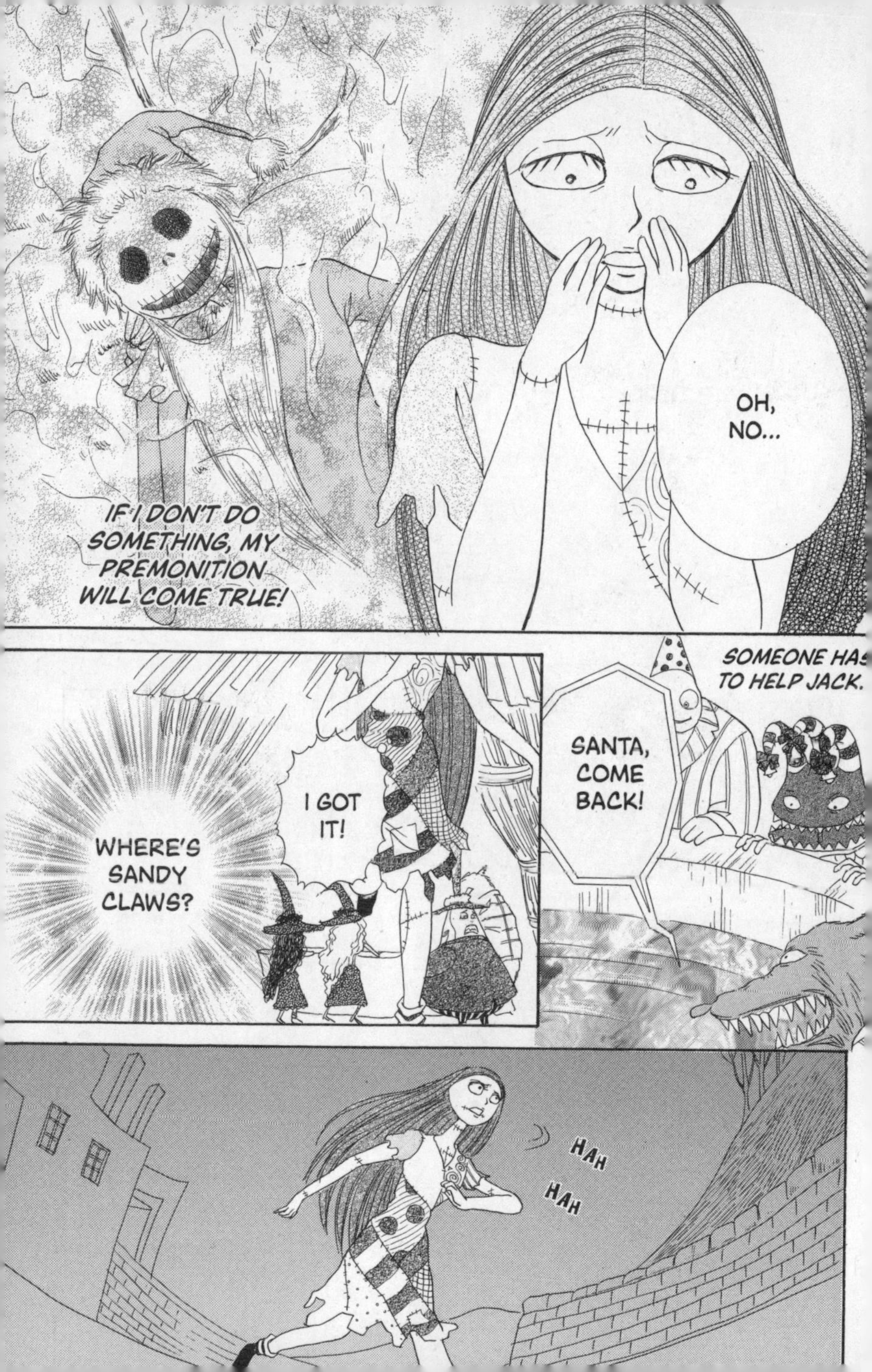
OH, NO...
IF I DON'T DO SOMETHING, MY PREMONITION WILL COME TRUE!
SOMEONE HAS TO HELP JACK.
SANTA, COME BACK!
I GOT IT!
WHERE'S SANDY CLAWS?
HAH
HAH

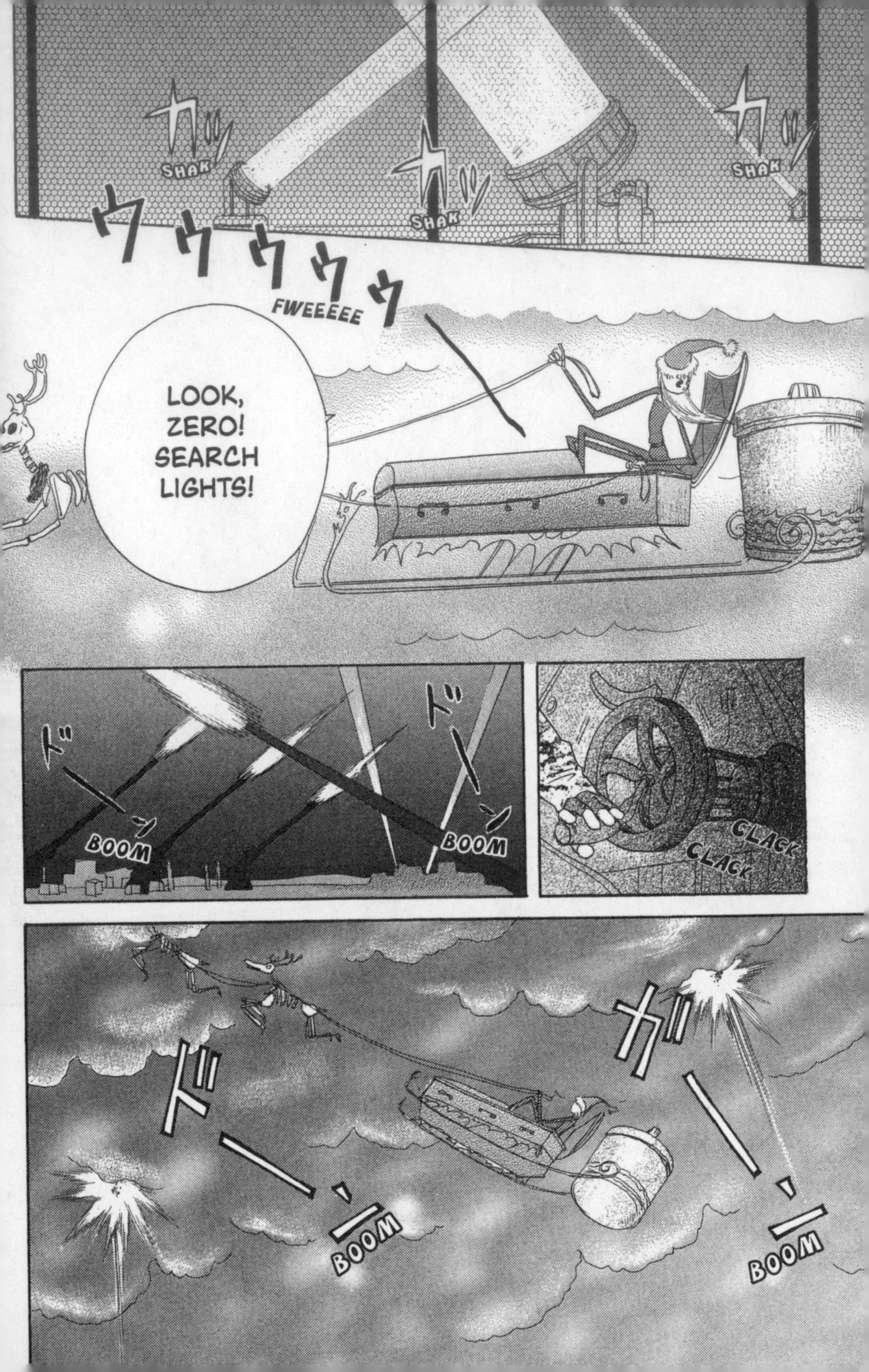
SHAK
SHAK
SHAK
FWEEEEE
LOOK, ZERO! SEARCH LIGHTS!
CLACK
CLACK
BOOM
BOOM
BOOM
BOOM

READ THIS WAY

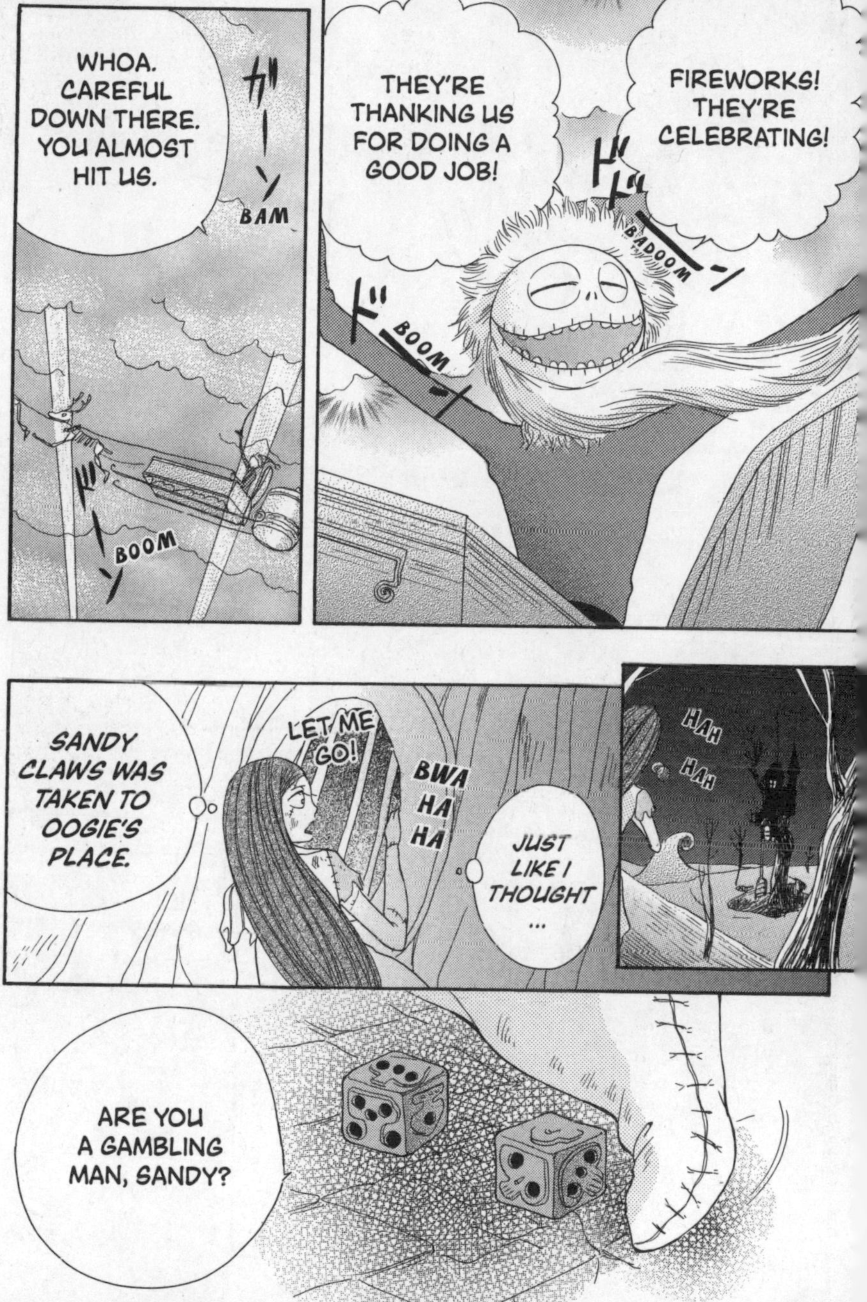
FIREWORKS! THEY'RE CELEBRATING!
THEY'RE THANKING US FOR DOING A GOOD JOB!
BADOOM
BOOM
WHOA. CAREFUL DOWN THERE. YOU ALMOST HIT US.
BAM
BOOM
HAH HAH
LET ME GO!
BWA HA HA
JUST LIKE I THOUGHT ...
SANDY CLAWS WAS TAKEN TO OOGIE'S PLACE.
ARE YOU A GAMBLING MAN, SANDY?

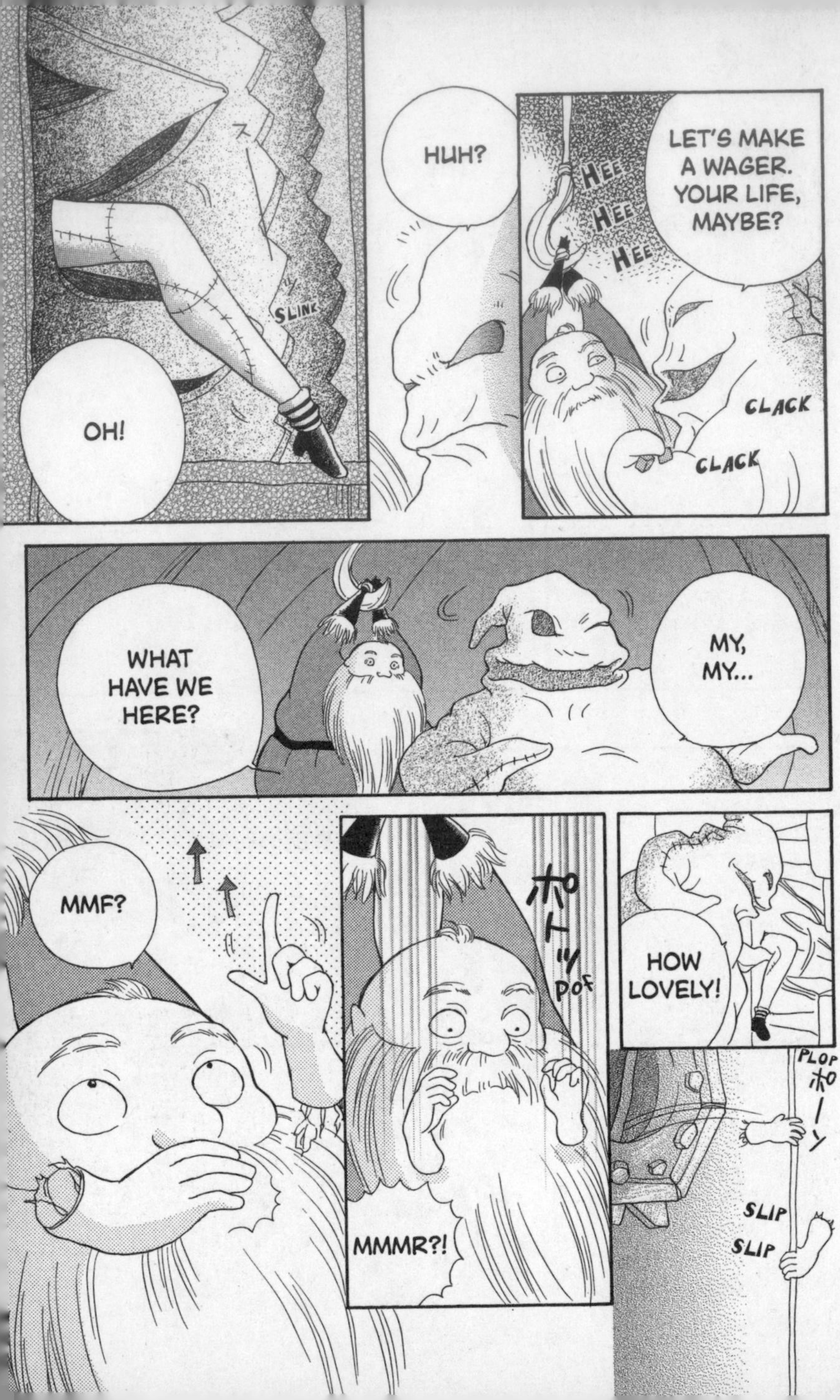
LET'S MAKE A WAGER. YOUR LIFE, MAYBE?
HEE HEE HEE
CLACK
CLACK
HUH?
SLINK
OH!
MY, MY...
WHAT HAVE WE HERE?
HOW LOVELY!
PLOP
ポーン
SLIP
SLIP
ポトッ
POF
MMMR?!
MMF?

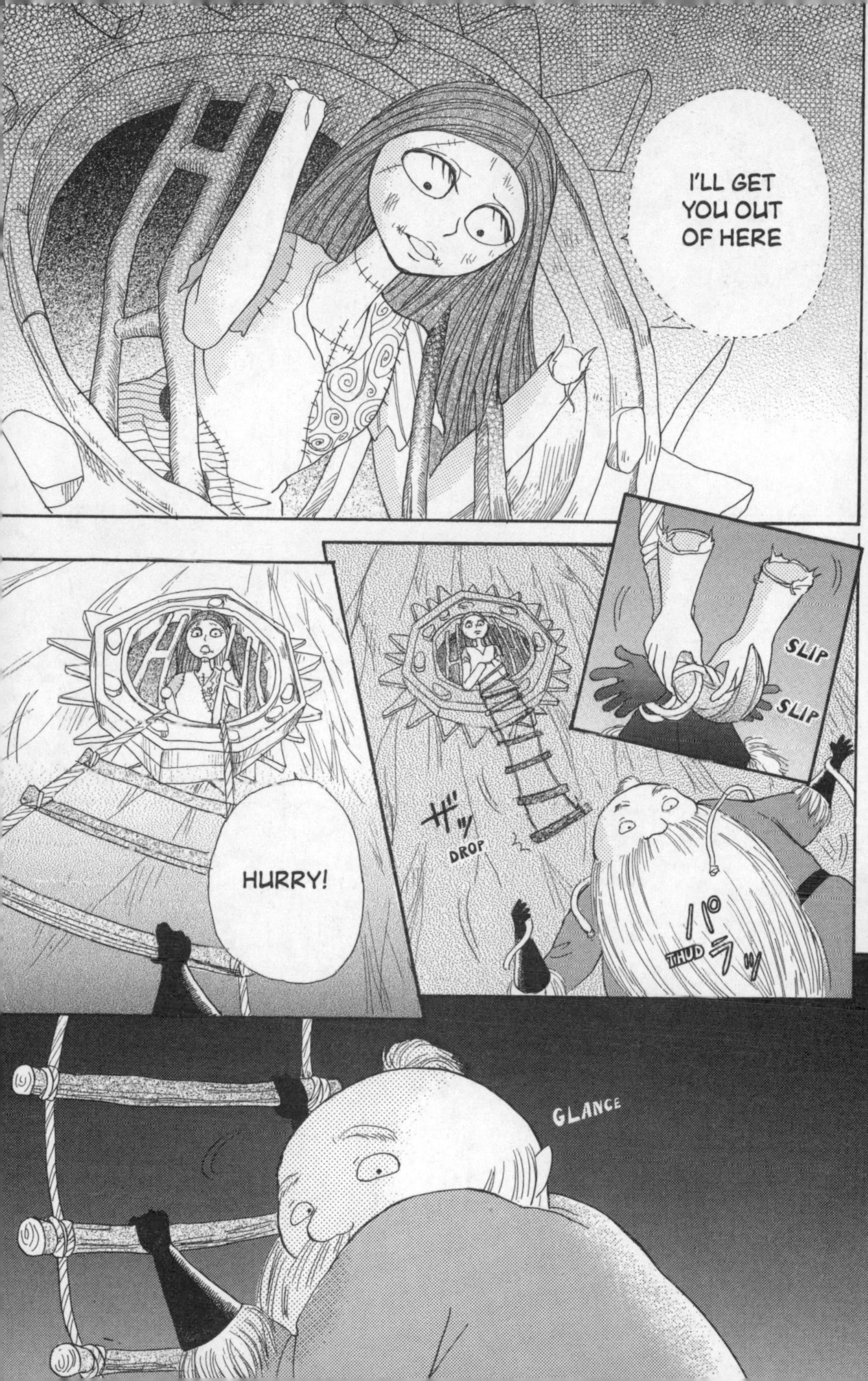
I'LL GET YOU OUT OF HERE
SLIP
SLIP
ザッ
DROP
パラッ
THUD
HURRY!
GLANCE

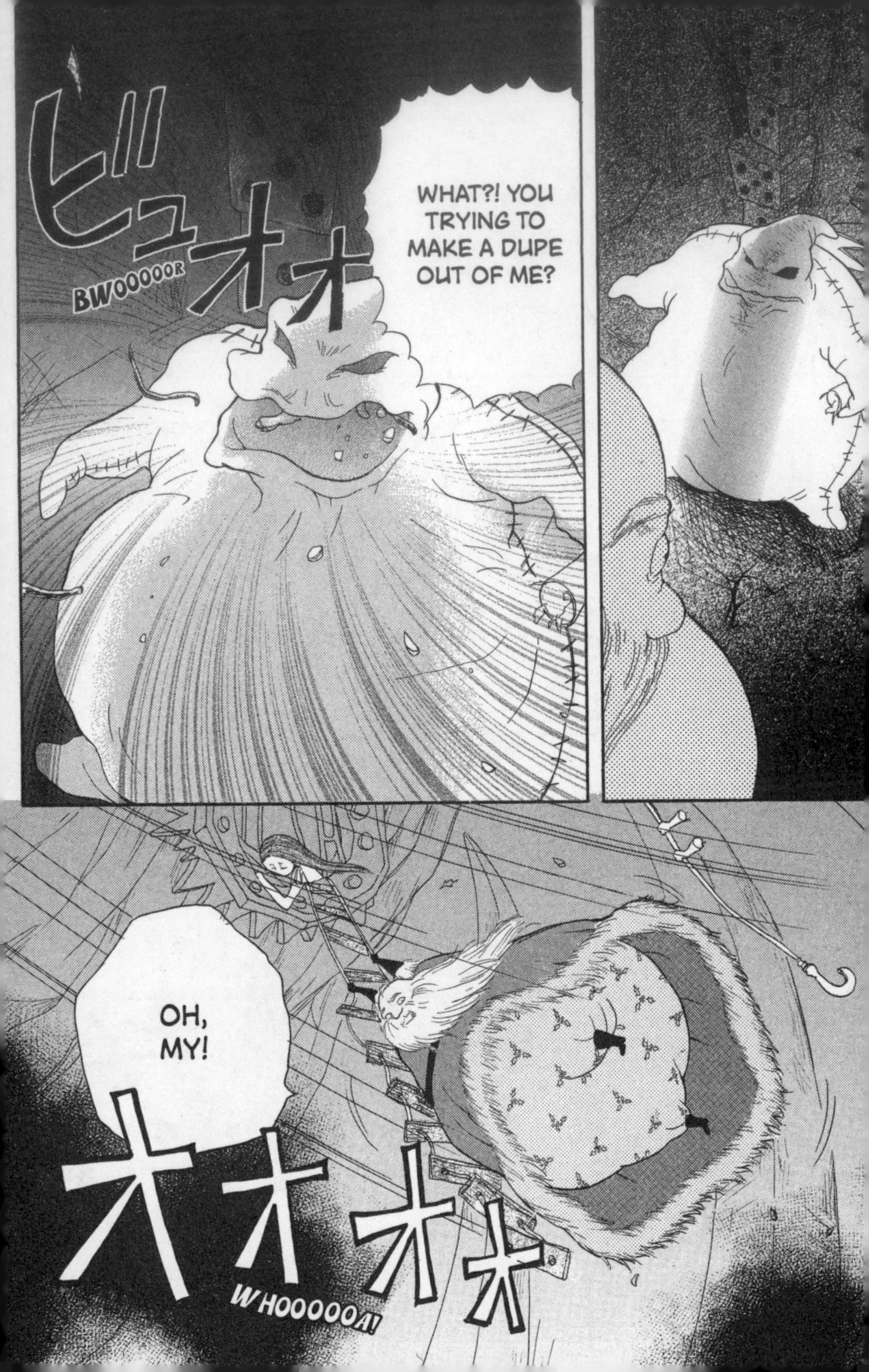
WHAT?! YOU TRYING TO MAKE A DUPE OUT OF ME?
ビュオオ
BWOOOOOR
OH, MY!
オオオオ
WHOOOOOA!

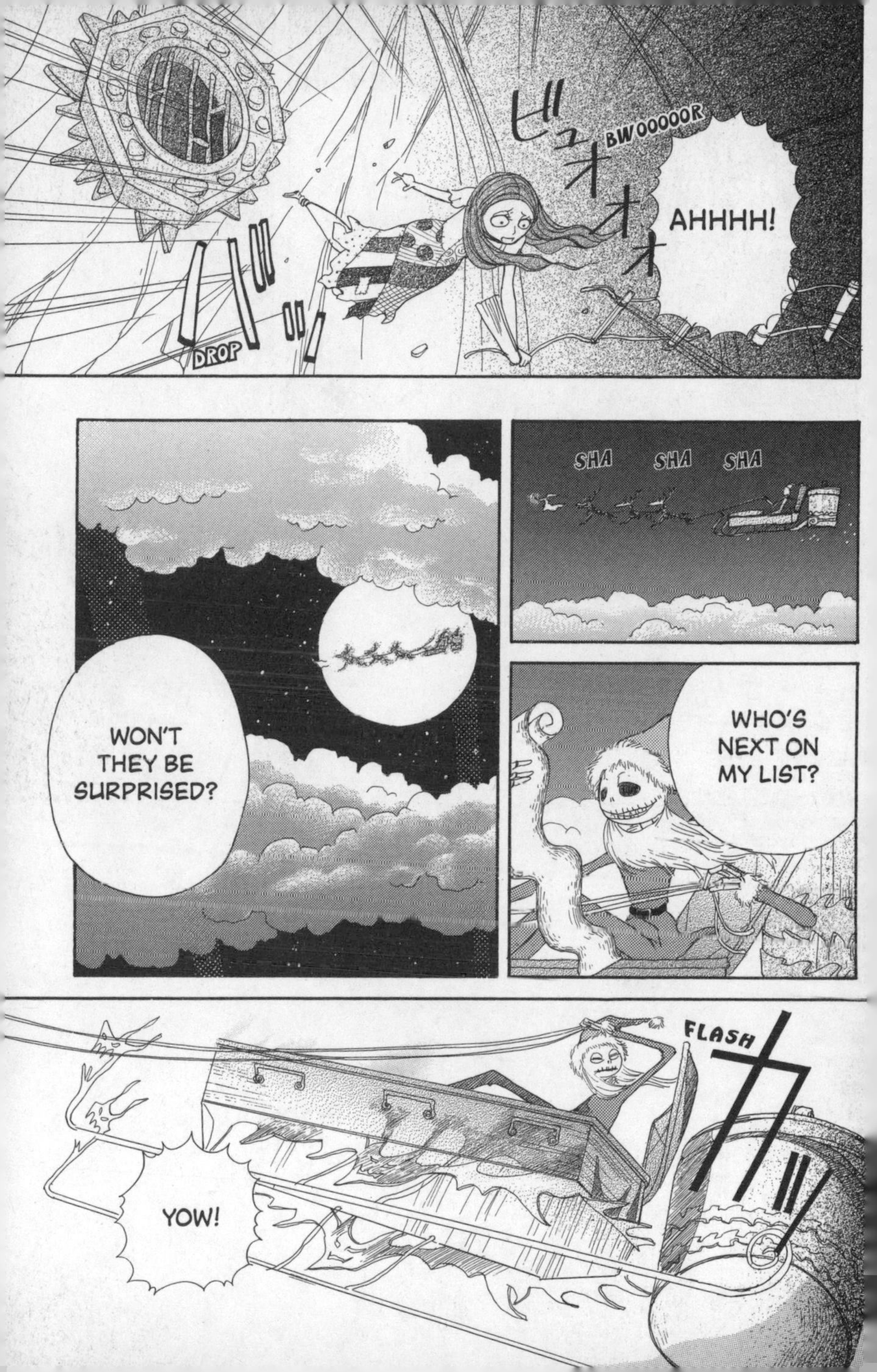
ビュオオオ
BWOOOOOR
AHHHH!
DROP
SHA SHA SHA
WHO'S NEXT ON MY LIST?
WON'T THEY BE SURPRISED?
FLASH
カッ
YOW!

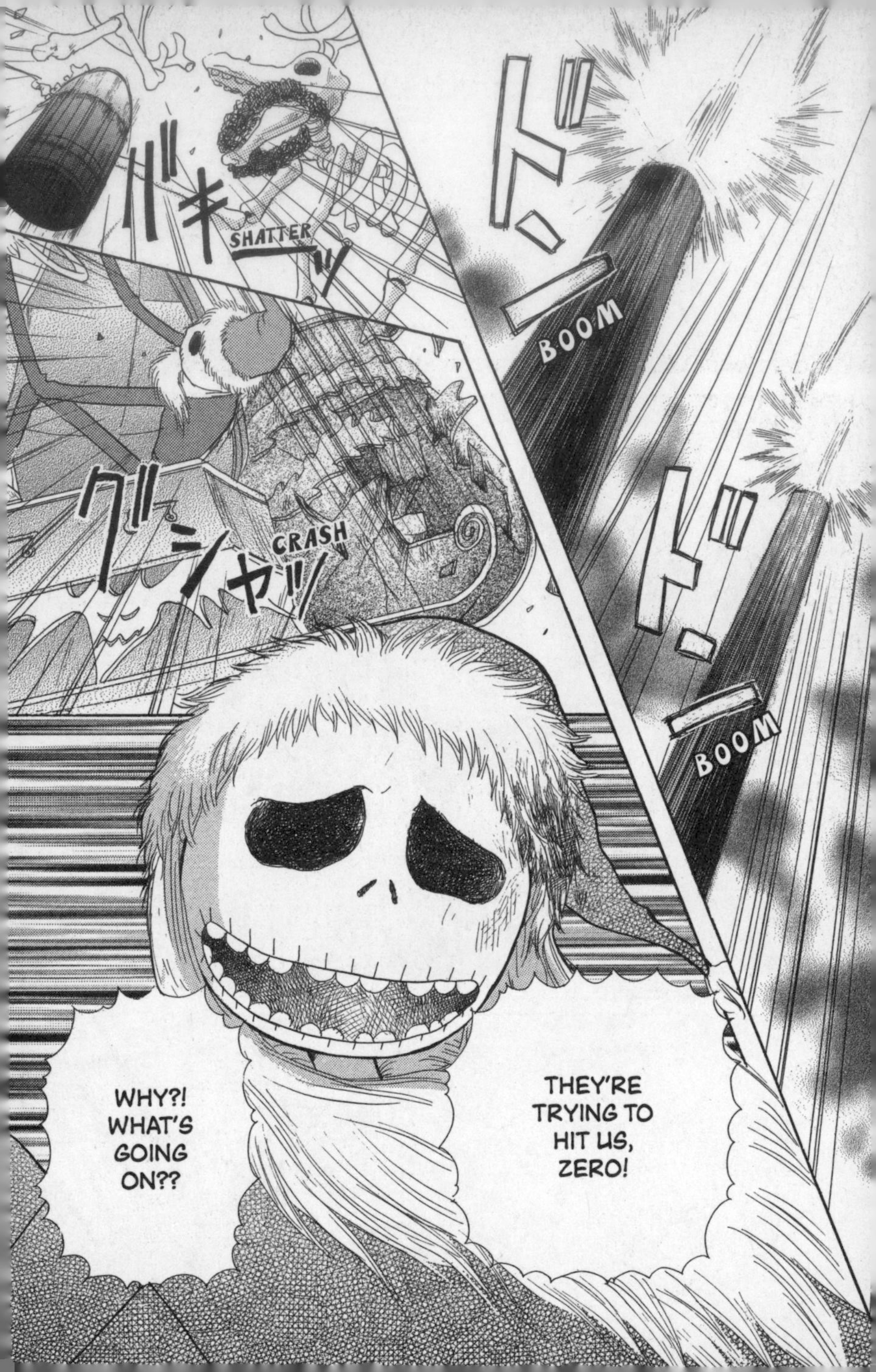
ドーン
BOOM
ドーン
BOOM
バキーッ
SHATTER
グシャッ
CRASH
THEY'RE TRYING TO HIT US, ZERO!
WHY?! WHAT'S GOING ON??

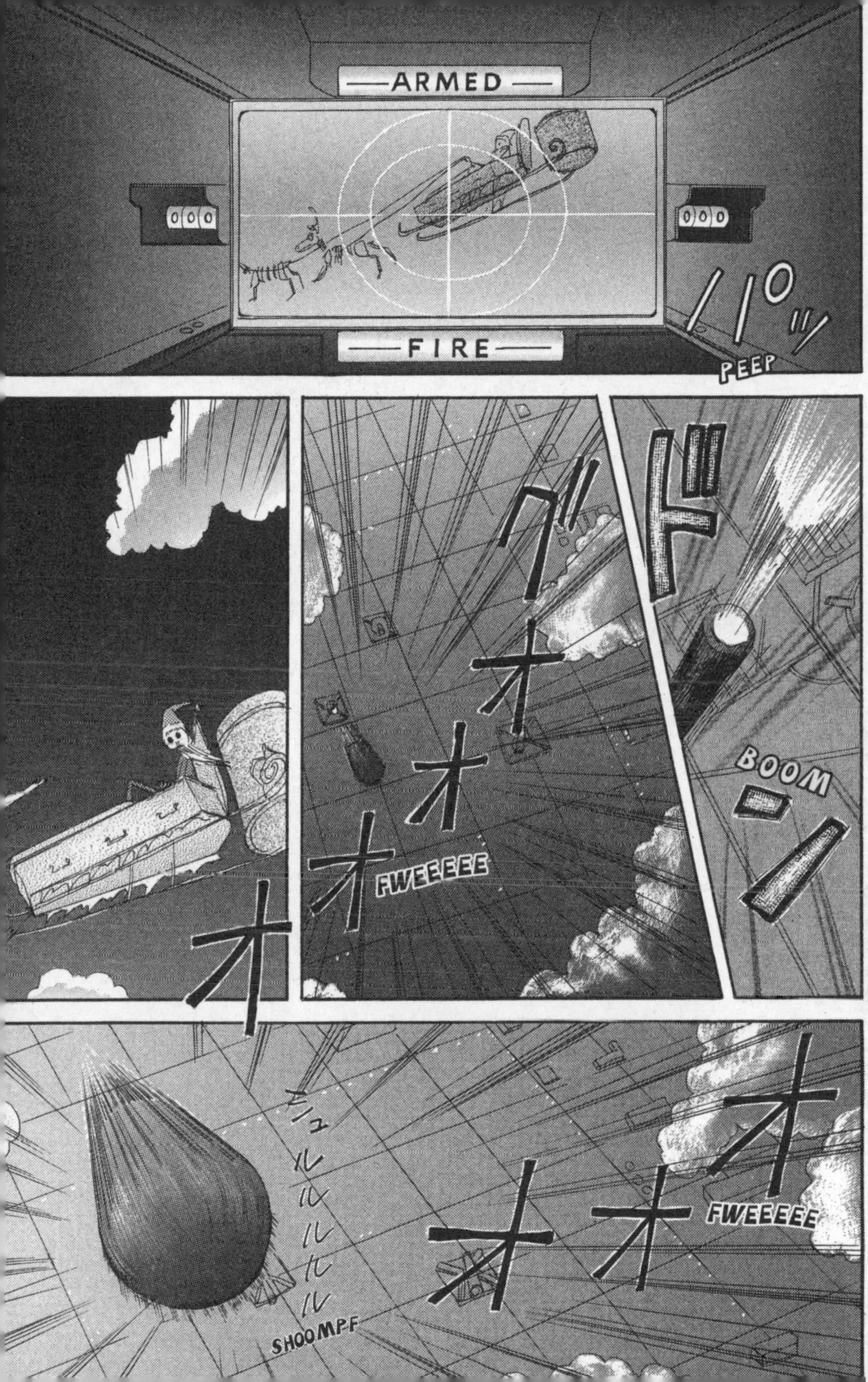
ARMED
000
000
FIRE
パッ
PEEP
ドーン
BOOM
グオオオオ
FWEEEEE
ヒュルルルルル
SHOOMPF
オオオ
FWEEEEE

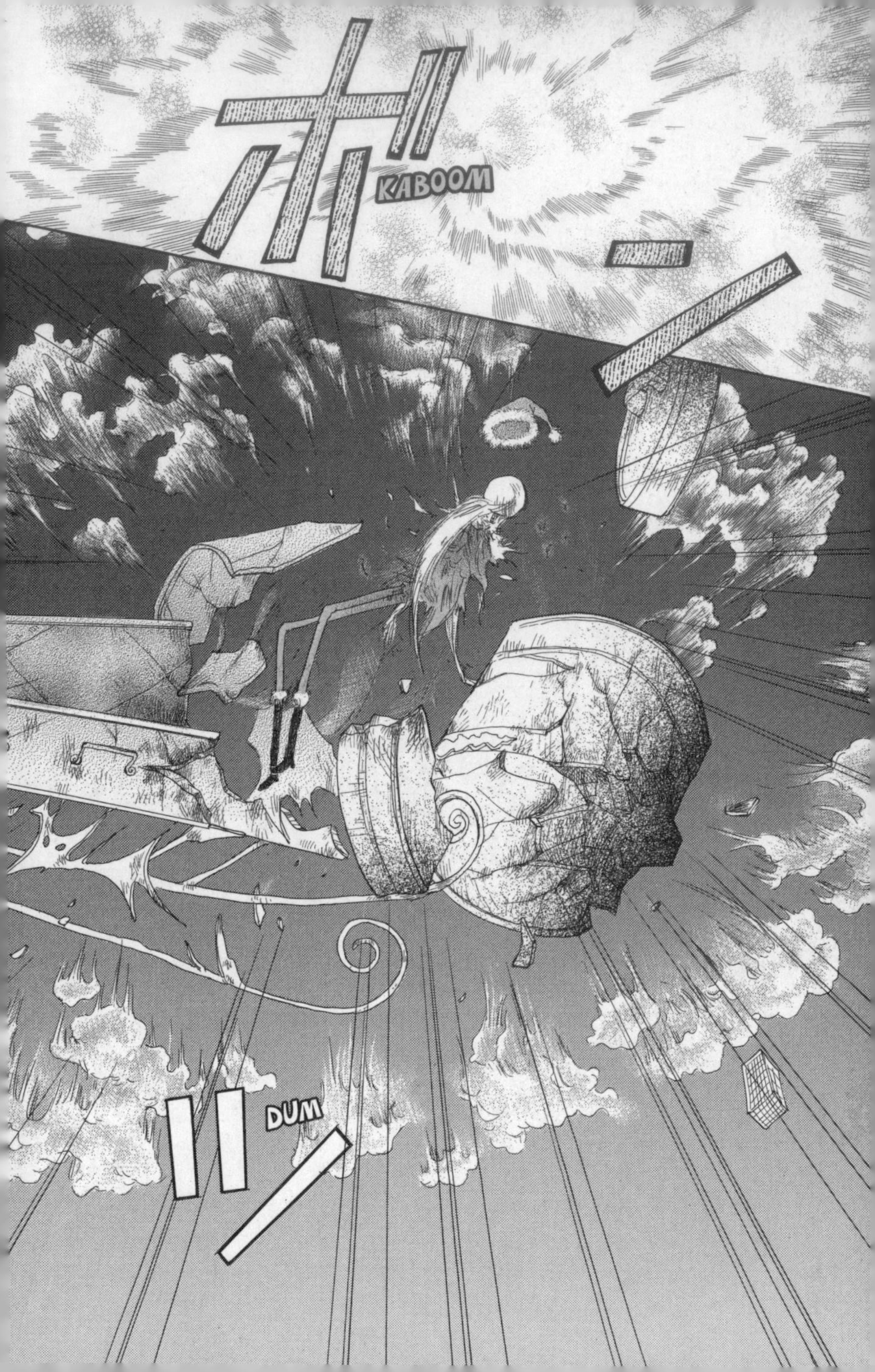
KABOOM
DUM

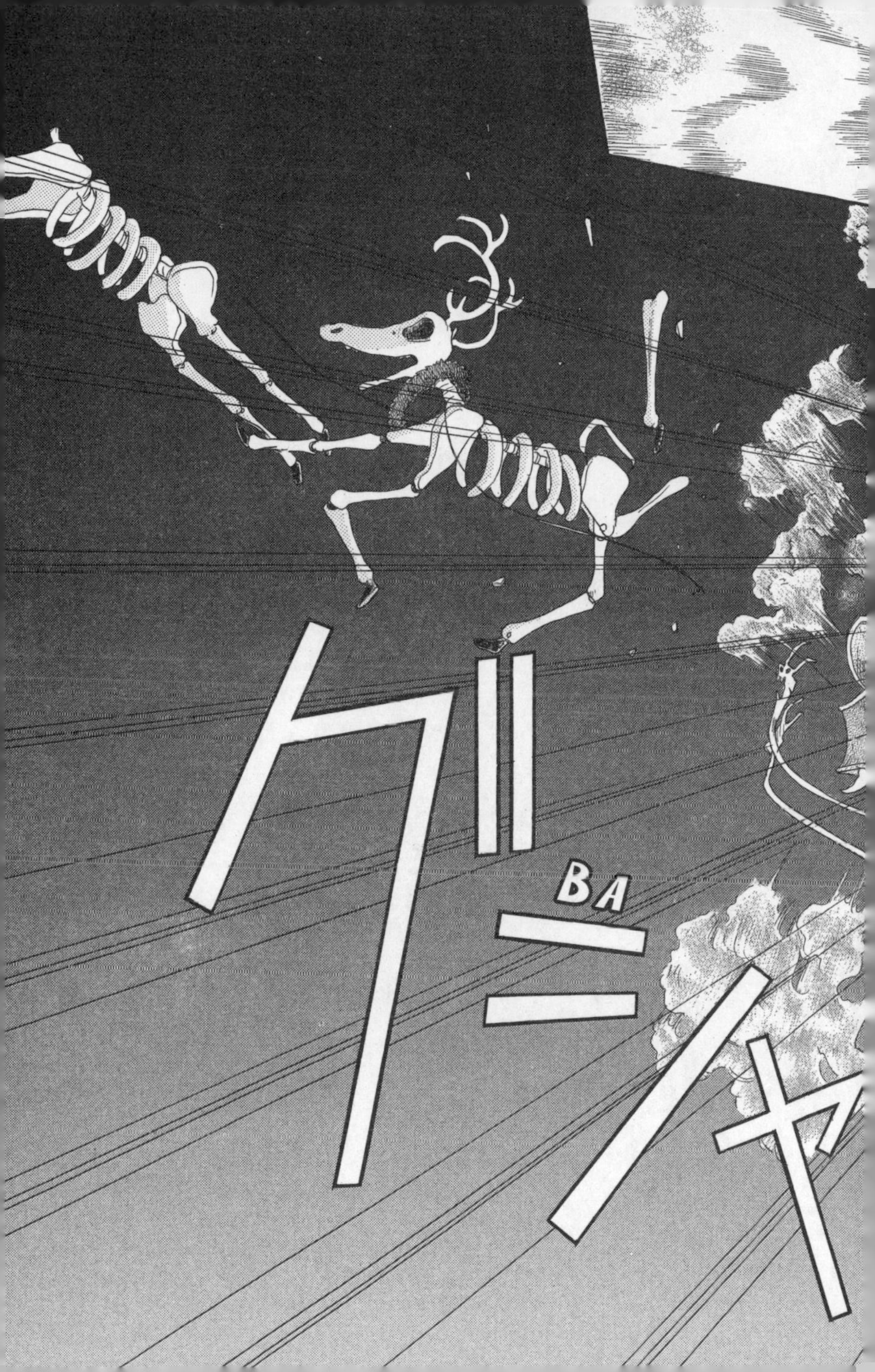
BA

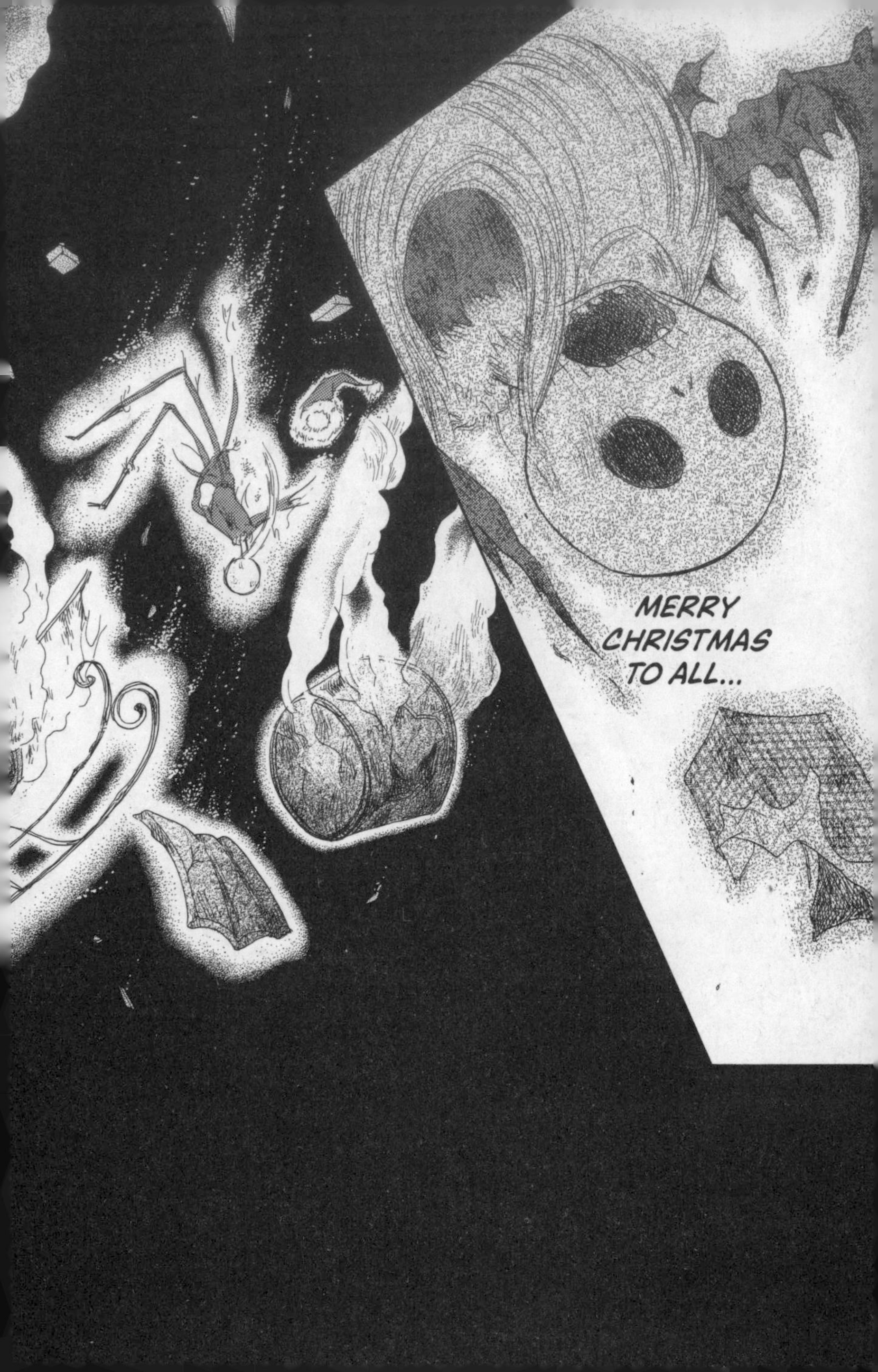
MERRY CHRISTMAS TO ALL...

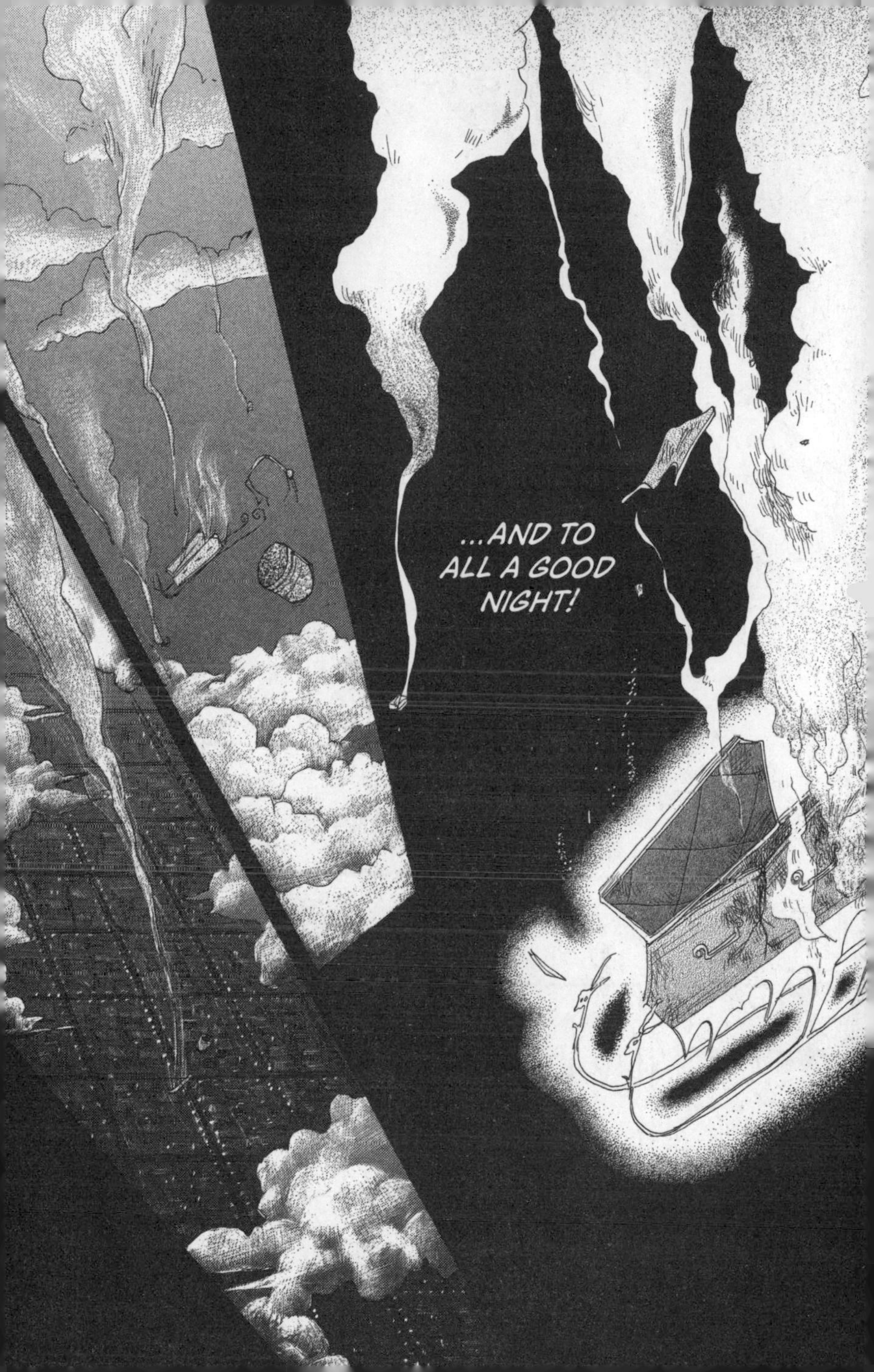
...AND TO ALL A GOOD NIGHT!

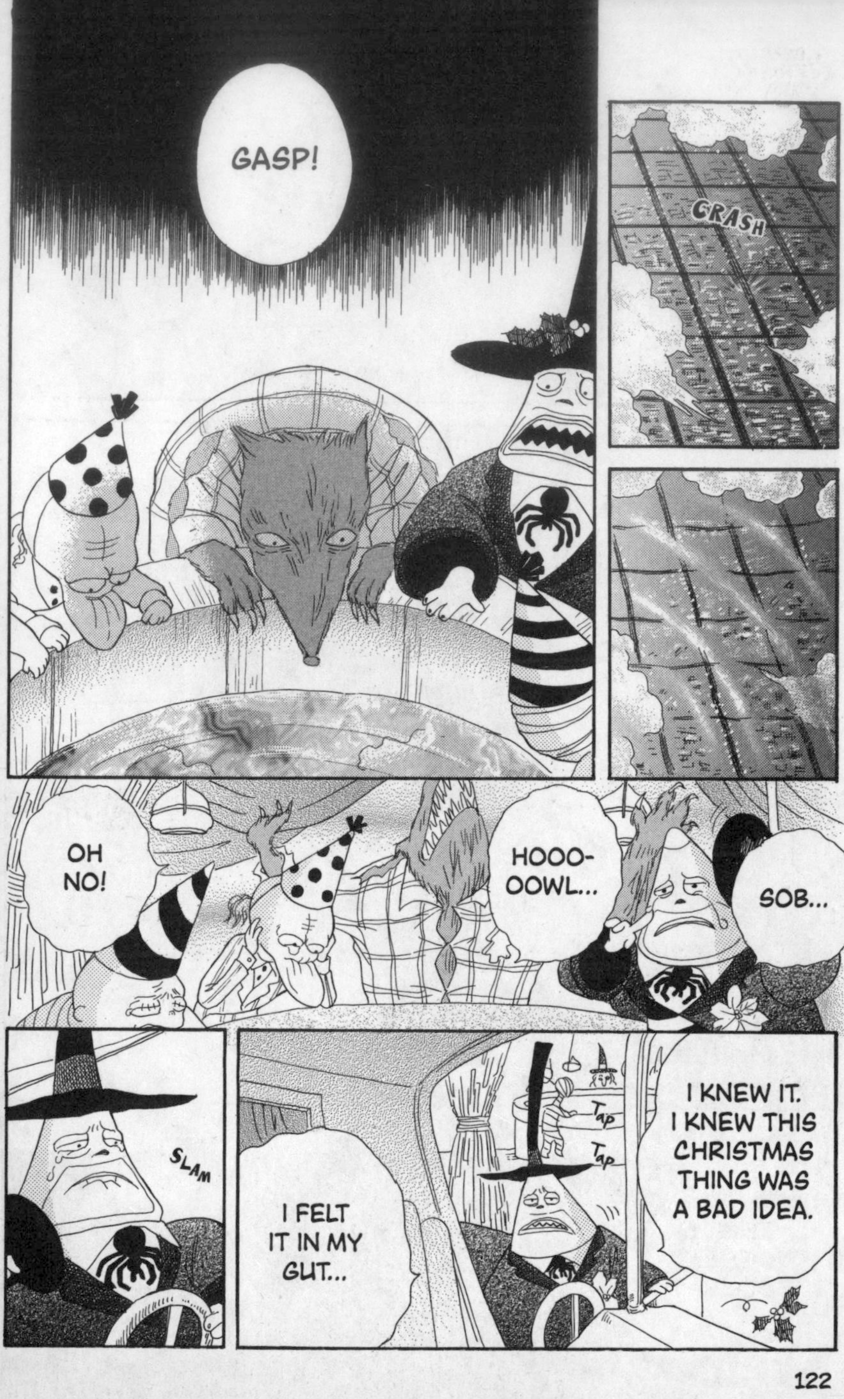
CRASH
GASP!
SOB...
HOOO-OOWL...
OH NO!
I KNEW IT. I KNEW THIS CHRISTMAS THING WAS A BAD IDEA.
Tap
Tap
I FELT IT IN MY GUT...
SLAM

READ THIS WAY

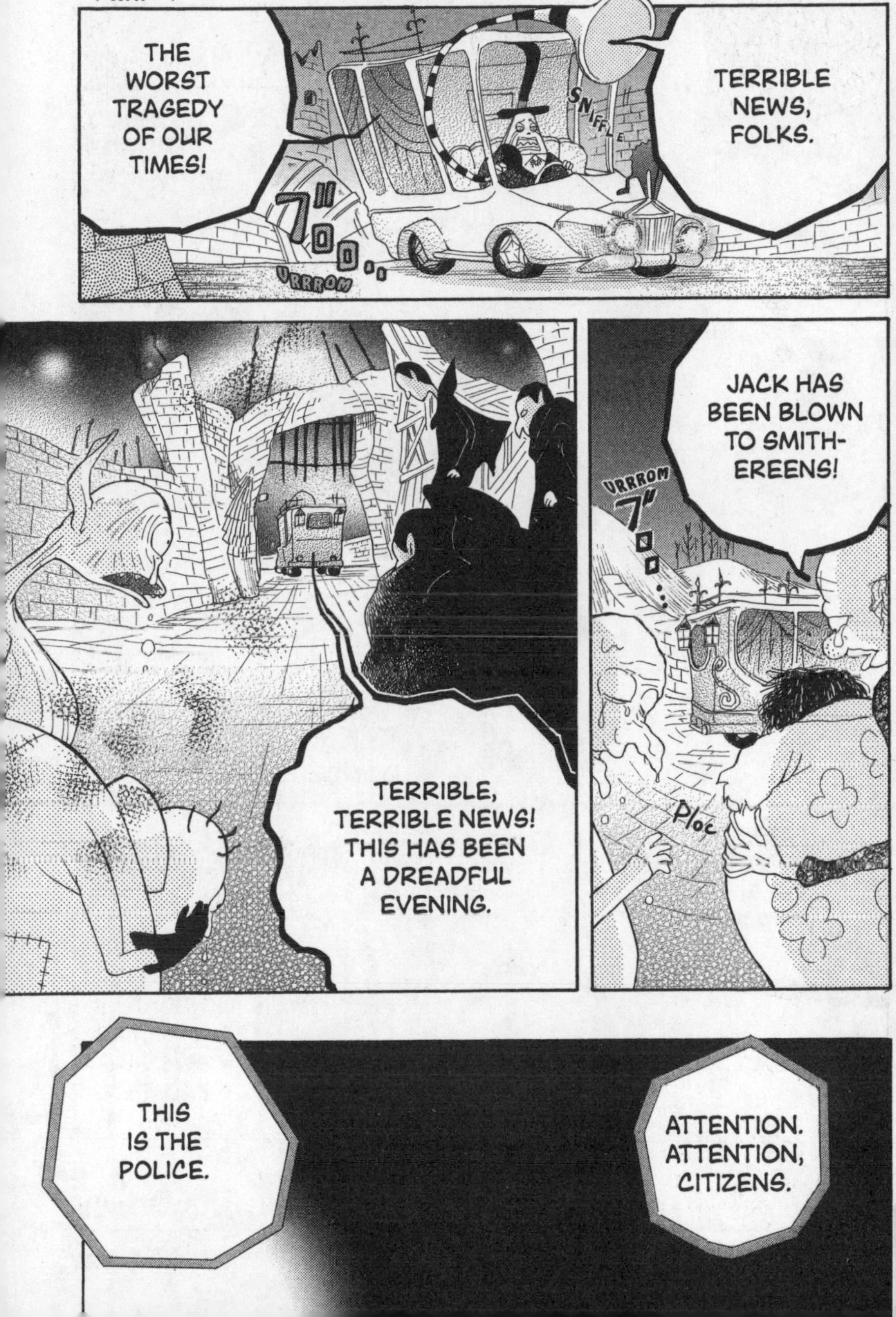
SNIFFLE
TERRIBLE NEWS, FOLKS.
THE WORST TRAGEDY OF OUR TIMES!
VRRROM
VRRROM
JACK HAS BEEN BLOWN TO SMITH-EREENS!
Ploc
TERRIBLE, TERRIBLE NEWS! THIS HAS BEEN A DREADFUL EVENING.
ATTENTION. ATTENTION, CITIZENS.
THIS IS THE POLICE.

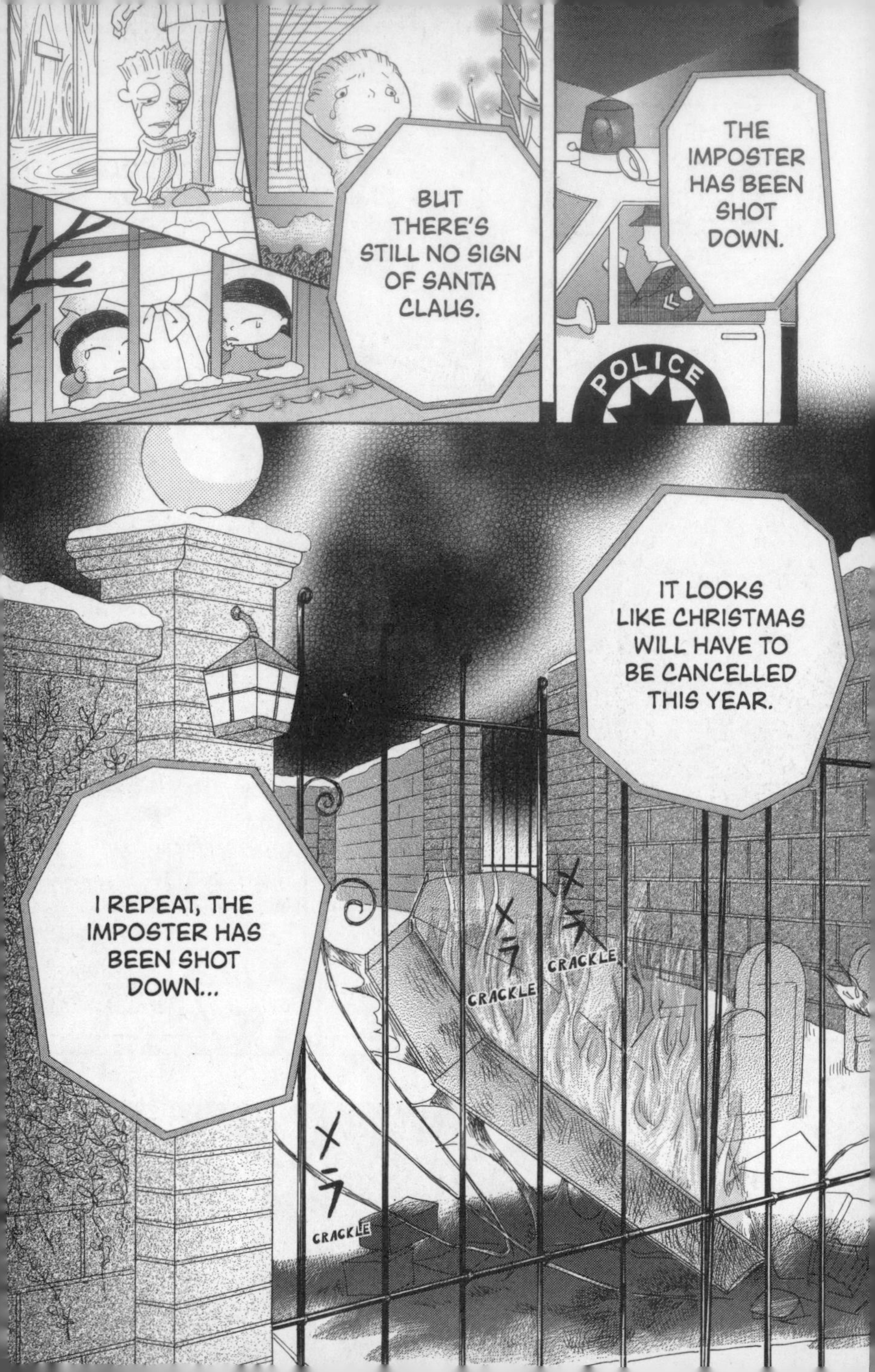
THE IMPOSTER HAS BEEN SHOT DOWN.
BUT THERE'S STILL NO SIGN OF SANTA CLAUS.
POLICE
IT LOOKS LIKE CHRISTMAS WILL HAVE TO BE CANCELLED THIS YEAR.
CRACKLE
CRACKLE
I REPEAT, THE IMPOSTER HAS BEEN SHOT DOWN...
CRACKLE

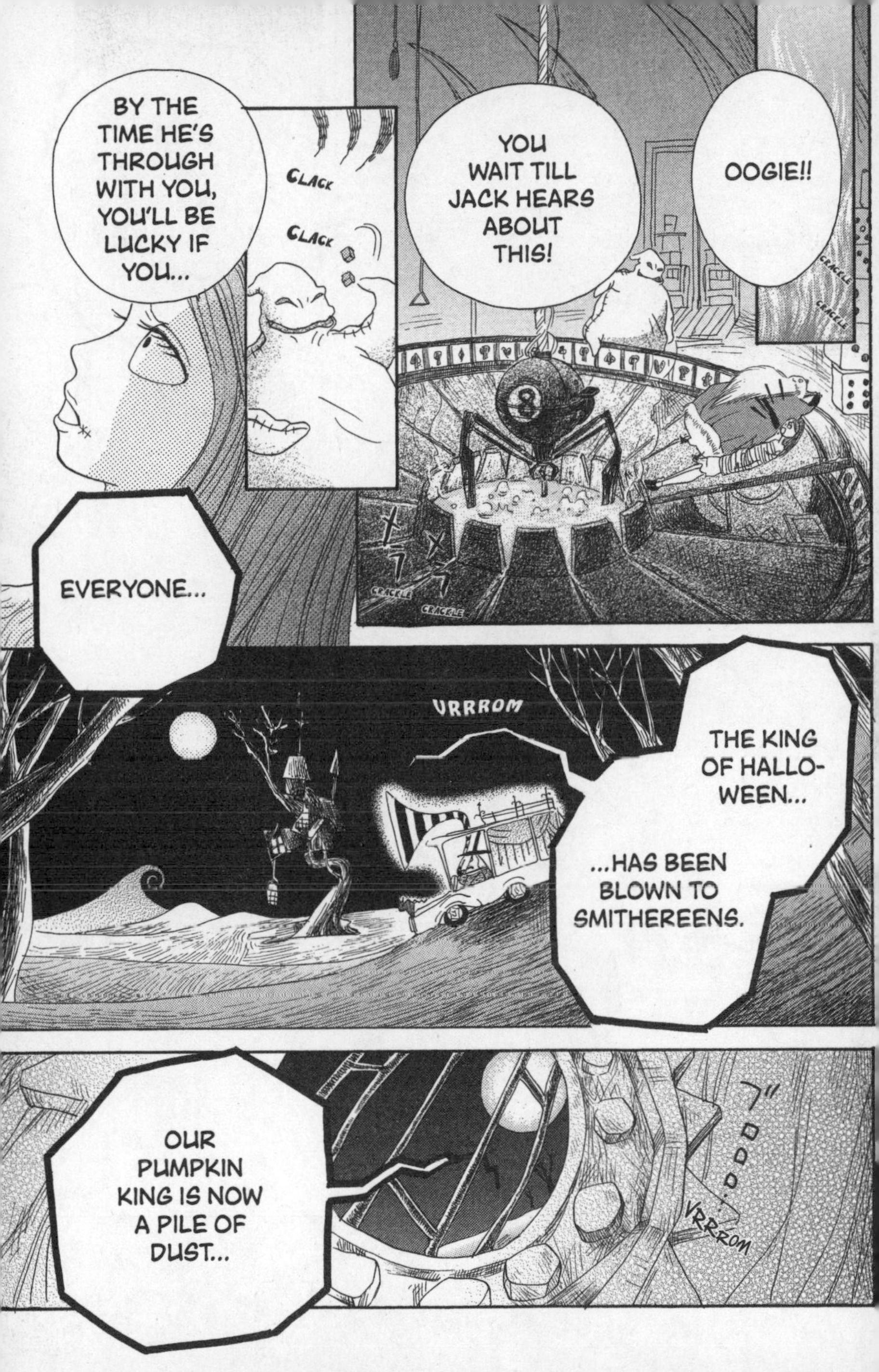

OOGIE!!
YOU WAIT TILL JACK HEARS ABOUT THIS!
CRACKLE
CRACKLE
CLACK
CLACK
BY THE TIME HE'S THROUGH WITH YOU, YOU'LL BE LUCKY IF YOU...
CRACKLE
CRACKLE
EVERYONE...
VRRROM
THE KING OF HALLO-WEEN...
...HAS BEEN BLOWN TO SMITHEREENS.
VRRROM
OUR PUMPKIN KING IS NOW A PILE OF DUST...

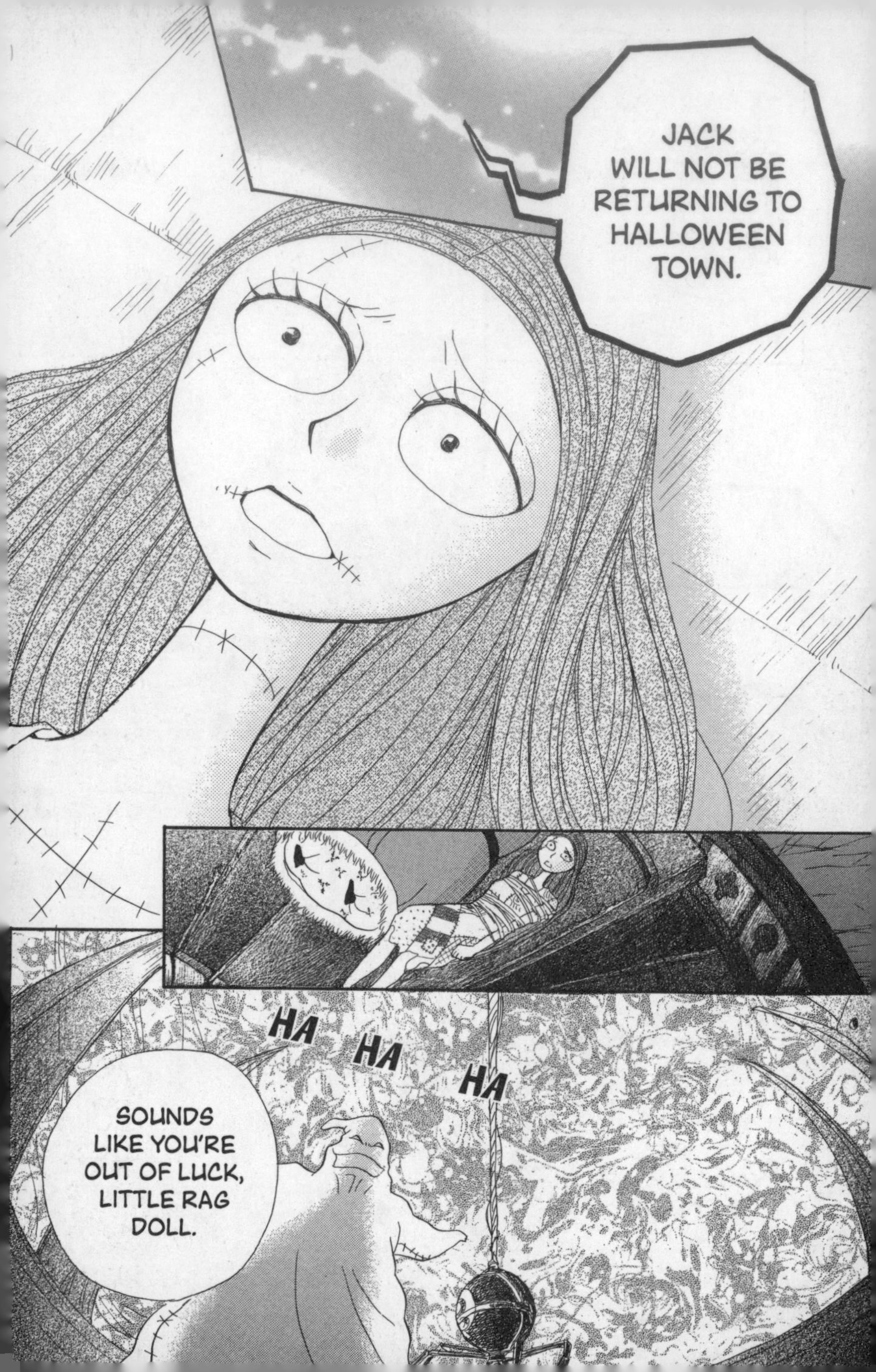
JACK WILL NOT BE RETURNING TO HALLOWEEN TOWN.
HA HA HA
SOUNDS LIKE YOU'RE OUT OF LUCK, LITTLE RAG DOLL.

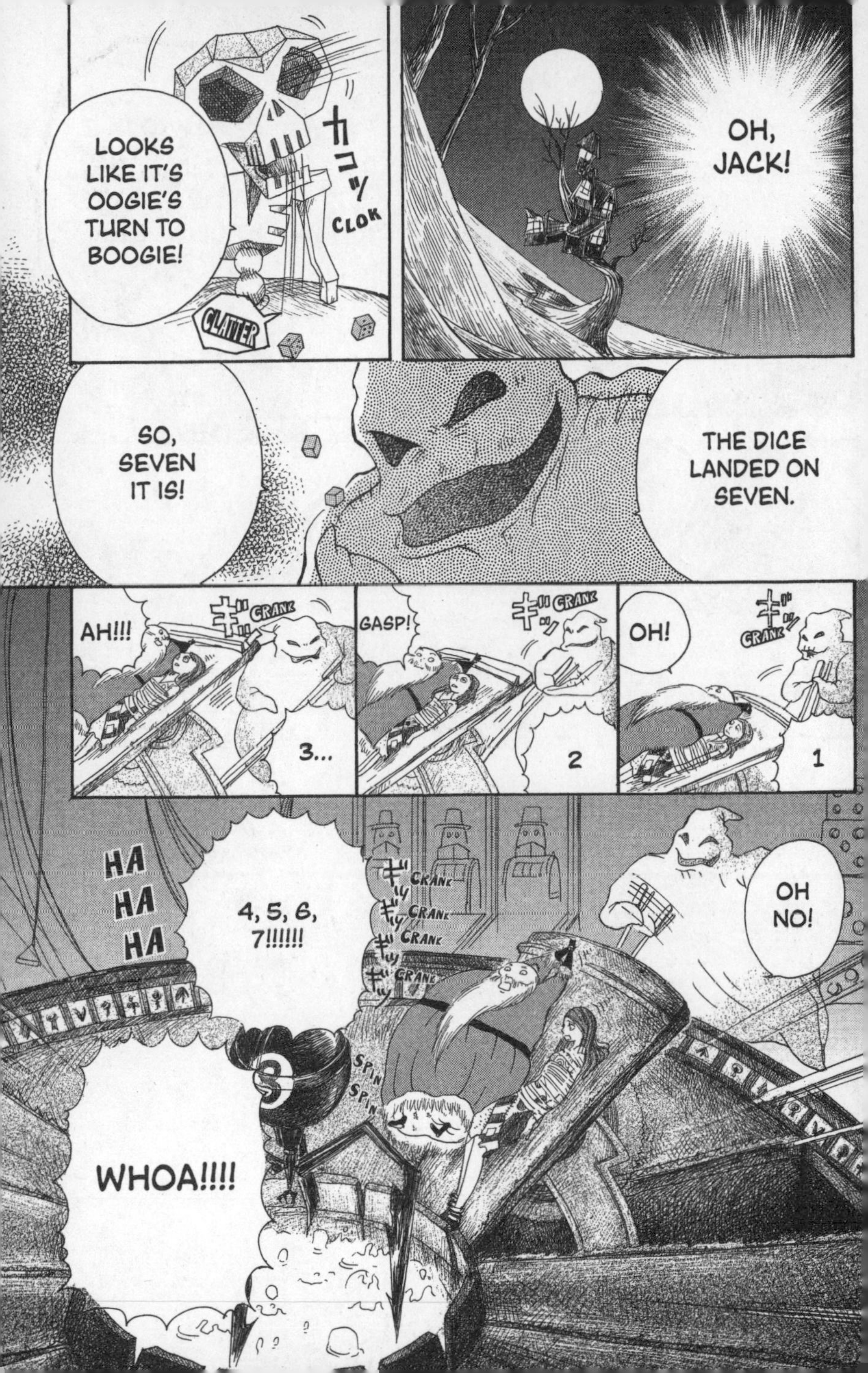
OH, JACK!
LOOKS LIKE IT'S OOGIE'S TURN TO BOOGIE!
カコッ
CLOK
CLATTER
THE DICE LANDED ON SEVEN.
SO, SEVEN IT IS!
OH!
ギッ
CRANK
1
GASP!
ギッ
CRANK
2
AH!!!
ギッ
CRANK
3...
OH NO!
CRANK
CRANK
CRANK
CRANK
4, 5, 6, 7!!!!!!
HA
HA
HA
SPIN
SPIN
WHOA!!!!

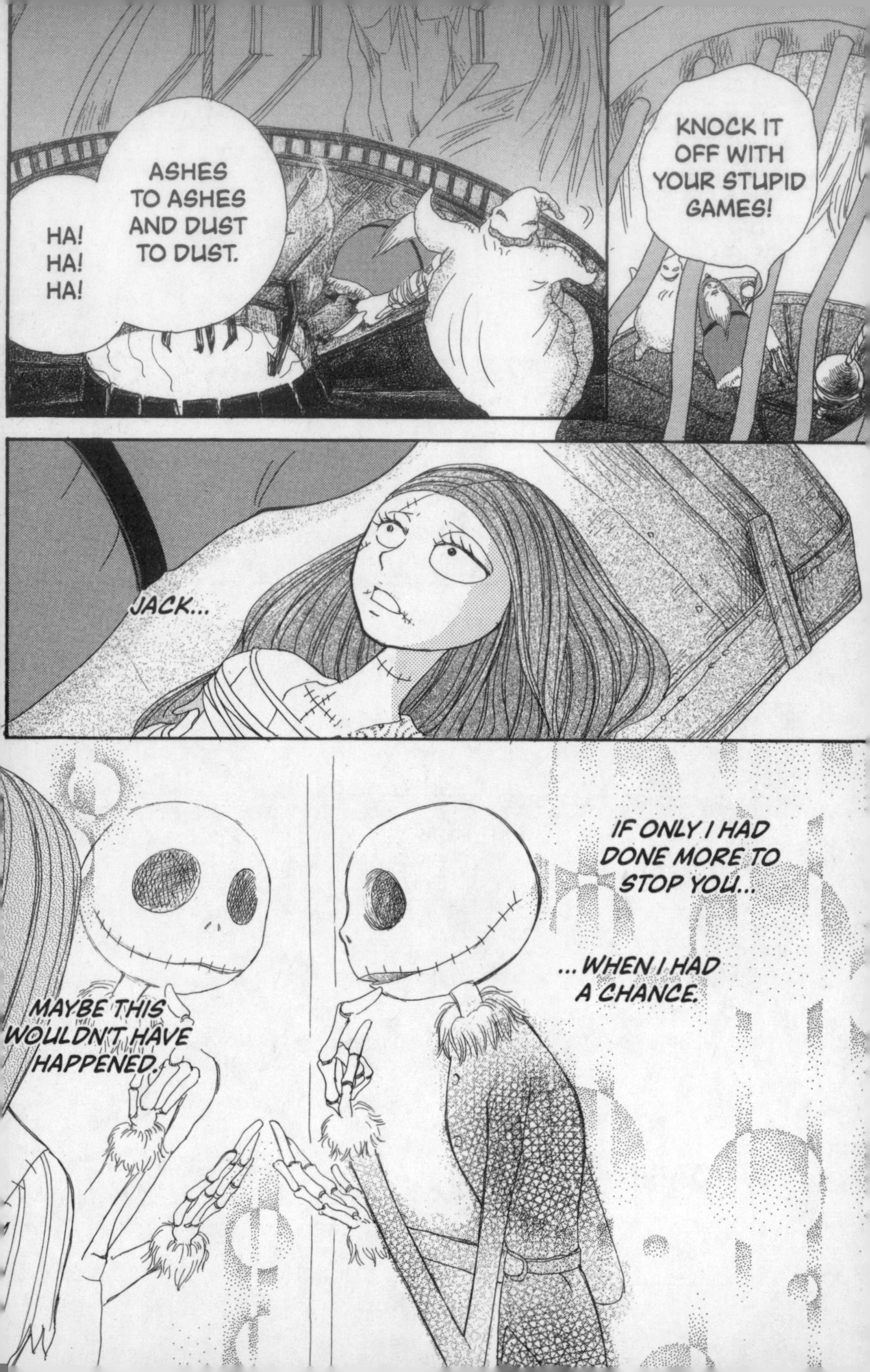
KNOCK IT OFF WITH YOUR STUPID GAMES!
ASHES TO ASHES AND DUST TO DUST.
HA! HA! HA!
JACK...
IF ONLY I HAD DONE MORE TO STOP YOU...
...WHEN I HAD A CHANCE.
MAYBE THIS WOULDN'T HAVE HAPPENED.

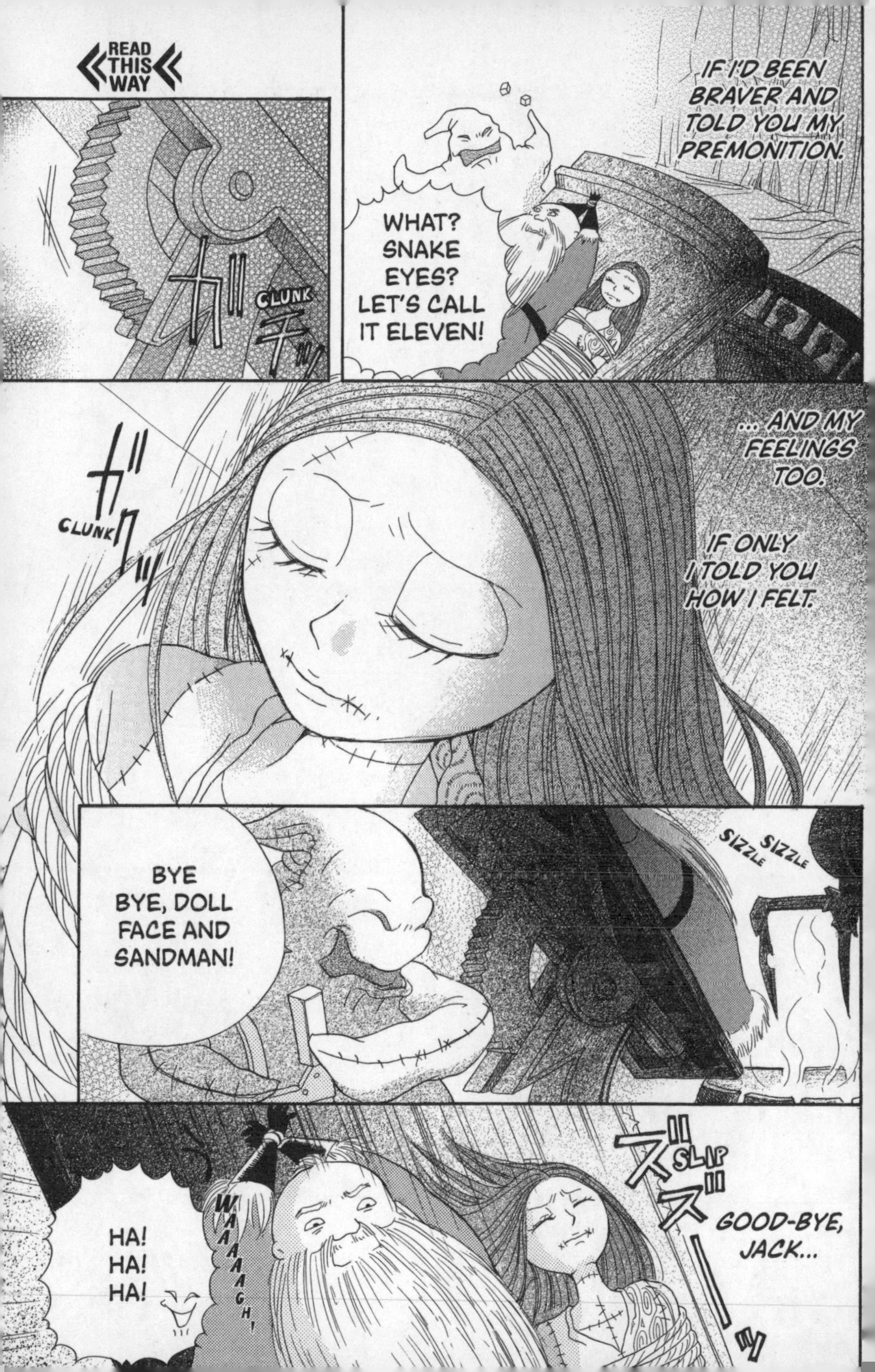
READ THIS WAY
IF I'D BEEN BRAVER AND TOLD YOU MY PREMONITION.
WHAT? SNAKE EYES? LET'S CALL IT ELEVEN!
CLUNK
... AND MY FEELINGS TOO.
IF ONLY I TOLD YOU HOW I FELT.
CLUNK
SIZZLE SIZZLE
BYE BYE, DOLL FACE AND SANDMAN!
SLIP
GOOD-BYE, JACK...
WAAAAAGH!
HA! HA! HA!

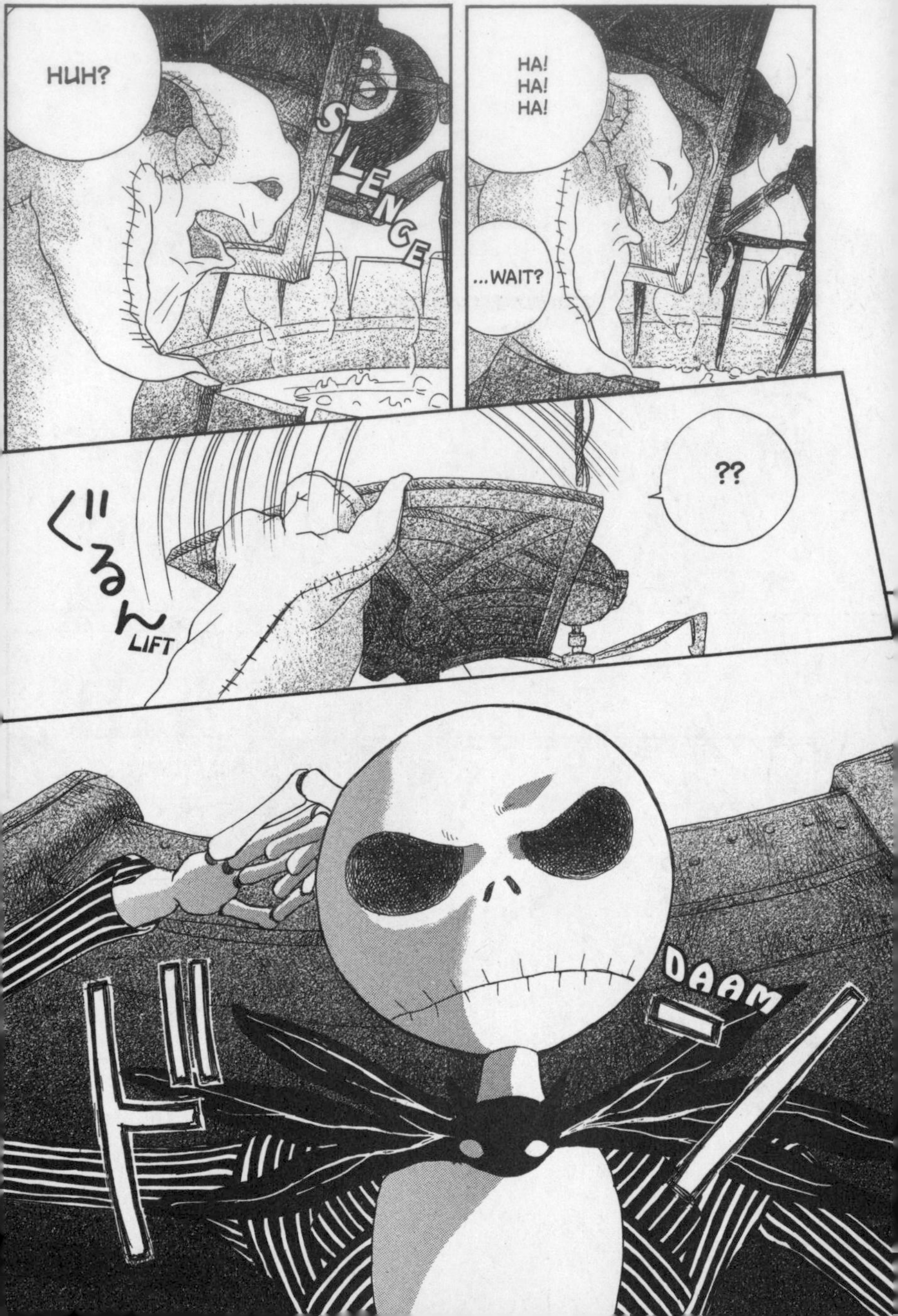
HA! HA! HA!
...WAIT?
HUH?
SILENCE
??
ぐるん~
LIFT
ドーン
DAAM

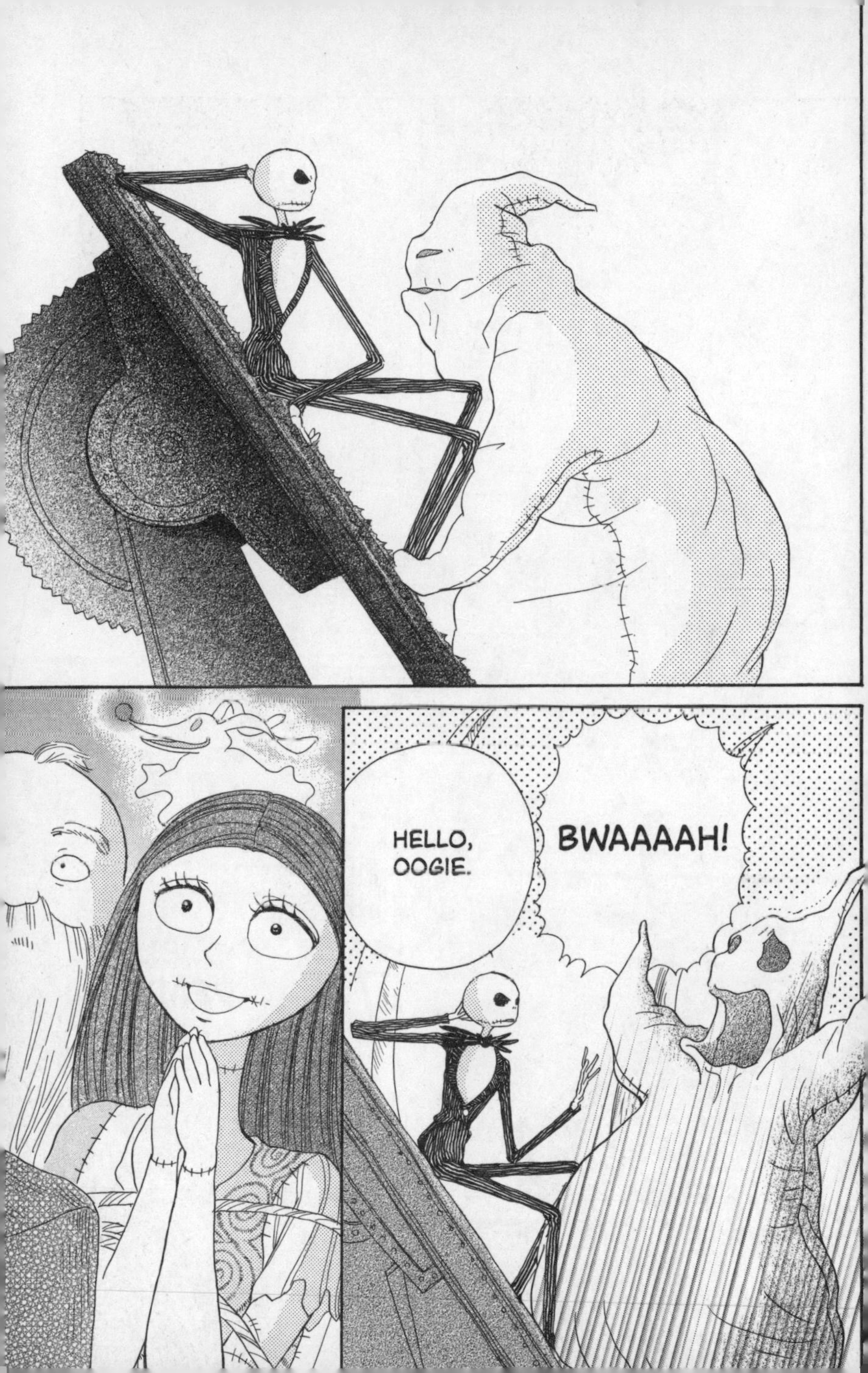
BWAAAAH!
HELLO, OOGIE.

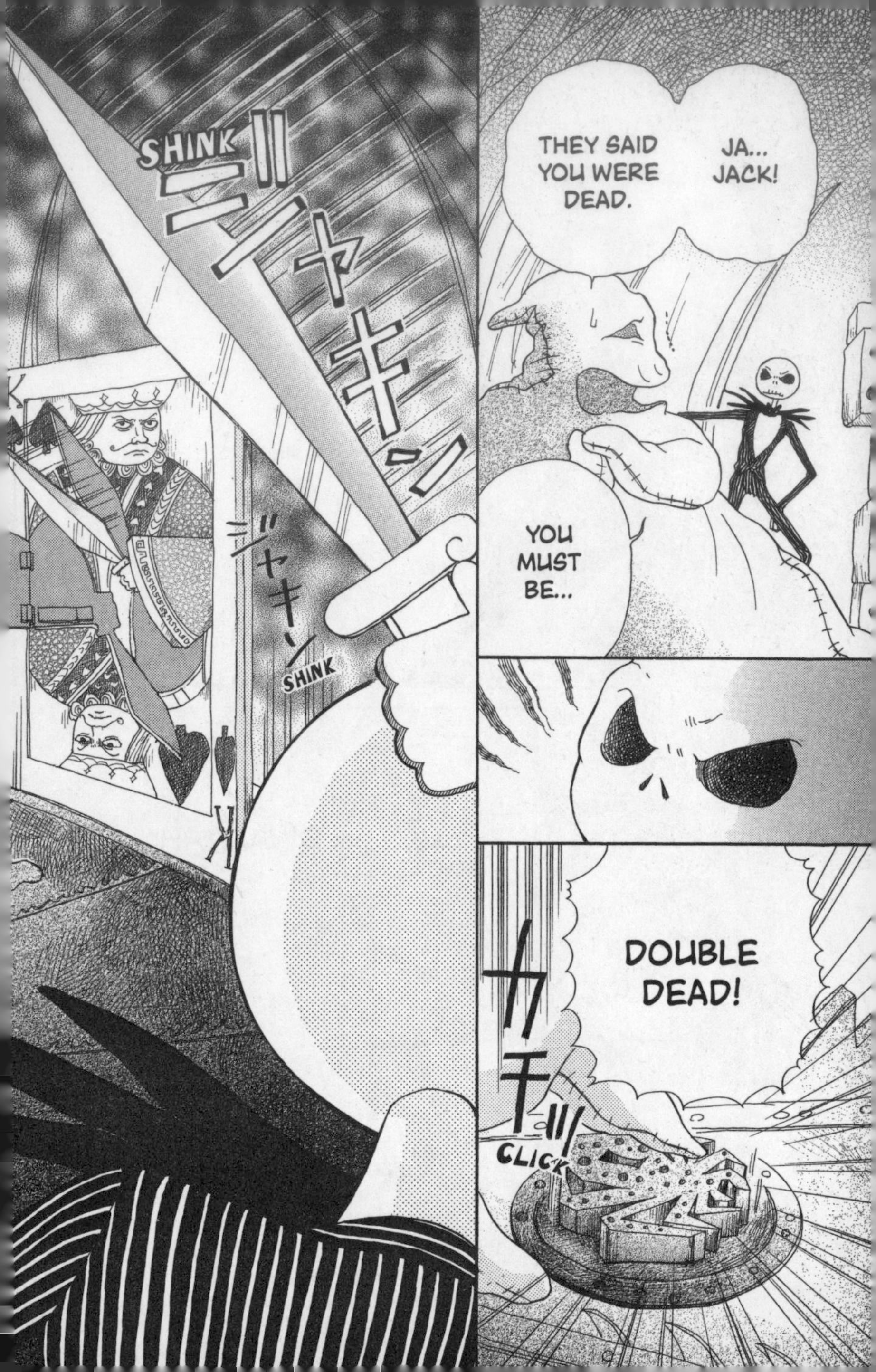
JA... JACK!
THEY SAID YOU WERE DEAD.
YOU MUST BE...
DOUBLE DEAD!
CLICK
SHINK
SHINK

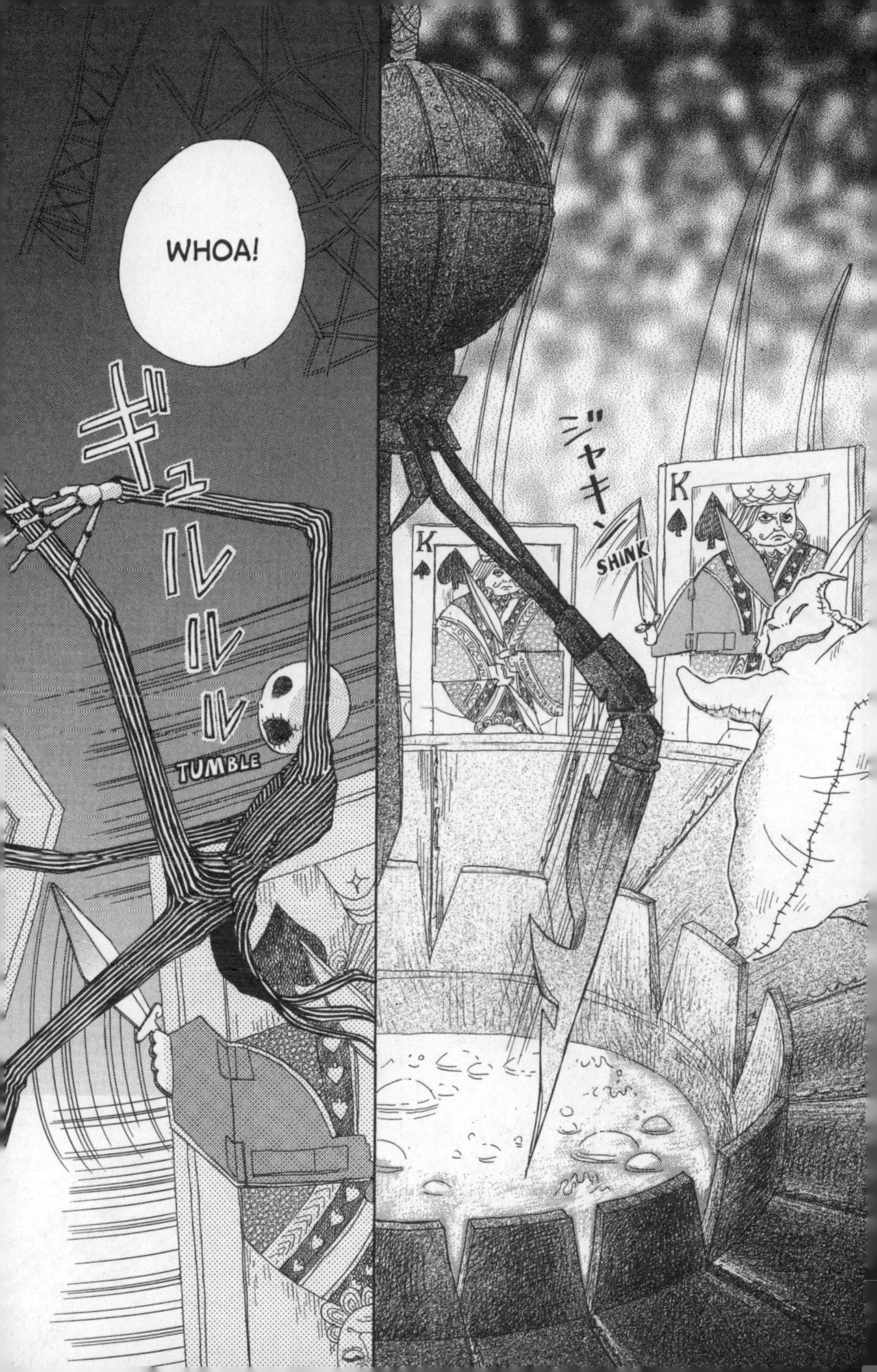
ジャキ
SHINK
WHOA!
ギュルルル
TUMBLE

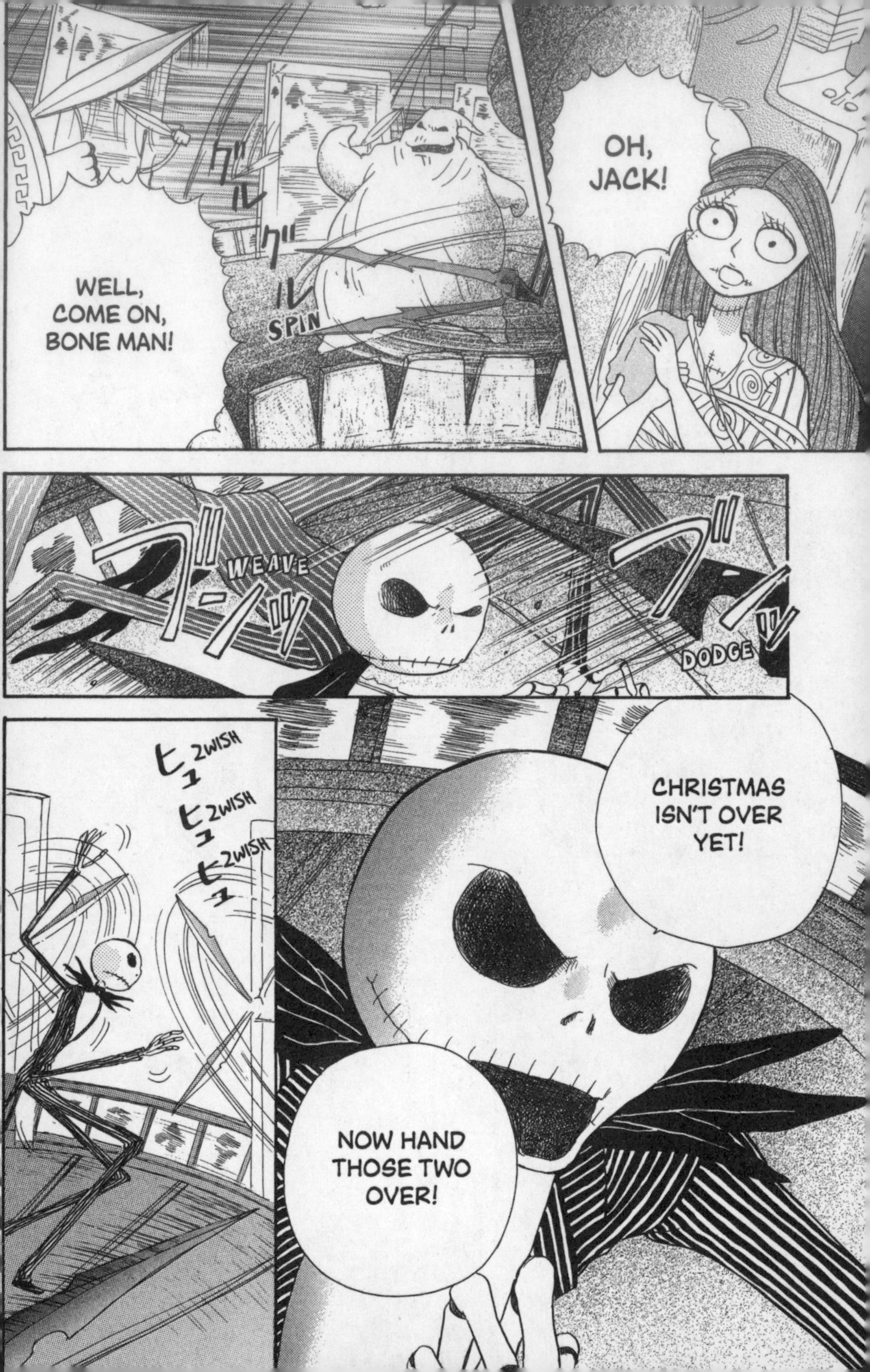
OH, JACK!
グル
グル
SPIN
WELL, COME ON, BONE MAN!
DODGE
WEAVE
CHRISTMAS ISN'T OVER YET!
NOW HAND THOSE TWO OVER!
ヒュ ZWISH
ヒュ ZWISH
ヒュ ZWISH

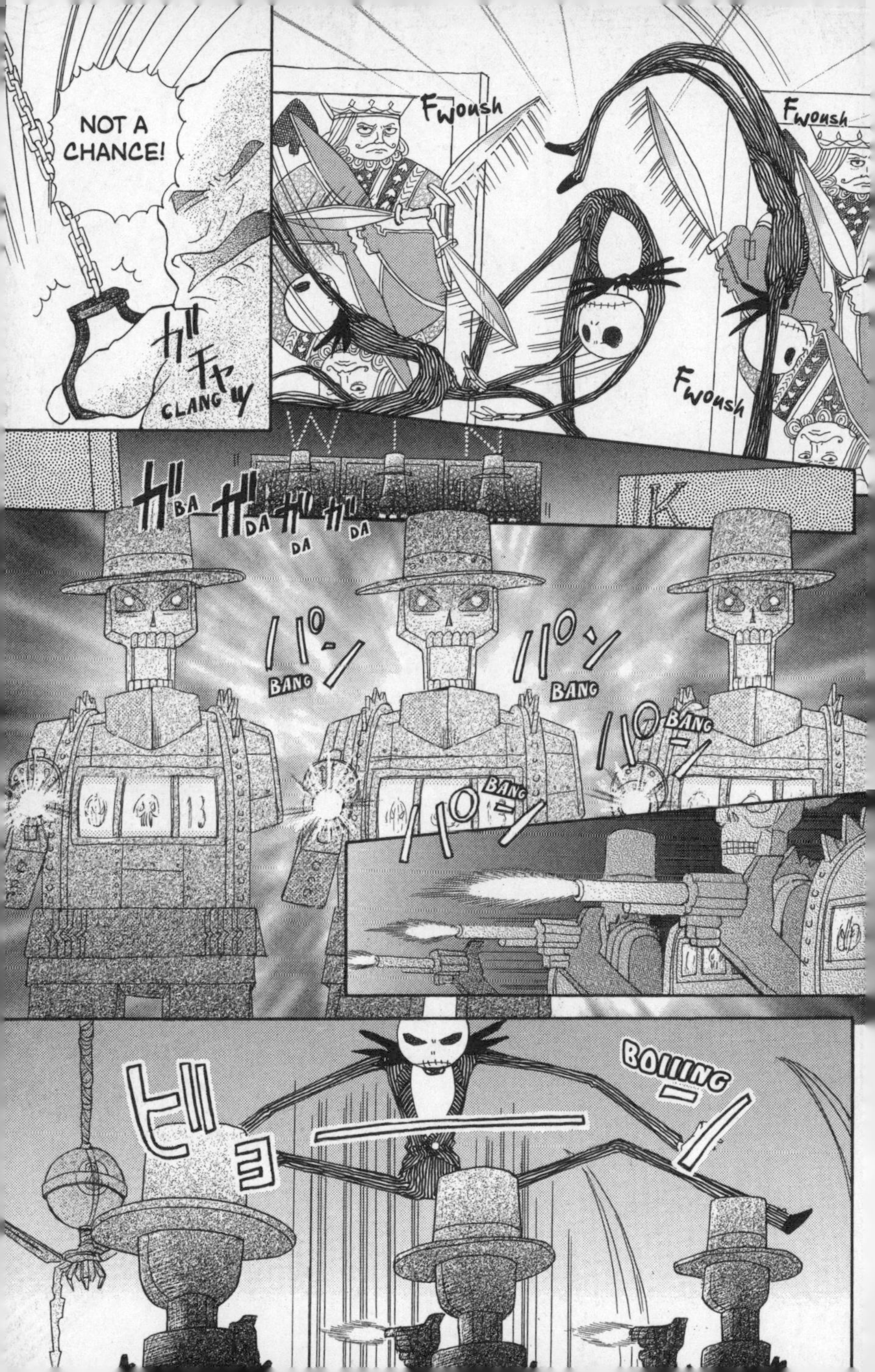
Fwoush
Fwoush
Fwoush
NOT A CHANCE!
CLANG
BA DA DA DA
BANG
BANG
BANG
BANG
BOIIING

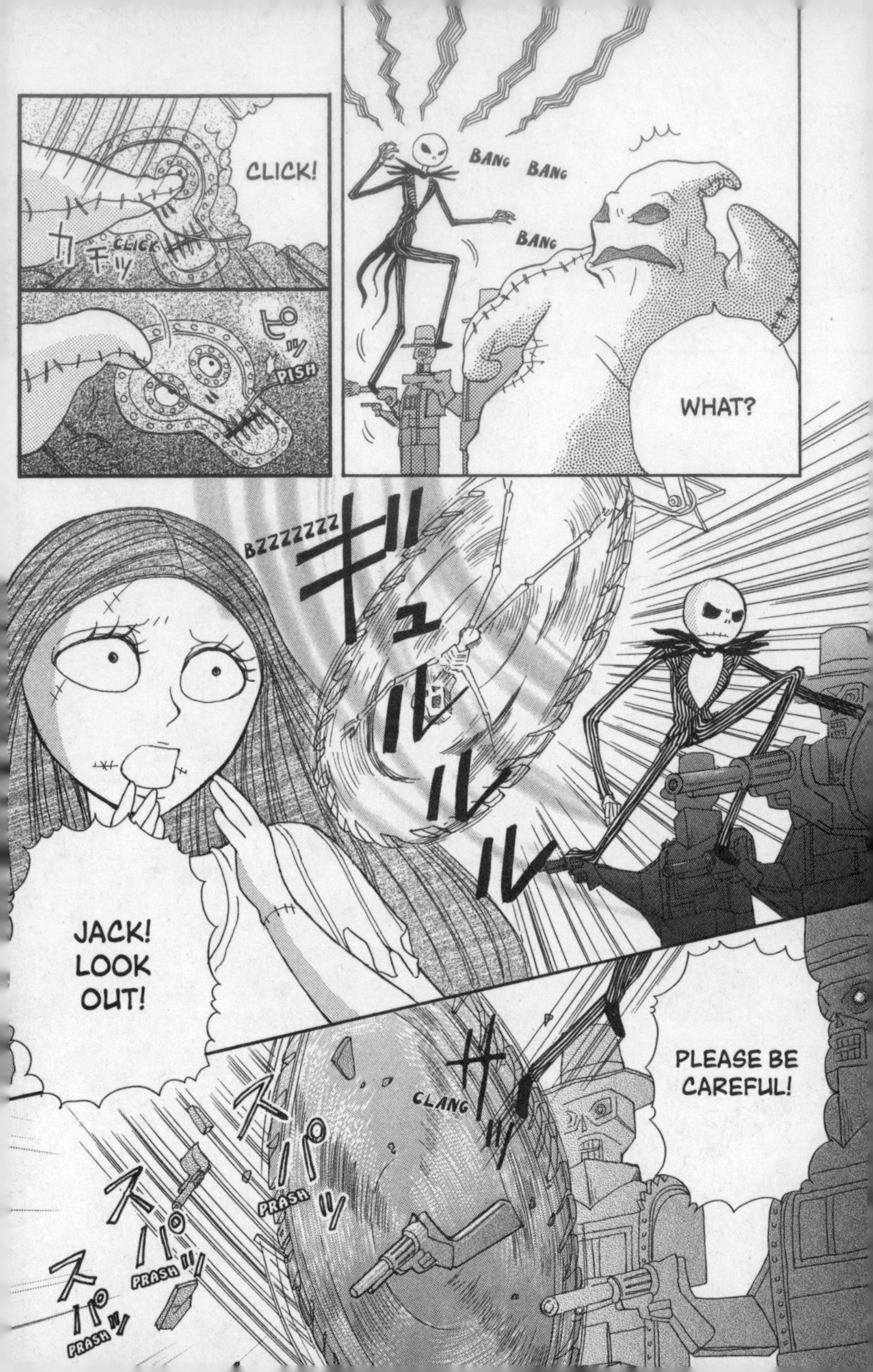
BANG
BANG
BANG
WHAT?
CLICK!
カチッ
CLICK
ピッ
PISH
BZZZZZZZ
ギュルルル
JACK! LOOK OUT!
PLEASE BE CAREFUL!
CLANG
スパッ
PRASH
スパッ
PRASH
スパッ
PRASH

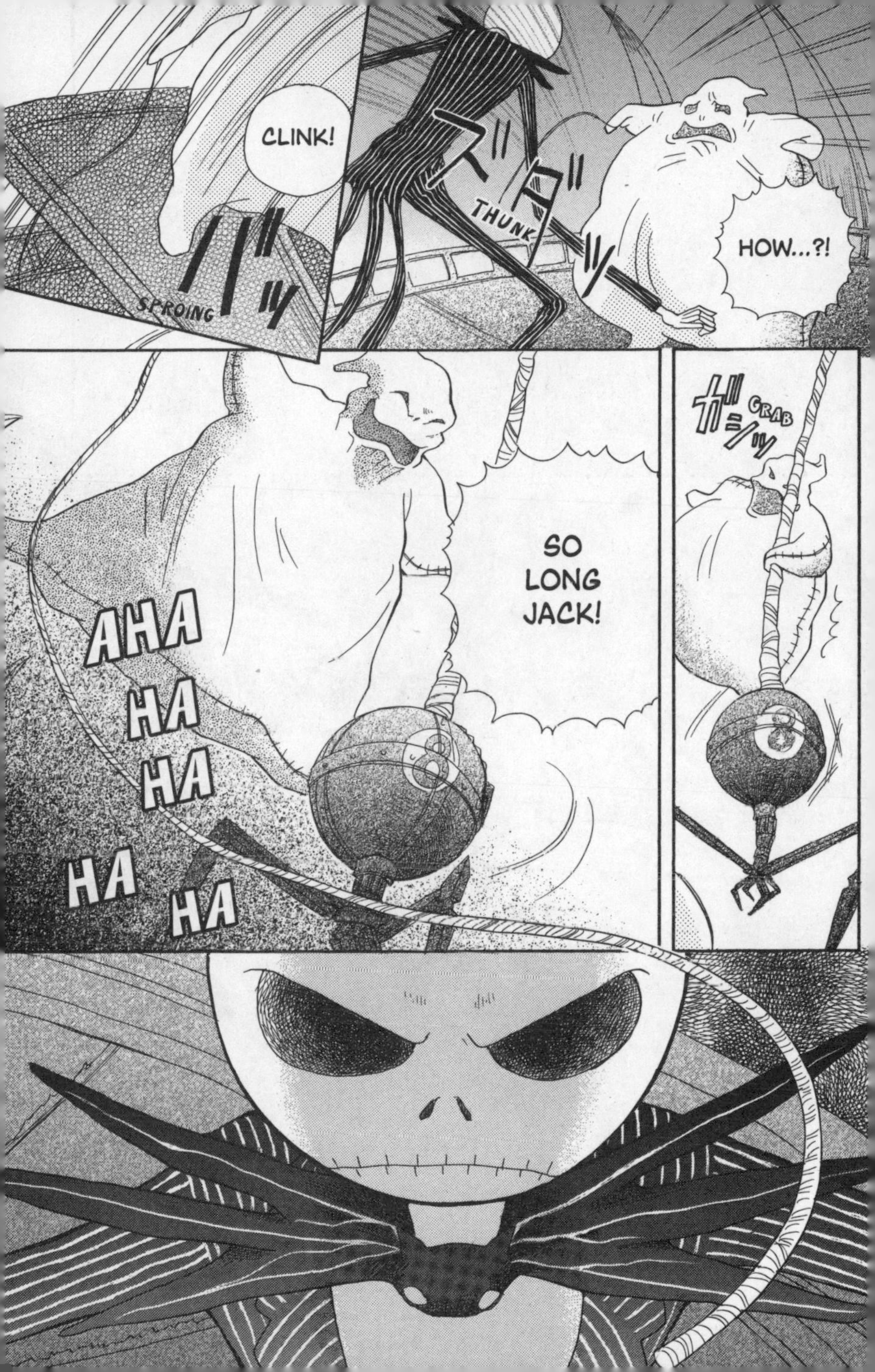
HOW...?!
THUNK
CLINK!
SPROING
GRAB
SO LONG JACK!
AHA HA HA
HA HA

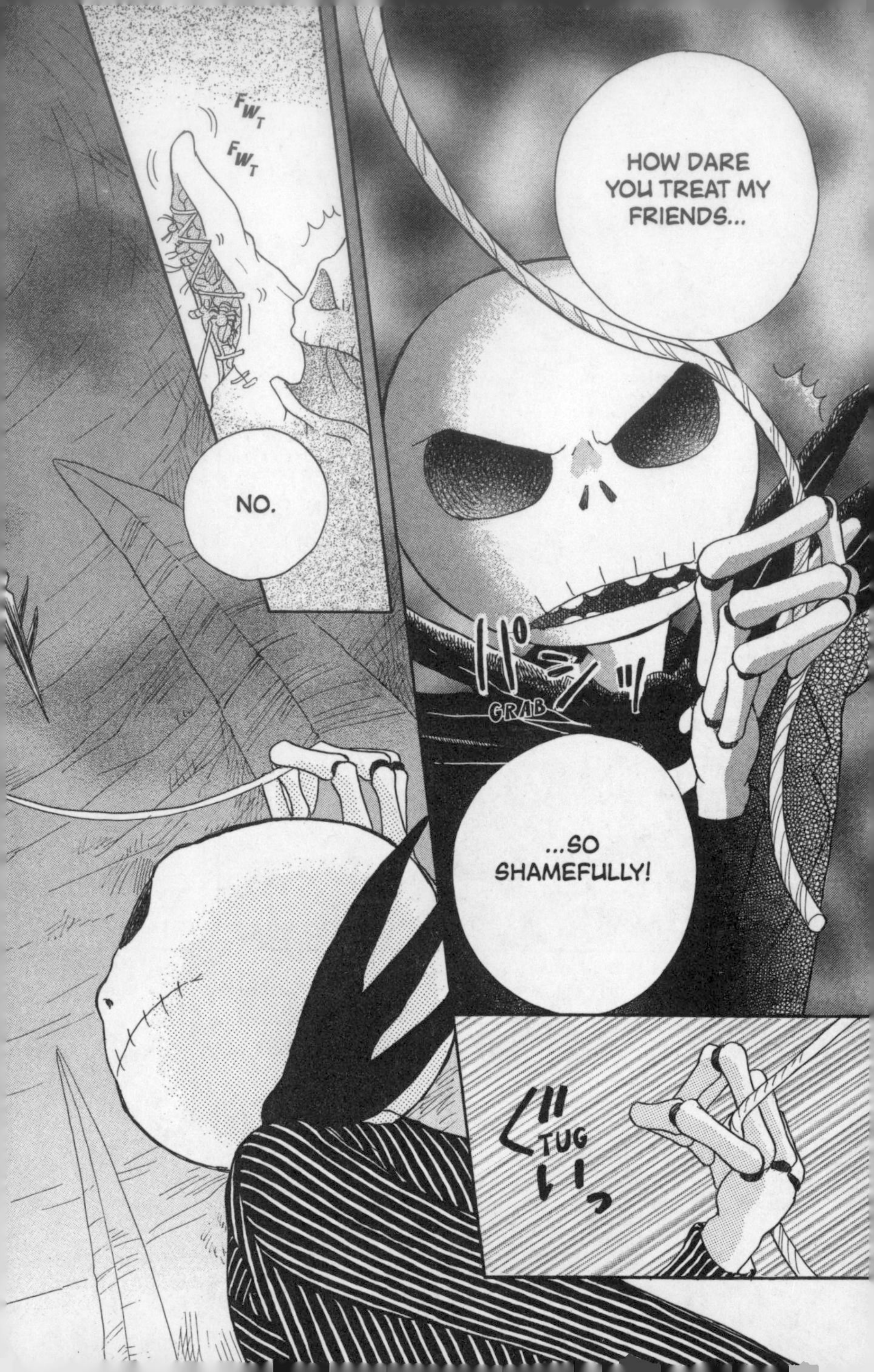
HOW DARE YOU TREAT MY FRIENDS...
GRAB
...SO SHAMEFULLY!
FWT
FWT
NO.
TUG

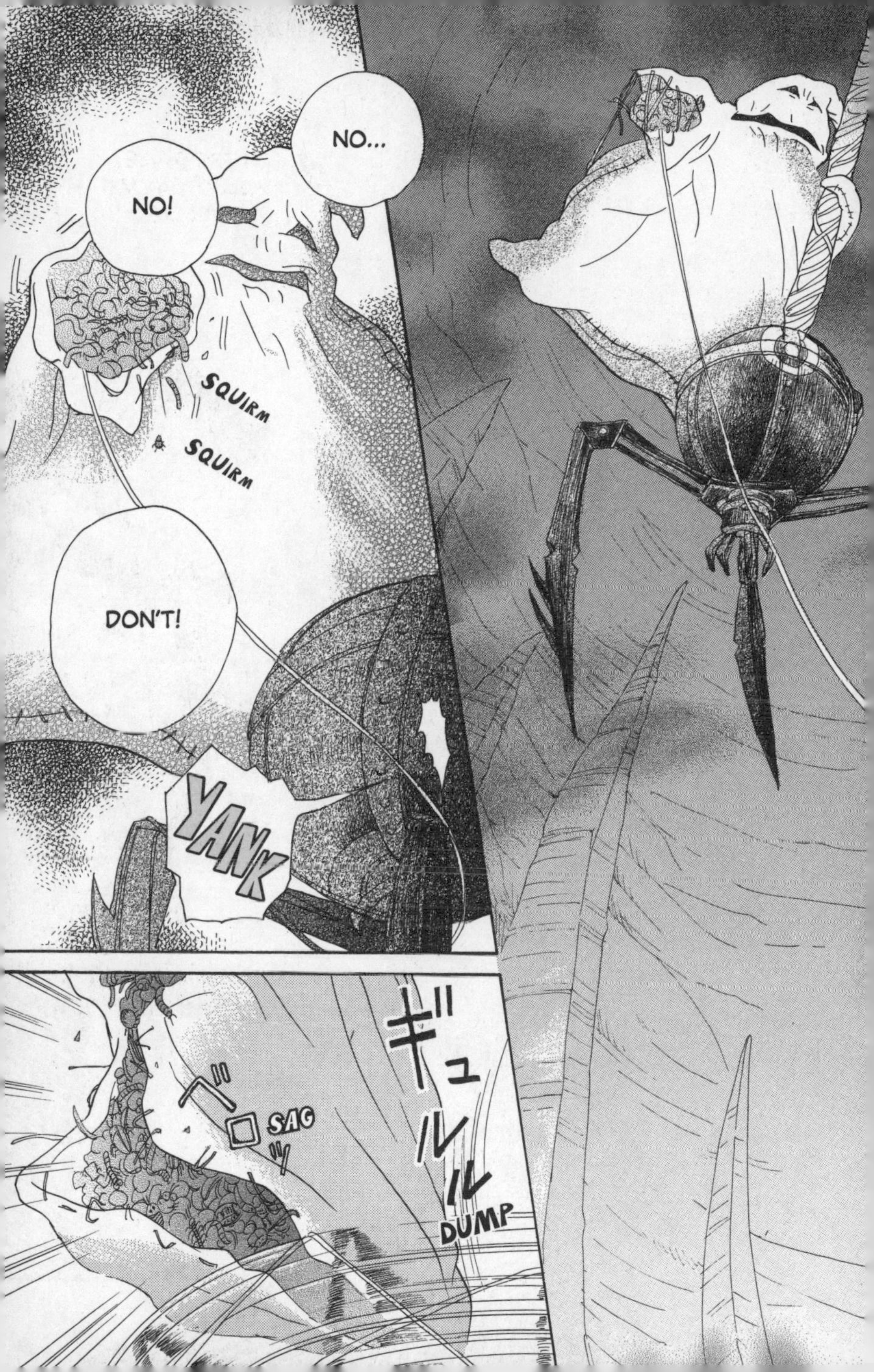
NO...
NO!
SQUIRM
SQUIRM
DON'T!
YANK
ギュルル
DUMP
ベロ
SAG

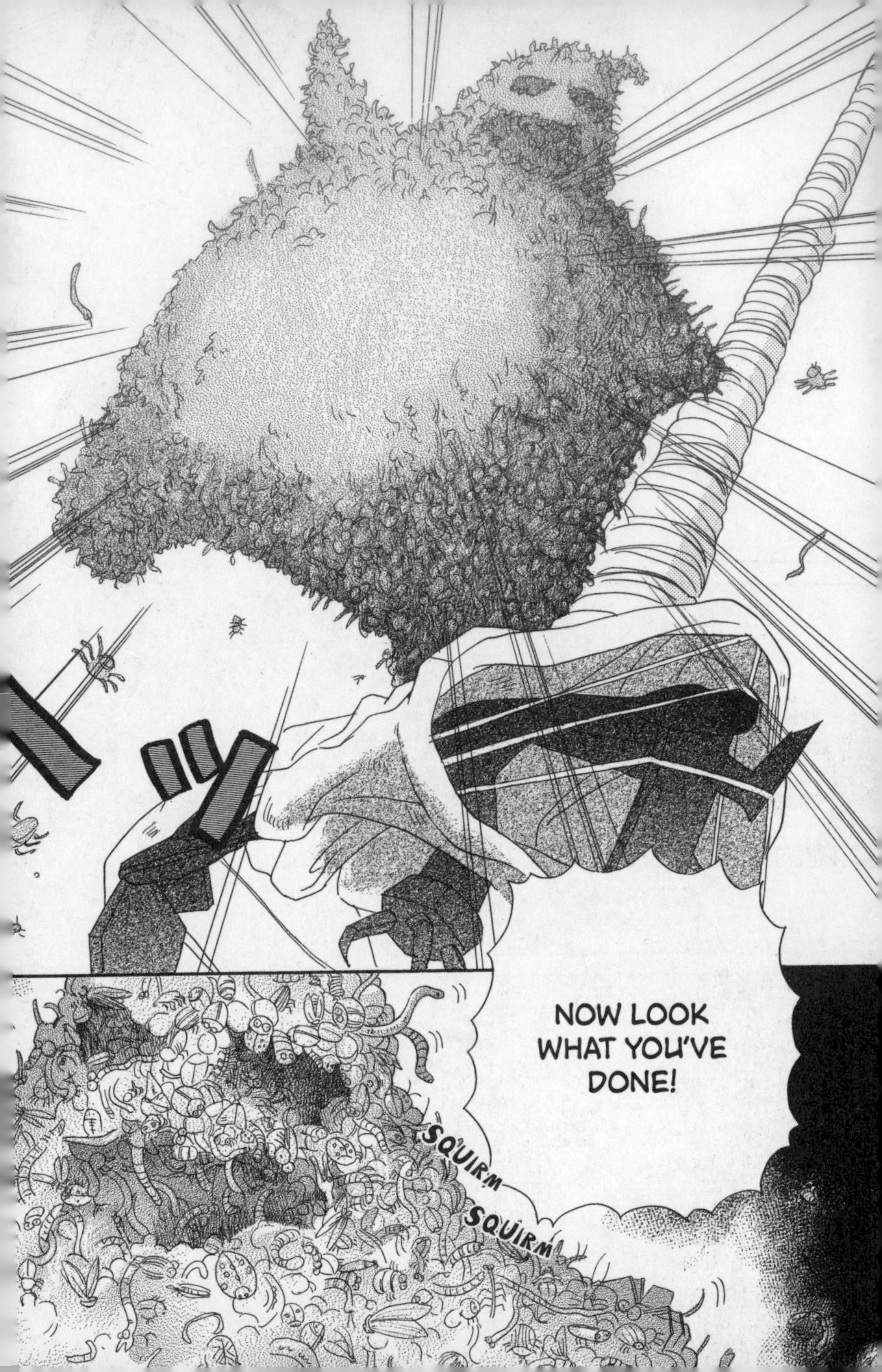
NOW LOOK WHAT YOU'VE DONE!
SQUIRM
SQUIRM

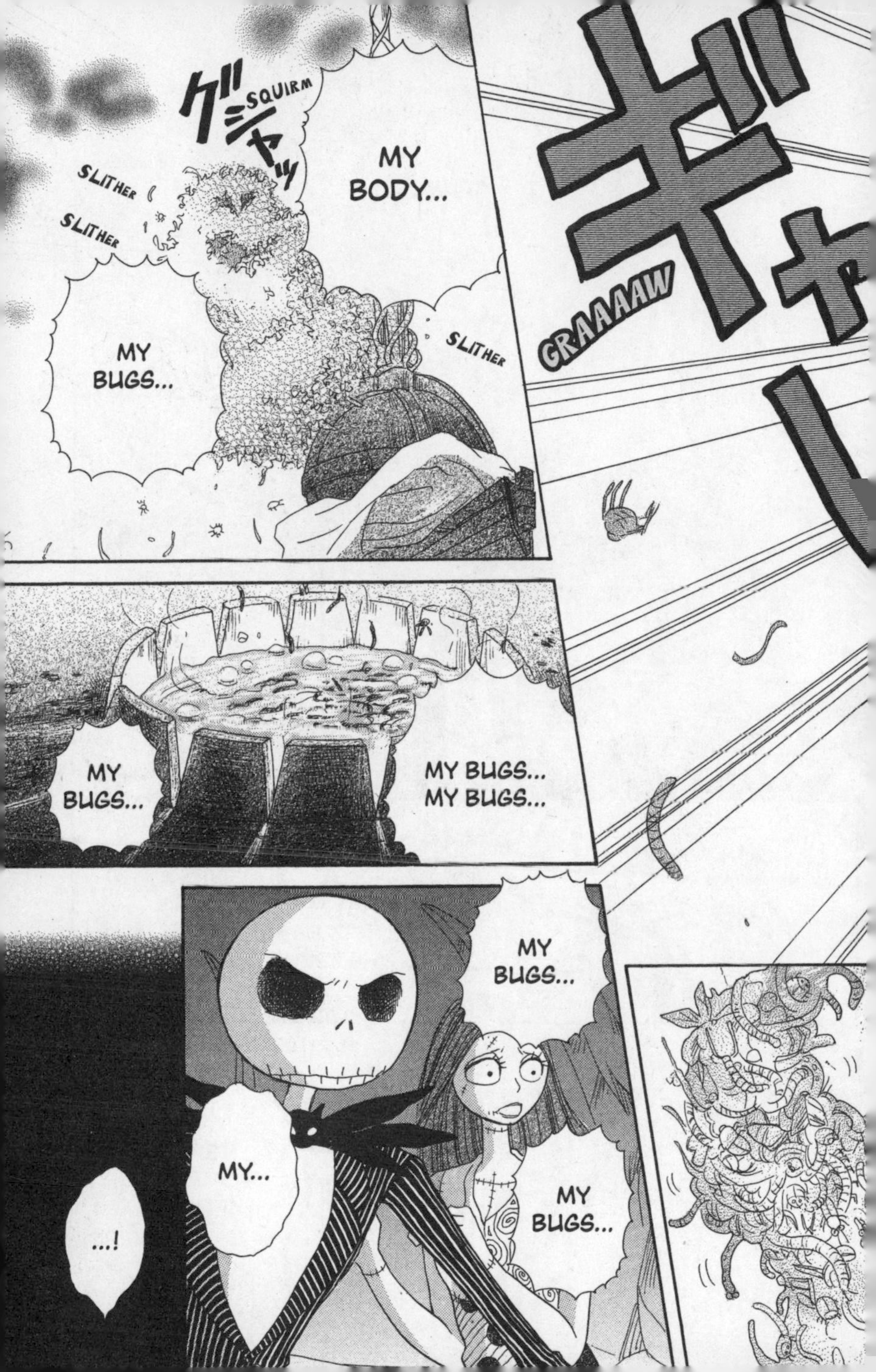
ギャー
GRAAAAW
グシャッ
SQUIRM
MY BODY...
SLITHER
SLITHER
SLITHER
MY BUGS...
MY BUGS... MY BUGS...
MY BUGS...
MY BUGS...
MY BUGS...
MY...
...!

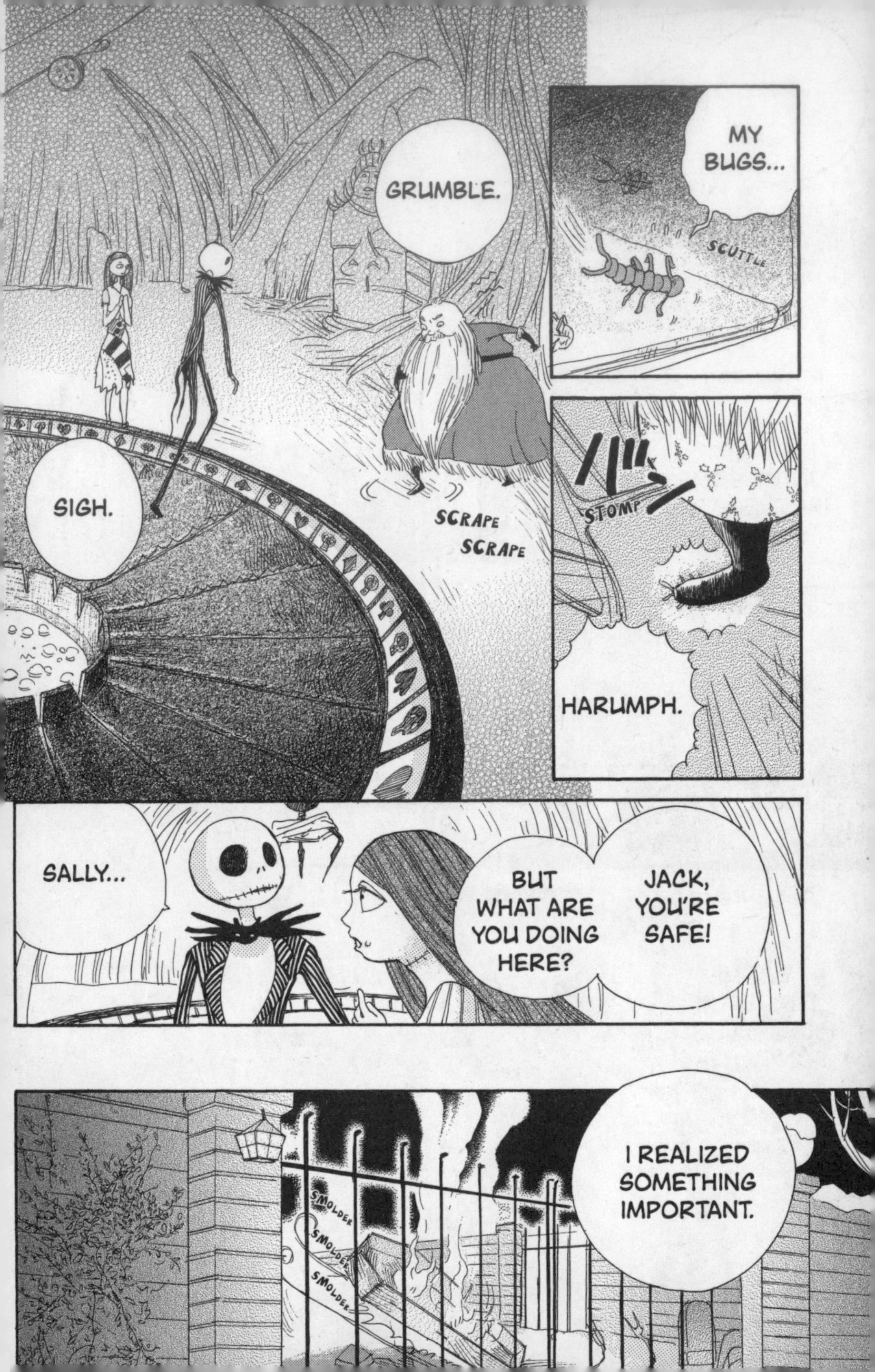
MY BUGS...
SCUTTLE
STOMP
HARUMPH.
GRUMBLE.
SCRAPE SCRAPE
SIGH.
JACK, YOU'RE SAFE!
BUT WHAT ARE YOU DOING HERE?
SALLY...
I REALIZED SOMETHING IMPORTANT.
SMOLDER
SMOLDER
SMOLDER

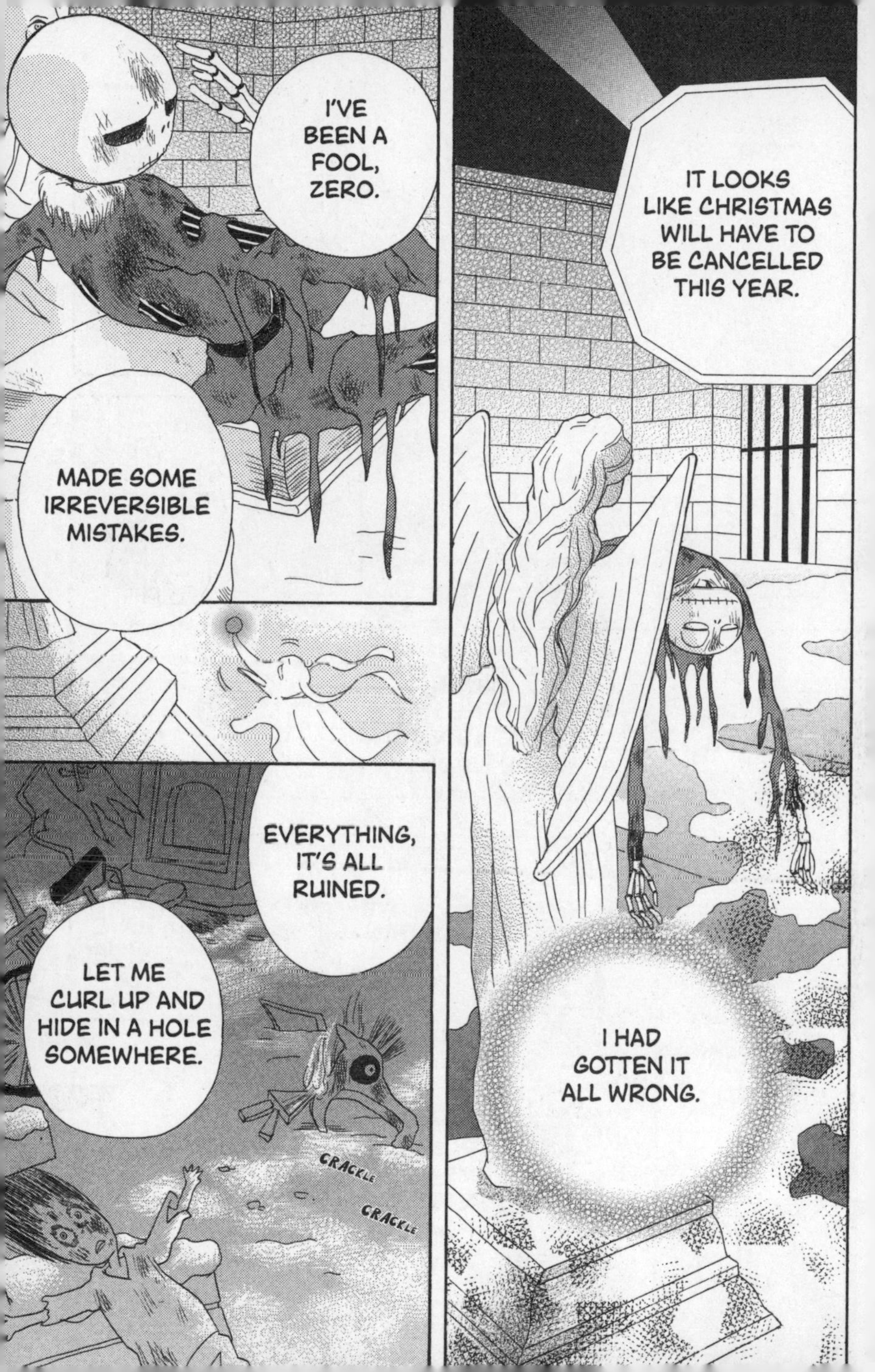
IT LOOKS LIKE CHRISTMAS WILL HAVE TO BE CANCELLED THIS YEAR.
I HAD GOTTEN IT ALL WRONG.
I'VE BEEN A FOOL, ZERO.
MADE SOME IRREVERSIBLE MISTAKES.
EVERYTHING, IT'S ALL RUINED.
LET ME CURL UP AND HIDE IN A HOLE SOMEWHERE.
CRACKLE
CRACKLE

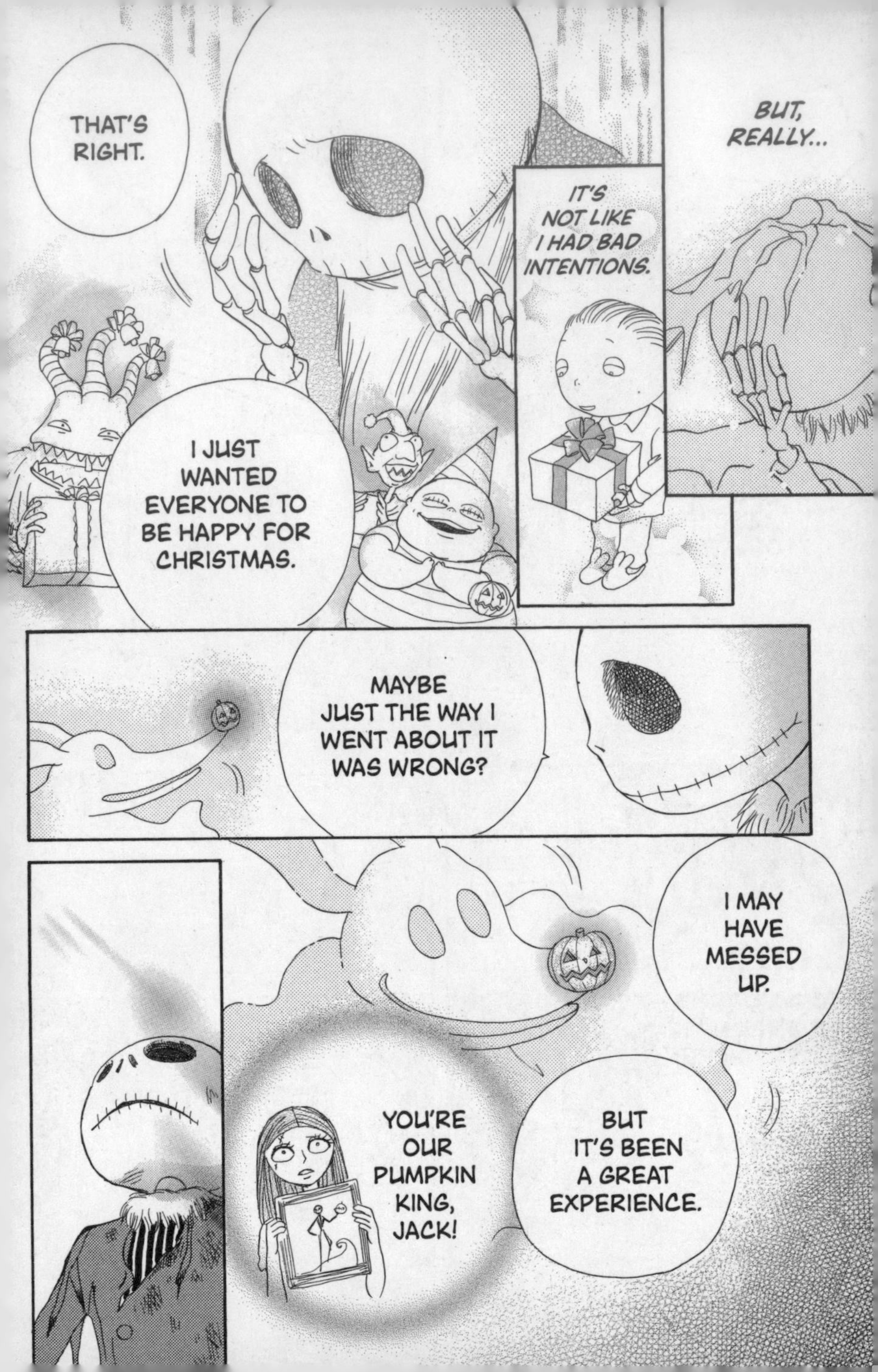

BUT, REALLY...
IT'S NOT LIKE I HAD BAD INTENTIONS.
THAT'S RIGHT.
I JUST WANTED EVERYONE TO BE HAPPY FOR CHRISTMAS.
MAYBE JUST THE WAY I WENT ABOUT IT WAS WRONG?
I MAY HAVE MESSED UP.
BUT IT'S BEEN A GREAT EXPERIENCE.
YOU'RE OUR PUMPKIN KING, JACK!

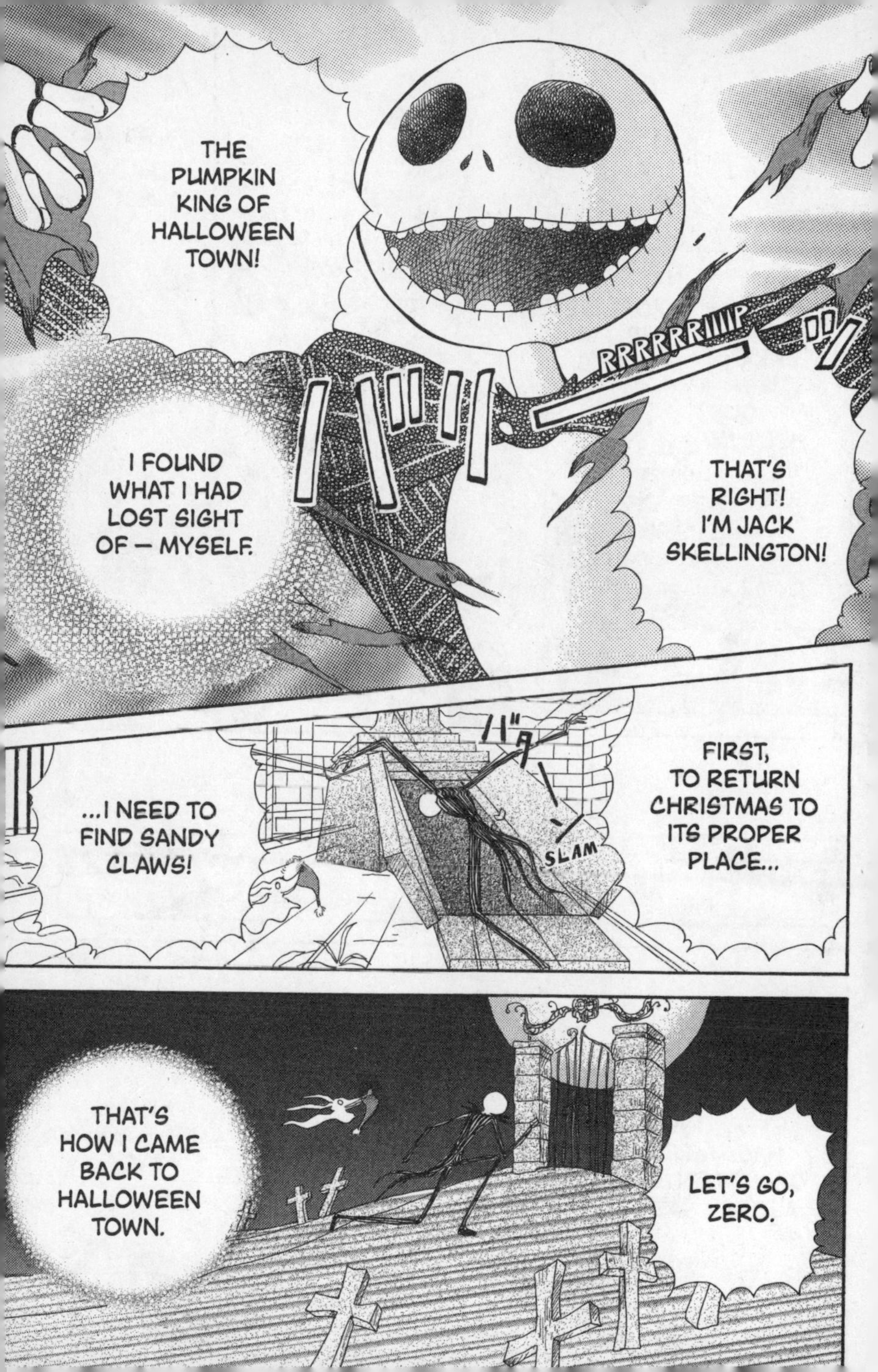
RRRRRRIIIIP
THAT'S RIGHT! I'M JACK SKELLINGTON!
THE PUMPKIN KING OF HALLOWEEN TOWN!
I FOUND WHAT I HAD LOST SIGHT OF — MYSELF.
FIRST, TO RETURN CHRISTMAS TO ITS PROPER PLACE...
SLAM
...I NEED TO FIND SANDY CLAWS!
LET'S GO, ZERO.
THAT'S HOW I CAME BACK TO HALLOWEEN TOWN.

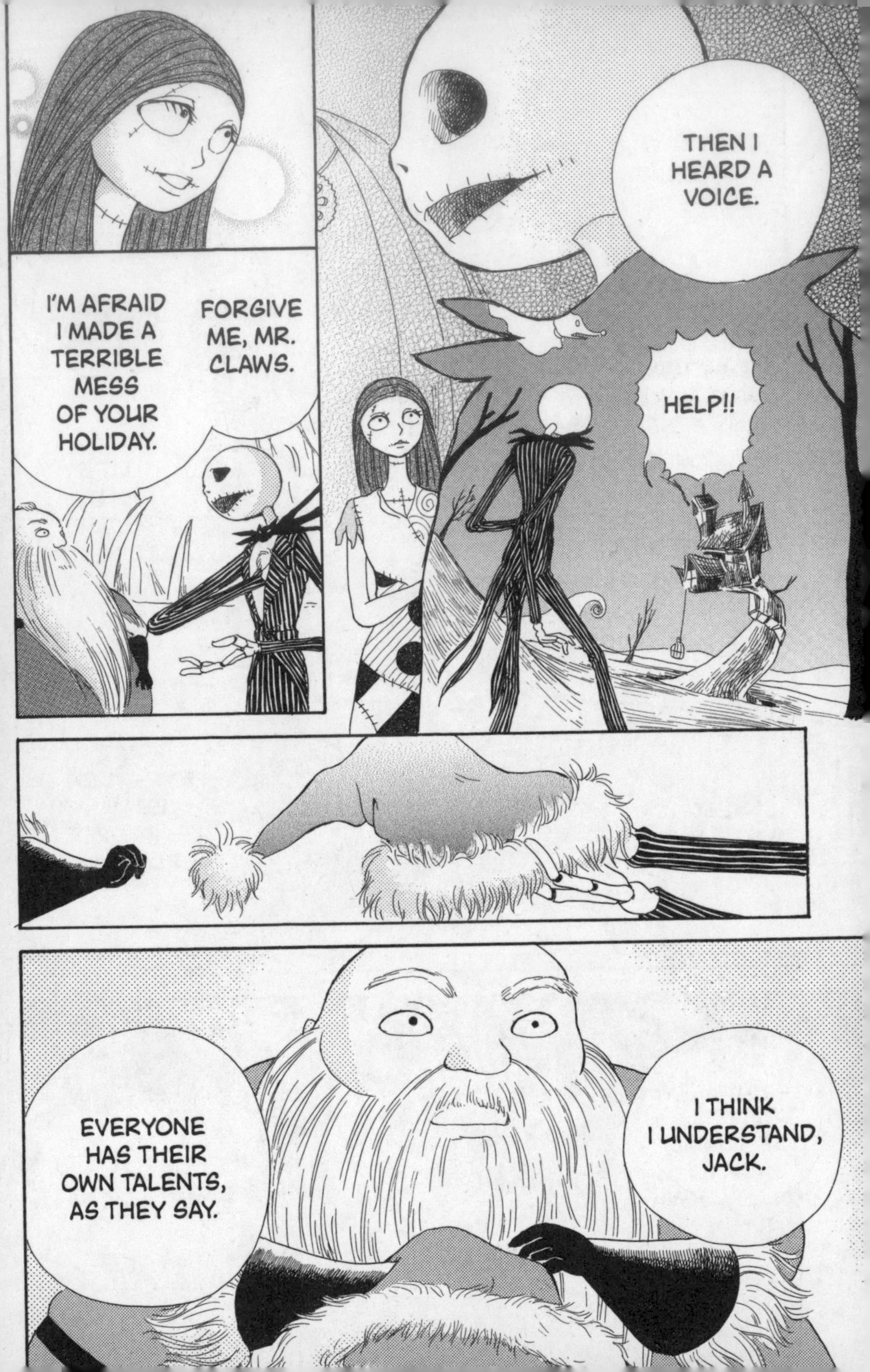
THEN I HEARD A VOICE.
HELP!!
FORGIVE ME, MR. CLAWS.
I'M AFRAID I MADE A TERRIBLE MESS OF YOUR HOLIDAY.
I THINK I UNDERSTAND, JACK.
EVERYONE HAS THEIR OWN TALENTS, AS THEY SAY.

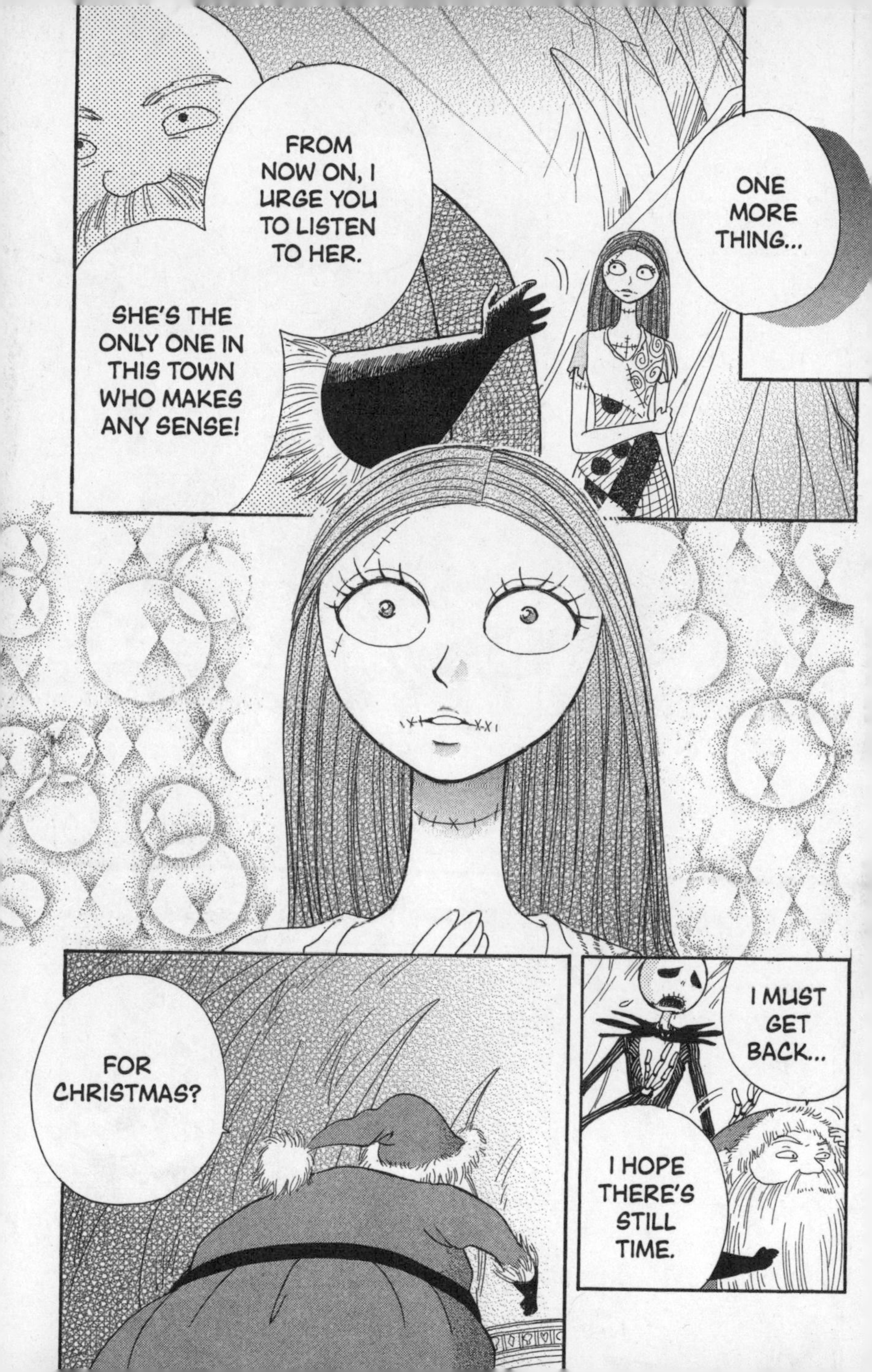
ONE MORE THING...
FROM NOW ON, I URGE YOU TO LISTEN TO HER.
SHE'S THE ONLY ONE IN THIS TOWN WHO MAKES ANY SENSE!
I MUST GET BACK...
I HOPE THERE'S STILL TIME.
FOR CHRISTMAS?

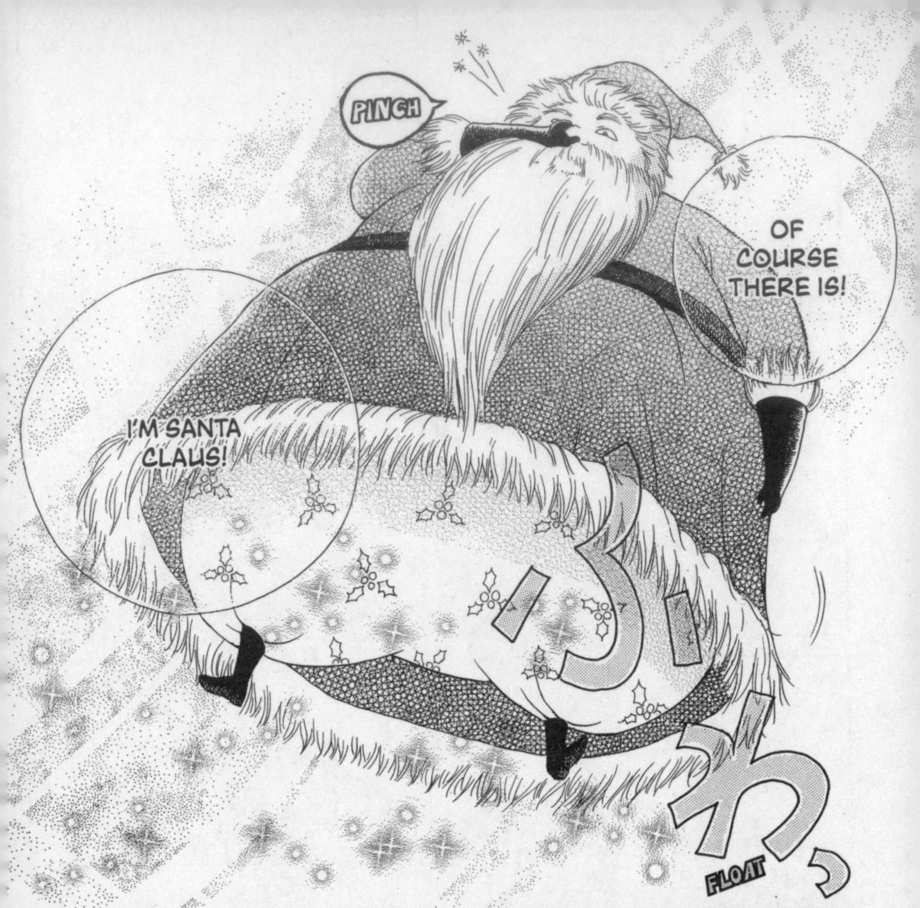
PINCH
OF COURSE THERE IS!
I'M SANTA CLAUS!
ふわっ
FLOAT

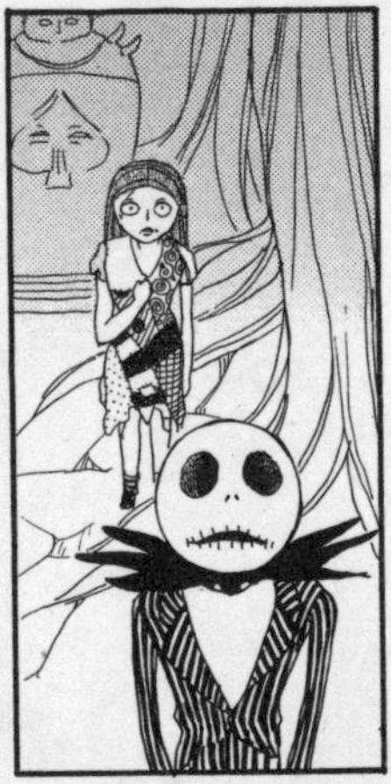

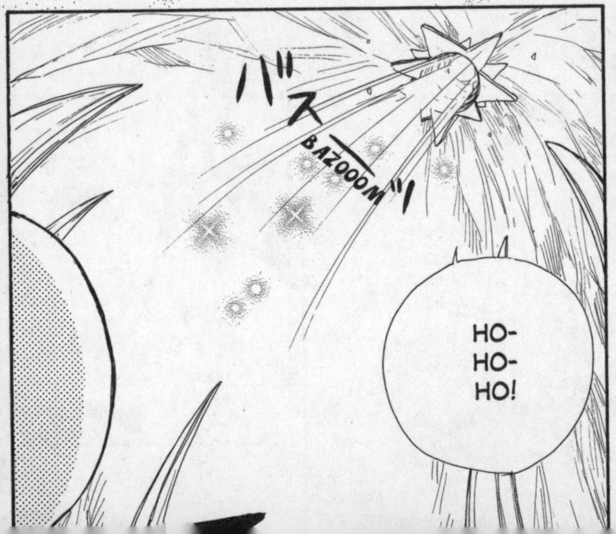
BAZOOOM
HO-HO-HO!

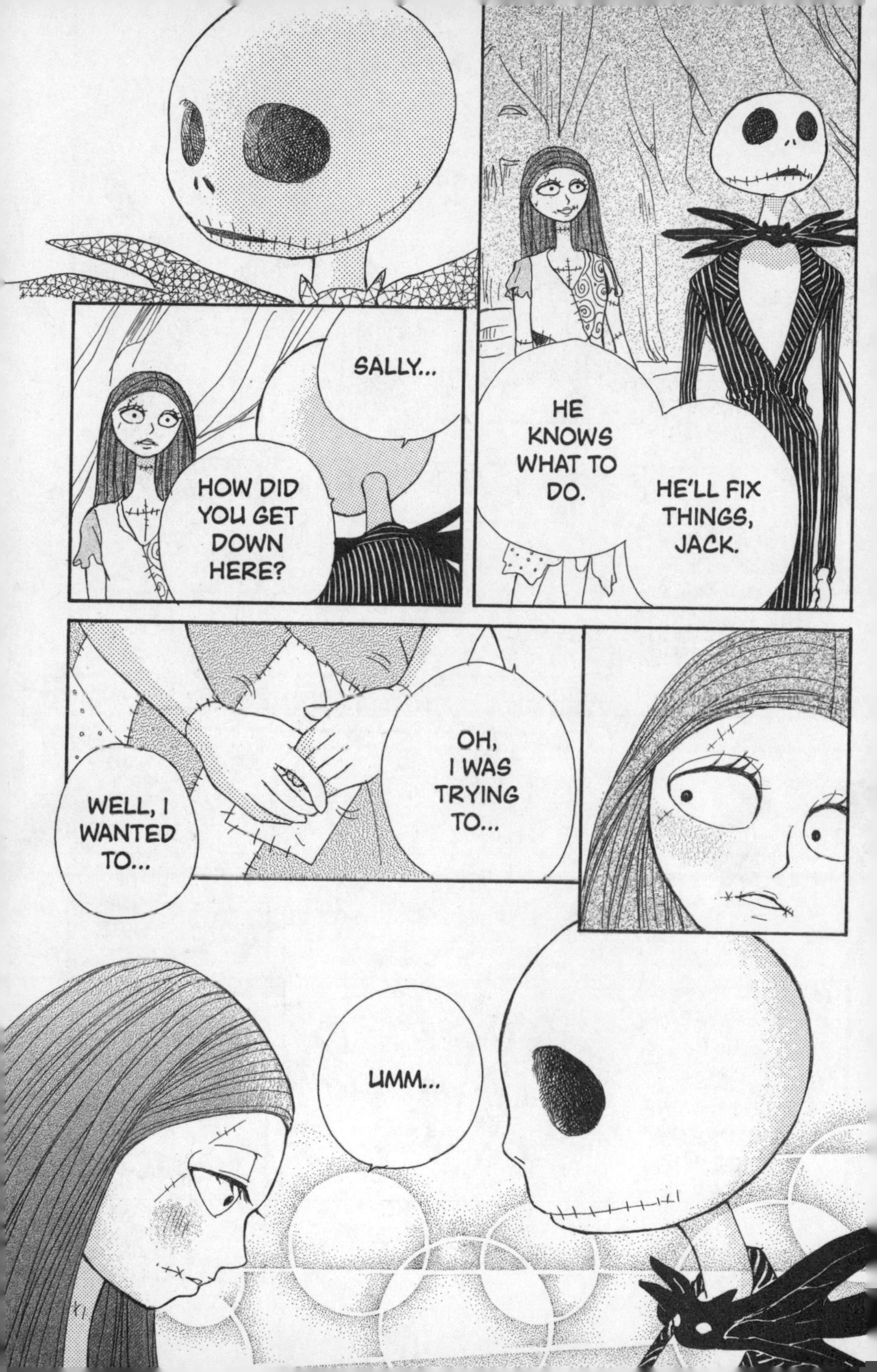
HE KNOWS WHAT TO DO.
HE'LL FIX THINGS, JACK.
SALLY...
HOW DID YOU GET DOWN HERE?
OH, I WAS TRYING TO...
WELL, I WANTED TO...
UMM...

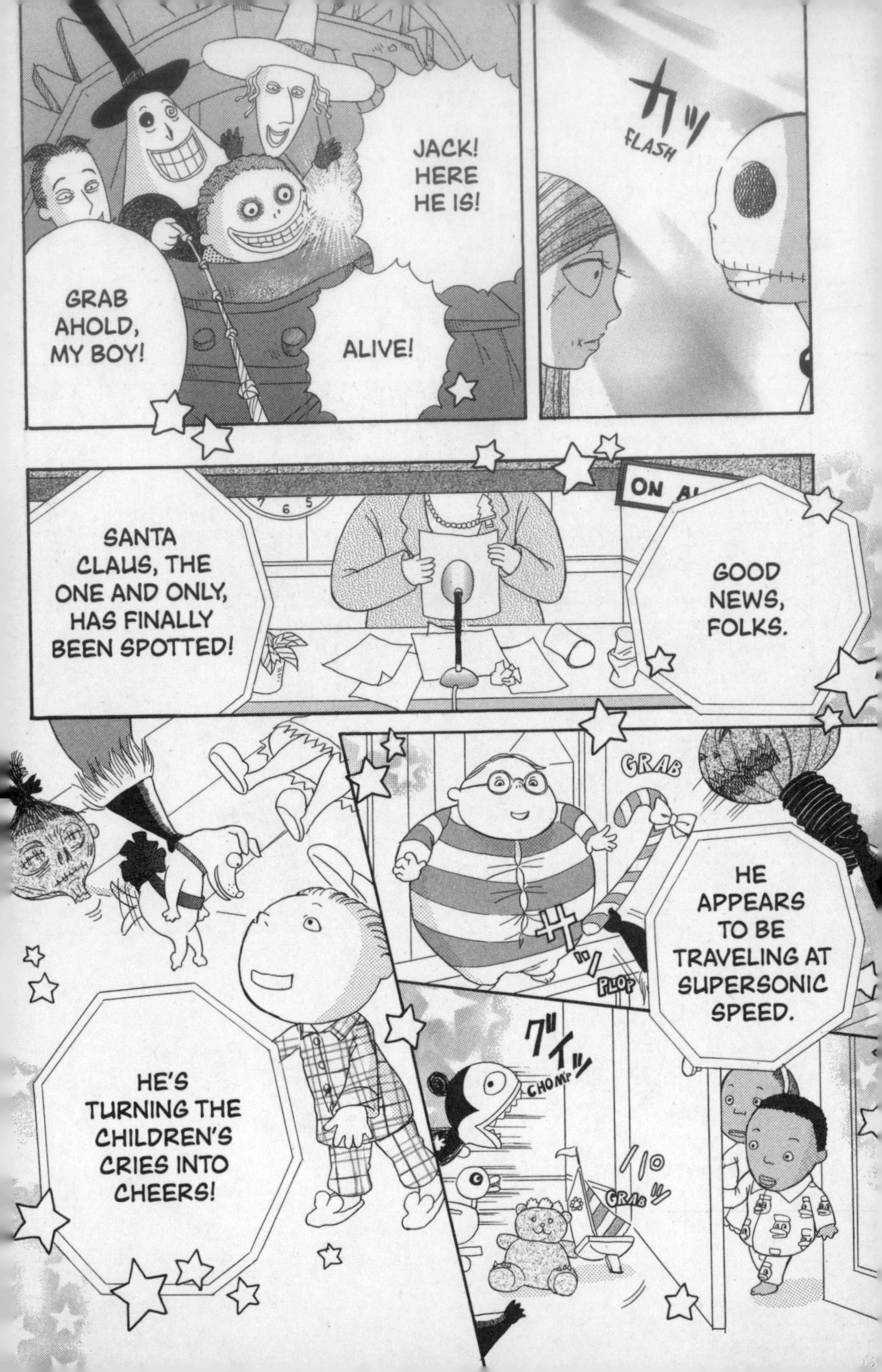
カッ
FLASH
JACK! HERE HE IS!
ALIVE!
GRAB AHOLD, MY BOY!
ON AI
GOOD NEWS, FOLKS.
SANTA CLAUS, THE ONE AND ONLY, HAS FINALLY BEEN SPOTTED!
GRAB
HE APPEARS TO BE TRAVELING AT SUPERSONIC SPEED.
PLOP
グイッ
CHOMP
GRAB
HE'S TURNING THE CHILDREN'S CRIES INTO CHEERS!

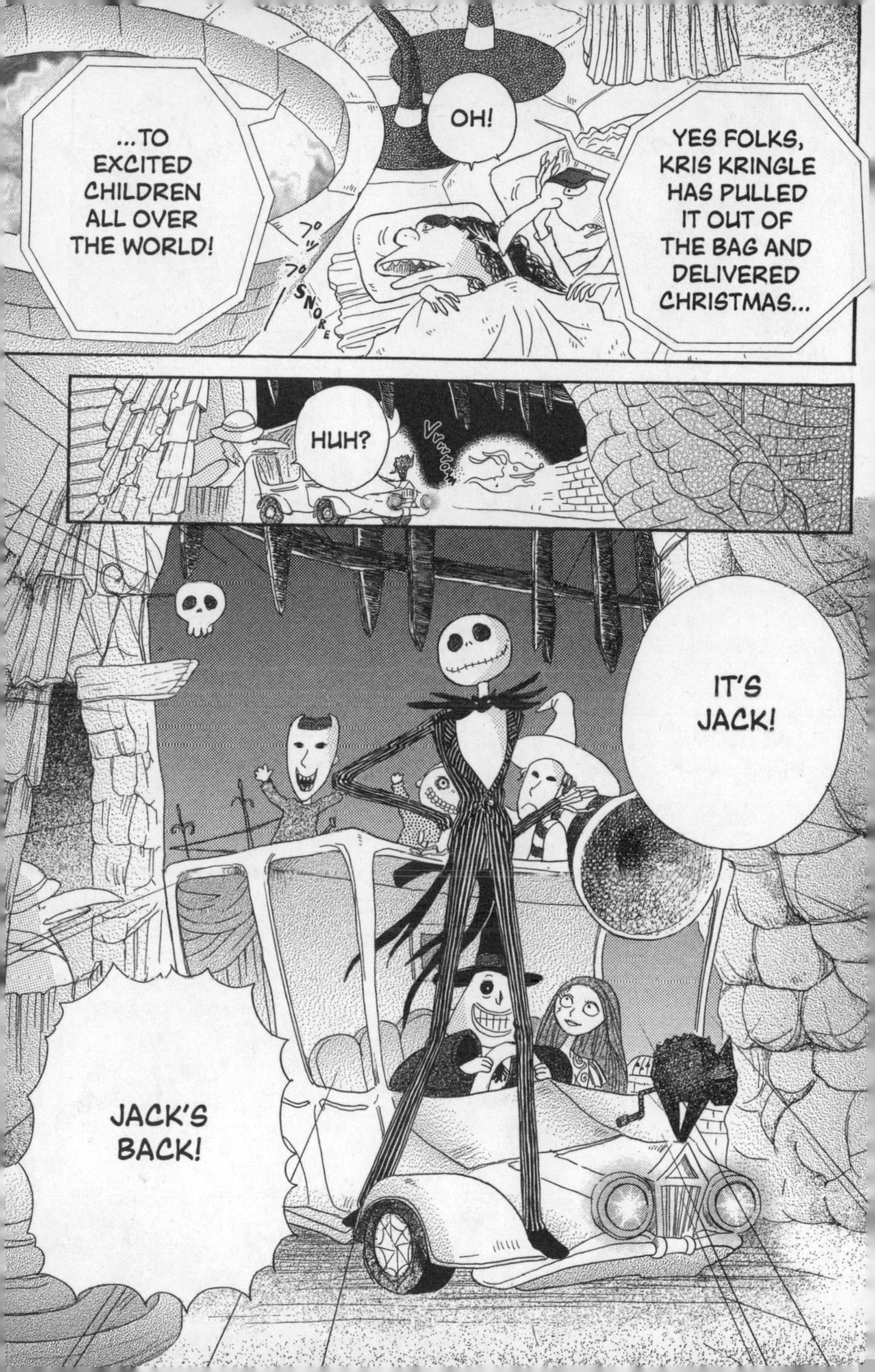

YES FOLKS, KRIS KRINGLE HAS PULLED IT OUT OF THE BAG AND DELIVERED CHRISTMAS...
OH!
...TO EXCITED CHILDREN ALL OVER THE WORLD!
SNORE
Vrrrroom
HUH?
IT'S JACK!
JACK'S BACK!

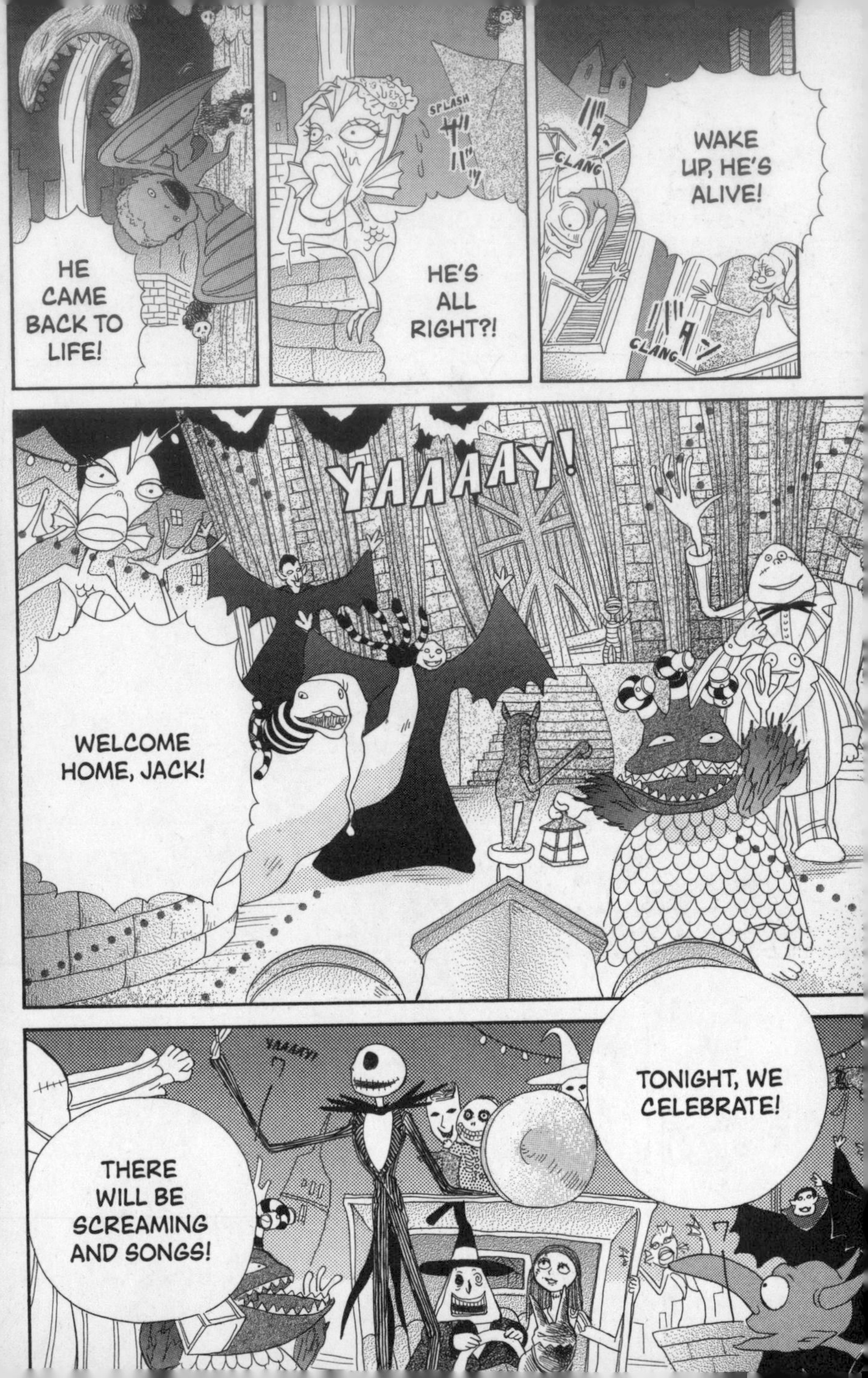
CLANG
WAKE UP, HE'S ALIVE!
CLANG
SPLASH
HE'S ALL RIGHT?!
HE CAME BACK TO LIFE!
YAAAAAY!
WELCOME HOME, JACK!
TONIGHT, WE CELEBRATE!
THERE WILL BE SCREAMING AND SONGS!

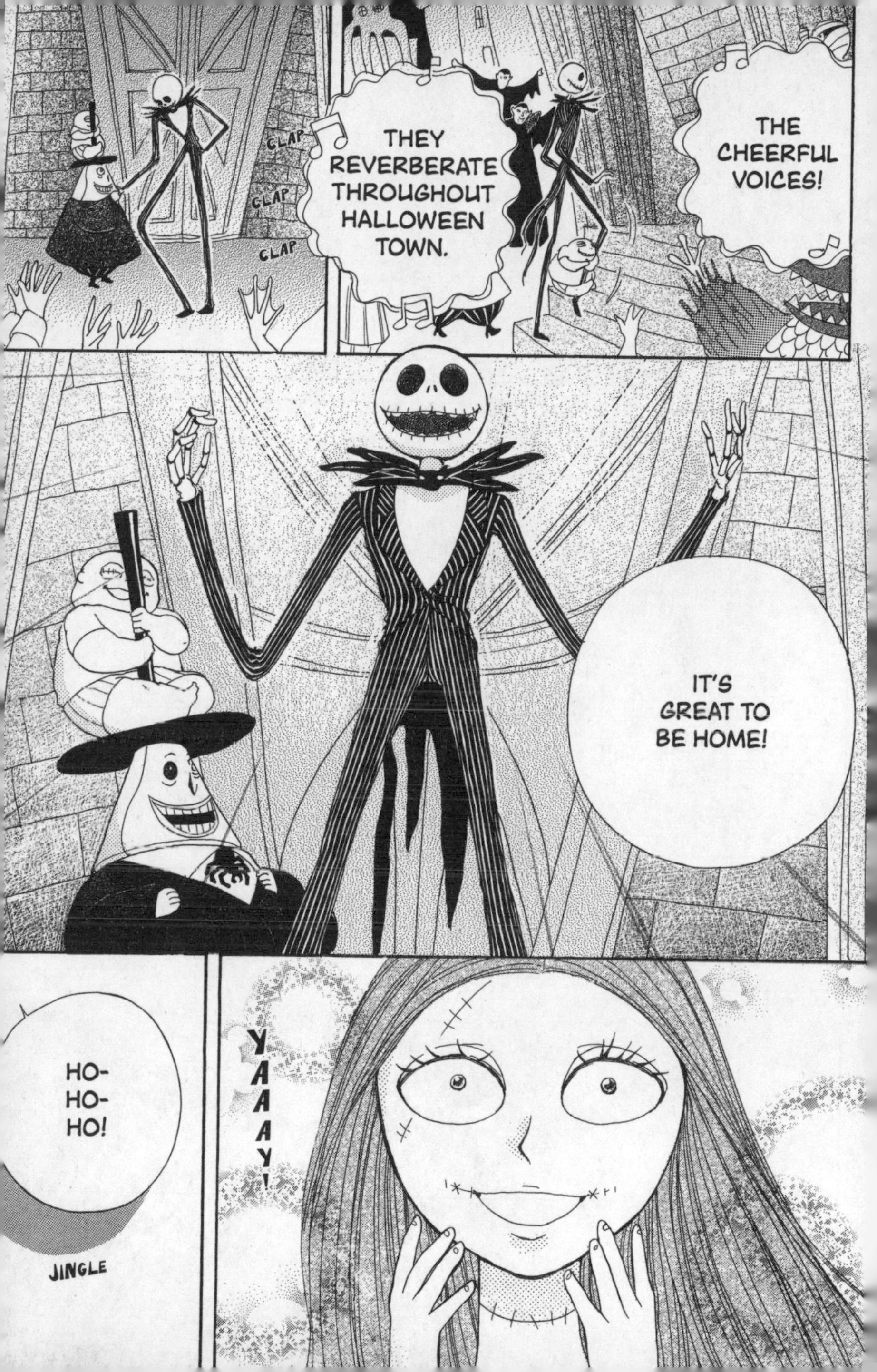
THE CHEERFUL VOICES!
THEY REVERBERATE THROUGHOUT HALLOWEEN TOWN.
CLAP
CLAP
CLAP
IT'S GREAT TO BE HOME!
YAAAY!
HO-HO-HO!
JINGLE

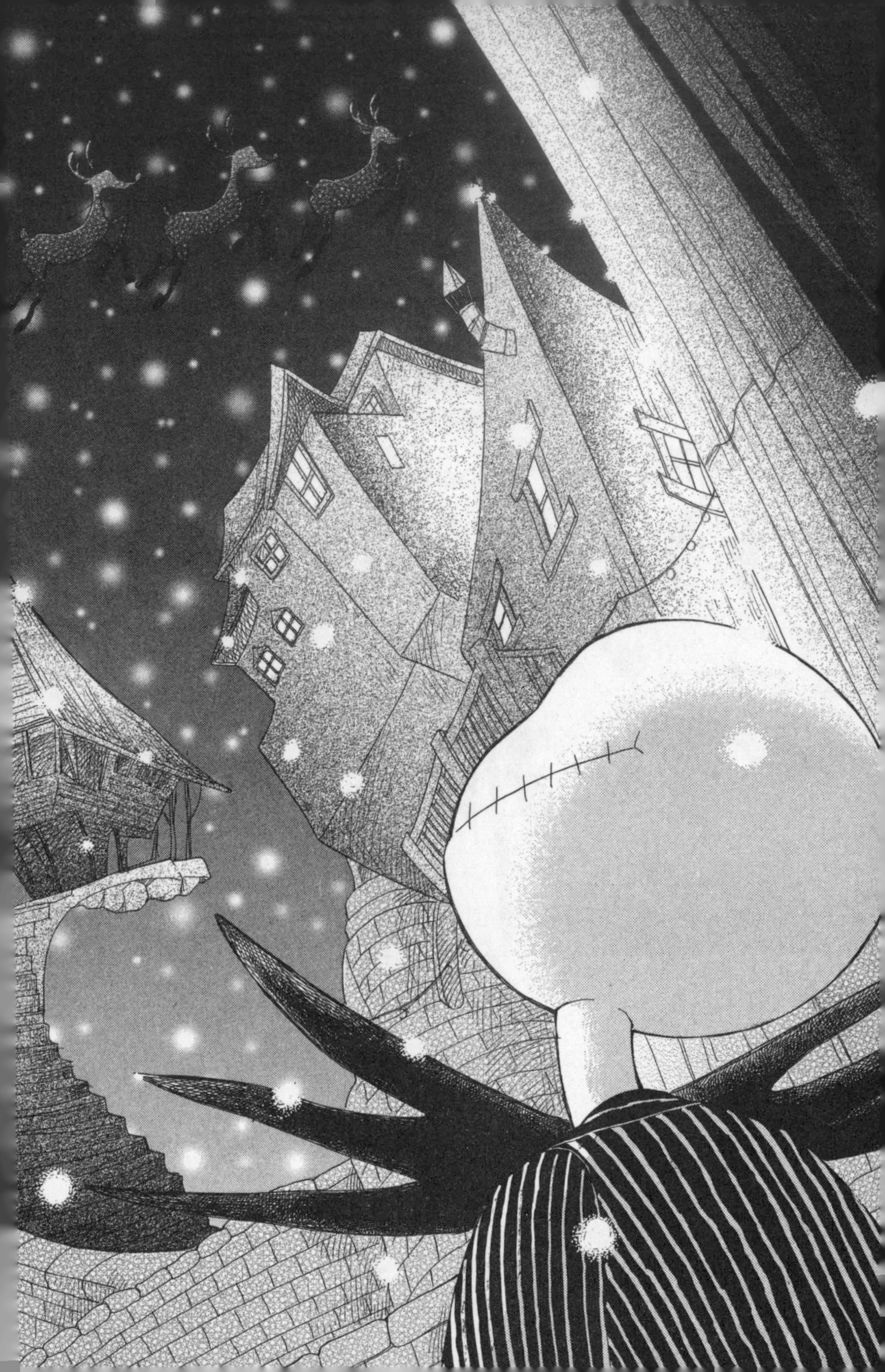

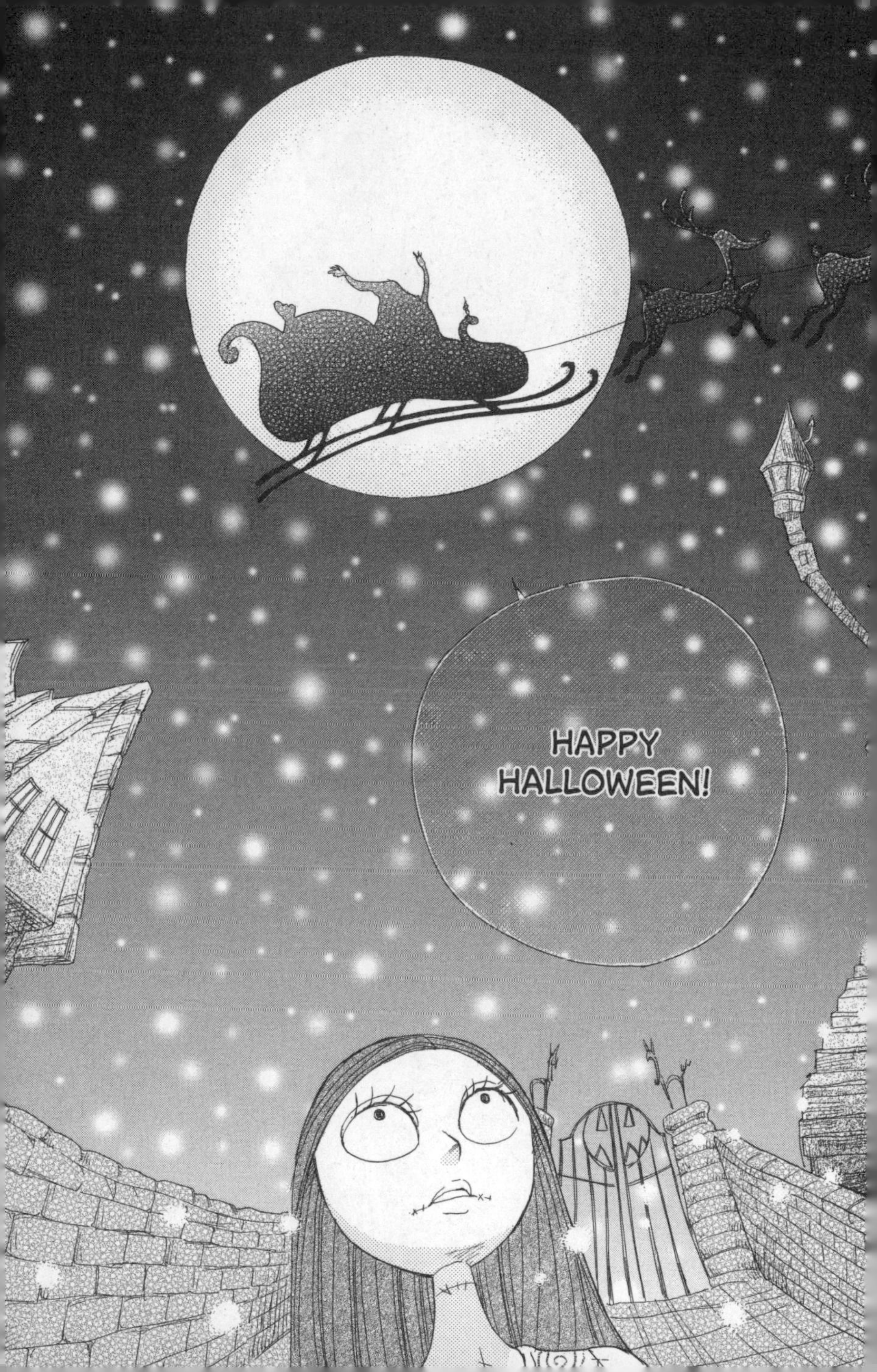
HAPPY HALLOWEEN!

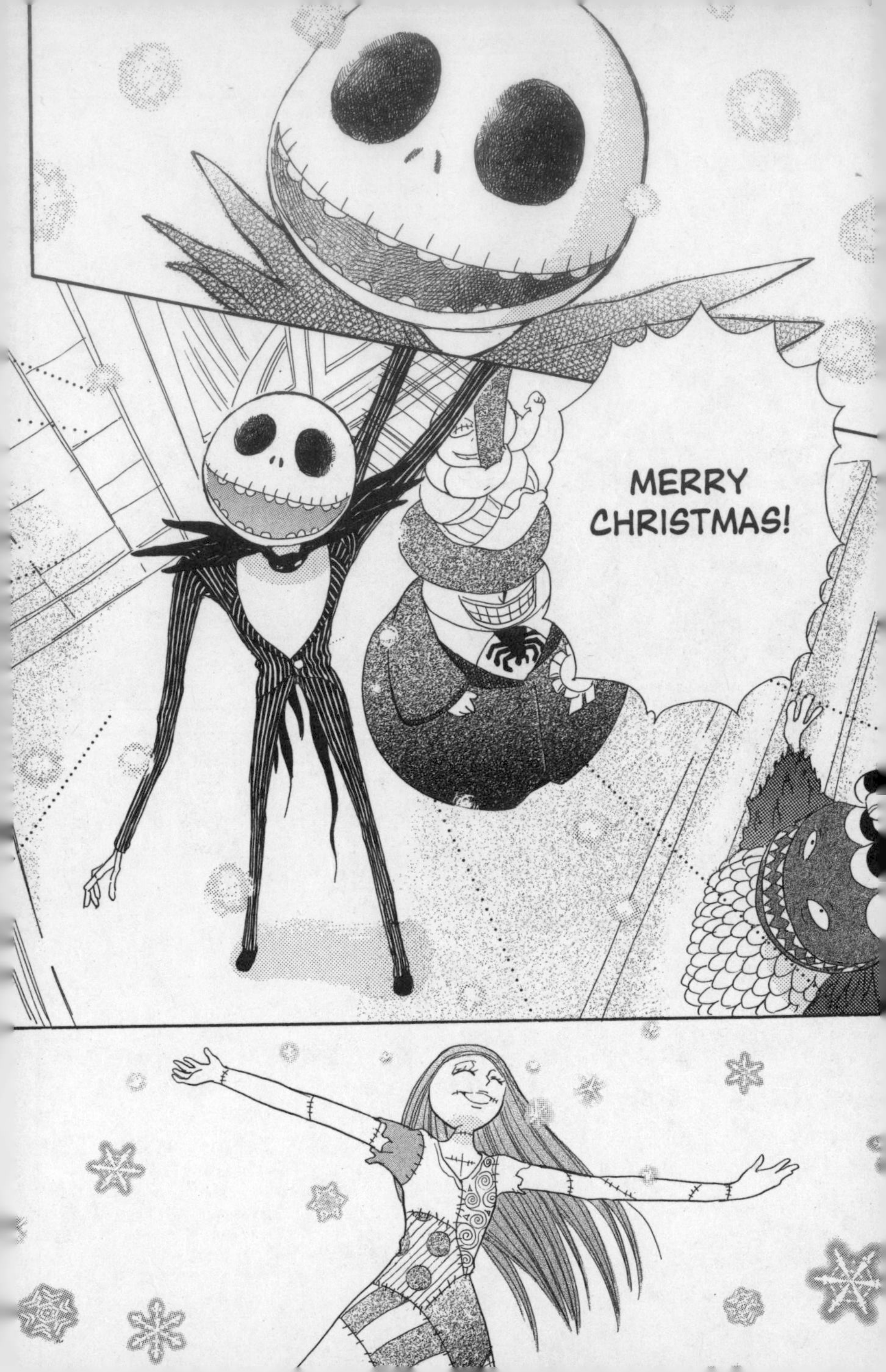
MERRY CHRISTMAS!

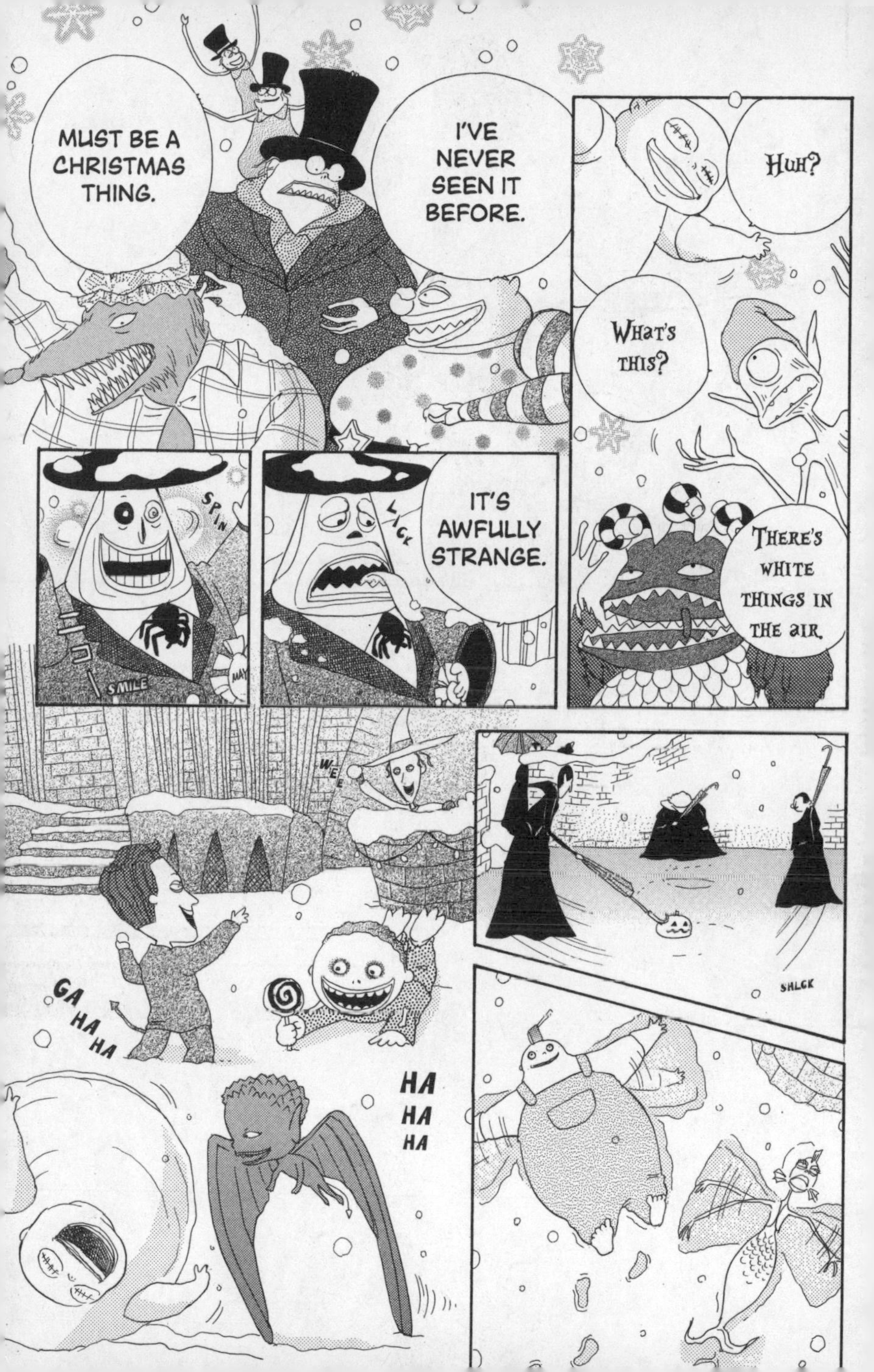
HUH?
WHAT'S THIS?
THERE'S WHITE THINGS IN THE AIR.
I'VE NEVER SEEN IT BEFORE.
MUST BE A CHRISTMAS THING.
LICK
IT'S AWFULLY STRANGE.
SPIN
SMILE
MAY
SHLCK
WEE
GA HA HA
HA HA HA

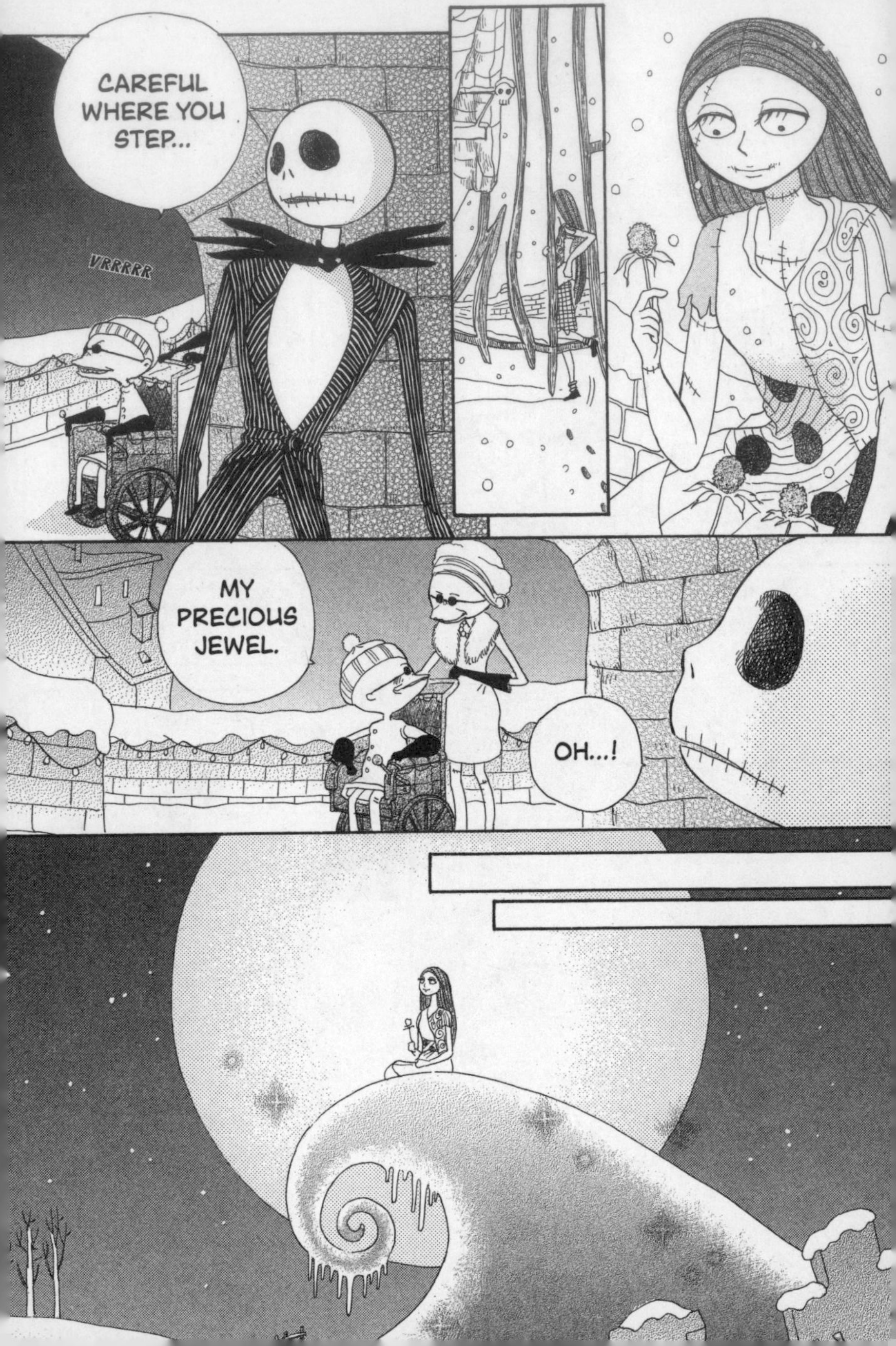
CAREFUL WHERE YOU STEP...
VRRRRR
MY PRECIOUS JEWEL.
OH...!

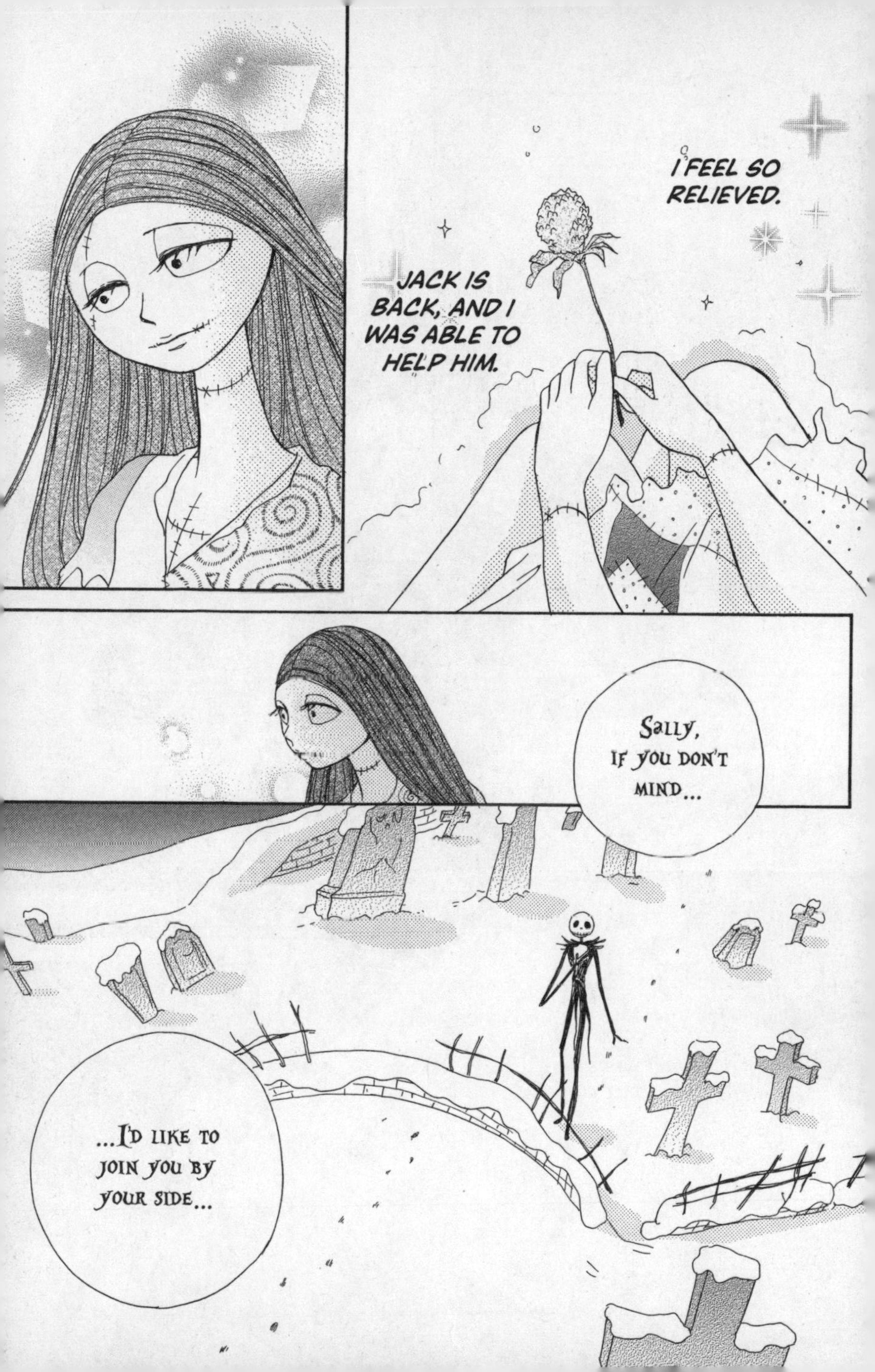
I FEEL SO RELIEVED.
JACK IS BACK, AND I WAS ABLE TO HELP HIM.
Sally, if you don't mind...
...I'd like to join you by your side...

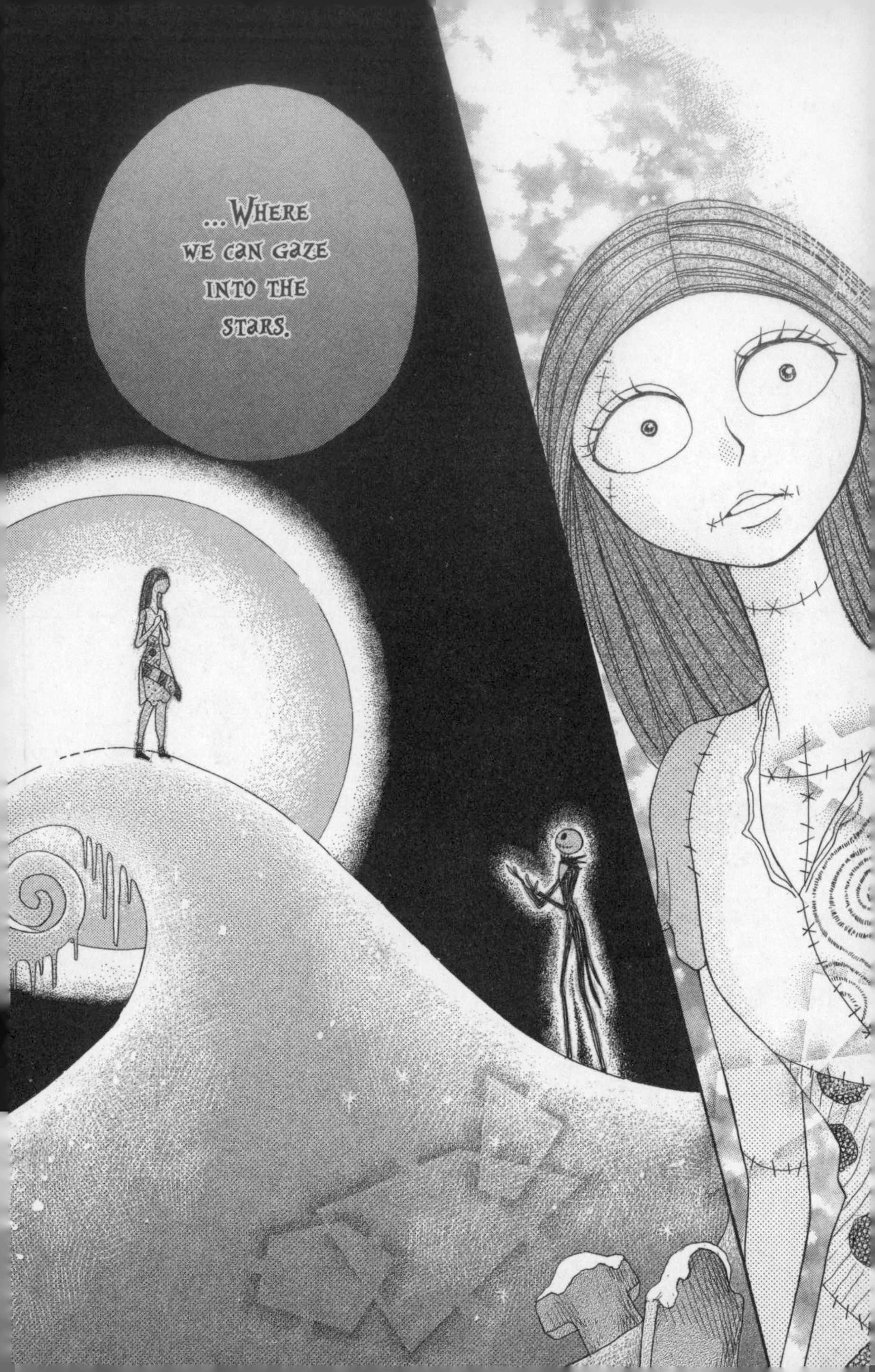
...WHERE WE CAN GAZE INTO THE STARS.

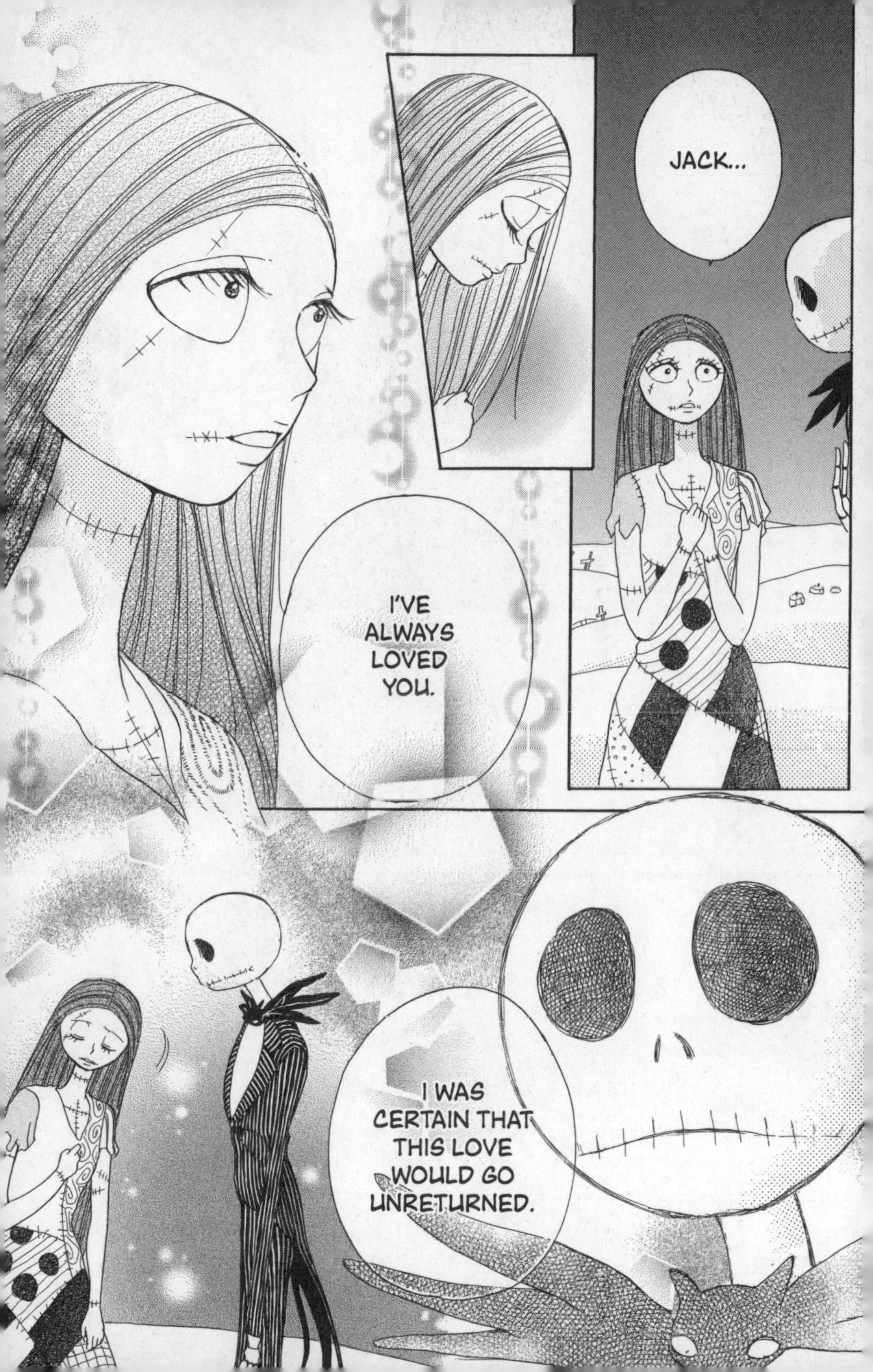
JACK...
I'VE ALWAYS LOVED YOU.
I WAS CERTAIN THAT THIS LOVE WOULD GO UNRETURNED.

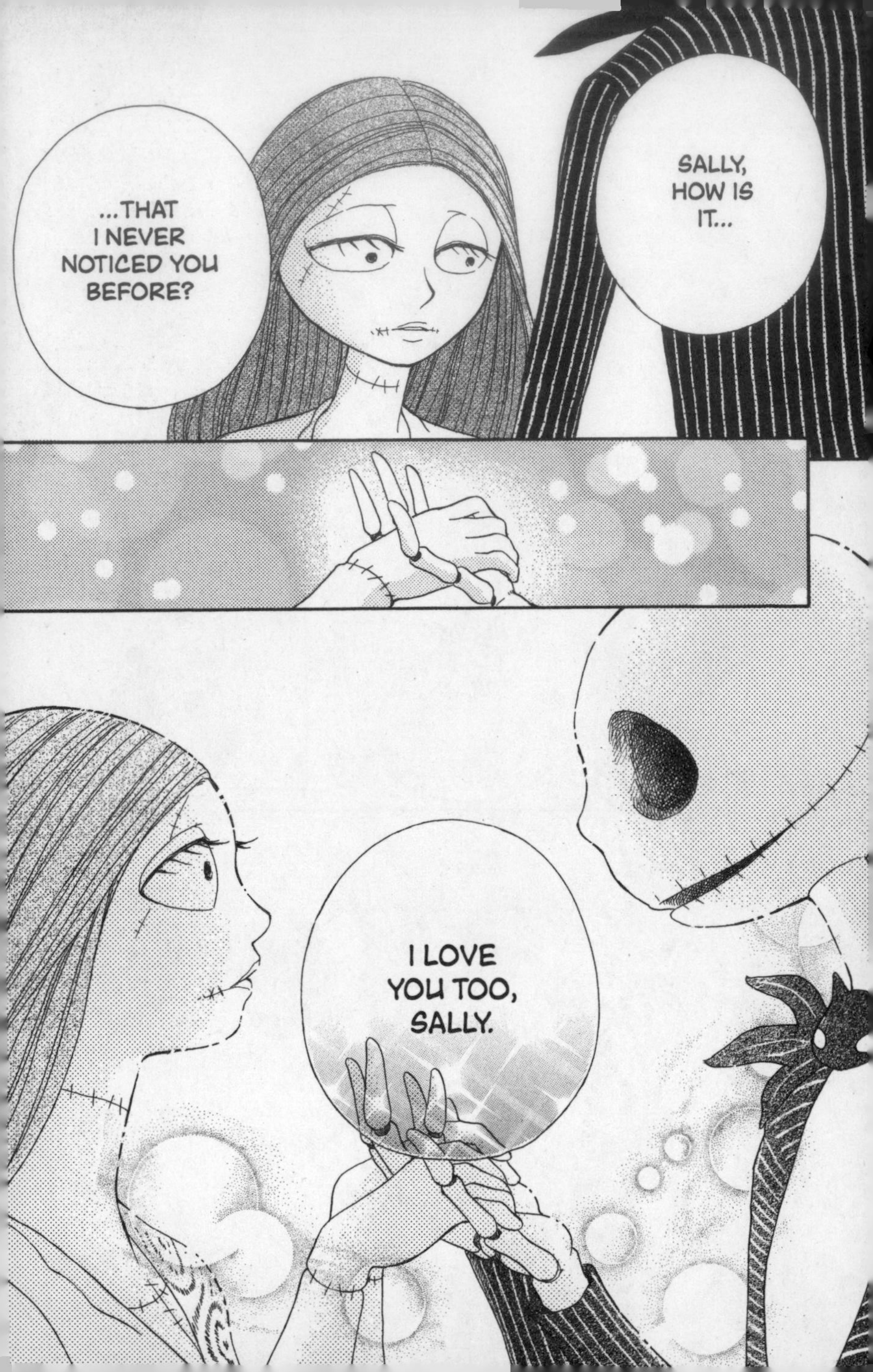
SALLY, HOW IS IT...
...THAT I NEVER NOTICED YOU BEFORE?
I LOVE YOU TOO, SALLY.

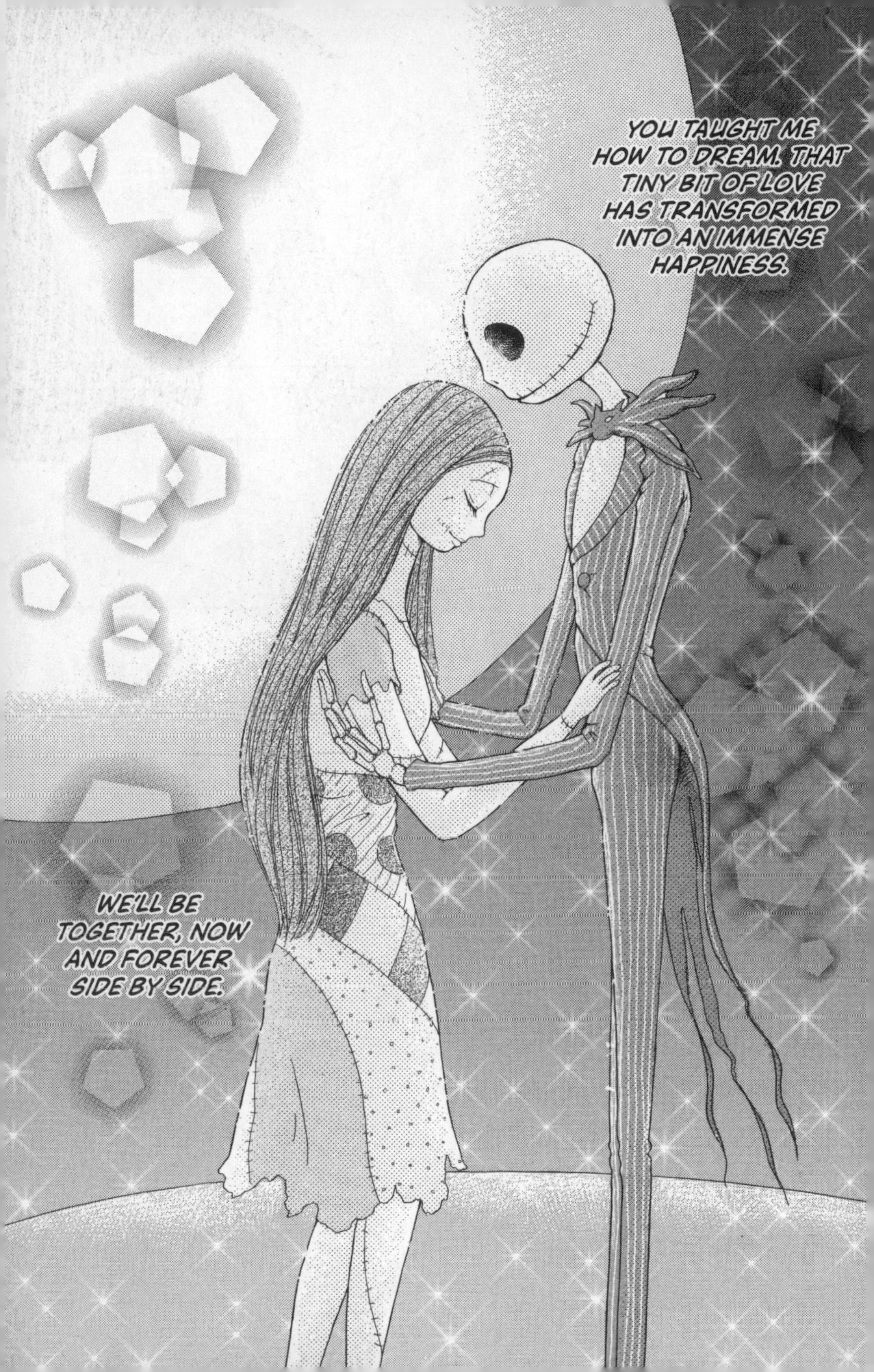
YOU TAUGHT ME HOW TO DREAM. THAT TINY BIT OF LOVE HAS TRANSFORMED INTO AN IMMENSE HAPPINESS.
WE'LL BE TOGETHER, NOW AND FOREVER SIDE BY SIDE.

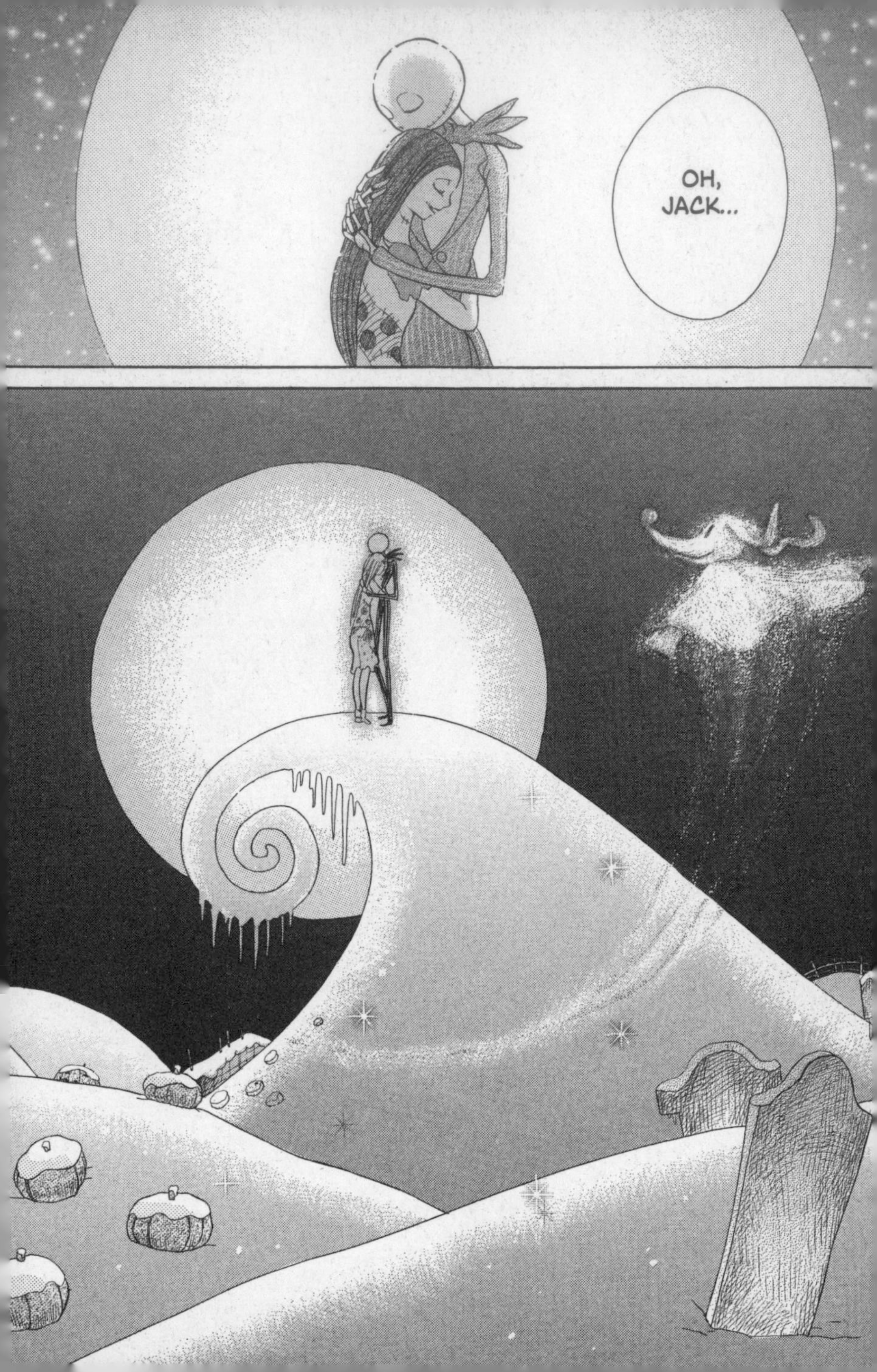
OH, JACK...

MIRACLES AWAIT THOSE
WHO BELIEVE IN THIS
HALLOWEEN FAIRY TALE.

THE END

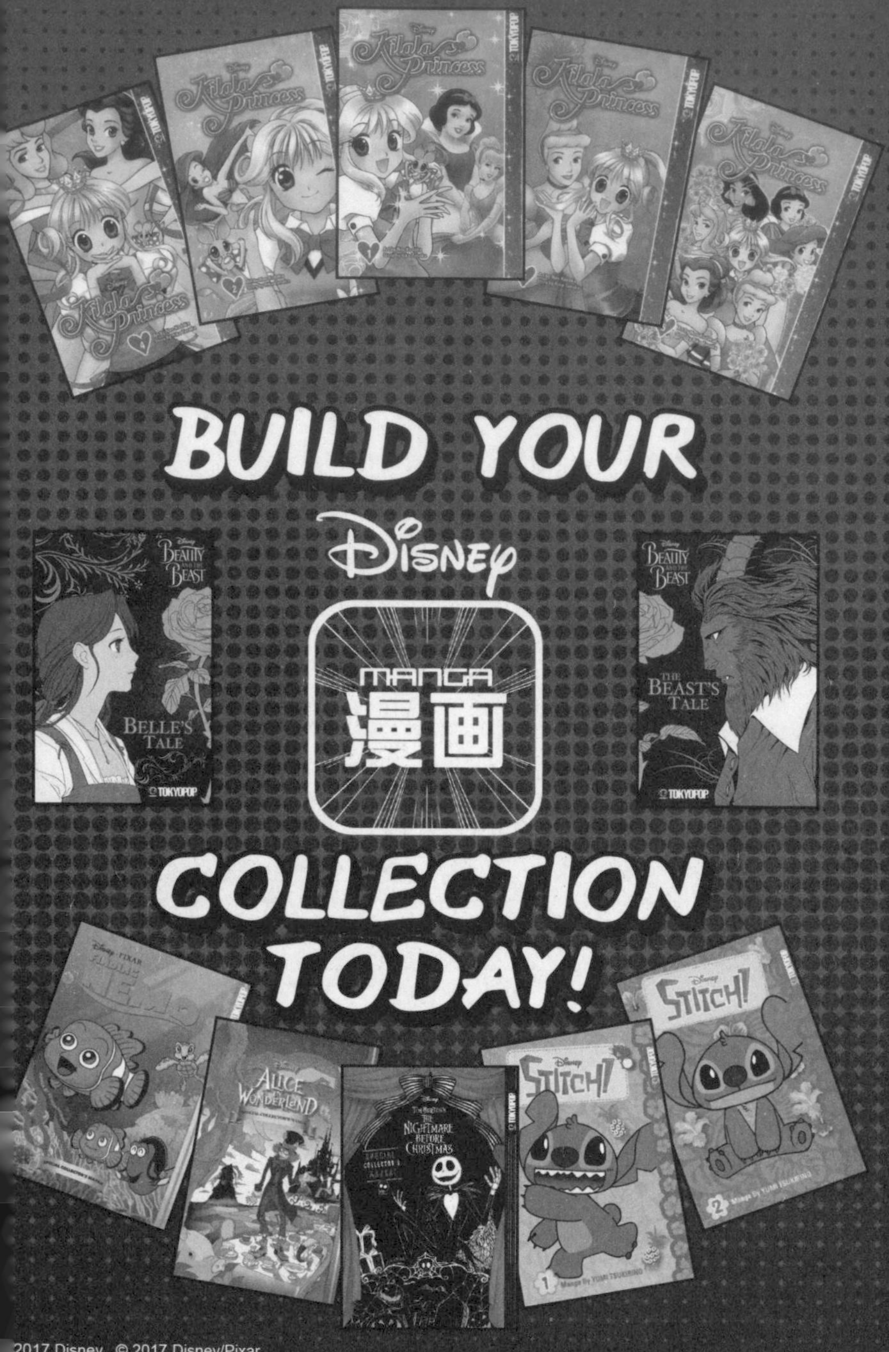
Kilala Princess
BUILD YOUR
Disney
MANGA
漫画
COLLECTION
TODAY!
Beauty and the Beast
Belle's Tale
The Beast's Tale
TOKYOPOP
Stitch!
Alice in Wonderland
The Nightmare Before Christmas

A BRAND NEW MANGA SET IN THE SPOOKY WORLD OF

Disney

TIM BURTON'S THE NIGHTMARE BEFORE CHRISTMAS

ZERO'S JOURNEY

Who says you can't teach an old dog new tricks?

COMING IN 2018 FROM DISNEY MANGA BY TOKYOPOP!

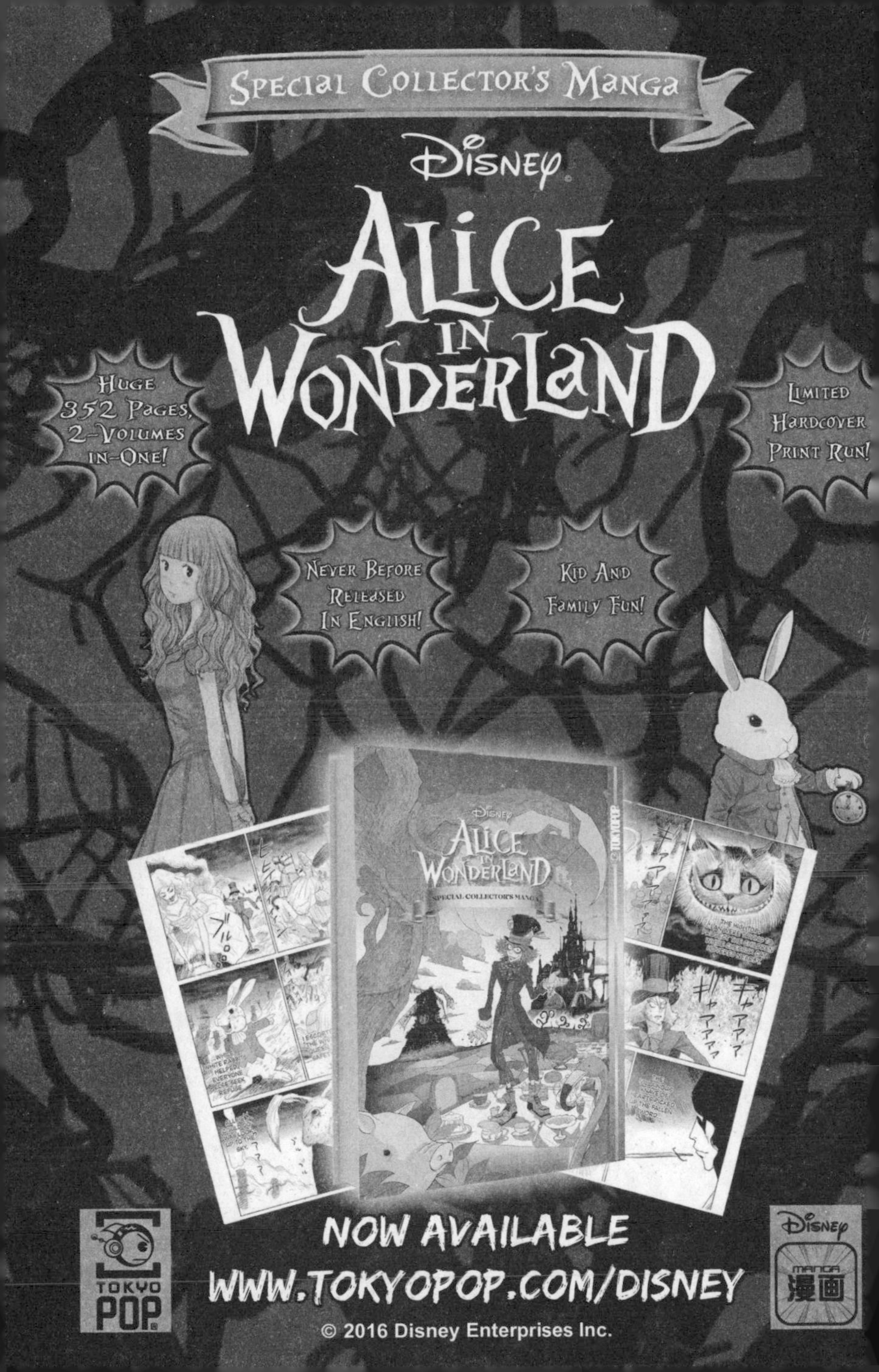
Special Collector's Manga
Disney
Alice in Wonderland
Huge 352 Pages, 2-Volumes in-One!
Limited Hardcover Print Run!
Never Before Released In English!
Kid And Family Fun!
NOW AVAILABLE
WWW.TOKYOPOP.COM/DISNEY
© 2016 Disney Enterprises Inc.

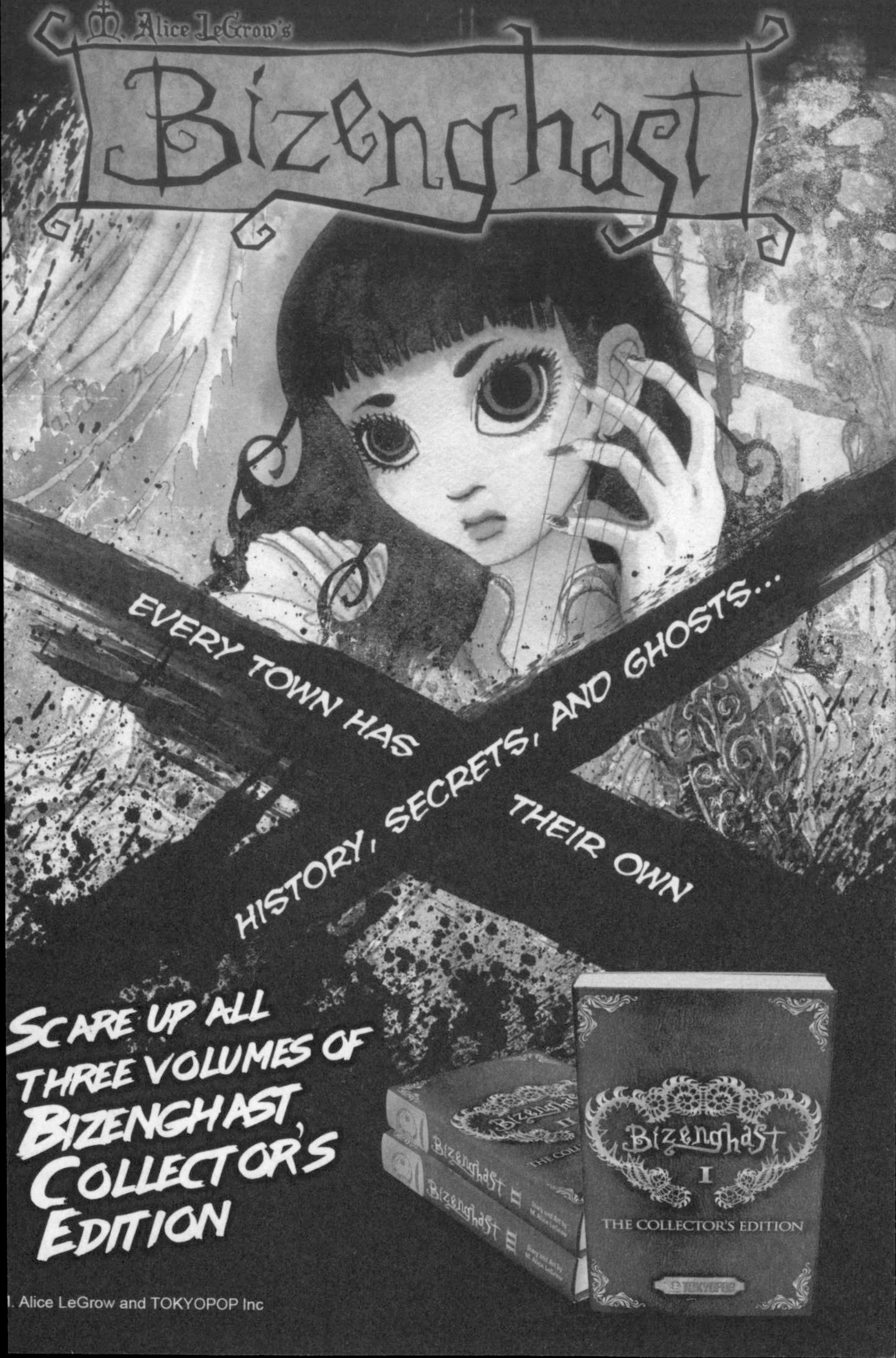
Alice LeGrow's
Bizenghast
EVERY TOWN HAS
HISTORY, SECRETS, AND GHOSTS...
THEIR OWN
SCARE UP ALL
THREE VOLUMES OF
BIZENGHAST,
COLLECTOR'S
EDITION
Bizenghast
I
THE COLLECTOR'S EDITION
TOKYOPOP
Bizenghast
II
Bizenghast
III
M. Alice LeGrow and TOKYOPOP Inc

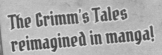

The Grimm's Tales
reimagined in manga!

Beautiful art by the talented
Kei Ishiyama!

Stories from Little Red Riding Hood
to Hansel and Gretel!

READ FOR FREE ON

POP COMICS

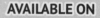